A Fairy Tale

Also by Shanna Swendson

The Enchanted, Inc. Series:

A Fairy Tale

Shanna Swendson

NLA Digital, LLC

A FAIRY TALE. Copyright © 2014 by Shanna Swendson. All rights reserved. Printed in the United States of America. No part of this book may be used or reproduced in any manner whatsoever without written permission except in the case of brief quotations embodied in critical articles and review. Address requests for information to NLA Digital, 1732 Wazee Street, Suite 207, Denver, CO 80202.

Production Manager: Lori Bennett
Cover art by Kirbi Fagan.
Cover design and book design by Angie Hodapp.

ISBN 978-1-62051-129-9

*To the adult ballet class at the
Ballet Academy of Texas.
Because ballerinas are tougher than they look.*

One

The Theater District, New York City—Fay's Diner
Wednesday, 1:30 a.m., Eastern Daylight Saving Time

"It's official—you're magical and enchanting."

Emily Drake leaned forward eagerly at her friend's words, resting her forearms on the table. "Really? You're not just messing with me?"

Olivia Washington turned her iPhone to face Emily and pointed to the screen. "There it is on one of the biggest Broadway blogs."

Emily's other friend, Will Carter, raised his hand and waved imperiously at the waitress. "Garçonette, another round of coffee for my good people here, *s'il vous plaît.*"

The waitress rolled her eyes at him as she topped off the cups on the table. "You keep that up, and you'll find itching powder in your dance belt the next time we're in a show together." She smiled at Emily. "So, the word is good?"

"It doesn't sound like I sucked." Emily was almost afraid to say it out loud. She couldn't help feeling she might wake up at any moment and learn that this whole evening had been a dream.

"You definitely did not suck," Olivia insisted, then she added to the waitress, "Becky, she was brilliant. You should have seen her."

Becky sighed. "And now she'll become a star and forget all of us still toiling in chorus after chorus—when we can even get a job." She brightened. "But hey, that means a chorus spot just opened, huh?"

"That's if the show doesn't close now that the big name has left," Emily said, worried they were tempting the Broadway fates. "We may all be looking for jobs again soon, no matter how much the blogs like me."

"Let's hope not," Olivia said. "I've enjoyed not going on auditions for a while. You know, this could be like a *42nd Street* understudy-becomes-a-star story, only instead of the leading lady breaking her ankle, she went off to Hollywood to be in a teen vampire TV series."

"I'd rather break my ankle," Will said dryly, tossing his blond hair out of his eyes.

A silver-haired man sitting across from Emily and her friends looked up from his apple pie and studied Emily intently. His gaze sent shivers down her spine—not bad shivers, but a very funny feeling. It was a vaguely familiar sensation, but she couldn't quite place it.

Becky shoved a paper menu and a pen in front of Emily, drawing her attention away from the man. "I want your first autograph as a star," Becky said.

Emily signed the menu with a flourish. The silver-haired man got up from his table and approached Emily's table tentatively, holding a *Playbill* from her show. Up close, he didn't look as old as she'd thought. The hair that had looked silver was really more of a white blond, while his face was smooth and youthful. And yet he dressed like an old professor, in a threadbare tweed jacket with a faded and sagging sweater under it. "You are Emily Drake?" he asked, his voice soft and shy. "You were Emma?"

"Yes," she said, trying not to giggle at the thrill of being recognized.

He put his *Playbill* on the table in front of her. "I saw your performance. I would like you to sign this."

"Oh, wow, my first real autograph." Her stomach fluttered in pleasure. "Who do you want me to sign it to?"

He didn't seem to understand the question. Frowning in confusion, he said, as though it should be perfectly obvious, "Me."

"Do you spell that M-E?" she asked with a laugh, then she added, "Or do you just want the signature so you can sell that *Playbill* on eBay when I'm famous?"

Now sounding unsure of himself, he said, "Yes, that."

She signed the *Playbill* carefully, using the autograph she'd been practicing since high school, then handed it back to him. "There you go. I hope you enjoyed the show."

He smiled and gave her a slight bow. "I did, very much. It was the bee's knees." He frowned, then said, "No, that's wrong. Radical? No." He shook his head. "It was very good." He abruptly turned and walked away, muttering under his breath.

"You've got a fan!" Olivia whispered with a glance at the man. "And he's cute, too."

"Cute, but kind of weird." Emily checked the time on her phone and said, "Oh, no, I was supposed to call Sophie, but she'd kill me if I called her at this hour. But would that be worse than her killing me for *not* calling?"

"I think you're safe from your sister up here," Olivia said with a grin. "But we should probably call it a night. We've got a matinee tomorrow, and you have hype to live up to."

They got their checks and settled up before heading out. Olivia tried to flag down a taxi, but it passed them by. "You'll be sorry when she's famous!" Will shouted after it.

Laughing, Emily struck a haughty pose and added, "Yeah, don't you know who I am?"

The next two cabs that came by were occupied. "We may as well hoof it uptown," Olivia said. "Then we'll be heading in the right direction if another cab comes along."

The strange silver-haired man had left the diner around the same time they had, and he'd made no move to hail a cab for himself or to walk away. He approached them. "If you are planning to walk uptown, would you mind if I joined you?" he asked. "I do not believe it is prudent to walk alone at this time of night. I read the newspapers. I know what can happen."

Emily and her friends glanced at each other. This wasn't a city where it was wise to trust strangers at any time of day, no matter how polite they were. As if sensing their doubts, he smiled and spread his hands helplessly. "The three of you outnumber me," he said. "I believe I am more at risk in trusting you than you are in trusting me."

"Well, come on, then," Olivia said with a shrug and a wry glance at Emily as she started walking. "Home isn't getting any closer with us just standing here."

As they walked, Emily studied the man out of the corner of her eye. Olivia was right; he was cute. He was definitely a fixer-upper, but with raw material like that, it would only take one good shopping trip to make him more than presentable. Granted, he was a little strange, but not in a creepy way. It was more like he was unearthly, from some other time or place. Based on his wardrobe, Emily guessed that he might be an academic who seldom left his ivory tower. Not her usual type, but variety was the spice of life.

"I'm sorry, I didn't catch your name," Will said to him.

The man hesitated, then finally said, "I am called Eamon."

"Thank you for coming to our show, Eamon," Olivia said.

"Do you think our Emily's going to be a huge star and forget all her friends?" Will asked.

Any normal person would have said something like, "Of course she'll be a huge star, but I doubt she'll forget her friends." Eamon said, "They do often forget," his voice solemn and mournful.

"Okay!" Will said in a "changing the subject now" tone. He, Olivia, and Emily continued chatting about the show as they walked. Eamon listened attentively, smiling as though he enjoyed hearing the conversation, but he made no effort to join it.

They reached Columbus Circle without running across an available cab. "So, park side?" Will asked. "That'll put us in position for an uptown cab. I don't know about you people, but I have no desire to walk thirty more blocks."

"Good idea," Olivia said. "We'll put you big, strong men between the park and us ladies, so you can protect us from things that lurk in the darkness."

"If some lurking thing leaps out at us, you're on your own," Will said. "I figure all I have to do is outrun the rest of you."

It was Eamon who walked between the group and the park wall as they headed up Central Park West. When they reached the old Tavern on the Green, Will called out, "There's a cab coming!" He stepped toward the street, waving his hand. Emily turned to see if the cab stopped, and while she was distracted, she missed her footing and would have fallen if Eamon hadn't caught her elbow.

Emily felt oddly dizzy—whether from the near fall, the events of the day catching up with her, or Eamon's touch, she wasn't certain. She was sure she was still walking, but it felt more like floating, and it seemed as though she was covering great distances with each step. She closed her eyes for a moment and gave her head a good shake. When she opened her eyes, everything was different.

For one thing, her friends were nowhere in sight. For another, she was deep in the park, not on the sidewalk next to a major street. Grass and trees surrounded her, as far as she could see. And she *could* see. It had been dark before, but now it was daylight. Not midday, but more like the time just before sunset, although the shadows didn't stretch the way they did at sunset. In spite of the waning light, the colors were intensely saturated. The grass was much greener, the sky was much bluer, and there were brightly colored flowers everywhere. It was as though she'd left sepia-toned Kansas to enter Technicolor Oz, and everything had burst into the most vivid hues she'd ever seen.

The one constant was the man with her, and even he had changed. She'd thought he was cute before, but now he was so beautiful he was beyond human. His pale skin had an opalescent shine, like he was lit from within, and the white-blond hair glowed a metallic silver.

This was all really, really strange, but she had a sneaking suspicion about what had happened. The details were different, but the incident was hauntingly familiar. Her pulse sped up like she was about to step onstage on opening night. "Oh my God," she breathed. "It was *real!*"

She'd been in a place like this before, long ago when she'd wandered off the path in the woods back home in Louisiana. At times over the past fourteen years she'd wondered if it had actually happened, if it had just been a dream or a delusion of her sister's that she'd heard about so often that she had a mental image of it as vivid as a memory. But it *was* real.

She'd been brought back into the realm of the fairies—not the cute winged sprites of greeting cards and Disney movies, but rather the Gentry, the fae, the Sidhe, whatever people called them in places where these creatures were feared or respected. According to her sister Sophie, they were beautiful, horrible, greedy, selfish, and utterly amoral. The last time, Sophie had brought her back to the real world and had impressed upon her the danger she'd narrowly escaped, but ever since then, Emily had felt incomplete, like she longed to return to a place where she'd once been truly happy.

Now she was back, and Sophie was nowhere nearby to drag her away this time. Could a place this beautiful really be *that* dangerous? Okay, so Eamon had pretty much kidnapped her instead of inviting her, but it wasn't as though he'd done it in a mean way. This time she knew the rules: never give direct thanks and don't eat or drink anything they offer. She might as well enjoy herself, and then if it worked like the time before, she could be back home before anyone knew she was missing.

"So, you've brought me back to fairyland," she said to Eamon.

If he was surprised that she knew the score, he didn't show it. "I have brought you to the Realm." He held his arm out to her, and she let him escort her across a park that was almost like Central Park in the real world, only more so. The real one was but a shadow of this place.

"I've been dreaming about this for fourteen years," she said as they walked. "Last time, I just stumbled into the Realm. Did you come after me, specifically?"

"I was looking for you, Emily Drake."

She didn't notice the transition, but suddenly they were indoors, in an apartment. It wasn't a real apartment, at least, not a real New

York apartment, cramped and filled with books. It was a Hollywood sound stage version of the living room in a New York apartment, with a raised area at the back where doors opened onto a terrace with a geographically impossible view of the city, all of the landmarks of the skyline showing at once, and in the wrong proportions. The room was open and airy, filled with mid-century modern furniture.

A Holly Golightly-style party was in full swing. Women wearing retro cocktail dresses danced with men in suits with skinny ties. It looked like a scene out of a Doris Day movie. This was the kind of place where she could imagine Doris Day sputtering in righteous indignation at Rock Hudson while wearing a fabulous frock.

But here the people were too beautiful, even for Hollywood, and in a strange way. Their hair was done in the right styles, but it didn't look quite like real hair. It was metallic-looking, or else like spun glass. The people seemed insubstantial, like they might vanish in a puff of smoke at any moment. The music they danced to should have been early sixties jazz, but it was a wild Celtic-sounding music that was the wrong accompaniment for the twist the dancers were doing.

Her memories of the Realm had been more like *A Midsummer Night's Dream* than *Pillow Talk*, but the unearthly people and their eerie beauty were the same. She felt awfully out of place in this setting. Her jeans and the souvenir show T-shirt her former chorus mates had given her for an understudy-taking-over gift weren't appropriate party attire.

Then she looked down and saw that she was wearing an early-sixties cocktail dress–heavy green silk, off-the-shoulder, fitted to the waist, with a full skirt. Funny, but she still felt like she was wearing jeans. It was probably a glamour, she thought, recalling Sophie's fairy lectures. She wished she could do that in the real world. It would be wonderful to look like she was dressed to the nines in evening wear and stiletto heels while she felt like she was wearing jeans, sneakers, and a T-shirt.

Now, this was the kind of opening-night party she should have had, she thought with a grin. A fairy handed her a drink, but she dumped it into the nearest potted plant as soon as the fairy's back was turned. Sophie had warned her that eating or drinking what the fairies offered her would make it nearly impossible for her to leave their world, and while coming to a party here was fun, she had a career on the rise back in New York.

Eamon stayed by her side. He looked as out of place in this party as she felt–possibly even more out of place than he'd seemed in the diner–but he was just as beautiful as any of the fae at the party. His silver hair gave him a shimmering halo. Although his face looked young, his eyes were ancient. They were the color of the mercury in old thermometers, a quicksilver color that shifted with light and motion. They were the most bewitching eyes she'd ever seen, and she felt as if she could have stared into them for hours–until she reminded herself that mercury was poisonous.

"Something tells me this isn't just an opening-night party for me," she said to him. "So, what's the deal? What do you want with me?"

"I wish nothing of you. I'm bringing you to one who sought you."

Emily shook her head in confusion. "But why? Was there unfinished business from before? Was something supposed to happen before Sophie showed up and ruined everything?"

He looked like he had no idea what she was talking about. "You have been sought for years. You were lost, and now you are found."

The room suddenly went quiet. Even the music stopped. The party guests all faced the rear windows. Emily turned to see a fairy woman standing on the upper level. The woman's golden hair was pulled into a French twist, and she wore a skin-tight dark green dress that cupped her breasts in a heart-shaped bodice and then flared into a mermaid-style tail just below her knees. She was tall enough to make Emily feel short, and so slender that her body couldn't possibly have held the normal human organs. Emily had seen her before, during her last visit to the fairy realm, although she'd been dressed differently then.

The woman paused to pose until she was certain that every eye was on her before she stepped gracefully down into the room. She sashayed across the floor to Emily, then stood in front of her for a long time, studying her with eyes that were as hard and as glittery as diamonds. She reached up a hand to stroke Emily's cheek, and it took all of Emily's self-control not to wince at the icy touch. Other memories were now returning. They were hazy, but Emily recalled being afraid, and it had been because of this woman.

The woman frowned and tilted her head to one side before turning to Eamon. "Are you quite certain?" she asked. "She doesn't feel right."

He took the *Playbill* from his jacket pocket and showed the autograph to the woman. "She gave me her name."

The woman studied the signature, then gave him a brilliant smile. "Eamon, darling, you've done it," she purred. "You've brought me my prize, at last." She turned back to Emily and said conspiratorially, "You have no idea how gratifying it is to learn that there is someone competent around here, after so many failures."

Eamon gave a stiff bow. "I am honored to have pleased you."

The woman laughed and swatted at his arm. "I'd ask you to give my court lessons in competence, but you're such a dreadful bore that I couldn't stand more like you." She gestured toward a flunky, who handed Eamon an old, leather-bound book. "Here is your reward, as I promised. Now, run along, back to your library."

Eamon seemed more relieved than insulted to be dismissed like that, and his attention was already more on the book than on his surroundings. He gave the woman another stiff bow, nodded to Emily with a faint smile, then left the party. Emily felt a pang of loss at his departure. She'd thought he liked her, but she was nothing more to him than the object of a quest. *That's the last time I let a fan walk home with me,* she thought.

The woman took her hand and gave it a squeeze, sending a chill all the way to her elbow. "Now, my pet, we never got a chance for proper introductions before. I'm Maeve, but you may call me Your Majesty." Still holding Emily's hand, she led her to the sofa, which immediately cleared as the other fairies scattered, returning to their party. Once she and Emily were seated, Maeve continued, talking as though this was a normal conversation happening in a normal place. "How have you been doing? And how is your sister?"

Now Emily remembered more from that time before, something about a confrontation between Maeve and Sophie, and although Emily had hated to leave the fairy world, she'd been glad to be away from Maeve. Fear welled up inside her. This wasn't about a party at all. There was something else going on, and she wished for the first time this evening that her big sister would show up and get her out of the Realm again. She gave Maeve what she hoped was a steely smile. "Sophie's probably on her way here already. She always knows when I need her."

Maeve returned Emily's smile and said, "Good. I've been looking forward to seeing her again for a very long time."

A chill that had nothing to do with Maeve's touch surged through Emily's veins. This was the first time she'd ever encountered anyone who'd had a run-in with her sister who had any desire to repeat the experience. She knew then that she was in big trouble.

Sophie, come get me! she screamed inside her head even as she tried not to let her panic show.

 TWO

Maybelle, Louisiana—The Drake Residence
Wednesday, 1:30 a.m., Central Daylight Saving Time

Sophie Drake woke with a start, gasping for breath. Then she buried her face in her pillow and groaned, "Oh, Emily, not again."

With a deep sigh, she rolled out of bed and crossed her bedroom, yanked her closet door open, pulled her suitcase down from the top shelf, and began packing to go to New York. Maybe this time she could settle things once and for all.

Three

The Realm—The Apartment
Soon Afterward

Maeve didn't seem to notice Emily's fear. "Now, how long has it been?" she asked. "You've become an adult since I last saw you."

"It's been fourteen years," Emily said tightly.

"Oh, really? Is that a long time?" According to Sophie's fairy indoctrination, time did funny things in fairyland. Emily could spend what felt like months here and return to the real world at the moment she left it, or she could spend what felt like minutes, only to return to the real world and find that a century had passed.

Needless to say, she preferred the former option. It would be far less detrimental to her career.

It was possible, then, that to Maeve it had only been a day or two since her last visit. "It's about half my lifetime," Emily replied.

"Then that charming sister of yours should be an adult now, too."

"Well, yes. She's nearly four years older than I am." This was the kind of conversation Emily could follow with only half her brain, so she concentrated the rest of her mental capacity on thinking about how to deal with her current situation. She resorted to the problem-solving method that had worked for her since she was a child. "What would Sophie do?" she asked herself.

It was a trick question. Sophie wouldn't be in this situation because she'd have known Eamon was a fairy and would have sent him running in terror instead of going with him. But if the fairies got smart and hired a bunch of mercenaries to sneak up on Sophie in a dark alley and surround her, and if one of the survivors managed to whack her on the head so the fairies could haul her into fairyland, and if she were then stuck in a crazy fairy queen's lair for some unknown purpose, then what would Sophie do?

"What is your sister doing now?" Maeve asked. "She used to visit us all the time, but she stopped coming and we miss her. She's a lovely dancer. Of course, she did have the best training."

That got Emily's attention. She knew Sophie knew a lot about fairies, but she'd thought that was just part of Sophie knowing pretty much everything about everything, not because she was a regular in fairyland. In spite of her wish just a moment ago that Sophie would come to her rescue, she felt a pang of the familiar "It's not fair!" younger sister lament. If Sophie went to the Realm all the time, then why did Emily have to stay away? She supposed that Maeve could have been lying, but if she didn't know Sophie beyond her rescuing Emily before, how did she know Sophie was a dancer? Not that Emily wanted to let Maeve know this was news to her. "She's teaching dance now," she said.

Maeve's smile was creepily reptilian. "Is she, now? Really? You mean she's not dancing anymore?"

"She does that, too. Sometimes."

Maeve threw back her head and laughed. Emily didn't know what was so funny. Yeah, Sophie had been on the fast track toward international ballet stardom and had surprised everyone by staying home to teach instead, but she had her reasons. Come to think of it, Emily had never actually asked her sister about that. She'd been too grateful that Sophie staying home had made her own escape easier.

With a wave of her hand, Maeve summoned a serving girl

who bore a tray of cocktail glasses filled with pastel liquids. Maeve took a glass, then said to Emily, "Have a drink."

"I'm not thirsty," Emily said firmly, even as her mouth seemed to fill with cotton.

Maeve laughed again. "I suppose your sister taught you not to eat or drink here." She gave a smug smile. "I don't think it will make much difference."

Her smile vanished instantly as she turned back to the human serving girl. "Why are you still here?" Maeve snapped. "She doesn't want a drink. Leave us." Emily tried to give the girl an encouraging look, but the girl didn't raise her eyes as she scuttled away. "I shouldn't expect too much from her," Maeve said with a weary sigh. "She *is* only human."

Her mood shifted abruptly again as the apartment door opened and two women entered. She waved them over to the sofa. "Oh, good," she said, "just in time. Here are some people I want you to meet."

The women were dressed in the same Doris Day style as all the fairies, one wearing a pale blue dress with a full skirt and the other a buttery yellow sleeveless sheath. Both of them gave deep curtsies to Maeve as they chorused, "Your majesty."

"Hello, my pets," she crooned to them. "I've brought you a new friend."

Emily felt like she was at a casting call where they'd specified a particular physical type. The women fit her general description, even though they didn't look much like her. They were both in their twenties and were tall and slender, with reddish hair. Although they were pretty, they didn't have the unearthly beauty of the fairies. They were human.

"You've come to join us!" the woman in yellow said. "We'll have so much fun!" She turned to Maeve and asked breathlessly, "Is she the one?"

"Yes, she is, finally."

"They thought we were the one, but her majesty said we

weren't," the one in blue explained to Emily. "She let us stay, though. She's very good to us."

Emily cringed at the realization that these women must have been kidnapped because they resembled her. She hoped they weren't angry that their lives had been disrupted.

They didn't seem to mind. They jumped up and down like demented cheerleaders, crying, "Yay! You're here at last!"

A fairy man in a Rat Pack suit approached the sofa and bowed deeply to Maeve. She sat up straighter, and her eyes lost even the slightest hint of warmth. "Do you have something for me?"

"Yes, your majesty."

Maeve rose gracefully from the sofa. "You girls have fun. Keep an eye on Emily for me." She took the man's arm and let him escort her out to the terrace.

Once she was gone, the two human women sat on either side of Emily. The one in blue crossed her legs daintily at the ankles. "Queen Maeve has been *dying* for you to get here," she said. "She likes us, but you're the one she wants."

"And when the queen is happy, everyone is happy," the one in yellow said. Although her tone was cheerful, Emily thought she saw fear in her eyes. If she was afraid, then maybe she was still rational enough to know what was going on. These two weren't ideal information sources or allies, but Emily knew she had to start somewhere.

"I'm Emily," she said. "What are your names?"

They frowned and looked at each other. "I forgot," the one in blue said, looking momentarily troubled.

"Me, too," the other one agreed.

"What do they call you?" Emily asked.

"They don't really talk to us," the one in yellow said with a shrug.

"You have to have names. What should I call you?"

They looked at each other again, then said, "Emily!"

Emily swallowed a scream of frustration. "No, you can't be Emily. *I'm* Emily. It would get confusing. Now, what else would you like me to call you?"

Her pretty forehead creased in a frown for a while, then the one in blue said, "I'll be Emma."

"And I'll be Leigh," the other one said.

"Okay, I can live with that," Emily said with a sigh of resignation. This looked like a hopeless cause, but she pressed on, asking, "How long have you been here?"

They looked at each other again. "I think it's been years," Emma said, then frowned. "Or has it been days? I'm not sure." She giggled. "You know what they say about time flying when you're having fun!"

"And we're having fun!" they chorused in unison. Emily shuddered. This was very Stepford Wives, sorority house edition. She noticed that although these women were clearly human, they had a hint of fae unearthliness about them. They must have been drinking the local Kool-Aid. Now she understood why Sophie said that was a no-no. Was this what she'd be like now if Sophie hadn't rescued her before?

"How nice for you," she said with a thin smile. "But don't you want to go home?"

"Why would we want to go home?" Leigh asked with a shrug. "Here we don't have to work. We just go to parties and dance and sing all day, and we get to be around her majesty."

Emma looked more wistful, like she was remembering something she'd lost. "What is it?" Emily asked gently.

"I forgot," Emma said with a sigh. "Sometimes I think there was something that made me happy before, but it can't have been as good as this, could it?"

"Did you ever try to leave?" Emily asked, but a handsome fairy with blue-black hair took Emma by the hand, pulled her to her feet, and danced off with her. Her wistfulness disappeared instantly. She threw back her head and laughed while she spun wildly with the fairy man. His hands strayed onto some rather intimate places, and she leaned into him. Pretty soon, they'd be in "get a room" territory, Emily thought. She turned her attention to the other girl and repeated her question.

"There's no way out," Leigh said.

"There has to be. My sister got me out before."

"Some of the Gentry come and go, but they tell us humans can't pass through the barriers on their own."

Well, yeah, they would tell you that, Emily thought. "Do you know why they were looking for me?" she asked, but Leigh was being pulled away by another fairy to dance. Emily shook her head at the fairy man who approached her, even though the music made her twitch with the desire to dance. Dancing might be giving in. She swore to herself that she absolutely would not go native.

Alone again, she was back to the question of what she should do. She imagined Sophie would figure out if she really was a prisoner, test the defenses to see if she could escape, gather and analyze information, and then come up with a plan.

Emily could do that. She glanced around the room, looking for potential exits. There was the front door, a door opening from the other side of the living room, and the terrace doors. Nobody stood at any of those doors in a guard-like pose, but there were also plenty of fairies between her and all the potential exits. She figured she should see if she really was a prisoner.

She got off the sofa and ambled across the room, aiming toward the buffet table but passing right by the front door. A fairy man moved between her and the door as she passed, his movement almost unobtrusive enough to be casual. She wandered by the interior door as she went to examine a painting on the adjacent wall and, again, someone just happened to move in front of the door. Yeah, she was a prisoner, all right.

Maeve had entered and exited through the terrace doors, so they had to lead somewhere other than just a terrace. While Emily didn't want to run into Maeve, she thought she might learn something by heading in the direction Maeve had gone. But if that was a way out, she doubted they'd let her go.

What she needed was an excuse to be near the terrace doors. She could stand there and stare at the view until they got bored watching her and figured she was just looking out the window. They'd still probably do something if she tried to go outside, though.

Then an idea struck her. If they wouldn't tell her why they wanted her, then she had to guess, and why would they take a Broadway actress right after she made a stunning–if she said so herself–debut in a starring role? It was safe to assume (or pretend to assume) they wanted her to perform. She was pretty sure she remembered something about fairies stealing humans to make them sing and dance. She glanced around for something that would make a good prop while also being useful as a weapon. Unfortunately, the Doris Day life didn't come with many potential makeshift weapons. The best she could do was a big, frilly umbrella with a pointed end that she found in an umbrella stand by the door. That gave her an idea of something to perform.

After a mental rehearsal to make sure she remembered all the words, she sang the opening lines to "Don't Rain on My Parade." There was stunned silence as every fairy in the room turned to face her. As the song picked up steam, she danced forward, twirling the umbrella, then moved back and stepped up on to the room's upper level. The fairies turned out to be much like any other audience, and soon she felt she had them eating out of her hand. If this had been an audition, the part would have been hers for sure.

She treated the upper level like a stage, dancing along it. When she reached the bridge of the song, she moved to the heavy drapes hanging to the side of the terrace windows. She clung to the drapes while checking behind them to see that there was an open door there, and then she moved forward to the front of her "stage." She made another trip back to the drapes, then forward again, so they'd get used to the idea of her approaching the drapes and returning.

At the end of the song, while she was still holding the final note, she stepped behind the drapes, bending backward for a grand finale before making a dramatic exit. She heard the applause as she slipped through the doors and out onto the terrace.

But she wasn't really outdoors, she realized. It was like a sound stage, giving only the illusion of the outside world, and the terrace was incomplete. One more apartment doorway opened from it, but then the terrace shifted and became a balcony on an entirely different building. Through the windows she saw what looked like an Art Deco-era hotel ballroom full of people doing the foxtrot. That wasn't any closer to home for her, but the voices behind her meant she didn't have the luxury of picking her next stop.

She might be leaving the frying pan to throw herself into the fire, but she didn't think things back in Doris Day land would go well for her now that she'd tried to escape. Without a backward glance, she stepped through the French doors and into the ballroom.

Four

The Upper West Side, New York City—The Murray Residence
Wednesday, 3 p.m.

A persistent buzzing sound penetrated Michael Murray's sleep. He swatted at it to make it stop, but his arm was trapped and didn't work. Something wet touched his face, and he opened his eyes to find himself staring eye-to-eye with a glaring, slobbering bulldog. The dog barked once, as if to make sure he was awake. The buzzing noise repeated, and Michael gradually realized it was the front-door intercom.

"Hush," he told the dog sleepily. "Maybe if we pretend we're not home, they'll go away. Anyone who needs to see me has a key."

The dog grunted and sprawled on the floor beside the sofa. Michael let himself drift back to sleep when the buzzing stopped. He hadn't completely lost consciousness when there was a polite rapping on his apartment door and a female voice called, "Detective Murray?"

That was harder to ignore. If someone had made it past the front door, then he ought to see who it was. With a groan, he struggled to sit up and then get to his feet. That would have been easier if his right arm weren't in a sling and if he didn't have to worry about stepping on the dog. The painkillers that made his head fuzzy didn't help matters, nor did the fact that he was about a quart low on coffee for the day. Come to think of it, he hadn't had any. He couldn't be expected to function. Once he was standing, he waited a second to make sure he could remain vertical, then he staggered to the entryway.

Peering through the peephole, he saw a woman. She didn't look too threatening, and both of her hands were visible, so she was apparently unarmed, unless her umbrella concealed a weapon. That didn't make it any easier for him to open the door. Putting his hand on the knob, knowing there was a stranger on the other side, made his heart beat faster and beads of sweat break out on his forehead. Gritting his teeth, he unlocked the deadbolt and opened the door.

He instinctively made a mental note of the woman standing there, as though he was filling out a report: Caucasian female, somewhere between early twenties and mid thirties—she could have passed for eighteen physically, but there was a stillness about her that indicated greater maturity. About five foot three, slim build, red-gold hair, just past shoulder length, loose curls. Blue eyes. Wearing a flowered dress with a long, full skirt, a pale blue cardigan sweater, and flat shoes. He ran his good hand over hair that hadn't seen a comb in days in an attempt to smooth it as he suddenly felt intensely conscious of just how awful he must look.

"Detective Murray?" she said in a honeyed drawl. "I'm so sorry to disturb you. I'm Sophie Drake, Emily's sister."

He remembered Emily talking about her sister, though from the way Emily had described her, he'd expected an armored Amazon holding a sword in one hand, a bullwhip in the other, and shooting death rays from her eyes, not this pretty little thing.

"Emily, your downstairs neighbor?" she prompted, and he realized he'd just been standing there, staring at her.

"I thought you'd be taller," he said without thinking.

"Yes, well, genes can be funny that way. I understand you have Emily's spare key."

His head was gradually clearing, and that request put him instantly on high alert. "How did you get up here?" he asked suspiciously.

She waved a casual hand down the hallway. "Oh, one of your

neighbors was nice enough to let me in. He even carried my bag upstairs for me."

Michael gritted his teeth. He was always lecturing his neighbors about not letting strangers inside. Sophie Drake—or whoever she really was—didn't look like a serial killer or a burglar, but you never could tell.

"I really am Emily's sister," she said, as though he'd spoken out loud. "Would you like to see my ID?"

She wasn't what he'd expected, but she did look like a miniature version of Emily, and he recognized her umbrella as the gift Emily had bought for her sister last Christmas. When opened, it would have a painting of ballet dancers on it. Closed, there was a glimpse of a foot in a ballet shoe. "That's not necessary," he said. "But why do you need Emily's key? Is she not home?"

"No, she's missing, and I need to make sure Beauregard's okay."

"Beauregard?"

"Her dog."

"Oh, Beau." He really shouldn't be having a conversation like this on a coffee-free day. "He's fine. He's here." Responding to his name, Beau waddled up to the door and stuck his head out from behind Michael's legs. "See, here he is."

"Oh, *good.* That's a relief. I hope you don't mind watching him a while longer. Again, I'm sorry to have disturbed you." She turned to go, grasping the handle of her suitcase.

His painkiller-fogged brain finally caught up with the conversation. "Wait, you said Emily's *missing?*"

She turned back. "She didn't show up for the matinee today."

"How do you know?"

"It's on the Internet."

He had to grab the door frame to steady himself as his legs threatened to go out from under him. He was pretty sure he was awake, so this couldn't be another nightmare. "Oh. No, she wouldn't miss a performance," he said numbly.

"Definitely not," she agreed. "I could see her becoming

scarce if she'd been a flop, but girls who've spent years trying to get a big break on Broadway don't run away after getting rave reviews. Something has to be wrong."

He felt like he was living a horrible flashback about another actress who'd missed another performance. "She didn't come to walk Beau this morning like she said she would. I should have noticed that. I should have known something was wrong." A wave of dizziness struck him, making him sway. He'd have preferred to blame the painkillers and general weakness after his injury, but he knew it was probably a minor panic attack.

Sophie steadied him with a hand on his arm. "Oh dear, are you all right?"

"I'm just–I," he stammered.

She dropped her umbrella, put her arm around his waist, and bustled him inside, settling him on the sofa with a pillow behind his back. "You've had a shock," she said. "I'll make some tea."

Moving with a brisk efficiency, like she already knew where everything was and had no intention of wasting a single movement, she headed to the kitchen alcove that opened from the living room, filled a kettle, and put it on the stove. While the water heated, she went back to the entryway and brought in her umbrella and a suitcase big enough that she could have traveled inside it and been less cramped than in a coach seat. Michael had the disconcerting feeling that he'd completely lost control of the situation. He hadn't even invited her inside, and yet there she was with her luggage, and she'd taken over his kitchen.

Once he was past the initial shock, his instincts and training kicked in. "Have you notified the police yet?" he called into the kitchen.

She poured water into mugs, then came back out to the living room. "I *just* got off the airplane," she said, raising one delicately arched eyebrow. "And doesn't an adult have to be missing for a certain amount of time before the police will take a report? They'd probably laugh at me if I called so soon."

"It depends on the circumstances. When there are strong

indications that she didn't leave of her own accord, the sooner we take action, the better. I can make the call. If I say it's something worth looking into, that may make it a greater priority."

She blinked. "Oh. Well, that's very kind of you. But I don't want to be a bother."

It wasn't the first time he'd heard that from a relative of a crime victim, and in his experience, those were the people who either called him every other hour or turned out to be the perpetrators. He couldn't imagine Sophie Drake fitting into either category, so he wasn't sure why she was declining his help. Maybe it was a Southern thing, a polite demurral for propriety's sake. "It's no bother, really," he insisted. "I just have to make a phone call."

She hesitated, then said, "Well, in that case, I would appreciate any help you can offer." With that, she headed back into the kitchen.

He called the precinct and ignored the good-natured teasing about goldbricking before he reported the situation. While he spoke, he kept an eye on Sophie in the kitchen. To convince his colleagues that this was serious, he couldn't mince words, but he hated talking so bluntly about his concerns in front of Sophie.

A burst of classical piano music filled the room, and both he and the dog jumped, startled, while Sophie groaned out loud as she went to the purse she'd left on the coffee table and took out her phone. He got distracted while trying to simultaneously follow two conversations. "Oh, hello, Donna," she said into the phone. "Did you get my message? No, I'm afraid you'll have to. You see, I'm *already* in New York, so there's no way I can host the meeting tonight. Donna, honey, I'm sure you can do it. They'll probably beg you to take over permanently. Okay then. Take care. Bye-bye!" As she switched off her phone, she muttered, "You'd think I was the only one in the entire town who could host a book club meeting."

Michael forced his attention back to his own phone call and said, "I could bring her over if you like... Yeah, my place is fine. Okay, whenever you can get someone here."

As he hung up, Sophie brought over two steaming mugs, set one on a coaster on the coffee table, then handed him the other, making sure he had a secure hold before she let go. She sat on the other end of the sofa and picked up her own mug as she slipped one foot out of its shoe and tucked it up under her other leg. "Do the police think it's anything to worry about?" she asked, turning to face him.

He took a sip of syrupy sweet tea. It wasn't the coffee that would have really sharpened his mind, but it did revive him somewhat. "They'll look into it."

A flicker of something–he wasn't sure what–crossed her face, but she nodded serenely and said, "I'm sure they're horribly backed up, so it may be a day or so, right?"

"No, they said they'd get someone right over. I convinced them that this was serious."

She opened her mouth to respond, but another burst of piano music rang out and she reached for her phone. "Oh, hi, Mama," she said into it. "Yes, I thought I'd pay a surprise visit to Emily. I just *had* to see her show. No, you should be fine. Bess is there all day with Nana and puts her to bed. You'll just need to pop in a few times during the day. Now, I have to run. I'll talk to you later. Love you."

Michael watched her as the cheery smile she'd put on during the call faded. "You haven't told your mother about Emily?"

She switched the phone off and put it back in her purse before giving him a pitying look. "Oh, honey, no, and you should be glad of it. The last thing you need is my mother up here, fussing around in a panic, and that's exactly what would happen if she knew."

"Won't she find out eventually?"

Her other foot came out of its shoe and was tucked up under her skirt. "I'm not sure my mother knows how to work the Internet, she doesn't believe in television, and she hasn't touched a newspaper since Daddy died. We're safe for a few days." She studied him with a steady gaze, then said, "I didn't realize you weren't well, or I wouldn't have bothered you. What happened, if you don't mind my asking?"

"I knocked on a door. I guess they weren't happy to see me," he said, remembering too late that shrugging was a bad idea.

"Oh, dear. I hope it wasn't too serious."

"Nothing that a week in the ICU couldn't take care of."

"And Emily's making you dog-sit in your condition?"

"Actually, I think Emily's making the dog neighbor-sit."

A smile threatened to curve Sophie's lips, and she took a sip of tea before saying dryly, "I'm sure he's quite helpful around the house—cooking for you, cleaning up, changing your bandages."

"With some help from Emily. That's why I'm pulling any strings I can for her."

She put her feet back in her shoes, leaned forward to put her mug on the table, then stood up. "After all that hard work, Beau could probably use a walk. I'll take him out while we're waiting for the police to get here. Where do you keep his leash?"

At the word "walk," Beau tried to make himself invisible. "There's a hook by the door," Michael said. He found it odd that she was so concerned about a dog at a time like this, but she was flitting about the apartment so rapidly he couldn't quite focus on her enough to ask about that. Maybe she was just trying to distract herself from worrying about her sister, he reasoned.

She found the leash and came over to the sofa. "Come on, Beauregard, let's go out." Beau edged his way under the coffee table, and Sophie turned to Michael, frowning. "I thought dogs liked walks."

"That would be normal dogs. Beau is either the laziest dog alive or an agoraphobic. He hates going out."

"Come on, Beau," she urged, sounding frantic, like she needed to go out far more than Beau did. A knock on the door interrupted her coaxing. Michael shifted his weight forward onto his feet so he could stand, alarmed about not having heard the downstairs buzzer, but she put a hand on his knee and said, "No, don't get up. I'll get it," and headed to the entryway.

Before he could warn her to find out who it was first, she opened the door and Gene Tanaka, his training supervisor from his first year as a detective, stepped inside. Tanaka was a bear of a man, shorter than Michael but still towering over Sophie, and broad-shouldered enough to fill the entryway. "Hello, ma'am," he said to

Sophie, then he addressed Michael as he came into the living room. "Hey, Rev, I heard you called for some backup."

"That was fast," Michael said. "I feel special."

Sophie froze behind Tanaka. "You mean, this is the police, already?" she blurted, and the look on her face was panicked, not pleased.

Five

For a moment, Emily forgot she was being pursued. When she stepped through the balcony doors, it was as though she'd walked into the kind of movie she and Sophie used to watch on rainy Saturdays. She'd moved from the Doris Day universe to the world of thirties musicals. Glamorous couples in evening attire swirled around an Art Deco ballroom to the sounds of an ethereal orchestra. Waitresses in black uniforms with frilly white aprons moved around the perimeter of the room, where more fairies sat lounging at tables and drinking champagne—or the fairy equivalent.

The scene would have been more familiar to Emily in black and white, but this version had been inaccurately colorized, which was what told her she was still in fairyland. The skin tones weren't quite human and the hair colors not only didn't appear in nature, they were beyond anything that could come out of a bottle. The clothing hues were just a little too deeply saturated to be real. Combined with the highly polished floor, the mirrored walls and pillars, and the bubbles wafting through the air, the effect of all the color, sound, and motion was disorienting.

Remembering that there were people following her, Emily ducked behind a potted palm and looked for another way out. She scanned the room's walls, but every time she thought she saw a door, it turned out to be a reflection from somewhere else. The only way to find the exit was to work her way around the room.

And that would be a problem, she realized when she glanced down at herself. The green dress she'd worn at Maeve's party would have stood out here, but that glamour had faded, leaving her in jeans and a T-shirt, which were even more incongruous. She'd be spotted as an outsider the moment she ventured out from behind her palm.

She was pondering whether she could crawl around the room under tables when she noticed that her legs were now draped in blush-pink silk. This room's glamour must have kicked in. Her skin was fair and her hair was bright enough that she might be able to slip through the crowd without immediately being recognized as human. Keeping to the outside of the mirrored pillars that ringed the dance floor, she strolled casually around the room. It reminded her of a carnival funhouse. She practically had to touch the mirrored wall to be certain whether what she saw was real or a reflection, and there were times when she was fairly certain she saw something in a reflection that wasn't in the room.

A woman approached her, and Emily tensed. This woman was tall and quite sexy in a dress made of pale pink fabric almost the color of her skin that clung to every curve so that she appeared naked while being fully clothed, and she was heading so directly toward Emily that it would be terribly obvious if Emily tried to avoid her. Emily's only hope was to act like she belonged there and was on her way to an important destination. She forced herself to keep walking as though she didn't see the woman, but the woman didn't veer off her path. Emily was a split second from walking into a mirror before she realized that she was approaching her own reflection.

She paused to admire herself for a moment. "I have *got* to find a dress like this," she murmured. Then she noticed movement in the reflection and turned to see that some men in Maeve's Rat Pack style attire had entered through the balcony doors. They'd caught up with her, and she still hadn't found an exit.

She hoped they'd look for someone trying to hide, not for someone in the middle of the dance floor. She stuck her umbrella point-first into a palm tree's pot, then grabbed a tuxedoed fairy man who bore a striking resemblance to an otherworldly Clark Gable. "Dance with me, handsome," she purred. He obliged by pulling her into a dance hold and sweeping her onto the floor.

She and her partner hadn't even made one circuit of the floor before the music trailed off into silence. There were angry mutterings as the dancers stopped, and a voice rang out from near the bandstand, saying, "How dare you enter our domain?"

A man and woman who looked a lot like Nick and Nora Charles from the *Thin Man* movies stood on the stage by the band, glaring at Maeve's people. One of Maeve's men stepped forward. "We seek a fugitive on behalf of her majesty," he said.

The fairy Emily thought of as "Nora" laughed harshly. "Her majesty? Do you mean Maeve? I do not recall her earning that title. She rules only her own little court. She has no power here."

"And we have no treaty with her," Nora's counterpart "Nick" added. "You are not welcome here."

"Maeve's captive must be returned to her," the newcomer insisted. Emily felt like he was looking right at her. Surely he'd recognize her. She was the only human here not working as a waitress. She pressed against her partner's side, trying to hide behind him and willing the searchers not to notice her.

Nora smiled and ran one finger along the long strand of beads that hung around her neck. "If you tell us who it is and why it is so important to Maeve, perhaps we would oblige her by offering some friendly assistance."

Yes, please, tell her, Emily thought. Then she might finally learn what was going on.

Unfortunately, the man merely bowed, said, "We will inconvenience you no further. Apologies for the interruption." He and his colleagues left.

Nora raised one penciled-on eyebrow. "Maeve must be up to something," she said to her consort. "I wonder what it is this time." They laughed as she waved a gloved hand at the band and the music started again. Emily had a hard time focusing on the steps of the dance as she tried to keep an eye on Nick and Nora, who were talking intensely, their heads close together.

As Emily and her partner danced, Nick and Nora moved into the crowd. They didn't find partners, but both of them wove their way around the dance floor. Emily's breath caught in her throat from the fear that they were looking for her. If she was valuable to Maeve, she might be equally valuable to them, and she doubted they'd let her leave if they found her.

"You're trembling," her dance partner said.

"I felt a chill," she replied. Even though she knew she was still wearing her jeans and T-shirt and not a slip-like, nearly backless dress, she thought she felt his cold hand on the bare skin of her back.

"Do you need my jacket?" he asked.

She looked up at him and reminded herself that he didn't really look like Clark Gable. It was a glamour. Even with the glamour, he was odd, with eyes that didn't seem to have pupils or irises. They were disks of glossy black, and his hair had a bluish sheen. "I'll be fine if I keep dancing," she said, resisting the urge to look for Nick and Nora.

She spotted the exit when she saw people coming and going through a set of glass doors that were nearly invisible in the mirrored walls. She decided to dance the rest of this song, so her departure wouldn't be so obviously connected with the interruption by Maeve's goons, and then make her getaway.

The music shifted subtly from one song to another, and dancers changed partners or drifted to or from the dance floor. She was about to thank her partner for the dance, then remembered the rule about not thanking fairies. "That was a lovely dance," she said. He smiled and kissed her hand, and she turned to go, only to find herself in the arms of the man she thought of as Nick.

She instantly tensed, then realized that was a dead giveaway and forced herself to relax. They made one circuit of the floor before he spoke. "You dance divinely, my dear," he said, his voice low and seductive.

"That's quite a compliment, coming from you," she said flirtatiously, hoping she didn't sound as terrified as she felt. Why had he singled her out? He must have realized she was human. Did he know she was Maeve's escapee?

"I don't believe I've seen you before."

"I've been around, but I'm fairly new here."

"Ah. I'm sure I'd have noticed you if you had been here." He pulled her even closer in a way that her Cotillion teacher would have frowned upon, and they moved as one. He was an expert dancer whose lead was easy to follow. She was accustomed to dancing with professionals in choreographed numbers, but those dances weren't nearly as graceful and fluid as this impromptu whirl around a ballroom. If she could capture this motion on stage, her career would be made.

The music seemed to go on and on, and she wondered if it would ever end. She imagined that this was the equivalent of having the king dance with her, so she couldn't excuse herself in the middle of a song. She saw her umbrella in the potted plant as she passed by, and then the doorway, and then they were on the wrong side of the room again. She'd always thought Cinderella was foolish to linger dangerously close to midnight at the ball, but she was starting to understand just how difficult it could be to get away from a royal dancing partner. Every turn around the room brought her closer to pumpkin time.

The song finally wound to a finish, and she held her breath, waiting to see what Nick would do next. He bowed over her hand, released her, and after a long stare he turned and moved away, toward Nora. The two of them spoke softly as they stood in the middle of the dance floor, and while they were occupied, Emily hurried toward her umbrella, pulled it out of the pot, and moved swiftly for the glass doors.

Her back felt like it had a target on it as she forced herself to gracefully ascend the steps to the doors. At any moment, she was sure someone would call out, exposing her as an imposter, or capture her, but she made it to and through the doors into what looked like a fancy hotel lobby, only without the registration desk and bell stand. There was even a revolving door. She wondered where the door led–to yet another cinematic version of a historical era, or maybe to whatever passed for the outdoors in fairyland? It was too much to hope that the doorway would take her back to the real world. It couldn't possibly be that simple.

And it wasn't. She heard hurried footsteps behind her and turned to see a group of stern-faced tuxedoed men rushing out of the ballroom. She ran for the door, glad she still felt like she was wearing sneakers even as she heard the rapid click of heels on the marble floor. The footsteps behind her sped up, as well, and she dove for the revolving door, throwing her whole weight on it to start it spinning.

The door came to a sudden, shuddering halt before she was safely on the other side as her pursuers caught it. She wasn't entirely trapped, though. There was a narrow slit open to the outdoors, so she sucked in her stomach, turned sideways, and squeezed her way through. At the last second, her pursuers pulled back on the door, narrowing the gap and trapping her foot. She jerked away, freeing herself but leaving her shoe wedged in the doorway. "Oh, no, you're not using that to track me down. I've read that story," she muttered as she bent to grab her sneaker. She jammed her umbrella into the door to keep it from revolving, and then she ran for her life.

Six

Tanaka turned to face Sophie. "Miss Drake? I'm Detective Tanaka. I'll be looking into your sister's disappearance."

Sophie recovered her composure instantly and gave Tanaka a dazzling smile as she took his umbrella. "Please, call me Sophie. I must say, I didn't expect such special treatment. You got here so *quickly*." Although her honeyed drawl sweetened her words, Michael detected a tart edge of displeasure in her voice.

"Hey, anything for the kid here," Tanaka said, coming over to where Michael sat on the sofa. "How're you doing, Rev?"

"Better."

"Well, you still look like hell. I mean, heck. I'll have to tell everyone that you're not just taking a vacation here." His tone changed from teasing to real concern. "And this is probably the last thing you needed, huh?" The level of worry on his face and in his voice suggested to Michael that the rapid and high-level response had nothing to do with the potential seriousness of this case and everything to do with Tanaka's concern about how it might affect Michael's currently fragile health. In short, he was being humored.

Sophie joined them after setting Tanaka's umbrella in the bathroom to dry. "Can I get you anything to drink, detective?"

"No thanks," Tanaka said.

She gestured toward the chair facing the sofa. "Then please, have a seat." She seemed to have forgotten that this wasn't her home.

"I'll need to talk to you too, Rev," Tanaka said as he settled into the chair. "You're the neighbor, and you know her habits."

"I don't like being on this side of things," Michael grumbled.

Tanaka nodded. "I know."

Sophie paused for a second, watching the two of them, before joining Michael on the sofa. As soon as she sat, she started to lift her right foot out of its shoe, then she seemed to realize what she was doing and shoved her foot back down.

Tanaka took out his notebook and a pen, opened the notebook, and braced it on his knee. "Now, Miss Drake, I'm going to ask you both some questions. Please don't take offense, but there are some things I need to rule out. I'm not casting aspersions on your sister."

Sophie nodded. "I understand. And in the interest of saving time, I'll tell you that, to the best of my knowledge, my sister didn't have money troubles and wasn't in debt. I've never noticed any signs of substance abuse. She has no history of mental illness. She hasn't mentioned dating anyone, and that means she also hasn't mentioned any recent breakups. She wasn't planning a vacation, since she just took over the lead role of a Broadway show. She got a good response to her debut, so she isn't hiding in shame. Is there anything else you need to know?"

As Sophie went through this recitation, Michael watched her in something that felt uncomfortably like awe. He'd conducted hundreds of interviews, and he'd never seen anything like this. She sat perfectly still with her hands folded in her lap, staring steadily at Tanaka as she spoke. She didn't clutch or smooth her skirt, tuck her hair behind her ear, pick at her fingernails, or exhibit any of the other signs of nervousness he usually saw when he was questioning people. When it had been his turn in her place, he'd been a mess. He remembered grabbing his knees so it wouldn't be obvious how badly his hands were shaking.

But Sophie was the steadiest, calmest person in the room. Her unwavering gaze was getting to Tanaka, who had beads of sweat forming on his forehead. He kept his eyes down on his notebook instead of looking up at her, avoiding the intense eye contact. That was something Michael never thought he'd see–this delicate girl was making Tank sweat, just by looking at him. The most hardened psychopaths hadn't been able to get to Tank like that.

No, not a girl, Michael corrected himself. She was about four years older than Emily, as he recalled, so she was over thirty. She'd probably get carded in a bar, but no one would dare treat her like a child.

Tanaka shifted his shoulders uncomfortably and turned to Michael. "What about you, Rev? Does this fit with what you've seen?"

"Yeah."

Tanaka nodded. "Okay, that eliminates the usual reasons people go missing."

"Which means foul play, right?" Sophie asked.

Tanaka took a handkerchief out of his pocket and wiped his forehead, then shot a worried glance at Michael before answering Sophie. "Let's play it safe and investigate like it is foul play. Now, I need a physical description of your sister."

"She's twenty eight, five foot nine, very slender build, has strawberry blond hair a shade redder than mine. I think she's wearing it past her shoulders now. Her hair is a little curlier than mine. Blue eyes." She broke her focus on Tanaka, who sighed in relief, to take a photograph out of her purse and hand it to him. "This is the most recent photo I have of her. I printed it before I left."

Tanaka tucked it away in his coat pocket. "Thank you, that's helpful. Any tattoos or other distinguishing marks?"

"No tattoos, unless she got one recently that I don't know about. She is a dancer, though."

"So?"

"It gives her some distinguishing marks." Sophie pulled her right foot out of her shoe and extended her leg in front of her, her toes pointed. Michael would have expected a woman like her to have the kind of dainty foot that would slide easily into a glass slipper, but her foot was gnarly. Her toe joints were large and knotted, and there were calluses around her toes. The nail on her big toe was a purplish black. Two of her smaller toes were taped. "Dancers tend to have hideous feet," Sophie said, putting her foot back in its shoe.

Tanaka raised an eyebrow as he made a note. "I never knew you could spot a dancer by her feet."

"Oh, honey, ballet is *brutal*."

Tanaka flipped a page in his notebook. "When did you last talk to your sister?"

"Last night, shortly after ten my time, which would have been eleven here. She'd just come offstage, and she called to tell me how the show went. She was about to go out with some friends from the cast. She said she'd call me later, but she didn't, and she hasn't answered when I've called her, either at home or on her cell."

"Did she mention the names of these friends?"

"I'm sorry, no, but they're in the chorus of *Emma: The Musical*."

Tanaka turned to Michael. "And what about you? When did you see her last?"

"She came up yesterday evening before she left for the theater bring me some soup. She left Beau with me for the night and said she'd come by in the morning to walk him."

"She didn't come by?"

"No, but I didn't notice it at the time. I was kind of out of it. I fell asleep on the sofa, and Beau woke me up this morning when he wanted to go out. I took him for a walk, then I fed him, ate something, and I fell asleep again. Next thing I knew, Sophie was knocking on the door."

"Did you hear Emily come home last night?"

Michael shook his head. "Nope, but she could have had a wild party down there and I wouldn't have noticed."

Tanaka consulted his notebook. "Now, Sophie, Michael said you knew Emily was missing when she didn't show up for the matinee."

"That's right."

"You flew to New York from—where, exactly?"

"Maybelle, Louisiana. It's about forty miles northeast of Shreveport."

"Michael called us soon after three. The matinee started at two. How could you have known to come before anyone knew she was missing?"

Michael wanted to groan out loud. He hadn't even registered the time incongruities.

He wasn't the only one to react to the question. For the first time during this interview, Sophie's steely composure faltered. It wasn't an extreme reaction, just an overall tensing and a tightening of the muscles around her eyes, and for a split second, she broke eye contact with Tanaka, but it was more of a response than she'd shown thus far. She looked mildly furious, and Michael wouldn't have been surprised if Tanaka had turned to stone from her glare.

She lifted her chin ever so slightly, fixed Tanaka with her steady gaze, and said, "You wouldn't believe me if I told you."

"Try me."

"Okay, then, I had a feeling." She said it simply and directly, without stammering or looking at all embarrassed.

Tanaka raised his eyebrows and smirked. "A *feeling*?"

"A wake-up-in-the-middle-of-the-night-knowing-something's-horribly-wrong feeling."

"You mean a nightmare?"

She shook her head. "No. A feeling. That's the only way I can describe it. I knew something was wrong with Emily."

Tanaka cocked his head, radiating skepticism. "You flew to New York from Louisiana because you had a 'feeling' something was wrong with your sister?"

"My feelings tend to be accurate. It's a family trait. For instance, my father died of a heart attack in his office. I was out shopping with my grandmother, and right there, in the middle of the store, we looked at each other and knew something was wrong, so we headed to his office. We got there before his secretary found him. So, yes, a feeling is enough for me to take action." She shrugged. "I figured if I was wrong, Emily and I could have a good laugh and spend some time together, but if I was right, then the sooner I got here, the better." Her voice took on a sharp, challenging tone. "And, as it turns out, I was right, wasn't I?"

Michael was an expert at detecting lies. He spent a good part of his working days asking people questions and trying to figure out how much of what they said was true. Over the years, he'd learned to spot all the little clues that indicated a lie, from body language to facial expression to tone of voice and even the way things were phrased. And it looked to him like Sophie was telling the truth. This wasn't an elaborate cover-up.

Tanaka seemed to have the same assessment. His eyes widened, then after a momentary pause, he said, "When did you have this feeling?"

"At about half past one, my time, so that would have been two thirty here."

"So whatever happened to her would have happened at about that time?"

"That is the way it seems to work, yes."

"And whatever that was would have been bad?"

"I'm afraid so. She was terrified, and it was like she was calling me to come help."

"She hasn't mentioned any stalkers or overzealous fans, has she? To either of you?"

"I don't think she'd tell me," Sophie said. "She wouldn't want me to worry."

"She would tell me," Michael said, "but she hasn't mentioned anything." That earned him a quick glance from Sophie, the first time she'd acknowledged his existence since the interview began. "She once said she was glad to have a cop living upstairs," he explained.

"You haven't received any ransom demands, have you?" Tanaka asked.

"I believe that's the sort of thing I would have mentioned up front," she drawled dryly.

Tanaka got Sophie's contact information, flipped his notebook closed, then said, "Thank you for your time, and for your honesty. Now, I'd better get a look at Emily's apartment. I'll have to take her computer so we can see if there's anyone she's been communicating with."

She nodded. "Yes, of course. Detective Murray has a key."

Michael stood with some effort. He was long overdue for a painkiller, and he felt like someone was stabbing him repeatedly in the upper chest with a chisel. It would be good to turn the key and the situation over to Tanaka so he could return to the blissful oblivion of his sofa.

Sophie went with the two men to the door. "Once you've looked around, would it be okay if I stayed in Emily's apartment?" she asked.

"That depends on what we find there," Tanaka said. "It may be a crime scene."

"You think you'll find her body in there," Sophie inferred.

Tanaka flinched at her directness. "That is a possibility. The fact that no one's seen her since last night doesn't mean she didn't come home last night."

That didn't stop Sophie from following them down the stairs. When Tanaka turned to glare at her while Michael unlocked the door, she said, "I know I can't go inside, but I have to know."

"Wait out here. You, too," he added to Michael. "In this case, you're a civilian." It didn't take Tanaka very long to go through the studio apartment. He came back to the door a moment later. "She's not here," he announced, "but I can't let you in until I've checked things out."

She nodded her assent. "Maybe I'll go find something for dinner. I've been traveling all day and I'm suddenly starving."

Michael reached through the doorway and took two keys off the row of hooks just inside Emily's door. "Here's Emily's key to my place, so you can let yourself in when you get back," he said, handing it to her. "And this one opens the front door."

"Thank you," she said before running upstairs.

Once she was gone, Tanaka said, "You wanna help me poke around?"

"I thought I was a civilian here."

"Now I know it's not a crime scene, and you'd know better than I would if anything's different or missing."

There wasn't that much to search. While Michael scanned the one-room apartment for anything that seemed out of place, he asked, "So, Tank, what did you think of her?"

"Very pretty, in spite of her feet. Great legs."

"That's not what I meant. Don't you think she's kind of, well, odd?"

"Oh, you mean the woo-woo stuff? That 'feeling'?"

"That, and other things." He heard the front door close, went to the window, and saw the ballerina umbrella gliding rapidly down the sidewalk.

"Well, quite frankly, she scares the sh–heck out of me. That was one freaky stare. Her eyes are weird."

"You're allowed to curse in front of me. I won't tell anyone."

"Then I'd be lying, and I'd be corrupting the Reverend Saint Michael into lying, and that's worse than having to put a dollar in the jar."

Michael had long since given up fighting his department nickname and all the nonsense that went with it, so he asked, "What's weird about her eyes?"

"Didn't you notice? They're two different colors. One's blue and one's gray. I thought it was just the light at first, but the way she was staring at me, I couldn't help but see it. It was like I saw a different face depending on which eye I focused on." He shuddered.

Michael couldn't help but smile, in spite of the situation. "I never thought I'd see the day someone could make *you* sweat in an interview."

Instead of responding to that, Tanaka said, "Emily must be old school—a landline and a machine," and hit the "play" button on Emily's answering machine.

"Hey, Em, it's Sophie," Sophie's voice said, sounding much less steady than Michael had heard it so far. "I know it's really early, and you probably hate me for waking you up if you're there, but I got one of those feelings again, like when Daddy died, or that time before with you, and I'm on my way to New York. If you are around and I'm just being silly and paranoid, call my cell. I'll be changing planes in Atlanta, so that'll be your last chance to tell me to turn back. They're calling my flight now, so I have to go." Her voice took on a strained quality, like she was close to tears. "Call me, Emily. I love you."

The call clicked off, then the robotic voice of the machine gave the time stamp as seven thirty a.m., Wednesday. "Her story checks out," Tanaka said. There was another message from Sophie a couple of hours later, followed by one from a friend an hour after that and three from the show's stage manager, starting at one. "All these messages back up what she said. So she really did know in the middle of the night, all the way from Louisiana, that her sister was in trouble. Holy s—wow. That is freaky. I've dealt with a few of those psychics who volunteer to help in investigations, and none of them have been that accurate."

Michael thought the message also meant that Sophie was human, after all. She was as scared and worried as anyone might be in this situation, even if she hid it well. He took a framed photo off the bookcase to get a better look. The picture showed two little girls in ballet outfits. The older one, maybe about seven, stood tall and proud, her hair slicked back into a tight bun. The younger one, no more than three, was still pudgy with baby fat, and there was a bow stuck in her short curls. Her fingers clutched her sister's skirt. "I think it has something to do with them being family," he said. "It's not like she gets the Bat Signal whenever random people are in trouble."

"I didn't want to put you on the spot in front of the sister, but I have to ask, what's the nature of your relationship with the missing girl?" Tanaka asked as he searched a drawer.

"She's my downstairs neighbor."

"Her dog is at home in your place, and you have keys to each other's apartments. Look, I'm not prying into your personal life, but you know how these things go. There's no hiding anything in an investigation like this, and it's better if you come clean with it now."

"Yeah, I know, the husband, lover, or boyfriend is the first suspect. But there's nothing to come clean about. She's just my neighbor. You met Sophie. Now imagine her taller and more extroverted. If she wants to look after you, there's not much you can do to stop her that doesn't involve physical violence or moving out in the middle of the night."

"Uh, huh."

"Gene, I'm married. There's nothing going on."

Tanaka turned to face him directly. "Rev, don't you think it's time you moved on? It's been, what, seven years?"

"They found that girl in California after eighteen years. *Alive.*"

"That's why you're so keen on this case, isn't it? You find this girl, and it gives you hope."

"I'm so keen on this case because it's my downstairs neighbor, and I'll be stuck with her inanimate bulldog if you don't find her."

Tanaka opened the laptop on the desk in front of the window. "Hey, she left her computer on, and the e-mail's still up. I won't need the geeks to hack in."

Michael leaned over his shoulder. "Anything good?"

"No ransom notes or creepy stalker messages that I can see. Still, I'll take it and let the tech guys give it a once-over. I hope they come across something. Otherwise, it's like this girl disappeared into thin air."

"And those cases are nearly impossible to solve." As Michael knew all too well.

Seven

New York City. The Upper West Side
4:10 p.m.

Sophie forced back a rising tide of panic as she hurried down the sidewalk. She'd wasted far too much time talking to policemen who couldn't do anything because this was way beyond their jurisdiction. If she'd known that the dog was being cared for, she could have gone to a hotel instead of to Emily's apartment and avoided the police entirely.

Then again, it would have looked awfully suspicious if she'd been in town while her sister was missing and she hadn't contacted the police. It wasn't as though the police were likely to get in her way, since they'd be looking in all the wrong places.

In the meantime, she had other things to worry about. She didn't think the waves of fear assaulting her senses were just her worry-fueled imagination. Wherever she was, Emily was in danger and afraid. Sophie bit down hard on the inside of her lip to keep herself from screaming out loud from the frustration of not being able to act immediately. Sitting through that police interview while feeling that fear had been sheer torture.

It was hours before twilight, when she might be able to find a way into the Realm, so she couldn't stage a rescue immediately, but she could buy some time. Emily knew better than to eat the food where she was, and she might be able to hold out longer if she had human food. Sophie stopped at a corner grocery and bought a couple of energy bars, a packet of roasted peanuts, a bottle of water, and a half-pint container of cream, then hurried to Central Park, the most likely place in the city to have what she needed.

She doubted she'd find what she was looking for too close to the street, so she walked until the traffic noises faded and looked for an oak on a hilltop. When she found one, she investigated the roots. The ground was muddy after a day of rain, and she slipped and skidded as she searched. At last she found a hole in the earth under one of the larger roots.

She lifted her skirt, wrapping it around her thighs to keep it from dragging in the mud, then knelt on the ground and opened the cream carton. She poured a small amount on the ground inside the hole and set the open container nearby. "Good Neighbor, I bring you this offering," she said softly, hoping this worked. She hadn't ever tried it, but she'd read a number of mentions in her research. As she waited for a response, she considered whether she might be able to squeeze through the hole and make it directly into the Realm without having to find a gateway. It would be messy, and it would require braving the Borderlands, but it would mean less waiting.

Before she could convince herself to try, a small, gnarled creature emerged from the hole. The creature lapped at the cream on the ground, sniffed greedily, found the carton, and asked, "Who brings me this offering?"

"I do, Good Neighbor," Sophie said.

The creature looked up at her, then fell on its knees. "Your gift is welcomed, my good lady. What has one such as I done to merit your favor?"

"It's what you *will* do for me. My sister has been taken to the Realm. I need something brought to her, and I ask you to take it through for me."

"I could do that, my lady." The creature sounded surprisingly eager.

"Oh, good," Sophie sighed under her breath. She'd expected more haggling, based on her research, but she had no quarrel with doing things the easy way, and this task was minor enough that she didn't feel the need to look for traps or loopholes. She took a sheet from the memo pad in her purse and scribbled a note, then put it in the plastic grocery bag with the food. In the depths of her purse she found a ribbon from an old pointe shoe. She wrapped the ribbon around the neck of the bag, tied it in a bow, and handed the bag to the creature. "Please see to it that this gets to the human girl who just entered the Realm."

"I will do that, my lady," the creature said with a bow.

Taking care not to give direct thanks—which would have implied an obligation to the creature—she said, "Your assistance is gratifying. Please enjoy the cream I leave for you."

The creature dragged the package into the hole, then returned for the carton of cream. That mission accomplished, Sophie stood and let her skirt fall so that it hid most of her mud-streaked legs. A few good puddles would take care of her shoes and ankles. She hurried back toward the street. Now she really did need to find some dinner, because she hadn't been lying about feeling starved.

Eight

The Realm
Immediately Afterward

Emily's trick with the umbrella must have bought her a few minutes, as no pursuers had yet caught her, but she was under no illusion that the umbrella would hold a bunch of magical creatures for very long. So, she paused to put her shoe back on and then ran all-out, as quickly as she could.

She was running down a tree-lined avenue like the Mall in the real Central Park, but she wasn't sure where to head. Sophie said the gateways between the fairy world and the real world existed at right angles to reality, and you had to find them by feel. Emily had no idea what she was supposed to feel. What she needed was a white rabbit to follow down a hole, but there wasn't one in sight, and she wasn't sure she'd trust it even if there was. Since she'd been brought into this world from near Tavern on the Green, she struck out in that direction. The old restaurant might not be there in this skewed reality, but she hoped that if a gateway existed near there in her world, there might be a corresponding gateway in this reality.

Changing course allowed her to glance behind her. She saw no sign of the hotel or apartment building, but she did see her pursuers, who had been far enough behind her that they hadn't yet realized she'd left the Mall. She dove behind a nearby bit of shrubbery and watched as they ran past.

Once her heart quit pounding so loudly it drowned out everything else, she noticed a strange, wild, and beautiful music wafting through the park. It reminded her of her first encounter with the fairies, when she was fourteen. She'd been walking in the woods, trying to get lost, when she'd been drawn by music like this, music that sounded to her like freedom.

The music seemed to be coming from within a nearby grove of trees. The trees offered cover, she rationalized as she left her hiding place. She most definitely wasn't going in search of that soul-stirring music.

Within the grove was a clearing, and there the fairies danced. They weren't doing the twist that fit into Maeve's Doris Day fetish or the foxtrot from Nick and Nora's ballroom. These looked wild and free, wearing filmy garments made of spiderwebs and flowers as they danced in a circle to music played by fairy musicians on instruments made from nature–a fiddle carved out of a gourd and a harp strung on a curving tree branch. It was the most amazing dancing she'd ever seen, even more hypnotic and entrancing than Sophie alone in a studio when she didn't think anyone was watching and she dropped her rigid self-control.

The sound of a hunting horn rang out before the temptation to join the dance overcame her. The fanfare sent a surge of adrenaline through her body, but she wasn't sure if it was triggering fight or flight. Apparently, she wasn't alone in that response. The musicians stopped suddenly, and there was a flurry of rustling noises as swarms of little creatures disappeared into the underbrush. The fairies in the grove also scattered, running as if the devil himself pursued them. Emily didn't want to see anything that could scare fairies, unless it was her sister, and she doubted even Sophie could trigger a fairy stampede.

A fairy woman grabbed Emily's hand and dragged her away with the others. Emily resisted, not wanting to be kidnapped yet again. "You don't want to be caught out," the woman urged, "not if you don't want to serve them." That sounded reasonable to Emily, so she ran with the fairy woman. They crossed what might have been Bow Bridge, but which wasn't, and ran into the woods, where they crouched behind some large rocks that allowed them to see the bridge while remaining hidden.

The horn sounded again, this time closer, and soon the head of a procession came into view. Tall, thin soldiers led the way on horseback, one of them sounding the horn. They wore leather and golden armor, and their hair streamed down their backs. The horses were armored and draped in silk. Behind the soldiers rode a man and woman wearing crowns and solid black clothing that was somewhat medieval in style. Both had white skin, solid white hair, and silver eyes that made Maeve's eyes look warm and twinkly in comparison. Aside from the white hair, they showed no signs of age, but Emily still got the sense that they were absolutely ancient. Behind them rode more courtiers and soldiers, and red-and-white hunting hounds ran alongside the horses.

They passed within yards of Emily's hiding place. She held her breath, now understanding why the fairies had run for cover. These people had an air about them that said they saw the entirety of creation as existing to serve their whims. A hidden fairy not much farther down the lake's shore must have made some noise because the queenly woman gestured and one of her soldiers dismounted, then pulled the struggling fairy out of the bushes. He bound the captive's hands with a silver chain and fastened that chain to his saddle before remounting and rejoining the procession. The fairy captive was left to run alongside the soldier's horse.

The procession went on forever, with hundreds and hundreds of fairies, not all of them going willingly. Emily thought a few of the captives looked human. They all moved in total silence, aside from the occasional blast on the horn. None of the fairies spoke to each other. They just stared straight ahead. If this was the alternative, Emily could see why fairies might be drawn to Maeve's court. Maeve seemed like a lot more fun.

Finally, the tail of the procession passed. The hiding fairies waited several more minutes before tentatively emerging from their shelters. "I'm lucky you were there," Emily said to the fairy girl who'd helped her.

"I would not subject anyone to the whims of Niamh and Fiontan," the fairy girl said with a shrug.

"I don't suppose you know a way out of here—to the outside world?" Emily said, hoping the girl's helpfulness might go further.

The fairy pointed behind Emily. "There is a passage in the woods. Look for the roots of the oak tree."

"Okay, oak tree. Got it." Emily left the fairies behind and headed deeper into the woods. This was like the Ramble in her park, only it really was wild, not carefully cultivated to give the appearance of wildness. If she wasn't mistaken, it was also getting darker, and not just because the trees blocked the light.

It would have been easier if she knew what to look for. Would it be like a magic mirror with the real world on the other side, or would she hear traffic noises? Traffic noises would have been reassuring and definitely less creepy than the noises she heard now, which were wilder and fiercer than anything that came from the zoo.

She glanced up at the forest canopy to look for oak leaves, then realized she wasn't actually among trees. Roots came down from above to form what she'd thought were tree trunks. So, that was what the fairy meant when she mentioned the roots of the oak. Fairyland must be underground, and there must be a passage hidden in the tree roots. The trick would be finding it. How would she recognize an oak tree without being able to see the leaves?

She was so busy looking up as she walked that she tripped and fell. While she was still on the ground, something pounced. She swatted it away, but then something else came at her. Things pulled at her hair, and she felt sharp teeth pierce the skin of her neck.

Leaping to her feet, she shook them all off and ran back toward the light. Now she knew why she'd been able to escape. They didn't have to worry about her getting too far. The dark areas where the barrier between fairyland and the real world was thin were too dangerous for her to pass through on her own. She no longer had a destination in mind. She just wanted to get away from these attackers. She ran blindly, as fast as she could go, toward the only source of light she could see.

The light turned out not to be the flat twilight that counted as daylight in the fairy world. Instead, it was squares of windows. As she drew closer, she saw that the windows were set in a forest hut. Would it be a gingerbread cottage where a witch lured children to their deaths, or would it be the home of a kindly woodsman who would give her shelter?

Right now, she didn't care. She wanted these things with their sharp teeth and grabbing hands off her. If it was the witch, she'd just have to shove her in the oven. She reached the hut, wrenched open the door, and found herself in a library.

Bookcases rose from the floor to a ceiling several stories high—far taller than the cottage had looked from the outside. In addition to the leather-bound volumes she expected to find in a place that looked like it belonged in an Ivy League university, the shelves were filled with battered paperbacks, a few textbooks, lots of magazines—many of them torn or stained—and stacks of yellowed newspapers. It looked like a library made up of things people had left on park benches.

Once she caught her breath, a wave of exhaustion swept over her. Whatever time it was in fairyland, her body thought she'd been up all night. Even Sophie would be tired, and this library hut seemed like the last place Maeve would go, given the way she'd sneered at the book she'd given Eamon. This was probably about as safe as she'd get in this world.

Feeling like Goldilocks in the bears' home, she looked for a place to lie down. The bench by one worktable would be too hard, but there was an overstuffed chair by the fireplace that might be just right. She sat down, slumped against the back, turned sideways to drape her legs over one arm, and dropped off right away.

She didn't feel like she'd been asleep long at all when she woke with the sense that someone was watching her. When she got her eyes fully opened, focused, and adjusted to the light, she saw Eamon, her kidnapper, standing in front of her.

"What are you doing here, Emily Drake?" he asked.

Nine

New York City. The Upper West Side—Murray Residence
Wednesday, 5:00 p.m.

Michael saw Tanaka off, straightened Emily's apartment from the search, then locked up and headed up to his own place. He had to stop at the top of the stairs to catch his breath and fight off a wave of dizziness, and then a burst of panic struck when he unlocked his apartment door. His heart raced and his hand shook, and he had to remind himself that it was his own apartment. The only individual on the other side of that door was the world's laziest dog, unless Sophie had made it back without him noticing, and he didn't think she would shoot him. A door phobia would not be good for his career, so he told himself to get over it and opened the door.

Although he'd just feared finding someone on the other side of the door, once he was inside he couldn't help but hold his breath and hope that his apartment wouldn't be empty this time. But the only sound that greeted him was the jingle from Beau's tags as the dog lifted his head to acknowledge Michael's return. Michael let out his pent-up breath in a sigh. "I'm having flashbacks on multiple traumas today," he told the dog. "That doesn't sound good, does it? And I'm consulting a dog about my mental health. We'd better not share that with anyone, okay? I'd like to eventually be allowed to carry a firearm again."

His stomach growled, reminding him that he hadn't eaten anything since a Pop Tart sometime that morning. He headed into the kitchen and opened the refrigerator to see if any food had miraculously materialized. Alas, the only thing inside that didn't require cooking was a half-full container of the soup Emily had brought the night before.

"Whaddaya think, Beau?" he asked the dog, who'd joined him in the kitchen the moment the refrigerator door opened. "Soup, or call out for delivery?" Beau barked once, letting him know that he wasn't the only one who was hungry. While the dog danced eagerly around his dish–about the only time he showed much sign of life– Michael measured out dog food.

There was a knock at the door, and Sophie's voice called, "It's Sophie. Don't get up." He went out into the hallway as the door opened, just in time to see a bedraggled Sophie enter, holding a plastic bag. She put down her umbrella and stepped out of her shoes in the entryway. Her legs were spattered with mud from the knees down, and the hem of her dress was damp and muddy. "I brought dinner," she said, holding up the bag. "Has Detective Tanaka already gone?"

"Yeah. He said it's okay for you to go into the apartment. I've got the key. And Tank took your suitcase down."

She set the plastic bag on the dining table. "That was awfully kind of him."

"Did you have any trouble?" he asked.

She frowned and looked down at her damp and mud-spattered clothing. "Oh, yes, that." Without offering an explanation, she said, "I hope you like Chinese." Before he could answer, she headed into the kitchen and came back with plates and silverware. "I didn't get anything to drink. Is water okay?"

"Yeah, water's fine." He stood there helplessly as she went past him back into the kitchen and filled two glasses with water before bringing them to the table, where she unpacked the plastic bag, bringing out several to-go boxes. He had so many questions about what was going on with her that he didn't know where to start. Not that he'd get a straight answer out of her, so it probably wasn't worth trying, he decided.

"Since you've got a bad arm, I'll make a plate for you. I got cashew chicken and Hunan beef. Would you like a little of both?"

"Uh, yeah, that'll be good," he said, realizing that once again she'd taken over the role of hostess in his home. He got the feeling she did that everywhere she went. If she went to dinner at the White House, she'd welcome the other guests and ask the president if there was anything she could bring him from the kitchen.

She loaded a plate with food and set it in front of him with a fork and a napkin. "Soy sauce?"

"No, I'm good. And thanks for dinner. You didn't have to do this." Though he was glad she had.

She dished rice onto her own plate. "Nonsense. I've put you to so much trouble. It's the least I could do." She finished filling her plate, took her seat, then asked, "Did you find anything interesting in Emily's apartment, or are you not allowed to tell me?"

"If she came home last night, she left again and took her wallet and her phone." He recapped the rest of what they'd found, including the phone messages. "I'm sorry, but we don't have a lot of leads."

"It's still early," she said, sounding so calm that he would have been suspicious if he hadn't heard her frantic messages. "I can hardly expect instant results."

"I'm curious about one thing, though," he said. "Your phone message mentioned the feeling you had being like another time with Emily. Was that anything that might be relevant here?"

She reacted ever so slightly—so slightly that he couldn't read her reaction. Then she waved her hand dismissively. "Oh, it was something that happened when we were kids. She got lost in the woods when we were camping, and I knew she needed me to come find her."

"I bet that knack of yours comes in handy."

"It's brought me nothing but trouble. Trust me, you do *not* want to be the first one on the scene when someone dies."

"I know that. Crime scenes are my job."

"But how often are you the one to find the body?" Her eyes softened into something that looked a lot like pity. He noticed what Tank had meant about her eyes being different colors. The difference was subtle enough that it wasn't immediately obvious, but once noticed, it became disconcerting. "I'm sorry to put you through this," she said. "Emily didn't tell me about your wife, or I never would have involved you."

He nearly choked on the bite he'd just taken. "What?" he blurted before coughing as some rice went down the wrong way. She jumped out of her seat and came around to pound him on the back.

"Can you breathe?" she asked, and when he nodded, she handed him his glass of water and ordered him to drink.

Once he could get enough air to talk, he croaked, "How did you know?"

"I couldn't help but notice," she said, returning to her seat. "You wear a wedding ring and there's a wedding photo on your bookcase, but otherwise this looks like a bachelor's apartment. Detective Tanaka seemed far more concerned about you than he was about me, which gave me the impression you'd gone through something similar. In fact, I suspect he came here more because of you than because he thought this case needed immediate action."

He nodded weakly and forced a smile. "Have you ever considered an investigative career?"

She raised an eyebrow. "I'm sure the NYPD recruits a lot of ballet teachers." She hesitated, then asked gently, "What happened to your wife?"

Normally, he didn't like talking about it because he'd had to talk about it so much when it first happened and it came up again whenever any cop found anything so much as resembling a lead. Now, though, he found himself wanting to discuss it with someone who might understand. "It was a lot like this, actually. She was even an actress. She didn't show up for a performance one night. Sometime between having lunch with a friend and the cast call for that night, she vanished without a trace."

"That must have been very difficult for you, even as a police officer."

"Yeah, it was. When something bad happens to a woman, it's usually the husband or boyfriend who did it. That made me the number-one suspect. Luckily for me, I was working crowd control for a big event that day. I was surrounded by cops the entire time between when she was seen last and when she didn't turn up. I was on closed-circuit security footage that whole day. I had the most airtight alibi in the history of alibis. And the investigating detectives still acted like they thought I'd rigged the whole thing, or like I'd been so horrible that she'd given up everything to get away from me."

"She was never found?"

He hated to answer and possibly dash her hopes, but he didn't think Sophie Drake was likely to crumble from hearing the truth. "Not yet. I'm not giving up, though."

"How long has it been?"

"Seven years."

Her eyes went unfocused, and she said absently, talking more to herself than to him, "Seven years ago Emily had just come to New York. Mama was violently opposed to that scheme, but it was all Emily ever wanted, and she didn't see any point in waiting." She blinked back to the present and added, "It seems like so long ago, doesn't it?"

"Yeah, it does. And some days, it's like it was yesterday."

She followed his gaze to the wedding photo on the nearby bookcase, showing a man who now seemed like a stranger, so young and innocent, wearing a police dress uniform and smiling at a tall, red-haired woman in a wedding gown and veil. Sophie bit her lip as she looked at the photo, then abruptly pushed her chair back and stood. "Are you done with that?" she asked, indicating his plate.

He wasn't hungry anymore. "Yeah, thanks."

She gathered the dishes, took them into the kitchen, and came back for the to-go containers. "I'll leave you the leftovers so you'll have some meals for later." He felt like a heel for sitting there while she cleaned up and washed the dishes in his home, but he did have an arm out of commission. Even with two good arms, he doubted he could have matched her pace. She moved so briskly she practically blurred.

After she'd finished cleaning up, she came back to the table and said, "And now if you've got that key, I'll get out of your hair. I can take Beau. You've had to do enough dog-sitting."

"I don't mind. I should warn you that he snores. I can keep him out here and shut out the worst of it, but Emily doesn't have a separate bedroom."

"I've spent enough nights in my grandmother's room, and even a bulldog has nothing on her. But if you want to keep him..."

It occurred to him that she might want the company. "You go ahead, if you want to keep him with you. But I'll take him if he keeps you awake."

"Okay, then. Now, the key?" He took it out of his tracksuit pocket and handed it to her, but when he moved to stand, she shook her head. "You stay here. I'm quite capable of making it downstairs on my own. You need to rest."

She hooked Beau's leash onto his collar, picked up her purse and umbrella, and said, "Does Beau also have supplies at Emily's place, or will I need to take his things downstairs?"

"He should have everything he needs."

"Okay. Well, have a good evening, and thank you again for everything." Before he had a chance to respond, she was gone, and he was left with his head spinning. She'd suddenly gone frantic—or what passed for frantic in the unflappable Sophie Drake. Her mood had changed when she looked at the wedding picture, so he got up to get a closer look. What about it had upset her so much?

One glance gave him a good idea. Funny, he'd never noticed any resemblance between Jen and Emily. They were totally different types, but now that he looked at the photo, thinking like a cop instead of like a husband, he realized that he'd use the same words to describe them if he were writing a report. It was too much to be coincidence: Two women who lived in the same building, who fit the same general description, and who even had the same profession had vanished without a trace, almost exactly seven years apart. Was this the break he needed?

Or was he seeing patterns that weren't there, trying to find sense in something senseless?

He'd turned this case over to the police, and now it was none of his business. And yet, if they found Emily, they might find Jennifer, or at least they might learn what happened to her and he could put her to rest. He couldn't sit on the sidelines now.

He called Tanaka. "Say, Tank, there's something I'd like you to check," he said. "Could you run a missing persons search on all females in their late twenties at the time of their disappearance who are tall and have red hair? If you get any, see how many are actresses."

"You think this is connected to Jen?"

"It is a pretty staggering coincidence."

"Was Emily Drake living in that building when Jen disappeared?"

"No. But she was on the Upper West Side."

"Two points don't make a pattern, Rev."

"That's why I'm asking you to check for more points. I don't expect you to find dozens of cases, or else we'd have noticed, but it's possible that there have been others and they were too spread out for parallels to be obvious."

"Okay, I'll check. Now, remember, you're not working this case. Go lie down and take it easy. See if that little ballerina will cook you dinner. I bet she's the type who'll stuff you with home-cooked meals while she's here."

"She already brought me Chinese."

Tanaka laughed. "Of course she did. It probably softened you up for her interrogation."

Michael was glad Tanaka wasn't there in person, or he'd have surely seen from Michael's face that he was right. She *had* managed to get a lot of information out of him. "While I lie down, you get to work," he said.

But he didn't want to lie down. He didn't feel like this could wait. Tank was good, but he was as overworked as every other detective in this city, and Michael had a feeling that if he got Sophie on board, she might make more headway with the theater people. If they hurried, they might even be able to catch the cast as they arrived at the theater.

Ten

The Realm—The Library
Immediately Afterward

Emily tried to hide her surprise as she muttered, "Somebody's been lying in my bed, and here she is!" Eamon didn't seem to appreciate the reference. She sat up straight, swinging her legs around to plant her feet on the floor. With a glare she felt had to be as good as anything Sophie had ever dished out, she added, "What am I doing here? You *kidnapped* me!"

He smiled at her, but the firelight made his mercury eyes look demonic, which canceled out any friendliness from his expression. "I brought you to the Realm, but I did not bring you to the library. I asked what you are doing in the library."

"I was out for a walk and thought I'd drop by."

He didn't respond to her sarcasm, if he even caught it. "But how did you leave Maeve's court?"

She struck a dramatic pose. "With style and pizzazz."

"How did you find my library?"

"I just stumbled on it," she said with a shrug.

He frowned–that is, his eyebrows moved toward each other,

though his brow remained uncreased. "I find that unlikely. Few can find this library. You came from the Borderlands, didn't you?"

"If that's what you call the dark, creepy place with all the tree roots, yeah. I had these *things* after me, then I saw the light in the windows, and, well, here I am." Thinking about it made her brush at her shoulders and rake her fingers through her hair to make sure those things were all gone. "That's where your front door leads?"

"It is helpful to my work if I have easy access to the world above."

"What *is* your work?"

"I once was a scribe, but there has been little call for that lately. Now I am more of an archivist."

She glanced around at the library shelves. "It looks like you scavenge anything with words in it."

"That is the most recent part of my collection. It is only lately that the printed word has become so common among humans that it is so readily disposed of."

She was pretty sure she saw a *Life* magazine from the forties on a nearby shelf, which she wouldn't have considered "recent." Then again, if he was immortal, that might have felt like last week to him. "Why would you want old magazines?" she asked.

"I study humans."

If he was a student of humanity, he'd failed the test that night in the diner. Then again, she'd trusted him even if she'd thought he was strange, so he hadn't done too badly. "Why?"

He paused, frowning as he sat in the chair on the other side of the fireplace. His old-professor clothes were perfect for this setting, she noted. "Humans are so *real*," he said after a while. "Your lives are short, and that means everything you do matters so much more. We have almost forever and do nothing with it."

"How very philosophical of you." His appreciative smile indicated that he still wasn't getting her sarcasm. But while they were bonding, she thought she might as well try probing him for information. "I don't suppose you know why Maeve wanted me."

He looked surprised by the question, but he still answered.

"She sought you because you are a changeling." His tone had an implied "duh!" to it.

"What?"

"A fairy left in exchange for the human who is taken."

She shook her head. "I know what a changeling is. But me being one? That's impossible!"

"How would you know?" he asked calmly, tilting his head to the side as though he didn't understand her dismay.

"I'd know! How could I not know I was a fairy copy of a human girl?"

"If you were created to replace Emily Drake, the magic would make you think that's who you were. You'd never know."

Emily was glad her stomach was empty because she might have thrown up otherwise. It wasn't true. It *couldn't* be true.

Eamon leaned forward, his elbows resting on his knees. "Have you ever felt like you were different, like you were out of place?" he asked, his voice soft and gentle.

"Well, yeah, sometimes," she admitted. "But if feeling like I was too big for my hometown is proof of being a changeling, then fairies must have been systematically swapping out most children born in small towns for decades. Don't fairies ever feel like oddballs?"

He gave a rueful smile. "Not often, and feeling odd makes one even odder."

She must have hit a hot button she could exploit. Resisting the urge to grin in triumph, she said, "Does that mean you're probably a changeling, yourself, that maybe you're a human who was kidnapped by fairies long ago?"

"Of course not. I have magical powers that a human would lack."

"Oh, right. That would be a dead giveaway. But if you aren't a changeling, then maybe neither am I."

"But you are. You are Maeve's daughter. Her enemies took you and left you with humans, and she has been trying to get you back ever since."

Emily felt queasy again for a second, then she shook her head.

"Maybe that's what she told you, but why hasn't she said anything to me? When she tried to take me before, I'd have been *overjoyed* if that beautiful woman I met in the woods had told me I was her daughter. I'd have gone with her in a heartbeat, and not even my sister could have dragged me away. But she didn't say anything then, and she hasn't said anything now."

He studied her, making her feel like an insect under a magnifying glass. "It would not be easy to tell a long-lost daughter her true heritage," he said after a long silence. "Even Maeve might fear that you would react just as you have and reject her."

"You know what would have kept me from reacting this way? Actually *talking* to me instead of kidnapping me and playing games. But even assuming I *am* a changeling, what happened to the real Emily?"

"She would have been returned as soon as you entered the Realm. No one will know the difference."

"She won't remember living in fairyland all this time? She'd be the right age, have all my memories, be just like me, only fully human?" She shook her head in disbelief. "I don't think so. She wouldn't get past Sophie. Sophie would know." As soon as she said that, hope warmed her. "*Sophie would know!*" she repeated, more vehemently. It made her feel better to think that, but was it anything more than blind faith in a seemingly omnipotent older sister?

"Who is Sophie?" he asked.

"You haven't heard of Sophie? Wow, you are out of the loop. She's my sister, and she knows a lot about fairies. She got me away from Maeve before. I'm sure she'd recognize a changeling." Blind faith or not, once she had that one argument, others flooded her brain. "Besides, if I'm Maeve's daughter, why did they keep getting the wrong girl? I met those other girls who look kind of like me. Shouldn't your people have been able to recognize one of their own instead of grabbing the wrong humans?"

He stared at her for a long moment, looking like he was giving serious thought to what she said. Then, abruptly, he stood, crossed the space between them, and placed his hands on either side of her face. His cold touch took her breath away, and being that close to his unearthly eyes added to the breathlessness. "Your aura has been masked," he said with a confused frown. "This must be why they sought in vain for you for so long."

"What does that mean in human English?"

"We do not see as you humans do." He gestured at his own body, which shifted to look entirely human, the way he had in the diner. "Looking at the physical form is pointless." He changed back to his fairy glamour. "We recognize each other through our auras, no matter what glamour we wear. Humans have weaker auras, but they are still distinctive enough that we can recognize individuals. We are so accustomed to looking at the aura instead of the physical form that with your aura masked, you are practically invisible to our kind."

"Oh," she breathed. That explained why Maeve's people hadn't spotted her in the ballroom. "But does this have anything to do with whether or not I'm a changeling?"

"It means I can't tell what you are. Someone hid you from us."

"Someone?"

"The magic is not fae."

Sophie, maybe? Emily wondered. Sophie had sworn to keep her out of the fairies' hands, but magic? She had a way of getting what she wanted, but it wasn't magic. It was just a formidable intelligence and keen insight combined with an iron will and the occasional spooky moment. If not Sophie, who else? "How did you find me?"

"It was purely an accident. I usually do not go far beyond the park when I venture out of the Realm—it is draining to be away from the trees and among all that iron. But I was restless and walked too far, and then I saw the signs and decided to see the show because I had read the book. It must have been fated."

There was a light rap on the door in a musical rhythm. Eamon gestured for Emily to stay back as he went to open it. She ignored his gesture and followed him, but kept herself hidden behind a bookcase. He conducted a brief, murmured conversation, bent to take something, and shut the door.

She emerged from her hiding place as he turned, frowning curiously at the plastic shopping bag he held. "What's that?" she asked.

"It was brought here for you."

"For me? Who's it from?" Then she noticed the pink ribbon tied around it. Not caring how rude she was being, she grabbed the bag out of his hands. Her fingers trembled as she tugged the ribbon free and opened the bag to find a bottle of water, some energy bars, and a packet of roasted peanuts, along with a folded piece of paper. When she unfolded the paper and saw "Miss Sophie Drake" embossed at the top, she couldn't hold back a sob of joy.

"Em, hold on. I'm coming for you," the note read, written in her sister's elegant hand, but more sloppily than normal, like it was written in haste. The paper was water-spotted and the ink blotched in places, but it was the most beautiful thing Emily had ever seen. She clutched the note to her chest for a moment, breathing deeply until she got herself under control. Then she looked up to find Eamon leaning over her shoulder, uncomfortably close.

She handed him the note. "You know what it means? It means Sophie knows I'm gone. *I'm not a changeling.*"

He read the note, then handed it back to her, his face troubled. "But then why would Maeve say so?"

"Seriously?" How could a guy that old be that naive? "She played you."

Instead of answering, he paced the aisles of the library, his eyes narrowed in deep concentration. While he paced, Emily tore open an energy bar and devoured it. Normally, she thought those things tasted like sawdust, but it was amazing how good any food tasted when she was starving. She felt much clearer once she had food in her stomach. She never should have even considered the idea that she might be a changeling or Maeve's long-lost daughter. But that brought her back to square one: What *did* Maeve want with her?

Or was she the one Maeve wanted? How many times had she mentioned Sophie? Maybe this was more about Sophie than about her, which shouldn't have surprised her. *Everything* was eventually about Sophie. She just couldn't figure out where Sophie might fit into this, or how she fit in if it was really about Sophie. The fairies might not have been able to tell the other human women apart, but Maeve knew Emily wasn't Sophie.

Still mulling this over, Emily took a few sips of water and opened the packet of peanuts. She'd just put the first one in her mouth when Eamon returned.

"I should not have been so easily duped," he said stiffly. "I owe no allegiance to her, and I should not have done her bidding. I have wronged you."

"You could take me back home. That would make it up to me."

While he pondered her suggestion, she popped a peanut into her mouth. When he spoke, it wasn't to offer to take her home. "May I have one?" he asked.

"You eat human food?"

"I enjoy it, but I can only eat human food that is offered as a gift. Otherwise, it is poison. Alas, as the old beliefs have faded, few leave gifts of food for the fae anymore."

"You ate apple pie in the diner. I saw you."

He shook his head sadly. "Mere illusion. I have never tasted apple pie."

"Well, that's just sad." She shook a couple of peanuts into her hand and held her palm out to him. He carefully picked up one nut and placed it in his mouth. He chewed slowly and carefully, savoring the experience, before taking the second nut. "Was it good for you?" she asked, raising an eyebrow and wondering what he'd do with chocolate.

He nodded. "It was wonderful," he said breathlessly. Then he seemed to come to a decision. He took her hand. "We must go, now."

She wasn't going to argue with that. She let him lead her to the door, but before they reached it, another door flew open and Maeve's goons burst into the library. "There she is!" one of them said. "That *is* the one, right?"

"Yes, that's the one," the other said.

Eamon didn't have to tell her to run. She sprinted for the front door. But she couldn't reach it. No matter how hard she ran, she got no closer. It was like someone had thrown a rope around her waist and was pulling her backward into the goons' grasp. Her hand slipped from Eamon's as she was pulled away.

She expected him to fight for her and wouldn't at all have minded becoming the center of a tug-of-war, but all he did was stand there. As the goons dragged her out of the library, she shouted sarcastically, "Enjoy the rest of the peanuts!" She wasn't sure whether or not she wanted that to count as an official offering.

⌐Eleven⌐

Sophie nearly missed her footing on the stairs in her haste to get away from Michael's apartment, and she had to unlock Emily's door by feel because her vision was blurred by tears. She made it down the short entry hall and into the apartment's main room before her legs gave way and she collapsed, her skirt billowing, then settling around her as she fell. Once she was alone, she let her sobs shake her whole body.

She'd known Emily was in danger because of her, because she'd been so stupid and selfish and ambitious. She hadn't known at first that there would be a cost, but she'd realized it soon enough, and learning that hadn't stopped her until they'd gone after Emily. She'd given up everything then and hoped that sending her sister away would keep her safe. It had never occurred to her that anyone else would be affected, but now she knew. Detective Murray had lost his wife, merely because she bore a passing resemblance to Emily and fairies thought all humans looked more or less alike.

If they'd told her they'd make her the greatest dancer ever in exchange for her sister, she'd never have agreed to the bargain. But she'd assumed she'd be the one to pay the price, and she was willing. She should have known, though. In all the stories, it was someone else who was taken as payment for a favor—a first-born child, a beloved daughter, a lover, a sister.

Then again, there was always a loophole, a way to redeem the one who'd been taken or to sidestep the bargain entirely. She just had to find the loophole. Or maybe a more direct payment would suffice. It wasn't as though she'd be giving up much, and at least she wouldn't have to deal with the garden club anymore. Her sobs trailed off, and she got herself back under control.

Beau ambled over and dropped his head in her lap. She buried the fingers of her left hand in the wrinkles on the back of his neck and wiped the tears off her face with her right hand. She attempted a brave smile, even though there was no one there to appreciate it. "Those are turning out to be incredibly expensive dance lessons, and what good did they do me? I could have taught ballet to kindergarteners without going through all this."

The dog grunted and rolled onto his back, waving a paw to demand a belly rub. She gave him an absentminded scratch before reaching for her purse to find her phone. It had been off for hours, so she dreaded seeing how many calls she'd missed. As she expected, when she turned the phone on, the list of missed calls went on forever. Half the town had tried to reach her. "It'll serve them right if I never go back and they have to fend for themselves," she muttered.

She'd made it through an equally long list of text messages and was about to retrieve her voice mail when the phone rang, her mother's name appearing on the screen. She sighed, took a couple of deep breaths, and then put on a big smile before accepting the call. "Hello, Mama!" she said, keeping her tone bright.

"I've been trying to reach you all afternoon," her mother said, her voice sharp with accusation.

"Yes, I noticed. I just turned my phone back on. I've been tied up. Is there anything the matter? I got a message from Bess saying Nana was doing fine."

"Well, I–"

A knock on the door gave her a reprieve. "Can I call you back, Mama?" she said. "Someone's at the door." She disconnected before her mother could say anything, then turned the phone off. She'd pay for it later, but she had enough on her plate at the moment without having to mediate small-town crises from more than a thousand miles away.

"Sophie? It's Michael Murray," a voice said from outside.

"Just a sec!" she called out, her tone as bright as it had been for her mother. She wondered how bad she looked. Tears wouldn't be unexpected under the circumstances—he'd probably find it suspicious if she didn't shed a tear or two—but that didn't mean she had to look a fright. She nudged Beau off her skirt, got to her feet, splashed her face with cold water in the kitchen alcove, and dried her face with a paper towel before wiping her nose with it. She imagined she still was a bit blotchy and her eyes were likely red, but she wouldn't have obvious tear stains or visible snot.

She took a moment to collect herself before opening the door. The false cheer she'd put on when talking to her mother wouldn't be necessary with Michael. She settled on a wan weariness so he'd assume she needed to rest and would leave her alone. When she opened the door, she was glad she'd planned her approach because his appearance left her momentarily too stunned to think.

Michael Murray looked very different from when she'd last seen him less than half an hour ago. He was still drawn and gray, with dark circles under his smoky green eyes, but he'd shaved the several days worth of stubble and combed his dark hair, and instead of the rumpled tracksuit he'd worn earlier, he wore a real suit. His shirt was open at the collar, and he wore the jacket draped around his right shoulder, over the sling. He held a tie in his left hand.

"Do you need help with that?" she asked, taking the tie from him. She had to stand on her toes to get it around his neck. As she straightened the knot and smoothed his collar, she became conscious of how intimate those little actions were and grew mildly flustered because he was rather handsome and she didn't often get this close to a man. And he was married, she reminded herself, to a woman who had vanished because of her. She took a big step away from him and asked, "Now, where are you off to, all dressed up like that?"

"I had an idea."

"Oh?"

"We ought to go to the theater and talk to the cast, see which ones went out with Emily last night. Tank might not get to that tonight, and we could give him a head start."

It was a good idea, except that it was unnecessary. What she really needed to do was find a way into the local fairy realm so she could rescue Emily and Mrs. Murray. Twilight was the optimal time for that, when the barriers between worlds were weakest, and she might miss twilight if she went to the theater, which would delay her an entire day. "Are you really up to going out?" she asked, not having to fake concern. He'd cleaned up, but he still looked like death warmed over. "You should be resting."

"I thought some fresh air would be good for me," he said with a wry smile. More seriously, he added, "It may help if we can find out who saw Emily last, and where."

She had to admit that he was right—more right than he realized. Knowing approximately where Emily disappeared might give her an idea of where to look for a gateway, but she couldn't do that properly with him in tow. "I can go to the theater," she said. "You don't have to come with me. I studied dance in New York, so I can cope with the city."

"I have no doubts whatsoever about that. But I'd like to come. It would make me feel a lot better to actually do something."

Looking into his eyes, she could see that he needed this. It would be heartless to deny him. Maybe they could get it over with in time for her to get back and find a gateway. "Okay, but don't look at me if your recovery is set back. I can't go like this, though." She indicated her muddy skirt. "Give me fifteen minutes to change." She picked up the end of Beau's leash and handed it to Michael. "Take Beau for a walk before we leave him alone."

As soon as he was gone, she jumped in the shower and scrubbed the mud off her legs. After putting on a blue jersey dress, she coiled her damp hair into a loose knot at the nape of her neck, put on enough mascara to make her eyelashes visible, and finished her rapid makeover with a bit of tinted lip gloss. She'd just put on a pair of black ballet flats and was pouring fresh water into Beau's dish when Michael returned. The flurry of activity had restored her equilibrium, so she was back in total control of herself.

"We may have to walk over to Columbus to hail a cab," he said as they went down the front steps. "But at least it's stopped raining, so we might be able to find one."

She noticed someone halfway down the block getting out of a cab, so she stepped forward and waved. The cab came down the street and stopped for them. "How did you do that?" Michael asked as he opened the door for her with his good hand.

She slid across the seat and told the driver the address of the theater while Michael got in and closed the door. As the cab took off she said to Michael, "I waved my hand. It's not hard. I'll show you sometime. Or can you not do that left-handed?"

"I never see cabs on my street."

"Well, it's not like I brought it here with my magic powers." He didn't look like he was convinced, and she wished she'd invented a good reason for being in New York so quickly, so she wouldn't have had to tell how she'd known Emily was in trouble. Now he'd assume everything she did was uncanny. On the other hand, she thought while fighting back a smile, she might be able to make use of that. As long as he didn't burn her at the stake, it would be easier to keep him in line if he thought she was a witch.

When they got out of the cab near the theater, she said, "Oh dear," with a deep, groaning sigh. The place was a shrine to Emily, with candles, stuffed animals, flowers, hand-drawn posters pledging support, and enlarged photos of Emily. People wearing T-shirts from the show stood near the shrine, handing out fliers to passersby.

Michael took her elbow and guided her through the crowd

to the shrine. He dropped her arm and put his hand in his jacket pocket, then brought out and displayed a police badge. "Are you Emily Drake's friends?" he asked brusquely.

With a sidelong glare at him, Sophie said, "I'm Emily's sister, Sophie. She told me she was going out with some friends last night. Do you know who that would have been?"

A tall woman with skin the color of chicory coffee handed her stack of fliers to someone else and came over to Sophie. "I was one of them," she said. "I'm Olivia Washington."

Michael took a notebook out of his breast pocket, then fumbled one-handed for a pen while trying to hold onto the notebook. Sophie reached over and took the notebook from him, found a pen in her purse, and wrote down Olivia's name.

"Where did you last see her?" Sophie asked.

Olivia frowned in thought, looking confused by the straightforward question. "In the cab, I think. We went to a diner– Fay's, over on Eighth–then we couldn't get a cab, so we started walking. A cab came along when we were about halfway there. Emily was the last stop, so she was still in the cab when I left."

"Who else was with you?" Michael asked while Sophie wrote down what Olivia had said.

"Will Carter. He's handing out fliers at the TKTS booth in Times Square, but he should be here soon because it's almost cast call time. He was the first one we dropped off, though, so I was the last to see Emily."

"Where did you catch the cab?" Sophie asked.

"Near Tavern on the Green, on Central Park West."

"Was there anyone else?" Michael asked.

Olivia looked confused again, then she shook her head. "No, it was just the three of us."

Sophie jumped in before he could ask a follow-up question. "Were you in the driveway, near a park entrance, or inside the park itself?"

Olivia shrugged. "I don't know. I wasn't looking at the scenery. I was watching to see if the cab would stop for us."

"And all of you got in the cab?"

That should have been another easy question, but Olivia wavered before saying, "Of course."

With a glare at Sophie, Michael asked, "What time did you last see Emily?"

"I think it was sometime around two thirty." He cast a glance down at Sophie at that, which she made a point of ignoring. Why did people always make a fuss about her little bursts of insight? They probably got them, too. They just didn't listen to them.

Michael got Olivia's contact information, which Sophie wrote down. "The detective who's in charge of this case will be in touch with you," he said.

"Thank you so much for your help," Sophie added.

"We're having a vigil tomorrow before the show—that is, if she hasn't been found by then," Olivia said. "We'd love to have you speak." Before Sophie could demur—since she hoped the vigil would be unnecessary—Olivia said, "Oh, here comes Will. Will! Over here!" A young man with fair hair that flopped rakishly over his forehead came to stand by Olivia. "Will, this is Sophie, Emily's sister. And…" She trailed off with a glance at Michael.

"This is Detective Murray," Sophie said. "He's Emily's neighbor, and he's been so kind to help me."

Will's eyes widened for a moment, and then he grinned and whispered out of the side of his mouth to Olivia, "It's Officer Friendly." Her eyes widened, too, and she shot a grin at Will. Michael made a valiant effort of pretending to ignore it. He hadn't shown any signs that his relationship with Emily was anything more than platonic, but Sophie could see how Emily's friends might wonder about the handsome detective upstairs.

Sophie took Will's contact information, and he repeated the story Olivia told, with the same occasional look of confusion as he described the evening's events. Then the two dancers said their farewells and headed for the stage door.

"They're lying about something," Michael said when they were gone. Sophie thought it looked more like they'd been magically befuddled, but of course she couldn't tell him that. "We should go check out that diner," he continued. "Maybe we can talk to someone who was working last night, and they'll know if anyone followed them from there."

Sophie heard him, but her attention was focused on her surroundings. She had the oddest feeling that she was being watched, and not merely in the sense that she was being observed at the center of a minor public spectacle. Moving in the direction of the feeling through the encroaching crowd of theatergoers, tourists, and arriving musicians and actors, she looked for the watcher. To give her that strong a tingle between the shoulder blades, someone would have to stare hard, and someone staring that hard should be noticeable.

The feeling grew more intense as she moved away from the theater, and then a hand brushed her arm, near her purse strap. She doubted a mere pickpocket would give her this degree of unease. She kicked out one leg and wrapped it around the interloper's leg while she whipped her body around and grabbed his wrist. Then she was glad that she'd caught him with her leg before she saw him because her grip faltered. She'd caught herself a fairy, right there on Forty-fifth Street. She wouldn't have thought they'd get that deep into a city.

He was taller than Michael, and he had silver hair and quicksilver eyes with a young/ancient face. The funny thing was, he looked just as shocked as she felt, even a little scared. He'd been watching her, but either he hadn't expected her to fight back or she wasn't what he expected.

"Are you Sophie?" he asked.

"Where's Emily?" she demanded, wondering if she could reach the miniature iron horseshoe on her keychain.

She didn't really expect the fairy to tell her, but he didn't get a chance. Michael's voice boomed behind her, shouting "Hey!" The fairy froze.

Twelve

The Realm
Soon Afterward

Maeve's men marched Emily through long hallways that didn't seem to belong in the same world as Eamon's library hut. She tried noting each turn, in case she had another chance to escape, but she soon gave that up. The Realm was impossible to map. She got the feeling she could go through the same door twenty times and never wind up in the same place twice. Her next step felt like it spanned an entire continent. When she blinked and cleared her vision, she found herself back in Maeve's apartment.

Emily braced herself to be berated by Maeve, but the would-be fairy queen was otherwise occupied. She lay on the sofa, dressed in a marabou-trimmed peignoir, and complained to a group of attendants who didn't fit the décor. "She should be here by now. This is taking far too long." Emily thought Maeve was talking about her, but then Maeve looked right at her and said, "Oh, good, they found you," before turning back to her people and saying, "Don't return unless you're bringing her to me."

The attendants scurried away, and another group approached Maeve. One said, "Your majesty, the Gentry are gathering, as you instructed. It will have to begin soon."

"I'm not ready," Maeve thundered, and the attendant shrank away. More calmly, Maeve added, "Let them wait. Have the musicians play."

Maeve made a few more decisions about what sounded like party plans, and when the attendants had all rushed off to do her bidding, Maeve finally turned her attention fully to Emily. "You should know better than to run off like that. The Realm is a very dangerous place. I shall have to reward Eamon for sheltering you until I could send someone to bring you back safely."

Emily stiffened at the implication that Eamon had been cooperating with Maeve. She'd thought she'd reached an understanding with him. Had he been playing her, or was Maeve deliberately making her doubt her one possible ally in the Realm? "I'm sure he'd love another book," Emily said with a careless shrug.

The front door opened and Maeve turned to face it, forgetting Emily's presence. A man dressed like one of the wild fairies out in the park entered and dropped to one knee in front of Maeve. "There has been no sign of her, your majesty," he said, bowing his head.

"No sign?" Maeve shrieked. "You must not be looking very hard. She'll be here, I know it. Go, go look for her," she ordered, pointing at the door. The man scrambled to escape, looking like he knew he'd dodged a bullet. Maeve took a few long, deep breaths through clenched teeth as her hands formed fists, and then she turned back to Emily, a cheerful smile on her perfect face. "What *are* you wearing?" she asked. "You've got to get ready for the celebration." She glanced down at herself and laughed, adding, "And I'm not much better." She waved her hand, and in a heartbeat, Maeve wore another fabulous Doris Day gown, this one a metallic gold to match her hair. Emily looked down to find that she now appeared to wear a pale blue dress with a lace overlay, like she was going to the prom in 1959.

"Ah, that's better, now, isn't it?" Maeve said with a satisfied smile as she rose gracefully from the sofa. "You're a pretty girl. You should dress like it."

More attendants arrived, updating Maeve on the celebration preparations and hinting that time was running out. "I'll be there," she insisted. "It's royal prerogative to keep the court waiting." When they were gone, she said to Emily. "I'm surprised your sister hasn't come for you yet. The last time, it was a matter of seconds before she came to whisk you away. She does still love you, doesn't she?"

"She's probably operating in stealth mode," Emily said, even as she couldn't help but wonder where Sophie was. She'd sent the food, so she was on the case, but why wasn't she here yet? "You won't see her coming. You won't even know she's been here until you notice that I'm not here anymore." Not that Emily believed a word of this. Sophie had a particular talent for shock and awe. If she was in the Realm, everyone would know about it. So where *was* she?

Strangely, Maeve seemed more distressed by Sophie's absence than Emily was. With a sick lurch of her stomach, Emily realized that Maeve was using her for bait. Sophie wasn't easy to trap, but she could be counted on to rescue her kid sister. But why would Maeve want Sophie?

The front door opened again and an attendant meekly poked her head through the gap, keeping her body shielded behind the door. "Your majesty, we can't wait any longer. They're expecting your announcement."

"I can't make the announcement because it hasn't happened!" Maeve screamed, her face momentarily losing its beautiful glamour and becoming terrifyingly ugly. An instant later, she calmed and said, "But it's only a matter of time. I will be down in a moment." The attendant nodded and ducked away, closing the door behind her.

Maeve raised her hand and snapped her fingers. The two goons who'd retrieved Emily went to stand on either side of the apartment's front door, which Maeve opened with a wave. The goons led the way, with Maeve following and the rest of the fairies who'd been in the apartment falling in behind her. Emily got swept up with the procession. She doubted she had a choice, but she went willingly with the hope that she'd finally figure out what was going on.

They trooped through the hallway to a wide staircase that led down to what looked like the lobby of one of the old apartment buildings on Riverside, but bigger and grander than any apartment lobby, more like a ballroom. It was full of fairies dressed in Maeve's midcentury style, caught up in the party to end all parties. Sophie had always sniffed haughtily that "party" wasn't a verb–which told Emily that her sister hadn't been much fun in college–but this gathering proved her wrong. This was *definitely* partying in verb form. There was music, singing, dancing, and vast quantities of food, with drink flowing freely from a fountain in the middle of the room. In spite of the energy bar and peanuts she'd had not too long ago, Emily's mouth watered.

The others from the apartment hustled Emily with them down the stairs and into the heart of the party. Maeve remained above, standing with her hands on the railing of a balcony that overlooked the lobby/ballroom. A soft buzz spread through the room, and without any fanfare or announcement, soon everyone was quiet and facing Maeve, who looked like she would burst into "Don't Cry for Me Argentina" at any moment.

When she was sure every eye was on her, Maeve said, "I have wonderful news, my people! I have it within my power to take the empty throne, and soon, very, very soon, I will rule the entire Realm. Once I unite the Realm under my rule, we will turn our attention to the world above. They no longer pay us tribute. They no longer make offerings to us. Most of them have forgotten us. But we will remind them, and we will rule them!"

Emily's stomach threatened to rebel at the thought of Maeve leading a fairy attack on humankind. The deafening cheering from Maeve's people only made it worse. It sounded like they thought attacking humanity was a great idea. Then again, she got the impression that they were a bunch of sycophants who'd have cheered anything Maeve said, and if that was the case, why had Maeve been so worried about her announcement?

As the cheering continued, Emily noticed that it wasn't as unanimous as she'd initially thought. She did a double take when she noticed some of the people who weren't cheering. She thought she recognized the Nick and Nora couple, dressed to fit into Maeve's court. Not too far away was another couple that looked totally out of place in Doris Day attire, and Emily was fairly certain they were the scary pair who'd led the procession that sent everyone fleeing in terror.

The two couples noticed each other, and Emily instinctively moved as far away as she could in that crowd because the hatred between them was so powerful it lit up the air around them. Even Maeve noticed it, as she interrupted her *Evita* moment to stare with horror down at her audience. "What are you doing here?" she hissed, her voice not much above a whisper but ringing over the sounds of the crowd. "Niall and Orla, Fiontan and Niamh, you are far from your courts."

"You've found the ancient palace, have you?" said the white-haired fairy woman–Niamh, the fairy in the park had called her. "But if you have found it, then I must wonder why you do not present yourself as the crowned sovereign rather than merely announcing your intentions."

And that, Emily realized, explained Maeve's nerves. Announcing her plan to take the throne must have been plan B, and her original plan had been to present it as a done deal. It sounded like not finding Sophie had something to do with plan A not working, and that meant that Sophie was somehow essential to making it happen.

But what could Sophie possibly have to do with taking the throne of the fairy realm?

Maeve didn't have a good answer for Niamh, and while she was still struggling to come up with one, Niamh and her consort exchanged a glance, then vanished in a shimmer of light. "You don't have that throne yet, darling," the one Emily thought of as Nora, but who must be the one Maeve called Orla, purred, and she and Nick–probably Niall–also vanished.

Maeve looked close to panic, her eyes going wide and white as her fingers grasped the balcony railing. "Find her, now!" she shouted.

Emily found herself in the odd position of hoping her sister *didn't* come rushing to her rescue this time.

Thirteen

"That diner is a few blocks this way," Michael said, then realized he was talking to himself. Sophie had vanished. He had a flash of panic at the thought of another woman disappearing on him. A tour bus had just disgorged a swarm of theatergoers, and black-clad musicians were flocking to the theaters with instrument cases strapped to their backs. In all that confusion, it was impossible to spot one small woman. Or so he told himself.

His heart racing furiously, he shouted her name as he sidestepped a cello. He forced his way through the crowd, leading with his left shoulder and guarding the injured side. Finally, he caught a glimpse of blue ahead. Fortunately, she'd worn a bright color. He'd never have seen her if she'd worn black. He nearly caught up to her just as a guy reached for her purse.

Michael's warning died in his throat when he saw her suddenly whip out a leg and spin to catch the guy. The would-be pickpocket looked utterly stunned. He was a weird one, with hair dyed a metallic silver color. The guy was tall, so Sophie had to be standing on her toes–on one foot, since she had one leg wrapped firmly around her assailant–and yet she seemed a lot steadier than her captive did. Michael had caught a few pickpockets and purse snatchers in his time, and even with a uniform, badge, and gun, he'd never made anyone look as scared as this kid was. He'd have given his good arm to hear what she was saying, but he suspected the kid would never grab another purse, ever again.

Michael felt like he ought to come to the rescue–of the purse snatcher, not Sophie. "Hey!" he called out, and her victim looked up to see him. Michael pulled out his shield and waved it, and the kid wormed his way out of Sophie's grasp and took off.

Sophie spun to face Michael, and if she'd looked at that kid the way she looked at him now, not only would he never grab another purse, he'd probably enroll in seminary or join the Peace Corps. Then she tore off after the purse snatcher.

"Sophie!" Michael shouted, but his voice was swallowed by the din of the city. He knew better than to even try running after her, since normal walking was about as much as he could handle. She wove her way expertly through the throngs on the sidewalk, and the crowds seemed to clear a path for her.

Michael figured he could stand there, waiting for her to return from her fit of vigilantism, or he could go on to the diner. She'd probably know to meet him there, and if not, he was sure she could find her way back to Emily's apartment. He headed toward the diner.

There, a ponytailed young waitress greeted him just inside the door. He flashed his shield and asked, "Have you heard about the disappearance of Emily Drake?"

The waitress pointed to the flier taped to the window. "Of course. Everyone's talking about it. I just saw her last night, and now..." She shuddered as her voice trailed off.

"If you were here last night, I'd like to ask you a few questions."

"No problem. I'm not too busy right now." She frowned as she looked at him. "Are you okay? Maybe we should sit down to talk."

He wasn't feeling very steady, to be honest. There was a reason he was supposed to be taking it easy. "Good idea," he said. She gestured him toward a nearby booth, where he took the seat facing the door.

Once he'd caught his breath and fought off a wave of dizziness, he said, "I understand that Emily and her friends were here after the show last night."

"Yeah, they hung around until about two."

He patted his breast pocket for his notebook, then remembered that Sophie had it. "Was anyone else here?"

"There were a few other theater people, a couple of cops, and a guy I hadn't seen before."

Michael perked up. "Do you know the names of the cops?" Witnesses within the department would help.

She shrugged. "Sorry, no."

"What about the other guy, did he interact with Emily and her friends?"

"Yeah, he asked her to autograph his *Playbill*. He'd been in the audience." She frowned, then said, "Come to think of it, he left around the time they did."

The bells on the door jingled, and he looked up to see Sophie entering the diner. She was a little flushed and a curl had escaped the knot of hair at the back of her neck, but she didn't seem to be at all winded. He returned his attention to the waitress. "Could you describe him?"

"He had light blond hair–really light. I thought it was white at first, but he was too young for that. It looked almost silver sometimes, depending on the light. Twenties, maybe, but it's hard to say. Tall, thin."

"We may have you work with a police sketch artist. I'm just asking some preliminary questions. Another detective will be in touch with you."

"Okay." She gave him a concerned frown. "Would you like a glass of water? You really don't look so good."

Probably not as bad as he felt. "Yeah, that'd be great, thanks," he said.

As soon as the waitress got up, Sophie slid into the seat across from him. "So, here's where you went," she said, like he'd been the one to run off.

"Did you catch him?"

"No," she said with a deep sigh.

"What were you thinking?"

"Wouldn't you say he fit the description of the person in the diner who left with Emily and her friends?"

"You think he's the same guy?"

"Maybe. And you let him get away."

"I was trying to save you from assault charges."

She swatted that excuse away with a flick of her wrist. "It'd never stick. He laid hands on me first, so it was self-defense."

"That was some move you pulled. What was that, ballet as a martial art?"

"A dancer is one of the best-conditioned athletes you'll find," she said primly. "To dance at a high level, you need strength, flexibility, speed, and endurance." She gave him a smug smile. "I can get air that would have made Michael Jordan green with envy. I merely applied a little speed and strength to our friend back there. I don't think he was expecting it."

His brain finally caught up to the conversation. "Hey, wait a second, you didn't hear the description of that guy until just now. The friends didn't even mention him. How did you know to chase him?"

"I caught him following me."

"Why didn't you say something?"

"I didn't get a chance before you started waving your badge around."

The waitress came back with a glass of water, then she saw Sophie. "You've got to be Emily's sister. I've heard so much about you." Michael noticed that the waitress took a tiny step backward, and he had to bite his lip to keep from smiling. Apparently, Sophie's reputation preceded her.

Sophie didn't seem to notice the waitress's response—or didn't react to it. She smiled and said, "Thank you so much for your help."

While he drank the water and tried to rally his last reserves of strength so he could get home, Sophie dutifully wrote down the waitress's contact information and the description of the mysterious diner patron. As they left the diner, he said, "I wonder why Emily's friends didn't mention that guy."

"I don't know," she said, her voice vague, like she was thinking about something else.

"They both seemed to be lying or hiding something, and they must have planned their stories because they had all the same details. I guess they didn't get to the waitress, though."

"Are we done here, or is there something else you want to look into?" she asked, handing him his notebook.

"What? Oh, yeah, I guess we're done. I've got enough to give Tank a good start."

Once they were in a cab and on their way home, Michael said, "Why would her friends lie to us?"

"You don't think they did away with her, do you?" she asked, her eyebrows arching skeptically. "They're the ones organizing the search."

"Yeah, but sometimes you get people who cause problems just to get attention."

"Your job must make you very cynical." She went silent, staring out the window. He leaned back against the seat and tried to make himself relax. His chest throbbed mercilessly. It appeared he wasn't yet ready to go off the painkillers.

He glanced at Sophie and saw that she'd fallen asleep with her head leaning against the window and one foot tucked up under her skirt. As they neared his street, he wondered what he should do. A gallant gentleman would carry her up the stairs, letting her sleep, but he wasn't sure he could get himself up the stairs. She resolved the dilemma by waking just before the cab stopped, and she paid the driver before Michael could grope for his wallet.

When he protested, she put a hand on his arm and said, "You're doing this for Emily, so investigative expenses are on me." He made it up the front steps without keeling over, so he decided to try to make it up to his apartment under his own steam. He said goodnight to Sophie and waited for her to enter Emily's apartment before he dragged himself slowly up the stairs.

He was too tired to have a panic attack as he opened the door, and the apartment felt even emptier than normal with Beau gone. The dog was lazy, but he was undemanding company. The first thing he did when he got inside was take one of his pain pills. While he waited for it to kick in, he checked messages and found one from Tanaka.

"Hey, Rev, I did a quick search, and there are three other women, besides Jen and Emily, who fit those parameters. One disappeared not long before Jen, and the others were pretty evenly spaced out since then. I'll look into those other missing women and see if any other parallels pop up. Take it easy, and say hi to the ballerina for me."

Michael dialed Tanaka's office number, knowing he'd get voice mail, and left the information they'd gathered. He left out the friends' stories because he wanted to hear what Tank got out of them without any preconceptions. "I know I'm a civilian here," he concluded, "but I thought it wouldn't hurt to track down those friends for you."

He was already feeling a little blurry around the edges, so he hurried—as well as he could with one good arm—to get out of his suit and into sweatpants and a T-shirt. He'd just climbed into bed when he heard the downstairs door close. On a hunch, he went to the window and pulled aside the curtains to look out. He was just in time to see what he thought was the swirl of a blue skirt turning the corner at the end of the block.

He shook his head. It was probably his imagination. It could have been anyone, and even if it was Sophie, there was nothing sinister about her going out. She was probably just giving Beau one last walk for the night.

But he still had the terrible fear that another redheaded woman was about to vanish.

Fourteen

After Maeve's rivals departed, the party intensified, as if in a frantic attempt to prove that there was nothing to worry about. Champagne flowed and music blared while the fairies danced, ate, and drank. Maeve came down the stairs and lounged on a sofa with a few of her courtiers. She acted as though she was already queen, but her gaze strayed anxiously toward the doors.

Emily figured that Sophie must have found or learned something that Maeve needed to take the throne, but what? It didn't matter, Emily told herself firmly, since it wasn't going to happen. She had no intention of sticking around and playing bait. Even if she couldn't get home, she could get away from Maeve, stir up a little chaos, and maybe run into Sophie. If Sophie was in the Realm, she'd be easy enough to find. Emily would just have to listen for the screams.

Feigning enjoyment, she ambled through the crowd toward the lobby's front doors. No one seemed to be paying any attention to her, and she concentrated on being invisible. If what Eamon said about her aura was true, maybe they wouldn't notice her in all the party excitement. Just before she reached the door, a large man in a skinny tie moved to block it, making direct eye contact with her as he did so, as if to send the message that she wasn't going anywhere. *Damn.* Not that she'd expected to be able to just walk out, but it would have made things so much easier. She changed course, as though she'd been heading that way all along and had never even considered going through that doorway.

Now what? If she couldn't get away, then she needed information. If she could figure out what Maeve was up to, she'd have a better chance of stopping her, and the info would definitely help Sophie. Spotting the guy who'd reminded her of Clark Gable from Niall and Orla's Nick-and-Nora ballroom gave her an idea.

Approaching him boldly, she grabbed his arm to turn him to face her and purred, "How about another dance, handsome?"

Without a word, he took her into his arms, and they began moving as one. Most of the other dancers were doing early sixties-style dances, but a few couples danced more closely together, so she and her partner didn't look too out of place. "So, we meet again," he whispered in her ear. "You left so abruptly before."

"I think you know why."

He raised one slightly slanted eyebrow. "You were the one Maeve sought."

"I'm very much in demand."

He dipped her, then pulled her back upright. "And I have to think that you have something to do with Maeve's scheme."

"Mmmhmmm," Emily murmured with what she hoped was an enigmatic smile.

"Which makes me think that my lord and lady might find you equally useful."

"How so?" Emily tried batting her eyelashes, but she was afraid she just looked like she had something in her eye.

He spun her around expertly. "You could help them win the throne. They would make it worth your while."

It didn't seem as though pretending that she already knew would trick him into opening up, so she decided to take the opposite approach. "I don't know anything about this. Maeve just kidnapped me. She didn't give me a briefing. You have to tell me what you want before I can decide whether or not to help you."

He missed his footing for a split second, but recovered within the space of the next beat. "You don't know about the lost throne?"

"Enlighten me."

They went all the way around the dance floor before he spoke again, and Emily noticed that they were on the opposite side of the champagne fountain from Maeve. "There are those who believe that the last queen of the Realm left instructions on how to claim the throne, when the time came. If Maeve found the palace, then all she needs is the instructions, which must somehow involve you."

Or my sister, Emily thought, but this still made no sense. Sophie was a know-it-all, but being the secret keeper of the instructions for claiming the fairy throne seemed beyond even her scope. She'd just opened her mouth to ask another question when "Clark" tugged her hand to spin her in front of him, then caught her with the other hand, keeping her spinning until their joined hands stopped her momentum, their arms fully outstretched. He did a little kick step, and she instinctively mirrored him. *Oh, boy,* she thought, *he's doing a Fred and Ginger.* She could barely think straight enough to come up with another question while keeping up with him, but she couldn't resist going along with the dance. She'd always dreamed of doing a Fred and Ginger routine, but she'd never met the right partner or run into the right situation. They didn't do much of this kind of dancing on Broadway anymore.

She felt like she was floating on air as he swirled her around and they moved in perfect unison. And then Emma and Leigh showed up to spoil it–probably sent by Maeve, who must have noticed her consorting with the outsider. The girls were all a-twitter as they pulled her away from "Clark." "Isn't this just the best party?" Emma asked.

"I'm glad to see you dancing and enjoying yourself," Leigh added.

"Let's find you a new partner!" Emma said.

"I think I'll sit the next one out," Emily protested, trying to wrest her arms from their grasp as she looked behind their shoulders for her erstwhile partner.

"Don't be silly!" Leigh said. "There's no reason for you not to have fun."

"I was having fun," Emily said through clenched teeth.

Emma dropped her voice and said, "Fun with the wrong person. You'll do better if you stop fighting Maeve." She nodded toward one of the servants. Emily noticed that the human servant was tall and had red hair.

"Another one," she said with a groan.

"She fought," Emma said. "Now she's a slave. We didn't. We get to dance and play, all the time."

"You're happy like that?"

"Of course! We don't have to work. We get pretty clothes. We get food. The men are very handsome." She giggled and blushed. "I don't remember much about before, but I'm sure I had to go to work."

Emily thought it sounded like the life of a spoiled poodle with a mercurial owner. It was a life of luxury, sure, but who wanted to spend a lifetime doing tricks for someone who was just as likely to kick you as kiss you? Then again, it sounded better than servitude. She smiled politely when Emma dragged over a fairy man for her to dance with. He was attractive in a somewhat feminine way—not Emily's type, but if dancing with him would keep her from being made a slave, she'd make the sacrifice. And maybe she could get him to talk.

Fifteen

Sophie and Beau were hardly the only ones out in the waning daylight, which made Sophie wonder if she'd find what she was looking for. Back home, they practically rolled up the sidewalks at six in the evening, so twilight was prime time for spotting fairies. Here, where there were more people out later, the rules might be different. In the city that never slept, when did the fairies come out to play?

She reached Tavern on the Green, where Olivia and Will had mentioned catching a cab. They'd both developed that fuzzy, confused look at that point in their stories. It had to mean something.

The gateway wouldn't be on the sidewalk, so she took the park entrance nearest the restaurant, followed the footpath for a while, then stepped off the path. Beau growled deep in his throat. "Yes, I feel it too," she said to him. Her skin tingled, and she trembled in anticipation. It had been a very long time since she'd entered the fairy realm. Folding her fingers around the laminated four-leaf clover in her pocket, she focused her senses to find the gateway, held the shape in her mind, and stepped through it.

She knew right away that she'd gone someplace *other*, but it didn't seem like the right place. Shivering as she pulled her sweater tighter about her, she studied the foreign landscape. Instead of the endless summer she recalled, this place seemed to be in late autumn—and late autumn during a severe drought, so the leaves were dead and dry rather than vividly hued. Her last experience in the Realm had overshadowed all her earlier memories, leaving her with the impression of darkness and danger. That wasn't what it had really been like, but it was the way it seemed now. The nearly skeletal trees beckoned and scolded her with clawed fingers, and desiccated leaves crunched under her feet as she resumed walking.

One thing that hadn't changed was the music wafting through the air. It brought back fond memories of nights spent dancing with teachers who were far more demanding, and yet far more encouraging, than the teachers at her hometown's small dancing school. In her classes, she learned the positions and steps. At night among the fairies, she learned to *dance*.

It had been fourteen years, but still the music made her feet want to move in rhythm. She yearned to kick up her legs and leap through the air. But she wasn't here for fun. She was on a mission. Unfortunately, she wasn't sure of her next steps. Her experiences in the Realm hadn't been broad. She'd always gone to the same place and done the same thing, and nothing about where she was now looked familiar. She decided to follow the music, since she'd never seen the fairy she sought when there wasn't music around her.

She forced herself not to walk in rhythm with the music, not to throw in the occasional dance step or move her arms with a graceful flourish. That was what had gotten her into this mess in the first place. She had a feeling she'd have plenty of time for dancing later.

The music came from a small grove of trees. Hiding behind a tree, she observed the circle of fairies dancing there. The sight brought on another wave of nostalgia. Dancing in such a circle had been a huge part of her childhood. She didn't recognize any of these fairies, though, and she didn't see the one she needed most. There were probably dozens—hundreds, even—of groves like this in the Realm. Finding the right one might be more challenging than she expected.

She'd thought she was being perfectly silent, but one of the fairies still dropped out of the dance and turned to her. "Will you dance with us?" he asked, extending a hand.

Stepping out of her hiding place, she said, "Not now. I'm looking for someone."

"You've found someone," he said with a cheeky grin and a gesture encompassing the rest of the group. The others stopped dancing and turned to stare at her.

She wasn't in the mood to play games. "I'm looking for a specific someone. Do you know Tallulah?"

"I might. And what would you trade for that information? Everything has its price, you know."

"Believe me, I am *well* aware of that," she said.

He came closer, moving in a graceful swagger. Beau growled a warning that he ignored. "Now, what might be a fitting price? Perhaps a kiss. I've heard that human lips are warm. I'd like to feel that. Or a dance—you are Tallulah's little dancer, are you not?"

While he spoke, the others also gathered around Sophie and Beau. One regarded her with a frown, and then turned sharply at the speaker's last sentence. Grinning, he backed away from the group and slipped off into the trees. The other fairies didn't seem to notice, and Sophie didn't know what to make of it. She doubted it was good, though. She knew fairies well enough to be fairly certain that he wasn't running off to bring Tallulah to her as an act of charity.

That meant she needed to stop fiddling around and do something. With a deep sigh of reluctance, she eased her mini horseshoe out of her pocket and said, "You mentioned a kiss?"

The fairy moved even closer. "I hadn't named my price yet, but I might consider a kiss. I'm not sure it would be enough, though. It sounds to me like this information is quite valuable to you." When he got within range, she dropped Beau's leash, gathered herself, bent her knees, and made a flying leap. She got an arm around his neck and brought him to the ground beneath her. Fairies were strong with magic, but they weren't very substantial. This one may have been a foot taller than she was, but she probably outweighed him. With the horseshoe so close to him, he couldn't use his magical strength against her, and at the sight of the iron, all the others backed away.

Leaning down to address her victim, she said sweetly into his ear, "Sorry about this, but I need some answers, I've already run up enough debts, and I do hope you'll cooperate because I don't want to have to get mean."

Sixteen

The Realm—Maeve's Lobby
Later

She laughed as the conga line wound its way through the lobby ballroom. This was the most fun she'd had in—well, she didn't know how long. The conga line broke up, and everyone went back to dancing in pairs. She was momentarily lost without a partner until someone took her hand and she turned to face him. He was very attractive. She thought she could get lost in the swirling quicksilver colors of his eyes.

"Hello there, handsome," she said. Rising to her toes, she put her hand behind his head and pulled him to her for a deep kiss. His lips were cool and dry against hers, and at first he resisted the kiss, but then with a soft sigh he gave in and kissed her in return. It only lasted for a second before he jerked away.

"Emily Drake!" he said, sounding shocked.

Emily? That name sounded familiar. Emily must be someone she knew. She looked around for this Emily person, sure she'd recognize her if she saw her, but she didn't see anyone who looked like an Emily. She did, however, see a tall, handsome man with silvery eyes and hair. "Dance with me," she said to him, taking his hand.

He pulled his hand out of hers, grabbed her by both shoulders and gave her a quick shake. "Emily! Please! You didn't eat or drink anything, did you?"

Wait, *she* was Emily? Oh, yes, that did sound right. "I'm Emily!"

"Yes, you're Emily. Did you eat or drink anything?"

"No, I've been too busy dancing." She plucked one of his hands off her shoulder and tried to lead him to the dance floor. "Let's dance."

He refused to budge, and although he was terribly skinny, she couldn't move him. "Now is not the time for dancing."

"You're Eamon," she said, coming gradually to her senses. "You let them take me away." She felt like she was waking up the morning after taking a double dose of allergy medicine. It took awhile for anything to make sense, and her tongue was so thick and heavy in her mouth that she couldn't express herself. She swayed and leaned against Eamon for support. "What happened to me?"

"You must have fallen into the enchantment."

"All I did was dance."

"You quit fighting. That is enough. Even I have to fight to maintain my independence in this court."

"They said it would be easier if I quit fighting."

"Who did?"

"The other human girls. I was acting like I was giving in so I wouldn't be turned into a slave."

"Perhaps you should act without immersing yourself so thoroughly in your role."

"Yeah, I'll keep that in mind. Oh, and sorry about the kiss."

"There is no need to apologize for that," he said solemnly, but when she looked up at him, his lips twitched ever so slightly.

"Don't laugh at me!" she warned. She wasn't sure if it was because of the enchantment, but it had felt like a really good kiss. Her body grew warm and tingly all over, just thinking about it. And then she remembered what had happened before she started dancing. "Sophie! She's what this is all about!"

He glanced around surreptitiously, then pulled her under the staircase where they were out of Maeve's view. "What do you mean?"

"Maeve announced that she's going to take some lost throne, and I think she needs Sophie to do that, possibly because of some information she needs to take the throne. I was just the bait so she could catch Sophie."

His reaction was violent enough to scare her. His eyes went dark, almost black, and his skin lost some of its luster. "She can *not* be allowed to succeed," he said in a low hiss.

"How do you lose a throne? That's not something that can just fall behind a bookcase."

"You may have noticed that the geography of the Realm shifts?"

"Yeah."

"That's how an entire palace could be lost. When the last queen left, those of us in the palace were cast out, and we couldn't find our way back."

"You said 'us.'"

"I was a scribe in the court."

"So you know about the queen and the palace and the throne, and all that?"

"I barely remember it."

"You worked for a queen in a palace, and you don't remember it?"

"It was hundreds of years ago, and we prefer to live in the present."

"Maybe it's like some Sleeping Beauty thing where a spell was put on the palace, and you have to find it to take the throne, and then throw in a little King Arthur, so there's some test you have to pass, like pulling a sword from a stone."

Before he could comment on her theory, the front door flew open and one of the wild fairies rushed inside. He was breathing heavily from a combination of exertion and excitement. "It worked!" he panted. "She's here! In the woods nearby."

Maeve bounced to her feet. Gesturing toward the door, she shouted, "Go! Bring her to me!" An army of guards rushed for the door.

Emily turned to Eamon and clutched the lapels of his tweed jacket. "See? She wants my sister. I just don't know exactly why."

"I may have an idea." He looked uncomfortable, twitching his shoulders like he had an itch. "After you were taken from the library—"

"No thanks to you," she interrupted.

"—I went into the human world and encountered your sister."

"And you survived? I'm impressed."

"I think…" he trailed off, then tried again, "You may not be a changeling." He leaned very close to her, his nose almost touching hers. "But your sister is."

Seventeen

Sophie's victim grunted, then stammered, "Y–you were looking for Tallulah?"

"You'll cooperate?" she asked, keeping her iron horseshoe near his neck.

"Yes."

She eased herself off him, allowing him to sit up while she still kept him in her grasp. "Do you know Tallulah?"

"I do," he said with an eager nod.

"Ah, so she's around here now," she said.

"Here?"

"Not in Louisiana," she clarified.

"Where?"

Giving up that line of questioning as fruitless and instead focusing on the fact that he at least knew of Tallulah, she asked, "Can you take me to her?"

Although he still eyed her warily, he regained a little poise. "What is your intention with Tallulah?" he asked stiffly.

"I have unfinished business with her that doesn't concern

you." She raised the horseshoe again with a hint of threat.

"Very well," he said with a sigh. "I will take you to Tallulah."

"There, now, was that so hard?" Keeping her grip on his arm to force him to his feet, she stood and brushed the leaves off her skirt with her free hand, then picked up Beau's leash. "Come on, Beau, let's go get Emily."

The fairy didn't move, though. He was busy staring at the ground where they'd been sitting. It was the one green patch in the area. The other fairies standing nearby also stared at it. Sophie was surprised she hadn't noticed it earlier, but then she had been preoccupied with tackling and threatening her victim. The condition of the local plant life had been a very low priority. And it still was. She had a deal to make. "Lead on," she said, giving him a nudge.

He moved his arm, forcing her to shift her grip so that it was more like he was escorting her than like she was holding him prisoner. "This way, my lady."

The others fell in behind them in a procession as he led her across the grove. Sophie got the feeling that something important had changed, but she couldn't think of what that might be. He'd known who she was from the start, so why was his attitude toward her so different now? She doubted they were acting this way out of fear. Perhaps she'd passed some sort of test.

A shout nearby startled both her and her guide, and Beau barked. The fairies formed a circle around Sophie. A group of fairy men in Rat Pack-era retro suits emerged menacingly from behind trees. They were like nothing Sophie had ever seen in the Realm. "What's happening?" she asked her guide.

"These are Maeve's people," he said, his voice tightening.

"Maeve?" she asked. The last time she'd seen Maeve, she'd been nothing more than Tallulah's errand girl. "She has people?"

"My lady, you should flee," her guide urged, and she had to agree with his suggestion. The suited men were nearly upon them. She whirled to run, but one of the attackers grabbed her, wrenching her away from her guide. She still had her horseshoe in her hand, and she ran it across the attacker's face. He released her instantly, screaming. Beau clamped down on a second attacker's leg. Sophie spun and ran at the third man before he could come after her. A swift kick in the knee brought his face to horseshoe range, and that was another one out of the fight. There were still two more, and if they teamed up, she'd be in trouble.

Unfortunately, they were clever, and both of them came after her at once. One grasped her wrist and knocked the horseshoe out of her hand. The other grabbed her around the waist. She struggled toward the fallen horseshoe, hoping that just being near it would even the odds somewhat. She heard a snarl and a snort, and soon Beau had another ankle in his jaws. His ancestors who'd fought bulls would have been proud, Sophie thought.

Even with Beau's help, Sophie couldn't shake off her attackers. It would have been nice if her former prisoner and his friends had helped, but she could hardly expect them to aid a stranger who'd threatened one of them. She noticed her attackers faltering and knew she was over the horseshoe, so she abruptly shifted her weight downward, but they didn't release her.

A sound like the war cry of an alien animal rent the air, and a whole army of fairies led by her guide and his friends joined the fray. They swung at the still-mobile Rat Pack members with branches and sticks. Taking advantage of the distraction, Sophie broke free and hit the ground hard. She rolled over to find her horseshoe before springing back to her feet. Her former captive was immediately at her side. "You must run now, my lady," he said.

She hated to run from a fight, but she felt that this was one time when a strategic retreat was in order. She whistled for Beau, who reluctantly released his victim and trotted over to her. "Good dog," she said, grabbing his leash and running after her former captive.

The sounds of battle followed as they raced through the park-like land. A glance over her shoulder told her that the battle was now mobile. The fairy Rat Pack kept chasing and the other fairies did everything they could to get in their way. "Faster!" her guide called.

She could run, but Beau was built for tenacity, not speed, and he was wheezing like a badly maintained engine. She stopped to scoop him up in her arms, resting him against her shoulder like a baby. Carrying a fifty-pound bulldog slowed her, but she was still faster than his pace.

She was starting to run out of steam when she felt the shiver and tingle of a nearby gateway. Setting Beau down, she reached into her pocket to clutch her clover. Before entering the gateway, she said to her guide, "Tell Tallulah Sophie needs to see her."

"I will pass on your message, and she may be able to arrange a safer meeting. Is there anything else you wish of me, my lady?"

"No, that should do it for now," she said, and then the fact that he'd been calling her "my lady" registered. He hadn't sounded sarcastic. She chanced one glance behind her and saw that Maeve's people were closing in. There was no time to ask for an explanation.

Just as one of Maeve's men reached for her, she and Beau ran through the gateway and came out into the gray light of early morning. They were in a park, and it was far from deserted, with a number of people jogging or walking their dogs. Sophie got more than a few odd looks as she and Beau materialized from the mists. She slowed to a more sedate walk and kept going like this was her morning routine. Her pursuers didn't seem to have come after her, but she didn't relax until she reached the sidewalk and crossed the street.

Then she didn't so much relax as nearly faint. That had not gone according to plan, to put it mildly. She had expected to walk in, offer to trade herself for the human captives, and be done with it. Now, though, she had no idea what was going on. The fairies she'd known back home were here in New York, Maeve had dangerous flunkies who'd tried to abduct her, and she didn't know where her debt to Tallulah played into any of this. And that meant she also didn't know where Emily and Mrs. Murray were or how she could rescue them.

Tears stung her eyes as the enormity of her problem struck her, but she blinked them back. She didn't have time for a cathartic cry right now. She needed to think logically. Before she could do anything, she had to get more information, but first she needed to go back to Emily's place, get some rest, and regroup.

Then she realized that she had no idea where she was. Or

when she was. According to her watch, it was nine thirty at night, but her watch only measured the time that had passed for her. Judging from the quality of light and the activity around her, she guessed it was somewhere around six in the morning. But which morning was it? Time passed differently in the Realm. The cars on the street looked familiar, and no one was flying around with a jet pack, so she hadn't been gone for centuries, but years could easily have passed.

She reached a street sign and found that she was on Riverside Drive, so at least she was still in Manhattan. The cross street was 105th, so she wasn't too terribly far from Emily's apartment. Now she needed a newspaper to tell her what day it was.

⸰Eighteen⸱

Emily's first reaction to Eamon's announcement that Sophie was a changeling was: "That would actually explain a lot."

Her second reaction was: "Oh God, you mean there are *two* Sophies? If they ever meet and team up, we're doomed."

Her third reaction was: "Wait a second–if there's a Sophie who's been living in fairyland all this time, there's no way that throne would still be empty."

"The human girl who was taken might not be quite as…" Eamon paused and shuddered, searched for a word, then finished his thought, "…formidable as the changeling you know as your sister."

"Yep, you definitely met Sophie." She paused to consider Eamon's revelation. Then she shook her head. "Nope. It doesn't work. For one thing, Sophie carries iron at all times. Some girls keep a canister of mace or pepper spray on their keychains. Sophie carries a mini horseshoe. A fairy couldn't do that, could she?"

"I doubt it." He frowned in confusion.

"How was she, by the way? Where was she? What was she doing?"

"She appeared to be in good health." He shuddered again, and

Emily could only imagine what Sophie had done to him. "She was near the theater. There was a man with her who had a badge of office."

That had to be Michael, Emily thought. In his condition, he shouldn't have been out like that, though, and she was surprised Sophie had let him. She consoled herself with the knowledge that if he tried to do too much with Sophie around, he'd find himself handcuffed to his bed and then tucked in gently under a down comforter with a pot of chicken soup nearby.

She shook herself out of that train of thought. "But changeling or not, why would Maeve need Sophie?"

"Your sister has a powerful aura. She could be a valuable ally in Maeve's quest for the throne."

"Sophie isn't the kind of person you want anywhere near a throne that you don't want her sitting on. She's not exactly the vice-presidential type. Whatever the reason Maeve wants her, I need to get out of here. I don't want to be a hostage. Sophie might actually go along with them if they threatened me."

"You don't understand the way our people think. Holding a hostage would never work in the Realm. We don't value any life over our own desires."

"But using me as bait works?"

"We will do anything to retrieve our treasures."

"Then we won't suggest the hostage thing to Maeve, okay? But I still want out of here. They're guarding the doors. Do you maybe know another way?"

He glanced behind him, but before he could say anything, the front doors opened, and some of Maeve's goons trudged in. The party stopped as everyone turned to stare. Their clothes were pristine–probably because they were a glamour to begin with–but two of them had angry-looking welts on their faces and several moved with distinct limps. All of them had cuts and bruises on their exposed flesh.

"Well?" Maeve demanded. "Where is she?"

The head goon bowed deeply, then said, "Forgive us, your majesty, but she escaped."

"Escaped? *Escaped?*" Maeve's voice rose into a shriek as she rose from her sofa. "How?"

"The wild ones, your majesty. They attacked us and helped her reach a gateway." He glanced sheepishly at the ground. "And she had a dog. He was vicious."

Emily had to clap a hand over her mouth to stop herself from laughing out loud. Leave it to Sophie to find instant allies and, apparently, a dog. It couldn't possibly be Beau. She doubted he could be bothered to bite an ankle. Licking a shoelace would be the extent of his help.

Maeve flew into a rage. "How dare they defy me?" she shouted. "I was one of them! When I am queen, I will punish them for their disloyalty!" With no wild fairies handy to punish, she took her anger out on the guards who'd brought the message, raising her hands toward them. They screamed and fell to their knees, their glamours stripped away to reveal ugly, shriveled creatures. She then stomped around the room, shouting and screaming, and everyone got out of her way.

Eventually, Maeve sank onto her sofa in a pique, and the party gradually resumed. "We should go now," Emily told Eamon. "Get me out of here while they're distracted. If I'm not here, Sophie won't have a reason to come back."

"I doubt Maeve will give up," he warned.

"Yeah, but we'll be on our turf then. Come on."

"I know a way that may not be guarded," he said, taking her hand to lead her through the crowd of revelers to the stairs. Under the stairs was a door that looked like it belonged to a utility closet. He put his hand on the doorknob and turned it, but nothing happened. "That is odd," he said, frowning. "This is how I got here." He released her hand so he could use both hands, and the door opened easily, but when he took her hand again, the door slammed shut.

"It's keeping me here," Emily said, her spirits sinking.

Eamon released her hand and opened the door again, then got his body halfway through and beckoned to her. Her toe barely crossed the threshold before the door swung at them. He jumped backward into the passage and she jumped backward into the lobby as the door slammed shut. She lunged for the doorknob, but it wouldn't turn. "Find Sophie and warn her!" she shouted through the closed door.

Nineteen

Michael and Emily's Building
Thursday, 6:30 a.m.

Having gone to sleep soon after eight, Michael woke very early the next morning. He also woke hungry, and although he thought it would be like Sophie to offer to make him breakfast, he suspected it was too early for that. She'd had a long day, and it was an hour earlier in her home time zone. He'd have to fend for himself, and he was completely out of Pop Tarts.

He was just coming down the stairs when the vestibule door opened and Sophie came inside, Beau trailing behind her. "Why, good morning!" she said, not quite managing to sound as perky as she seemed to be trying for.

He could understand the lack of perkiness. She was still wearing the dress she'd had on the night before, with a sweater over it. Her hair had come unpinned and hung haphazardly around her face, which was pale with dark circles under her eyes. He opened his mouth to ask where she'd been, but a warning voice in his head whispered *Don't ask,* and he suddenly felt compelled to close his mouth.

She held up a white paper bag. "Doughnut?" she offered. "I know I shouldn't, but I thought I deserved a treat."

"I don't suppose you have any coffee in there."

"I'm sorry, I don't drink coffee. I was about to make some tea." She hesitated, then added, "You're welcome to join me."

It wasn't the most enthusiastic invitation he'd ever received, and tea was no substitute for coffee at this time of the morning, but he wanted to know what she'd been up to, so he said, "Yes, I'd like that. Thank you."

She unlocked Emily's door, ushered him inside, then unhooked and hung up Beau's leash and stepped out of her shoes before heading into the apartment. She put the paper bag and a folded-up copy of that day's *Times* on the tiny bistro table and went to the kitchen to make tea. Beau collapsed on the floor near the table, panting like he'd just run a marathon.

While the kettle boiled, Sophie took off her sweater and folded it carefully over the arm of the daybed, which either hadn't been slept in or had already been made. Then she went back to the kitchen and brought plates to the table. When Michael couldn't stand it any longer, he asked, "What were you doing out all night?"

She turned to face him. "Out all night? What makes you think that?"

"You're still wearing the same clothes."

She poured tea into mugs, brought them to the table, then sat across from him. "I've got glazed and jelly. Which do you prefer?"

He started to demand an answer to his earlier question, but he reminded himself that this wasn't an interrogation and she didn't actually owe him any answers. Besides, he'd likely get better results if he let her set the pace and didn't make her feel pressured. "Glazed is fine," he said, trying not to let his tension come through in his voice.

She put a doughnut on his plate, took one for herself, took a bite, chewed, swallowed, and took a sip of tea, then glanced at her watch. "I was barely out for two hours," she said.

He studied her carefully, but his internal lie detector told him she wasn't lying. Even so, being out two hours at this time of day wasn't something to let slide. "Are you insane? The city's a lot safer than it once was, but not a lot of good things happen before dawn."

She gazed back at him, the blue eye looking wide and innocent while the gray one appeared shadowed. "Don't worry, I wasn't in any danger."

That was a lie. The needle on his mental polygraph shot straight up, going right off the paper. "Sophie! I'm serious. Do you realize that two women other than Emily and Jen who fit that same pattern have gone missing?"

She took another bite of doughnut and another sip of tea, then smiled at him. "But I don't fit the pattern. I'm not nearly tall enough, and I'm not an actress."

"We don't know what the important parts of the pattern are, and until we know what's going on, I don't think you should be out wandering the streets at night or very early in the morning. We don't need another missing person case."

"Nobody's trying to abduct me," she said with a roll of her eyes.

Lie, his mental polygraph said.

Wait a second, someone had tried to abduct her? He noticed then that she had red marks on one wrist, and there were faint scratches on her arms, hands, and face. She'd escaped, but it looked like it had taken some effort, and his instinct was to lock her up in protective custody.

She turned to the side in her chair and straightened her legs, pointing and flexing her feet and rotating her feet at the ankles. She also had a few scratches on her legs–legs that were solid muscle, he noted. "Besides," she continued blithely, seemingly oblivious to his scrutiny, "I have Beau to look after me, and he can defend me, can't you, boy?"

Michael was about to remark on Beau's unlikely abilities in that area when he realized she'd told the truth about that. Beau got up and flopped down next to her, and she rubbed his back with her bare toes. "Yes, you *are* a good boy," she crooned. Beau looked up at Michael, and it seemed like the dog was smiling smugly at him. Michael glanced back at Sophie, who regarded him with the same steady gaze she'd given Tanaka the day before. He got the distinct feeling that she knew he knew she'd been lying, and she was daring him to challenge her.

It was a dare he couldn't resist. "Then what did happen to you? I'd have thought a dancer would be graceful enough not to get this banged up on an early-morning doughnut run."

She gave him a rueful smile. "You'd think so, wouldn't you?"

"Let me guess, you ran into a door."

"You should see what the door looks like." There was a hint of something bloodthirsty in her thin smirk.

"So something did happen while you were out at oh-dark-thirty," he said, fighting back a smug smile of his own. "You were set upon by an evil door that failed in its attempt to carry you back to its lair, and you taught it a valuable lesson about messing with ballerinas."

"Yes, that about sums it up, though I did have help. Chivalry isn't dead, after all, and this city isn't as heartless as its reputation." He took a moment of studying her face before he decided that she was telling the truth, though probably not all of it.

"Sophie," he warned in a tone that was almost a growl. He looked straight at her until she was forced to make eye contact with him, and then they held each other's gaze. He wasn't sure how Tank had stood it for so long the day before, but he refused to blink, even though the direct stare from her odd eyes gave him chills.

She didn't blink or look away, but she broke the silence first. "Okay, you're right, it is dangerous out there at that time," she said with a weary sigh. "But as I said, someone came to my rescue, and Beau defended me, and as you can see, I'm fine. Just a few scratches. Dancing *Nutcracker* is a lot more painful. I didn't want to worry you. You've got enough on your mind."

He held her gaze a moment longer, waiting to see if she'd waver or give any sign she might be lying. She didn't, and he looked away with great relief. He still wasn't sure he really believed her, though. There was something she wasn't telling him, but did it have anything to do with Emily—or Jen? He intended to find out.

Twenty

Maeve's Ballroom
Later

Emily might have felt better if Eamon *had* abandoned her again.
Then she could have been angry at him instead of feeling scared
and trapped. This time, though, she could only hope he'd heard her
plea to reach Sophie. The party raged around her, but she resisted
the temptation to dance. Now that she knew how dangerous that
could be, she wasn't risking it. Being at the party to end all parties
but unable to eat, drink, or dance wasn't the most fun way to spend
an evening. Or a day. Or whatever time it was.

She wove through the crowd so she wouldn't stand out as
a wallflower. If she always seemed to be moving with a purpose
toward another part of the party, she might not get dragged into
joining the festivities.

The tone of the gathering shifted ever so slightly. Were the
fairies finally running out of steam? A low murmur spread through
the crowd, gradually building until it was clearly audible over the
music. Emily studied the throng and noticed a wave of movement.
The crowd parted and then coalesced, as though allowing someone to

pass, but all she could tell was that someone was heading toward the couch where Maeve had collapsed after her earlier temper tantrum.

Since the crowds didn't part for her, Emily elbowed and shoved her way around the lobby. Just when Maeve's sofa came into view, Emily saw a tall, flame-haired woman approach it. Without breaking stride, the newcomer appropriated the glass from a tray being brought to Maeve and seated herself beside the self-proclaimed queen. Maeve jolted to attention and flinched, but she didn't protest.

The newcomer leaned against the sofa back and languidly crossed her long, shapely legs. Her attire fit into Maeve's decorating scheme, but she wore it as though she was attending an early-sixties costume party where many of the other guests were men in Doris Day drag. "I see you've done well for yourself, Maeve," she said. After taking a sip of her drink, she added, "And I hear you're about to do even better."

Maeve jumped to her feet. "We should go up to my rooms and catch up," she said, smiling as though attempting to convey friendliness, even while her tone suggested she was inviting her guest to visit her torture chamber. "It's hardly fitting for you to mingle with the commoners, Tallulah."

Tallulah's smile in response said, "Ha! Knew it!" Emily silently prayed for her to refuse to move, but she rose gratefully to her feet. "I'd be honored."

Emily groaned as the crowd parted to allow the two fairy women to reach the staircase. She was sure this conversation would reveal something about Maeve's scheme, especially since Maeve had insisted on moving it to a more private venue. Emily doubted she'd be a welcome guest for this little tête-à-tête.

Once Maeve and Tallulah had passed, the crowd filled in behind them, which impeded Emily's progress while also making it less obvious that she was following them. People stood along the sides of the great staircase and on the balcony above, so nobody noticed her. She just had to resist the urge to elbow people aside in her impatience. She reached the hallway in time to see the two women go through a doorway. Emily remembered that the balcony behind the apartment spanned multiple rooms, so she took a chance and opened the nearest door.

The room she entered could only be called a boudoir. Calling it a bedroom sold it short. It was a room for lolling in sultry elegance on the satin-draped bed or maybe even for performing a musical number about falling in love while dancing around in cute pajamas. "I was born at the wrong time," she lamented softly to herself. They didn't make movie musicals the way they used to. But it looked like someone had tossed the place. The bed was unmade, and she'd have bet that the CSI guys from TV would find interesting stains on the sheets with their special lights. Pieces of clothing were strewn everywhere, which Emily found odd, considering that Maeve's attire seemed to be mostly glamour. Did she conjure up and scatter lingerie just for atmosphere?

But she wasn't there to analyze Maeve's wardrobe or critique her housekeeping. There was a wall of heavy curtains on the other end of the room that she hoped hid balcony doors, and she hurried over there. She was sidetracked along the way by a piece of paper on the nightstand. It had something drawn on it that looked like the maps at the beginnings of fantasy novels. She wouldn't have thought maps would be very useful in the Realm since the geography was so fluid, but why would Maeve have it if it didn't mean anything? Maybe it was a map to that missing palace and Eamon could make some sense out of it if he made it back. She didn't have time to study it, but she got her phone out of her pocket and found that although she didn't have network access, the camera still worked. She snapped a couple of pictures of the map, then headed for the balcony.

It was the way she remembered it from her earlier escape attempt. The next set of doors along the balcony were open, though blocked by the heavy curtains. She heard voices coming from within and recognized the tone of compliments thinly veiling cattiness as Tallulah remarked on Maeve's décor. Emily had heard similar conversations conducted in similar tones at many a small-town social. Sophie was a master of the art.

Emily found a slight gap between the curtains where she could glimpse Maeve's living room without touching the curtains. Tallulah finished her survey of the surroundings and seated herself on Maeve's sofa, patting the cushion beside her to indicate that Maeve should join her. Emily was surprised when Maeve did so without protest. She reminded Emily of a junior employee who'd been called into the boss's office but wasn't sure if she was going to be promoted or fired.

Tallulah kept Maeve sweating while she took a sip of the drink she still held. When it seemed as though Maeve was about to explode, Tallulah finally spoke. "As I said downstairs, I'm impressed that you're working so hard to move up in the world. Such initiative!" She took another sip, and her lips curled into a smirk behind her glass. "Though it is unlike you to make such a premature announcement. Usually, you have everything in place behind everyone's backs before you reveal your intentions. I expected to find you already sitting on the throne."

"All the pieces are in place," Maeve said stiffly. Emily wished she could see her face, but the tension in her neck and shoulders was obvious.

Tallulah raised an eyebrow. "Are they, now? *Something* must be missing, or you would have acted. I get the impression it involves a mutual friend of ours."

Mutual friend? Emily wondered. Did they mean Sophie?

Recovering some of her composure, Maeve gave a tinkling laugh and said, "Whatever gave you that impression?"

"The fact that she's been in the Realm, asking for me." *Definitely Sophie,* Emily decided. "You're making me look bad again. I haven't forgotten that your actions lost me something very valuable and wasted a great deal of work and potential. I don't appreciate being blamed for your schemes."

"You can't argue that something isn't needed," Maeve shot back. "I'm sure you've noticed. Time may finally be running out for us."

"And you think you're the one to save us?"

Emily pressed closer to make sure she didn't miss a word. Not that their cryptic conversation told her much. She must have moved too close, though, because Tallulah glanced up and looked directly at her. Emily held her breath and froze, hoping she hadn't disturbed the curtain.

"Someone has to," Maeve said. "No one else has come this close."

Tallulah sighed and shook her head. "Oh, Maeve, not again." She put her glass down and rose gracefully to her feet. "I'd better go warn my people. Some of them still haven't recovered from the last time." Then she smiled. "It's likely that I'll find her before you do. Have you planned for that possibility?" Without waiting for Maeve's response, she turned and strode briskly to the door.

Emily rushed down the terrace for the boudoir door, ran through that room and burst out into the hallway while Tallulah was still making her way down the stairs. "Please, wait!" she called out before Tallulah reached the lobby. "You know Sophie?" she blurted when Tallulah turned to face her.

"I once did."

"What did you want with my sister?"

"I wanted to make her the greatest dancer who ever lived."

That wasn't the answer Emily had expected, and it didn't explain anything. She tried a different question. "What does Maeve want with her?"

"I don't know. But I'll admit, I'm very curious." She turned to head for the exit, ending the conversation abruptly. Emily tried to follow her but was stopped at the door the same way she'd been when she'd tried to escape with Eamon. She felt like she'd gained some new clues, but she had no idea what to make of them, and now it seemed like there was yet another fairy who wanted Sophie.

Twenty-One

The Upper West Side
Thursday, 2:00 p.m.

A To Sophie's body, it had been nearly her bedtime when Michael left after breakfast, and the day before had been incredibly long and tiring, so when she finally went to bed, she slept far too long for all she needed to do and not nearly long enough to be well-rested. Losing all that time in the Realm had been worse than European jet lag. To force herself to full alertness, she did as many ballet exercises as she could manage in Emily's tiny apartment, took a long shower, and made a pot of tea. She'd just sat down with her teacup and the newspaper when Beau butted her leg with his head. "Do you need something?" she asked.

He trotted to the door, then looked back at her. "I thought you were supposed to be lazy," she said, getting to her feet and putting on her shoes. "This must be a real emergency."

She clipped his leash to his collar, then was barely able to hold him back while she shut and locked the door. At the foot of the front steps, he paused to water a tree, then he took off down the sidewalk at a rapid pace. "Do you have a train to catch?" she asked. He turned

the next corner at full speed, and she had to jog a few steps to keep up with him. If the world's laziest dog, according to Michael Murray, wanted to go somewhere that badly, she felt she owed it to him to let him go, especially after he'd defended her so valiantly.

Beau forged doggedly ahead without stopping to sniff the fire hydrants along the way. They crossed two streets and went down a mostly residential block, then the dog veered to the side and headed down a flight of metal steps leading to a shop on the building's ground floor. She followed Beau down the stairs and eased the shop's front door open.

She'd planned to leave Beau outside, but he charged past her into the shop like he owned the place, dragging her behind him. "Beauregard! No! Stay!" she called, then muttered, "Just what I need, a bulldog in a china shop." In her most commanding voice, she snapped, "I said *stay*." The dog immediately stopped and sat down. "That's more like it."

A tiny woman scurried to the front of the shop, saying, "Beau! I haven't seen you in ages!" A fat, solid white braid fell over the woman's shoulder to brush the floor when she bent to scratch Beau behind the ears. Beau's curled stub of a tail wasn't much use for wagging, but he wiggled his hind end in pleasure.

The woman straightened and looked up at Sophie. It was difficult to tell how old she was. Her skin had the crepey quality that comes with age, but it was mostly unlined, and her gray eyes were sharp and alert. She wore chunky dangling earrings shaped like apples, a string of beads that matched the earrings, an eyelet-trimmed T-shirt with an apple appliqué on the front, cropped jeans, and red Keds. She looked like a young kindergarten teacher who'd been dramatically aged by the class from hell, Sophie thought. She'd taught a few ballet classes like that.

The woman's appearance told Sophie where she was. Sophie smiled and said, "You must be Miss Athena Abercrombie. Emily has told me so much about you and your lovely shop." Emily worked at an antique shop when she was between shows and had made it sound far more elegant than this little den full of old china. Sophie wouldn't have recognized the place from Emily's description, but Emily had been dead-on in describing Athena Abercrombie's unique style. "I'm Sophie, Emily's sister."

Athena beamed at her. "I've heard a lot about you from Emily. It's a treat to meet you in person. How is Emily? I know she's been busy with her big starring role. Amelia and I were talking about getting tickets for later in the week. I suppose you've come to town to see her."

Sophie hated to dampen Athena's enthusiasm, but there was no easy way to break this news. "I'm afraid Emily's missing. She didn't show up for yesterday's matinee, and no one has been able to reach her since soon after her first performance."

Athena looked alarmed, but not all that shocked. She went pale and put her hand on the counter to steady herself, but there was no gasp of surprise. It was as though something she'd been dreading had finally come to pass.

Sophie dropped Beau's leash and took Athena's arm. "Maybe you'd better sit down," she said gently.

Athena shook her off. "I'm fine. It was just a bit of a shock."

Beau wandered behind the counter, and Sophie was about to call him back when she noticed the water dish with his name stenciled on it and the dog bed decorated with a bulldog appliqué, where Beau promptly curled up and began snoring. *No wonder he wanted to come here,* she thought.

The front door chimed, and a tall, glamorous woman entered. Sophie stepped out of the way so Athena could deal with the customer, but Athena rushed toward the woman, crying, "Oh, Amelia! Emily's missing!" The newcomer was likely Amelia Abernathy, Athena's younger sister and co-owner of the shop. She had the same ancient agelessness as her sister, with white hair in a French twist and aged but unlined skin, but she was dressed more appropriately to her years in a simple silk blouse and knee-length straight skirt, with silk stockings and sensible pumps. A single strand of pearls circled her long, slender neck. As she watched the two women together, Sophie was gratified to see that she wasn't the only woman whose "little" sister towered over her.

"Amelia, this is—" Athena began, but Amelia waved her off.

"Yes, I know, it's Sophie." She extended a hand for Sophie to shake. "How do you do? I'm Amelia Abernathy. Now, what happened?"

While Sophie told about Emily's disappearance, she assessed the shop. Most of the inventory consisted of mismatched pieces of fine china. A display case in front of the counter held an array of silverware, and a glass case on the wall behind the counter held antique-looking jewelry. There were also various ceramic decorative items on display.

But what Sophie found truly interesting was the amount of iron in the shop. The burglar bars in the front windows were perfectly understandable in an urban area, but filigreed bits of wrought iron also formed the backdrop for most of the displays. The sisters were keeping something out, and she didn't think it was burglars.

Therefore, it wasn't much of a shock when Amelia said, "The fairies must have finally got her."

Sophie was acutely aware that her response was being judged, so she tried not to react at all. "Yes, I believe a fairy named Tallulah has her. She's sent her people after Emily before, back in Louisiana, but she seems to have followed Emily here."

"There's no such thing as 'here' where the fairies are concerned," Amelia said. "The Realm is only tethered to physical reality in spots. The rest of it exists outside our concept of space and time. No matter where in the world you enter, it is still the same Realm."

"Which explains how I entered near Tavern on the Green yesterday evening and came out about an hour later this morning in Riverside Park," Sophie said with a nod. Then she sighed and leaned against the counter. "But it also means I was wrong when I sent Emily here to keep her safe from the local fairies back home."

"Do you mean you actually went inside, on your own?" Amelia asked, stepping closer to her, her sister right behind her, both of them wide-eyed.

"Well, yes. I used to do it all the time. I know the tricks to finding the gateways, and I have a four-leaf clover, so I can pass through into the Realm."

The sisters exchanged a look fraught with meaning. "I thought it took a bit more than that," Athena said softly.

While they were still caught off-guard, Sophie continued, watching their reactions carefully. "I went in last night to find Tallulah and arrange Emily's freedom. Before I could reach her, I was attacked. The fairies I was with said the attackers were Maeve's men. Maeve was the one Tallulah sent after Emily before. But they weren't dressed like Tallulah's people. They looked like something out of the Rat Pack era."

Amelia and Athena exchanged another meaningful look. "I'll get the chart," Athena said, hurrying to the shop's back room.

"Please, have a seat." Amelia gestured toward the bentwood chairs at a table in the corner. She went to the door, flipped the sign to "closed," and turned the lock. "This is best done without interruption," she explained.

Athena returned, hauling a roll of paper nearly as tall as she was. Amelia hooked a loop of ribbon from the top left-hand corner onto a bit of ironwork on the wall, then Athena unrolled the paper and hooked the right-hand loop of ribbon onto another bit of ironwork.

Oh dear, Sophie thought when she saw the poster. *She's made a collage.* It was like a giant scrapbook page, filled with photos cut from magazines, stenciled lettering, and fancy borders, all covered in clear adhesive paper. The two elderly sisters positioned themselves on either side of the poster, and Sophie, feeling like she was back in school, folded her hands in her lap and listened attentively.

"Contrary to what Edmund Spenser thought, there is no queen of all the fairies," Amelia began.

"Though there may have been in his day because we know there once was, but who she was and what happened to her has been forgotten," Athena interjected.

With the tiniest of glares at her older sister, Amelia continued,

"Instead, there are courts within the Realm, each having its own ruler. These rulers consider themselves to be kings or queens, but they only rule the fairies who have sworn loyalty to that court."

"They're like fairy gangs," Athena said. "They dress and act in ways that fit with the theme of that court. We've identified a few of these courts." She pointed to her poster, which contained pictures cut from magazine articles about the *Lord of the Rings* films, stills from old black-and-white musicals and Doris Day movies, among others. "They seem to be emulating human eras or trends–at least, some of them are. Some of the older courts may have influenced human trends of their time."

"Maeve has a court?" Sophie asked.

"Maeve's court is new–if you can even call it an official court," Amelia said. "There were no signs of it until perhaps fifteen years ago."

Athena pointed to the Doris Day photos. "She seems to have adopted the mid-twentieth century as the theme of her court–Doris Day, *Breakfast at Tiffany's*, and the Rat Pack."

"She was still part of Tallulah's clan fourteen years ago, though she may have been building a clique of her own," Sophie said. "Of course, there's no way of knowing how long ago that was to them. Then she was more like the wild ones. Who leads them?"

"Those are the free fairies," Amelia said. "They don't belong to any court, and they answer to no one. They make up by far the majority of the fairy population, and they include the small folk as well as some of the less humanoid denizens of the Realm. If they ever did unite behind a leader, they could easily rule the entire Realm, but they have no interest in either the power or the responsibility. You were accurate to call them wild."

Sophie nodded. "Those are the ones I know."

Athena came over and sat in the chair next to Sophie. "How do you know them?"

"I grew up with them. I found them dancing in the woods behind my grandparents' house when I was very small, and I kept going back until I was almost eighteen. Tallulah led the group I knew, but I stayed away after she tried to take Emily, presumably as her payment for teaching me to dance. Not that I agreed to that bargain, but that's how they work."

"They've been after Emily here, as well," Athena said. "We tried to protect her. We masked her aura so they wouldn't be able to identify her."

"You did *what?*" Sophie blurted before she could moderate her response. While fairies were commonplace to her and she didn't question her ability to know when something had happened to a loved one, she didn't know humans could do magic.

"The fairies see with senses beyond vision," Amelia explained. "They see a person's–fairy or human–aura."

"Yes, I know," Sophie interrupted impatiently. "But I didn't realize that could be changed."

"Not changed so much as hidden."

"And with unintended consequences," Athena put in.

"The other missing women," Sophie surmised. "Detective Murray said there were three other than Emily, including his wife."

Amelia sighed. "We discovered Emily not long after Jennifer Murray's disappearance when she visited our shop. The similarity was striking, and her tea leaves suggested that she was the one being pursued. That was when we offered Emily a job so we could look out for her, masked her aura, and suggested she look at the apartment downstairs from Michael Murray. We knew he'd keep a close eye on her, after what happened to his wife."

Sophie had thought she had a very high tolerance level for weirdness, but this was enough to make her dizzy. She turned the conversation back toward more comfortable areas, like fairy politics. "Why has the throne remained empty all this time?"

"That has been our job, in part," Amelia said. "We are enchantresses, and our assignment is to make sure no one takes that throne. It would not go well for mankind if the fairies were to unite, especially not now, when people have forgotten how to deal with fairies and protect themselves. So, we disrupt any effort by any of the rulers to seek the throne."

"How do you know so much about that world if you can't enter the Realm?" Sophie asked. She felt like she was being told a fairy tale, and these women had made up the whole thing.

"There are places where the worlds meet," Amelia said. "Not all fae live in the Realm, and most of those in the Realm don't venture outside. They meet at the markets, and we attend those to learn what's going on and attempt to influence events."

"You'll have to come with us to the next market," Athena said, far too enthusiastically. "We need you to round out our numbers, and I'm sure you're the one we've been looking for."

Sophie had hoped that she might have allies who knew what was really happening, but now she feared these two were insane, with just enough of the truth to sound marginally coherent. If they thought they were enchantresses tasked with influencing fairy politics, they had to be touched in the head. Sadly, most people who thought they knew about fairies turned out to be quite mad—or perhaps had been driven mad by the knowledge. Was that her future? She wondered if she could flee without looking rude. "I'm not an enchantress," she said as firmly as possible.

"Then what do you think you are?" Amelia asked. Sophie opened her mouth to say that she was a ballet teacher, but Amelia cut her off. "Don't play dumb. You consort with fairies. Ordinary people don't do that. You come and go at will from the Realm. Even we can't do that. We've heard Emily's stories about your uncanny knack for knowing when things will happen or what people are thinking—and for bending people to your will. Even if you've never been formally trained in its use, you have power."

Sophie was no longer worried about appearing rude. She stood, snapped her fingers to summon Beau, and said, "I'm sorry for taking up so much of your time. Thank you for your assistance."

Athena hopped to her feet and ran to get between Sophie and the door. "But we need you! We're one short."

"One short?" Sophie asked, already regretting the question but too curious not to ask it.

"We usually work in threes—it's a traditional thing. You know, the phases of woman, maiden, mother, and crone. Amelia's the mother, and I'm afraid I've become the crone after aging out of the maiden role. Amelia's daughter married and left us years ago. You're just what we need. You are a maiden, obviously."

Sophie felt her face flame. "I don't see how that's any business of yours," she said haughtily as she tried to sidestep Athena to get to the door. If she had magical powers, she would have used them to vanish from this place.

Athena took her arm in a gesture that appeared to be reassuring, even while it imposed an iron grip to keep Sophie from escaping. "It's nothing to be ashamed of, my dear," she said soothingly. "It's just rare these days. That rather complicates staffing for us."

If she'd tried to speak, she would have stammered or sputtered, so Sophie kept her mouth shut and held her head up high as she fought to will some of the blood to leave her face. Athena was right, it wasn't anything to be ashamed of. Besides, her hometown was hardly a target-rich environment for eligible men, and she was related to most of those who were halfway decent. Then there was the fact that most men were utterly terrified of her.

It wasn't as though she had time to date, either, not between school and ballet training, and then later her family and civic responsibilities. Even if there had been a man she found appealing who wasn't related to her and wasn't afraid to ask her out, she couldn't possibly have found time to develop a relationship.

She realized then that she'd been silent for so long that the silence had become as awkward as stammering and sputtering would have been. "I'm only here to find Emily, and then I have to return home," she said. "I'm therefore not a suitable candidate for the position."

She picked up Beau's leash and turned to leave. Her hand had grasped the door handle when Amelia said from behind her, "Do you think you'll be able to rescue Emily on your own?"

Sophie ignored her. "I need to be going. Good day." She opened the door and ran blindly up the steps and then down the sidewalk. If she'd known Emily was working for people that unstable, she'd have come to deal with the situation much sooner. Two crazy old women like that, responsible for keeping the fairy realm from uniting in order to protect mankind from a fairy invasion? Ridiculous! And they wanted her to join them because she was also an enchantress, with her pitiful lack of a love life a key factor in her qualifications? Impossible!

She was a ballet teacher in a small Louisiana town. She'd danced with fairies as a child, and as a result she knew a thing or two, but that was all. She certainly didn't have magical powers.

But they had been right about one thing. She wouldn't be able to rescue Emily on her own, not using her usual tactics. She'd need to be better prepared this time, armed with more than a horseshoe keychain and a bulldog.

Twenty-Two

Michael was dozing on the sofa when a knock on the door woke him. He sat up and smoothed his hair with his good hand, expecting the visitor to be Sophie, but then a voice boomed, "It's Tanaka, I still have a key, so don't get up." A second later, the door opened and Tanaka entered.

He raised a foil pan. "Marisol's mother sent enchiladas. And Copeland says you'd better get well soon because he doesn't think he can take much more griping about her mother."

"Tell him to get shot. That's how I got a break," Michael quipped.

Tanaka put the pan in the refrigerator, then came into the living room and sat in the chair he'd taken the day before. "I don't know why Mari's sending food if you're well enough to be back at work," he said, leaning back and crossing his right ankle over his left knee.

"Back at work?"

"Yeah, all that legwork you did last night. I told you to take it easy."

"I just went to the theater and got a few names. I was trying to help."

Tanaka nodded, then said, "It did give me a head start, but now you are off this case for good, you hear me?"

Michael raised his good hand in surrender. "Loud and clear. I saw the doctor this morning, and I've been resting since then. I'll leave the search for Emily up to you from now on. Is there any news on that front?"

Tanaka wagged a finger at him. "Ah, ah, ah. There you go again."

"Oh, come on, Tank, you only got involved in this because you were worried about me. Aren't you worried what I might do if I don't know what's going on?"

Tanaka sighed as his shoulders sagged. "Okay, but this is totally off the record. You didn't hear it from me. I've got a memo out to see which of our guys were at the diner that night, and the waitress is meeting with a sketch artist this afternoon. I talked to the friends, and I've gotta say, they don't add up."

Trying not to show any reaction, Michael asked, "How so?"

"They seem surprisingly hazy about events after they left the diner. They didn't remember any other person joining them—didn't even remember the guy asking for an autograph, but they remember getting home with crystal clarity. It's weird."

"I was wondering if you'd catch that."

"You got the same thing?"

"Yeah. Do you think they're behind it?"

"My gut says no, but I've gotta go with the evidence and consider them persons of interest, at the very least. Not only do they not have alibis, but they were with her when she vanished and claim not to have noticed." He paused, then asked, "Have you talked to your ballerina today?"

"I had breakfast with her. Why, haven't you?"

"Not yet. Haven't heard a peep from her."

Michael wasn't sure he should say anything, but Tank needed to know, so he said, "I get this strange feeling that she's not all that interested in the investigation. She flew all the way here, but I had to talk her into calling the police. It was my idea to go to the theater and talk to people. She rolled her eyes at the fliers the theater people were handing out. She hasn't called you for updates. She seems to care about Emily, but she's not trying too hard to find her. Not through the normal channels, anyway."

Tanaka was too good a detective not to pick up on the way he worded that. "What do you mean?"

Michael wished he'd kept his mouth shut, but now that he'd brought it up... "I caught her coming in early this morning. She said she'd only been out a couple of hours, but she was wearing the same clothes she had on last night, and she was all scratched up. I think she's investigating on her own, and whatever she's looking into, she didn't tell you about it."

"She may have just been going around to Emily's favorite places, looking for her."

"At that time of day? And coming back scratched and bruised?" Michael shook his head. "No, there's something about her that doesn't add up, something I don't get."

Tanaka nodded slowly. "I ran her for priors, and she's so clean she squeaks. Not so much as a parking ticket. I did a quick Internet search, and from the looks of things, she pretty much runs her hometown. She's all over the local paper. It's a miracle the place hasn't collapsed in the day she's been gone. Otherwise, she teaches ballet and dances with a regional company. There's some mention of a bunch of international dance awards, which makes it look to me like she way outclasses everyone else in the company, but I don't know anything about that stuff."

"See, she doesn't add up," Michael said.

"Last I heard, lack of ambition wasn't a crime."

"Can you really imagine *her* lacking ambition? She'd see world domination as an achievable goal."

"I checked with the airline, and she's on the passenger list for a flight leaving Shreveport early yesterday morning. She was in the air at the time Emily didn't show up for cast call at the theater. Unless she hired a hit or is part of some conspiracy, she couldn't have been involved in her sister's disappearance."

Michael shook his head. "No, I don't think that. I just feel like there's something very important—crucial even—that she hasn't told you and that she's doing on her own."

Both men flinched guiltily when there was a knock on the door and a voice called out, "Detective Murray? It's Sophie."

"Come in," Michael said.

She burst into the apartment, looking nearly as frantic as she had when she left the night before, then skidded to an abrupt stop when she saw Tanaka. "Oh, Detective Tanaka, hello. I didn't realize you were here," she said. After a pause, she added, as though just then thinking to ask, "Has there been any progress in the investigation?"

"I've been following up on the leads you two got last night," Tanaka said.

She nodded. "Good, good. That's good to hear."

"Was there something you needed?" Michael asked.

"Oh! Yes, I was wondering if you have a skillet I could borrow. Preferably cast iron. You can't make proper corn bread without it, and Emily doesn't have a very well-equipped kitchen."

Michael was starting to get used to Sophie's non sequiturs. "Actually, I have Emily's skillet. She usually cooks in my kitchen because it's bigger than hers."

"If you have an Easy-Bake oven, you've got a bigger kitchen than she does. Do you mind if I take the skillet?"

"Be my guest. I'm not using it."

She went into the kitchen and emerged seconds later with the skillet, holding it by the handle and hefting it like she was preparing to brain someone with it. "Sorry to have interrupted," she said, heading toward the door.

"I'll see you at the vigil tonight," Tanaka called after her.

She stopped and turned around, frowning. "The vigil?" Then the light dawned in her eyes. "Oh, yes, that. You're planning to attend? That's very considerate of you." There was the slightest hint of sarcasm in her voice.

"It's actually very cynical of me," Tanaka replied with a grin. "You'd be surprised by the number of kidnappers and killers who can't seem to resist showing up at these things. And, you never know, I might find more witnesses."

"I'll see you tonight, then, Detective," she said with a forced smile. Pointing at Michael, she added, "And you should rest. I think yesterday was too strenuous for you." She escaped rapidly enough that neither of them had a chance to say anything else.

Tanaka stared after her for a moment, then he turned to face Michael and the two of them exchanged a look. "Okay, you're back on the case, but only for this one thing," Tanaka said. "See if you can find out what she's hiding. But don't do anything stupid or dangerous. Talk to her, see if you can get her to open up. If you find anything interesting, let me know."

Twenty-Three

The shrine to Emily had grown to include laminated posters of reviews and newspaper articles, photos of Emily in costume, her headshot, and several pictures of her with friends. Banks of flowers surrounded the posters. Sophie took a picture of the shrine with her phone because she knew Emily would want to see it. Olivia, Will, and other cast members wearing show T-shirts handed out candles with little paper holders, like the ones used for the Christmas Eve candlelight service at church. The sun was still up, which made candlelight seem pointless, but the news truck parked beside the theater explained why they'd chosen this time—it was the perfect time to appear live on the evening news.

Olivia saw Sophie and came over to her. "Oh, good, you're here!" She turned to the others and said, "This is Sophie, Emily's sister."

They all took a step backward, but Sophie didn't let her smile drop. *What* had Emily been telling her friends about her? They'd have to talk about that when Emily was safe. "Thank you all so much for doing this," she said.

"We'll do anything to help find Emily," Olivia assured her. "Have a candle."

Sophie stood beside the shrine, holding her candle and feeling rather silly. A couple of cast members handed fliers to tourists on the sidewalk. The vigil began with Olivia saying a prayer. Sophie stayed on the fringes of the group, keeping watch for the silver-haired fairy she'd caught the day before. So far, there was no sign of the fae here. There was, however, a police presence, as she noticed Detective Tanaka standing to the side, observing the vigil participants and bystanders.

A young woman sang a song Sophie didn't recognize but that she assumed was from the show, based on references in the lyrics. Others picked up the tune as Will lit his candle and touched it to the candles held by the people beside him. The song swelled as the light spread around the group. The ritual was strangely affecting, and Sophie was surprised to find her eyes stinging with tears. She'd been so busy dealing with the situation that it hadn't occurred to her to miss her sister, and now she suddenly felt the absence acutely.

The news crew moved through the crowd, filming as the candles were lit. Olivia approached Sophie and took her by the arm. "Come on, they want to talk to you."

The last thing Sophie wanted to do was make a spectacle of herself. She let the tears that had been welling up in her eyes brim over and trickle down her cheeks. "I–I don't think I can," she whispered. "I'm sorry."

Olivia gave her a hug that squeezed the breath out of her. "Oh, you poor thing. I'm sure they'll understand. Do you mind if I talk to them?"

"Please do. Thank you."

Sophie gave a sigh of relief as Olivia headed back to the news crew, but then she noticed Detective Tanaka watching Olivia standing in front of the camera and talking into a microphone. Michael had been suspicious of Olivia and Will because their stories didn't add up. Olivia taking the spotlight wouldn't look good. Publicity might count as a motive for an actress. Now Sophie regretted letting Olivia do the interview. She knew Olivia and Will were innocent, and she couldn't let them become prime suspects.

She edged her way around the crowd until she reached Tanaka, then said, "Oh, Detective Tanaka!" as though she was surprised to see him. "Thank you so much for coming tonight. Have you noticed any suspicious characters yet?"

"Nothing extraordinary," he said, his attention mostly on Olivia.

"It was very kind of Olivia to speak for me," she said. "I just couldn't face the camera. It was too much for me."

That got his full attention, and he raised his eyebrows, as if to say he couldn't imagine anything being too much for her. "You're not a fan of publicity, I take it?"

"Does something like this ever help an investigation?"

"We sometimes get leads."

"How many of them pan out?"

"Not many," he admitted.

"I suspect it's like a funeral," she said. At his look of surprise, she explained, "Not because I think Emily's dead, but because the event is more for the benefit of the ones left behind. It lets them feel like they've done something, even if it does no practical good."

He nodded slowly. "I never thought of it that way, but you may have a point."

"You suspect her friends, don't you?" she asked as his attention drifted to the news crew.

He jerked his head back to her. "What makes you think that?"

"You're watching them like a hawk ready to swoop down on a field mouse."

"That obvious, huh?" He scratched the back of his neck. "Their story doesn't add up. They didn't mention the guy who left with them, and although they claim Emily was with them in the cab, I tracked down the driver, and he said it was only the two of them."

"I'd think if they were up to something, they surely would have mentioned another person who made a better suspect, and why do you believe the driver over them? Not that the driver is lying, but he may not have noticed."

"All good points, and I haven't arrested anyone yet."

Sophie pressed on. "Neither of them has anything to gain from Emily's disappearance."

"I checked out the understudy who's had to step into the role. She has a good alibi. But for those two, well, I've never met an aspiring star who didn't want publicity."

"Do you really think that appearing on the evening news under these circumstances will land someone the role of a lifetime?" Sophie was afraid she wasn't making headway with him, but she was also afraid to push further.

"Like I said, I'm not arresting them."

"But you're watching them."

"I'm watching everyone. Michael tells me you've been busy."

She wished she knew exactly what Michael had said so she'd know how to address it. "I've been searching. I've gone anywhere Emily's ever mentioned to me, like the place she sometimes works."

"No leads?"

She wasn't sure how well he could read her truthfulness, but she still chose her words carefully. "Nothing that would be of much use to you, I'm afraid. I've mostly learned how many people care about Emily. That's nice, but not very helpful."

"That's what you were doing before dawn this morning?"

My, someone is a tattletale, she thought. "The dog wanted to go out, and I couldn't sleep." Sort of true. "When I took dance workshops here, I liked early mornings the best, when the city was quiet." Also true, even if not applicable in this situation.

But it seemed to satisfy Tanaka. "You'll have to forgive Michael. He's edgy about cases like this."

"Yes, he told me about his wife. I can see how he'd worry about the well-being of any women in his vicinity."

Tanaka laughed. "That's putting it mildly. I thought his partner would deck him when they first started working together and he was so concerned about keeping her safe."

"This situation *is* hauntingly similar, don't you think? I can understand why he'd be edgy about it. But don't worry, I'll try to keep him out of it as much as possible." A crease formed between

Tanaka's eyes and his lips thinned slightly. She got the strangest feeling that she'd said exactly the wrong thing, and that was something that happened very seldom to her.

"Yeah, you do that," he said gruffly.

Olivia rescued her by coming over and saying, "We were live on the six o'clock news, so let's hope that gets the word out and you'll get plenty of leads, Detective. Oh, and the reporter would like a word with you so she can put together something more extensive for the late news."

Tanaka grunted and said, "Well, okay then. Excuse me, ladies."

Olivia turned her attention to Sophie. "Now, is there anything you need?"

"I'm fine," Sophie insisted.

"This is all so unfair. She finally got her big break, and then this happens. I wonder if it was someone who saw the show. She was amazing, and I guess that could have sent some unhinged fan over the edge. Though you'd think that kind of person would have grabbed her at the stage door, not hours later."

"People who kidnap other people can't be expected to think the way the rest of us do."

"Good point," Olivia said with a nod. She kept talking about what had happened the night of Emily's disappearance, but Sophie lost track of the conversation when she noticed a silvery head on the edge of the crowd.

She watched for a moment, made sure it was the fairy she captured the night before, then placed a hand lightly on Olivia's arm as she interrupted to say, "It's been lovely talking to you, but I just saw someone I need to go torture and interrogate. Please excuse me."

As she hurried toward the fairy, she heard Olivia say to someone else, "I always thought Emily was exaggerating about her, but now I don't know."

Sophie was more amused than insulted, but her focus was on the silver-haired fairy. She palmed her iron keychain, then grabbed his arm and demanded, "What do you want?"

He hissed in pain and jerked his arm out of her grasp, but he made no move to run. Before she could grab him again, he pulled a length of frayed pink ribbon from his pocket. She recognized the ribbon she'd tied to the package she'd sent Emily. Either he was working with Emily or he was her captor. "I bring you a message from Emily. And a warning."

"Where is Emily?"

"She wants you to stay away."

"That wasn't what I asked." She moved toward him again with her horseshoe and wished the cast-iron skillet had fit in her purse.

He backed away from her. "I can assure you that Emily is not being harmed, and I will bring her home as soon as I can."

"So you're friends, is that it?" Sophie knew she needed to get Emily out of the Realm soon. If Emily was ignoring everything she'd taught her and making friends with fairies, next she'd be eating the food, and it would be like detoxing an addict to return her to the real world.

The fairy tilted his head to one side and frowned in thought for a moment. He was unlike any fairy she'd ever seen before. If it hadn't been for the unusual coloring and the unreal level of attractiveness, he might even have passed for human. He dressed like an absent-minded professor, and she noticed a folded newspaper stuck in his jacket pocket. "Friends? Yes, I do believe we are," he said at last, as though he was as surprised by the thought as Sophie was.

"But you're the one who took her."

He looked her straight in the eye and said, "For that I am sorry. I was told she was a changeling who needed to be restored to her people, and I thought her masked aura was proof of that–the reason she'd been lost to us."

"Her aura is masked?" she asked, fighting to keep her voice steady. That was what the crazy old women had said. It was true?

"She is practically invisible to our kind. I only recognized her by her name when I saw her show. I do not know how it happened. It isn't fae magic."

"Why are you helping her?" she asked, suddenly suspicious.

There was another long pause as he put serious thought into his answer. "My name is Eamon," he said somberly.

Sophie knew he was putting himself at her mercy by giving her his name, though it was largely a symbolic gesture, since she couldn't really do anything with it. Still, it required a response beyond the usual "How do you do?" She gave him a slight bow and said, "I am honored to make your acquaintance."

He bowed in response and said, "I am helping because I feel responsible. I was too easily duped. And I do not want Emily to become like the other human captives. I want to bring her safely home."

That was good enough for Sophie. "Then I am happy to accept whatever aid you offer."

"You will stay away?"

"Why should I?"

"I will take care of her until I can get her away."

"Who has her?" she asked, but then she noticed Detective Tanaka staring right at them and starting to move in their direction. She could just imagine what he'd think about seeing her with someone who fit the description of their prime suspect. "You have to go, now," she said. "And can you change your glamour?"

"I don't have that power now. It is difficult for me here in daylight."

He did look awfully pale, she realized. She gripped his arm with the hand not holding the horseshoe and steered him through the crowd. "Then we'll have to find another way to get you out of here. The police know you were with Emily in the diner." His eerie silvery eyes widened as he glanced over his shoulder. "Don't look so suspicious," she scolded. She couldn't resist her own glance and saw that Tanaka had picked up his pace and was hurrying toward them. "Are you sure you can't do anything?" she asked.

"I can barely maintain a human glamour, and my strength is fading."

She remembered something from her childhood and dug in her purse for the plastic-wrapped chocolate-chip cookie that had come with the hideously overpriced airplane snack pack. "Please take this offering of food," she said, holding the cookie out to him.

He accepted it with a bow. "Your generosity is most welcome."

It took him a couple of tries to rip open the plastic while they kept
on the move, and then he took a cautious bite. After chewing, he
shuddered in pleasure. "Oh, this is good."

"Did it work?"

He didn't answer, but she felt a subtle change in her sense of the
universe, and her next glance backward showed Tanaka looking around
like he'd lost his quarry. "I have hidden both of us," Eamon said.

"Good work. Now, about my question: Who has Emily?"

"My glamour will not last long. I must return to Emily." Then
he disappeared even from Sophie's eyes. By the time she refocused
her senses and found him again, he was too far away to catch.

She heard someone calling her name and realized that his
disappearance meant the glamour on her must have dropped, and
now Tanaka could see her. "Oh, look somewhere else," she muttered
under her breath. She didn't have a good explanation for chatting
with the prime suspect, so she darted around the next corner and
lost herself in the crowd of arriving theater patrons. She didn't see
Tanaka behind her, but she still hurried down the street to the next
corner, where she hailed a cab and flung herself into the backseat,
crouching so she wouldn't be visible.

In spite of Eamon's warning, she knew she had to get Emily back
that night, or else Sophie might find herself in trouble with the police.

Twenty-Four

The Murray Residence
Thursday, 7:00 p.m.

When Michael saw Tanaka's number on his Caller ID, he eagerly grabbed the phone. "Did you get something?" he asked.

"Has the ballerina come home yet?"

"I think she might have. She didn't come up to see me, though. Why?"

"If I'm not mistaken, she just had a little chat with our prime suspect at the vigil, and then she helped him get away."

"Are you sure? She might have dragged him into her lair to torture him. I saw how terrified he was when she caught him last night."

"I didn't hear the conversation, but she was talking to a guy who fit the description, and when I headed toward them, they walked away in a hurry, then vanished. When I caught up, Sophie was alone, and she gave me the slip."

"I know she's weird and a little scary, but you don't think she's in on it, do you?"

"It wouldn't be the first time a family member did an end-run around the police to pay a ransom. It may not be anything. It may be a different guy, and she realized that after talking to him, but do me a favor and keep an eye on her. Let me know if she does anything suspicious. It may take a while to get a warrant to track her phone."

Feeling only slightly guilty for spying on Sophie, Michael positioned himself near the living room window so he could watch the front door downstairs. Shortly after eight, she left with Beau, a tote bag slung over her shoulder. Michael knew he should call Tank, but he'd probably lose her if he stopped to make a call. He could always call once he saw where she was going. He bolted for his door and hurried downstairs, reaching the sidewalk just in time to see her round the corner. He followed, staying far enough behind not to be noticeable.

She went down Columbus, turned onto Eighty-first, then crossed Central Park West and headed downtown. The sidewalk there was fairly empty, as most of the dog walkers and joggers were inside the park instead of along the street, so he had to fall back to remain inconspicuous. She entered the park at Seventy-seventh, followed the path along the lake, then headed to the Imagine mosaic, where she melted into a cluster of tourists. He watched the edges of the crowd, but didn't see her again until she was already well down the path heading south into the park.

She'd apparently noticed him, and he'd have aborted if this had been an official operation. But it wasn't, and if she wanted to know why he was following her, she could let him catch up and ask him.

Or she could try to lose him, which was what she seemed to be doing. The paths twisted and turned through the trees, and the sun had set enough that the light was dim within the park. He was also tiring rapidly. He hadn't done this much walking since he'd been shot, and she kept a brisk pace. She was losing him just by walking quickly. He couldn't keep up.

He had to pause and catch his breath while fighting off a dizzy spell, and by the time he recovered, she was so far away he could barely see her. She cut across the grass north of Tavern on the Green, but then he lost her completely. He reached the spot where he'd last seen her, and she was nowhere in sight. It was as though she'd vanished into thin air.

He wasn't sure if it was his overexertion or the setting sun, but he couldn't fight back a shiver.

Twenty-Five

Sophie came out of the gateway under a full head of steam, not so much because she was trying to lose Michael but rather because she was afraid that if she let herself slow down or hesitate in the slightest, she wouldn't be able to go through with her plan. She was in such a hurry, in fact, that it took her a while to notice how cold it was, colder even than in her previous visit. Shivering, she pulled her sweater tighter around her as she noticed a few snowflakes dancing in the air. It was as though months had passed in the Realm since the night before.

She didn't recognize her surroundings, which made it difficult to get her bearings. Then again, bearings were irrelevant in the Realm. If she kept walking, she'd end up where she was supposed to be–or where whatever powers that ruled the Realm wanted her to be. Sure enough, she soon found herself in a more familiar setting: the woods behind her grandparents' house. Or, rather, the fairy world that she'd entered through the woods behind her grandparents' house.

It was exactly the way she remembered. The clearing surrounded by tall pine trees was open to a sky of rich blue, just dark enough for stars to be visible. In the middle of the clearing was a patch of marble floor ringed with carved pillars, like the ruins of a temple. Some of the pillars had fallen into just the right position to serve as benches. Broad pediments topped the standing pillars, so the place had always reminded Sophie of the fairy circles of toadstools that grew in the lawn.

The music was even the same as she remembered, seemingly emanating from the trees themselves. The feathery branches of the pine trees sighed and sang like a string orchestra. Their sound brought back memories of long-ago nights spent dancing. She caught herself swaying to the music, then snapped herself out of the spell. She wasn't here for fun. She had a mission to accomplish—or she would if anyone showed up. The clearing was annoyingly empty. In spite of her stern mental lecture, her toes twitched and she shifted her weight from foot to foot. She'd never wanted to dance so much in her life. She rationalized that Tallulah would require a dance before she'd talk as a payment for the conversation, so she might as well warm up.

She took off her sweater, sat on one of the fallen pillars, and took an old pair of pointe shoes that were still serviceable—but too frayed around the toes to be presentable—out of the bag she'd borrowed from Emily's closet. She put on the shoes, then stood up and moved to the center of the floor.

After a few warm-ups, she started with an adagio suited to the plaintive tone of the forest music. The music grew livelier, as though welcoming her back, so she moved into a series of turns and jumps. In spite of the gravity of her predicament, her heart soared with the dance. At the same time, tears spilled from her eyes with the awareness of what she'd given up. She hadn't let herself go free like this in years. She kept up her skills with classes, but a routine of teaching little girls with big dreams and dancing the Sugar Plum Fairy every December didn't stretch her fairy-honed talent. She was getting old for a dancer, but she didn't feel it in her body. It was like she was seventeen again.

The music built to a crescendo and she crossed the floor with a chain of soaring grand jetés, her legs in a full split. As she'd told Michael, she could get some serious air. Sometimes she felt like she was just short of taking flight. She finished with some big fouetté turns, whipping herself around by kicking her leg in and out as she spun. This was the move that had been so helpful in snaring Eamon, and she couldn't help but smile at the thought. She landed in fourth position, breathing hard, tears streaming down her cheeks.

That was when she realized she had an audience other than Beau. The sound of one pair of hands clapping came from the trees surrounding the clearing, but she didn't see anyone. Beau dropped the stick he'd been gnawing on and growled. Squinting, Sophie could make out a few figures hiding among the trees. One finally stepped forward.

She was a statuesque fairy woman with flame-colored hair that fell to her hips and wafted around her like she was caught in a stiff breeze. Her gauzy dress, unaffected by the wind that stirred her hair, clung to her curves. "You have not forgotten everything I taught you, I see," she said.

Sophie returned the gaze of her former mentor, refusing to let herself be cowed. "No, I haven't."

"You will excuse my friends if they are wary of approaching. I'm sure you understand their fear."

"Yes, I suppose I was rather…" Sophie's voice trailed off as she tried to think of a good way to describe the way she'd acted the last time she'd met Tallulah and her people.

"Angry?" Tallulah suggested.

"That's putting it mildly." Sophie didn't apologize because she still wasn't sure that her fury hadn't been justified. "And it's happened again."

"Your sister," Tallulah said with a nod, stepping up onto the marble floor and coming to stand in front of Sophie.

"Among others. And I'm here to get them back." Her heart pounding madly at the enormity of what she was about to propose, Sophie steeled herself and said, "I know what you taught me had a price, and I'm willing to pay that price myself. I'll stay here with you, as long as you want me, if you'll let Emily and the others go."

Smiling sadly, Tallulah placed the palm of her hand against Sophie's cheek. "My poor child, your sister was not the price for my teaching."

Sophie jerked away from Tallulah's cool touch. "Then why did you take her? Why have you been trying to take her for years—and taking the wrong women along the way? Why do enchantresses feel the need to protect Emily from you and your people by masking her aura?" Sophie still wasn't sure about that last bit, but she wanted to see how Tallulah reacted.

"Do you think so little of me?" Tallulah said, arching one slightly slanted eyebrow. "If I wanted your sister, I would have found her, with or without an aura. I would have made no mistakes." She held up a hand to silence Sophie before she could protest. "No, it is Maeve who has taken your sister. It was she who tried to take her before—as you would have known if you'd listened to me instead of terrifying my people. It was she who mistakenly took the others."

"But Maeve was part of your family."

"Maeve had already left my family the first time she tried to take your sister. She was not acting on my orders or on my behalf."

Sophie's vision swam. She pulled her feet into fifth position and tightened her muscles so her legs wouldn't buckle under her, and still she felt she might collapse. She had to remind herself to breathe, and then her breath came in short gasps. "You mean, all that time..." she whispered, then she shook her head, blinking back tears. She'd given up everything that mattered to her to keep her sister safe, and it had all been for nothing? Fourteen years, stuck in a small town, teaching kindergarteners how to do pliés, when she could have been dancing her way around the world. It was too much to bear. She opened her mouth to release the scream that felt like it was coming up from the depths of her soul, but instead a laugh came out. She doubled over with hysterical laughter, unable to stop herself, even as her sides ached and the tears she'd been fighting spilled out of her eyes.

With every ounce of will she had, she forced herself to stop and straighten to look Tallulah in the eye. "Well, I suppose that was silly of me, wasn't it? It'll teach me to play the martyr without fully understanding the situation." On the bright side, it apparently wasn't her fault that Jennifer Murray had gone missing—at least not directly.

"You were correct that there was a price, though," Tallulah said in a tone that chilled Sophie's soul.

"What was your price?"

"I hadn't decided. Not your sister. I don't know what I would have done with her. I am not quite altruistic enough to say that seeing you dance was reward enough, though it does bring me great joy. Even if you'd asked me, I'm not sure I could have said what I wanted from you. You were wise to leave me when you did. The price would have become steeper than it already is." A trace of a smile crossed her lips. "And you do still owe me, little one." She frowned, tilted her head as she studied Sophie, then cupped Sophie's face with both hands. A glimmer of recognition flickered in her eyes, and she released Sophie's face. "It is time for you to make good on that debt."

"What do you want?"

"A song." She swept away from Sophie and went to sit on one of the fallen pillars.

"A song?" It was more customary to ask for a first-born child, a loved one, or years of a person's life. A song was small change.

"It is a beginning, not the whole payment." Tallulah turned and beckoned to the fairies hiding in the trees. "Come out, children. I don't believe she will harm you today. She's in a relatively good temper."

Beau, however, wasn't, and he growled again, then barked. Sophie leapt to grab his leash and pull him back from the fairies who were creeping out from behind the trees. She recognized many of them from her childhood, but there were several new ones. There were also some missing: Maeve and those who had gone with her.

The fairies settled on the ground around the circle. "Now," Tallulah said imperiously as she faced Sophie, "I recall that there was a delightful song you sang for us when you were a child, something your grandmother taught you. I would like to hear it."

Feeling like there had to be a catch, but unable to see the danger in a song, Sophie sang the old folk song about finding a lost love. She could practically hear her grandmother's voice in her head, not cracked and broken the way it sounded now, but strong and vibrant, the way it had been when Sophie was very little and her grandmother sang while rocking her to sleep.

At the end of the song, her fairy audience applauded. Tallulah regarded her quietly, her face somber. Then she abruptly smiled and clapped her hands. "Music!" she called out. "Dance for us, my child. Show me what you've been doing since you left me."

The last thing Sophie felt like doing was dancing, but she was afraid of what Tallulah would ask if she refused. At least no one she cared about would be harmed by her dancing. This was a far lower price than she'd feared. She nudged Beau off to the side with an admonition to behave. He growled at the fairies and lay glaring at them, but he stayed put. It didn't take long for the lively music to find its way to her feet, and soon she forgot about her wasted sacrifice, her lost dreams, and her worries about the future as she submerged herself in the dance. Once she was dancing, the fairies joined in, twirling and spinning around her.

Someone took her arm, and she rose onto one toe, prepared to let him turn her or support her in an arabesque, but he grabbed her so hard he threw her off-balance. Someone else grabbed her from the other side, and she knew this wasn't about dancing anymore. She dropped off her toes and planted her feet, refusing to budge as her captors tried to drag her away. Tallulah and the others hadn't yet noticed anything amiss, and Sophie took quick action to rectify that. She lifted one knee and then brought her foot down, toe first, onto the bare foot of one of her captors, just behind the toes. The reinforced toe box of a pointe shoe wasn't something one would want slammed into one's bare foot with any degree of force. The fairy instantly released her with an impressive scream, which brought the rest of the group to silence.

That was what she'd hoped would happen—she'd always found it far more effective in a struggle to get attention by making her enemies scream rather than doing the screaming herself. Screaming took energy that she could better devote to defending herself, and then there was the psychological advantage of putting the other person in the role of victim. It was just as true in a fairy war as it had been in junior high. When she knew Tallulah was looking at her, she said, "Was this your plan? Are you working with Maeve, after all?"

Instead of answering Sophie, Tallulah glared at the fairy still holding her. "Release her!"

"We no longer answer to you," Sophie's captor said in a way that made Sophie want to jab her elbow into his ribs. Unfortunately, the way he held her made that impossible, and he was smart enough to move his foot before she could stomp on it. She leaned into him while he was still off-balance from trying to avoid her pointe shoe. He wasn't ready to support her weight as well as his own, and both of them fell. She scrambled frantically away, wondering why no one was helping her. Not even Beau had joined the fight, though she could hear him barking.

When she looked up, she saw why she was on her own: All the other fairies, Tallulah, and Beau were behind a shimmering barrier and couldn't reach her. She got to her feet and ran toward them, but she couldn't get through the barrier, either. She was trapped, and her bag containing her iron horseshoe and the skillet was on the other side of the barrier.

The fairy whose foot she'd stomped grinned as he moved his hand in a throwing motion and a silver chain appeared, circling her right wrist. "You're coming with us," he said, reeling her in. She fought every step of the way, and then when he was pulling on the chain with his entire weight, she stopped fighting and rushed forward, which sent him reeling backward. The other one went to his aid, grabbing higher up the chain and giving it a good jerk. Once he got her close enough, he slapped her hard across the face, sending her sprawling to the ground.

Gravity was on her side, so she grabbed the chain with her left hand and pulled with all her might, bringing the fairy down on top of her. Before he could react, she rolled over to straddle him and stretched the chain across his throat. "Didn't your mother teach you that a gentleman never strikes a lady?" she said.

She sensed the other one coming up behind her and shouted, "Back off!" Surprisingly, he did so. She turned her attention back to the one who was starting to gasp for breath. "You work for Maeve, don't you?" she asked, forcing her tone to remain calm and pleasant, like they were chatting over tea.

He didn't answer, and the chain writhed in her grasp. She got it back under control and wound it around his neck for good measure. "What does Maeve want with my sister—or with me?"

He gasped and sputtered, and the other one approached again. "I said, back off!" Sophie shouted in a burst of fury. She was surprised to see him go flying until he bounced off the shimmering barrier. Did she do that?

She eased the chain away just enough for her captive to speak, but all he did was clutch at her arms. The chain still wound around her wrist and in her grasp grew warm, then hot, then scorching. She let go, but it remained on her wrist. Her eyes watering with the pain, she brought her chained wrist against the face of the captive, who had tried to get up the moment she released the chain. Then she couldn't take the pain anymore and shook her wrist, trying to get enough air circulation to cool it.

Much to her surprise, the chain uncoiled. She was pretty sure she'd done that. Not necessarily on purpose, but she'd hoped to be free of it, and now she was. In other circumstances, she might have been startled by her ability to do these things, but this wasn't the moment to question it. She needed to use it.

She held her hand out to the fairy beneath her, willing him to leave her alone, and he fell backward. The other one approached, and she willed him back, as well. She struggled to her feet, put her hands on her hips and said, "I don't know what Maeve's game is, but I want you to tell her something: She can release my sister, and then we'll talk, but until then, I will do everything in my power to get my sister back." She couldn't resist a grin. "And you may have noticed that I do have power."

She waved at the shimmering barrier, and it vanished. Beau rushed forward, barking madly, and Sophie stopped him with a raised hand. That time, she felt the power surge through her. The odd thing was, it was a familiar feeling. Had she been doing this sort of thing all along, thinking she was swaying people by the force of her personality? She shoved the question aside as one of many things she needed to think about later.

She moved to stand over the fairy she'd been strangling. "Now, get out of here, and if I see you again, I won't be nearly as nice. This was a warning. From here, I play dirty."

He started to get to his feet, but Tallulah intervened. "No. He is mine. You are part of my family, Padraig. And now you betray me by attacking my guest?"

"I have sworn allegiance to Maeve," he said, though he looked somewhat ashamed of himself.

"That makes you a traitor, and you know what I do to traitors."

Sophie stopped her with a hand on her arm. "No, I want him to take that message for me. He'll suffer enough for failing in his mission, I'm sure." She turned back to Padraig and shouted, "Go!"

He didn't need urging. He and his colleague ran for dear life. Sophie couldn't help but notice that many of Tallulah's people had also disappeared into the woods. She released her mental hold on Beau, who came straight to her side and took up a protective position between her and Tallulah.

The fairy glared fiercely after the fleeing traitors. "I wonder how many spies Maeve left in my family," she snarled. Her eyes softened, and she took Sophie's right hand, raising it to nearly eye level and studying the angry, blistered burn on her wrist. "Fiona!" she called over her shoulder. "Bring the balm." To Sophie, she said, "I will tend your wound."

"What will that cost me?" Sophie asked. The pain had been washed out by the adrenaline rush but was returning, and seeing how ugly the burn was made her queasy.

"For the healing, nothing. You have paid me with the most entertaining show I have seen in far too long. There will be songs and stories about this."

A fairy who was even shorter than Sophie brought a small crystal container. Tallulah passed a hand over the top of it, flipped the lid up with her thumb, dipped her fingers into the container, brought them up to her lips and blew on them, then gently drew them around the burn on Sophie's wrist. It stung at first, then cooled, dimming the pain. Soon, the blisters were gone and the flesh was left smooth, though red and shiny, like a days-old burn that was healing. When she was finished, Tallulah sent Fiona away.

Still holding Sophie's hand, Tallulah said, "While I ask no payment for the healing, I have another demand of you to settle our debt. You were made an offer earlier today, or perhaps you thought it to be a challenge. You must accept it."

Sophie suddenly felt cold. She shivered and wished she could free herself from Tallulah so she could wrap her arms around herself. "Do you mean…they're for real, not crazy?"

"Yes, they're real," Tallulah confirmed. "You must do this."

"I can't!"

"We've seen here that you can." She drew herself even taller, looming over Sophie and speaking in a voice that lost all gentleness and warmth. "I could demand your first-born child, your sister, that nice young man you're becoming fond of, or even your own future. This is not such a big thing I ask. That is your task, and then we will almost be even."

"Almost?"

"I will ask one more thing of you soon." She released Sophie's hand and rested her hand on top of Sophie's head. "You were born for this, my fierce little one. Now, run along."

Once, during a sisterly squabble, Emily had accused Sophie of being a robot because she was so calm in situations that would make most people scream, cry, or curl up in a corner in a fetal position. Sophie countered that in a crisis it did no one any good to scream, cry, or withdraw. She merely pushed her emotions aside to deal with at a more appropriate time so she could focus on the matter at hand. She was sure she looked robotic now as she bent to pick up Beau's leash and made her way calmly over to where she'd left her bag, but everything that had just happened was so overwhelming that if she even let herself consider it, she'd be tempted to find the gateway that led back home so she wouldn't have to deal with any of this.

She sat down and mechanically unwound the ribbons from her ankles, took off her shoes, wrapped the ribbons around them, and placed them in her bag. She slid her feet back into her street shoes, then put on her sweater, buttoning the bottom two buttons at her waist. Slinging her bag over her shoulder, she stood, took Beau's leash, and left the clearing, sensing for the gateway.

A rustling in the underbrush nearby told her that someone was coming. But where was the gateway? It was hard to find it when her senses were more occupied with the potential threat. She put her hand in her bag and gripped the handle of the iron skillet.

It was Beau who found the gateway. His snorting and sniffing, followed by a low growl, told her he'd sensed something, and as she followed him she felt the distinctive shiver down her spine that told her she was being watched. The rustling grew louder and someone shouted, "There she is!" Hoping she'd come out not too long after she'd left, she stepped through.

A cold, tingling sensation made her gasp, and her first thought was that something had gone wrong with the gateway, but then she realized that it was raining in the real world. She was in the park, exactly where she'd left, and the light was dimmer, but not entirely gone. If it was still the same day, then she hadn't been away long, and that meant Michael might still be around, so she'd need to be careful.

She released the skillet so she could pull her umbrella out of her bag, then she looked around the park. She didn't see Michael, and with any luck, she could get home without having to deal with him. After everything that had just happened, that would be the proverbial last straw. She wondered if she could use her newly discovered magical powers to keep him away or make herself invisible.

A hysterical giggle threatened to escape at the thought of even having magical powers, and she clasped a hand over her mouth to stifle it. This wasn't the time or the place to have a meltdown, she told herself sternly.

She reached the path, and there ahead of her was a tall, dark-haired man with his right arm in a sling. "Oh, dear," she muttered under her breath. Deciding that the best defense was a good offense, she approached him and said with a hint of scolding in her voice, "Detective Murray, what on earth are you doing out in this weather?"

Twenty-Six

Emily avoided falling into the spell this time. It might have made the waiting more bearable, but she didn't want to lose herself again. She hovered on the fringes of the party, feeling like a wallflower who couldn't get a date to the prom. Time had lost all meaning for her. It seemed as though she had always been at this party and would spend the rest of eternity there.

She started to protest when a passing man swept her into his arms, then she realized it was Eamon, wearing a glamour that fit the room, even though she felt the rough tweed of his usual clothes when she placed her hand on his shoulder. "Is it my imagination, or are you warmer?" she asked as she fell into step with him..

"I have been in the outside world."

"Did you find Sophie? Oh, gosh, I never told you how to find her, did I?"

"I found her. I went to the theater, and she was there, where all your friends were mourning your loss."

"They don't think I'm dead, do they?" she asked in alarm, forgetting to keep her voice low as they danced cheek-to-cheek.

"I believe it is what the newspapers call a candlelight vigil."

"And Sophie was there? I guess she'd have to be, but she'd have hated every minute. Obviously, you survived the encounter. How did it go?"

"I warned her to stay away."

Emily snorted. "Yeah, that'll do a lot of good." At his blank look, she explained, "When I was feeling lonely here in the city and missed my big sister, I got a bulldog to keep me company. Do you get the picture?" He obviously didn't, so she clarified further, "Sophie can be stubborn."

"But I didn't tell her *why* she should stay away."

"You think that's a *good* thing?"

"If I'd told her she was the one Maeve really wanted, do you think she'd have stayed away?"

"Wow, you understand her pretty well." They danced a few steps in silence, then she said, "While you were out and about, did you figure a way to get me out of here?"

"Maeve's court seems to be enchanted so that no human may leave without permission."

"So, I'm stuck. Do you want to know what I learned while you were out?"

"You learned something?"

"I did." She glanced around the party. "Is there somewhere we can talk privately?" He steered her off the dance floor to a secluded corner, and after one more glance around, she got out her phone to show him the map. "Does this mean anything to you?"

He squinted at the image on the screen. "It's the palace. She's found it." He sounded stunned, and his breathing became more rapid. "Where did you find this?"

"In Maeve's room. But I thought you couldn't map this place."

"There are some markers…but if she knows where the palace is and she hasn't acted, there must be more to it than that."

"Like drawing a sword from a stone. But that still doesn't explain why she needs Sophie." Her stomach growled, and she winced in embarrassment. "I don't suppose you brought me any food?"

He smiled. "I have cookies. And milk."

"You spoil me."

"Your sister gave me a cookie, and I liked it well enough to bring them to you."

"If she's giving you food, she likes you."

"It was an emergency. Someone saw us together, and she thought that was bad. I was too weak for glamour without human food."

"I wonder who that could have been," she said as he handed her a cookie from his pocket. She devoured three cookies and half a small carton of milk before thinking to offer him a cookie. His reaction was a visual representation of sheer bliss. His eyes went heavy-lidded, and all the tension drained from his face as the corners of his mouth turned up. She tried to memorize his expression to use the next time she needed to portray that kind of ecstasy in a role.

"Perhaps I could go find this palace, and that would help me learn what more might be needed," he mused after he'd finished the cookie. "Though I hate to leave you alone again."

"No, go!" she urged. "It's more useful than you hanging out here with me. Anything you learn could help." She looked up at him, and the way he looked back at her made her shiver. "I know I'm not supposed to thank you directly," she said, suddenly feeling shy with him, "but, well, I don't know what I'd have done without you—other than not being here at all, I guess, but you know what I mean."

He tilted his head and studied her before saying, "Do I?"

"You've brought me food and carried messages, and you've tried to help, and I—well, I'm glad, I guess." That still sounded empty. She was a good Southern girl whose mother had forced her practically at gunpoint to write thank-you notes for every gift she received or party she attended, and expressing appreciation without direct thanks didn't feel right. "Aw, hell," she muttered as she placed her hands on either side of his face and kissed him. He froze for a moment before responding and pulling her against him.

"I didn't realize this was how humans customarily expressed gratitude," he whispered, his face still so close that his lips brushed hers as he spoke.

"Only when we're dealing with people who'll be insulted or think we're obligated to them, or whatever your deal is, if we dare use the words 'thank you,'" she said. "And only when—" She broke off when the front door opened and two fairy men limped into the lobby, followed by a few others who seemed relatively unscathed. The one with the slightest limp had red burns across his neck and on his cheek, while the other walked like he had a broken foot. "Something tells me you didn't convince her to stay away," Emily remarked.

He kept his arm around her waist as she turned to watch the proceedings. "Perhaps I underestimated her stubbornness."

"They must have really pissed her off. Usually, she doesn't have to get physical. They give up when she destroys them psychologically."

Maeve soon appeared at the top of the stairs and forgot to look regal as she hurried down, demanding, "Where is she?"

"She declined our invitation to join us," the one with the burned face said with a wince.

"She got away?"

"You might say that, your majesty. She had a message for you, though. She said that until you release her sister, she will do everything in her power to bring you down."

"Empty threats," Maeve said with a dismissive wave. "The two of you couldn't overpower one small human within our own realm?"

"Forgive us, your majesty," the limping one said, "but she does have power—magical power. She is an enchantress."

Emily barely bit back her exclamation at that, but it wouldn't have mattered because Maeve's shriek was loud enough to drown it out. "She can't be!"

"She broke every spell we used," the one with the burned face said. "Her power isn't controlled, but it is there. I would consider her threats to be real."

Maeve spun, searching the room, then spotted Emily and came toward her. Emily slipped out of Eamon's grasp and met Maeve halfway. "What do you know of this?" Maeve asked.

"It's the first I've heard of it, but it doesn't surprise me. It explains a *lot*. And I would take any threat my sister makes very, very seriously."

Maeve grabbed Emily by the face, held her for a second, then released her, hurling her away with such force that she stumbled. "You've been touched by magic, but I don't find it in you. How can that be? You are sisters!"

"I'm also about six inches taller than Sophie. Maybe I got the height and she got the magic. Or she could have learned something. I don't know."

Maeve turned back to her henchmen. "What else happened?"

While the two injured fairies told a long story about how helpless they'd been when confronted with a being of such magnificent power, Emily edged her way back to Eamon. "Is it true?" she asked him.

"I hadn't considered it. Perhaps that was the power I sensed in her."

"Well, if Sophie has magical powers, the world had better look out, that's all I can say. Maeve may have bitten off more than she can chew."

At the moment, Maeve was chewing out her henchmen. "Incompetent! That's what you are! All of you!" Her beautiful face screwed up into an ugly red mask of fury. "I don't care if she is an enchantress, you are *fae*! How many armies do I have to send after one small human girl?"

Eamon stepped forward. "I've found her."

That got Maeve's attention. "Where is she? Is she here?"

"I didn't say I have her, just that I've found her. I might be able to do so again, and she trusts me now."

Emily stared at him, open-mouthed. What was he up to? Sophie said you could never trust a fairy, but she'd thought he was different. He then gave her a sidelong glance that she interpreted to mean that he was up to something. She decided to play along. "No! You can't!" she shouted, grabbing his arm.

Maeve ignored her, focusing on Eamon. "You know I would be most grateful if you brought her to me," she purred.

"I'm sure you would, but I don't need more books. I do need to know why you want her. You lied to me about Emily Drake. I will do nothing more for you until you tell me the truth so I may decide if I want to be a part of it."

Okay, this was a pretty good plan, Emily thought, impressed. But would Maeve go for it?

Twenty-Seven

Michael whirled at the sound of Sophie's voice. His eyes widened when he saw her, then he frowned and glanced around, like he was trying to figure out where she'd come from. Still on the offensive, she said, "We need to get you home and dry." She tried holding her umbrella over both of them, but it required her holding her arm straight over her head. "Here, you hold it," she said, putting it into his left hand. "You're too tall for me to cover." He took the umbrella without protest, probably because he was too stunned to speak, then went along when she put her hand on his back and began walking.

He finally found his voice. "What are you doing out in this?"

"It wasn't like this when I went out. I thought Beau could use some exercise."

"How did you get Beau to come with you? I can't get him to go to the end of the block."

"Maybe he likes me better."

It felt like they were in their own little world under the canopy of the umbrella. She couldn't help but smile at the thought of the macho policeman holding the umbrella with Degas's ballerinas on it.

The dim light, the shadow of the umbrella, and the way she had to walk pressed against his side to stay in the umbrella's shelter meant he couldn't see her injuries and couldn't read her face. She wasn't sure what she'd do when they got home and he got a good look at her. Bruises took time to form, but the sleeve of her sweater wasn't long enough to cover the burn on her wrist, and her cheek still stung from the slap, so she was sure it had left a mark.

Although her hand on his back was meant to steady him, it grounded her, as well. She didn't know which of them was trembling– possibly both of them. He was at the end of his strength and she'd reached the point of emotional overload. His breathing had become ragged, like it took too much effort to get enough air, and that meant there was no conversation. When they reached the edge of the park, she said, "Are you okay? Maybe we should get a cab."

He shook his head. "I'm fine." But he gasped for air between words. "Besides, we'd never get one in the rain, with the dog. Even you couldn't pull that off." She was ready to argue, but she saw the number of people standing on the curb. She didn't know if there was a spell for getting a cab or if the way she always managed to find one had been magic all along.

By the time they reached his street, she'd put her arm around his waist to support him, and he leaned heavily against her. "We're almost there," she said encouragingly as they neared his building. She half carried him up the front steps, and then she leaned him against the wall where the intercom was while she opened the door. Instead of groping for her keys, she stood so he couldn't see what she was doing and touched the lock. She felt the now-familiar flow of power, and the door opened for her. *Okay, it works in the real world, too,* she noted.

She took the umbrella from Michael and held it to shield them while Beau shook himself dry. "Let's stop at Emily's place," she said. "I don't think I can get you up the stairs." That door opened at her touch, too, and she dropped Beau's leash, the umbrella, and her bag just inside the door so she could get Michael through the entry hall and onto the daybed. Then she stepped out of her wet shoes, unhooked the leash Beau trailed through the apartment, and found some towels.

Michael protested as she towel-dried his wet hair, but she ignored him. "You don't need to be chilled. What were you doing out wandering the park at this time of day? I was walking the dog. I don't know what your excuse is. Are you *trying* to catch your death of pneumonia?" She lifted the towel from his head and smoothed his hair back into place. "Now, I'll put on the kettle, then run up and get you a dry shirt. I doubt there's anything down here that would fit you."

Before she could turn to go, he caught her arm just above the burn on her wrist. "Sophie, what is this?" he asked, then he looked up at her and saw her face. She didn't need a mirror to know what a fright she looked because she could see it in his eyes. "What happened to you?"

"Beau saw a squirrel and took off, and he took me along for the ride. The leash gave me a rope burn," she said as airily as she could manage.

He tightened his grip and frowned at her. She could feel him assessing her, see the doubt on his face. "Sophie, I've seen a squirrel run across Beau's back–I guess it thought he was a rock–and he didn't move a muscle."

"You also don't think he wants to walk beyond the end of the block, and I'm seeing otherwise." She jerked her arm out of his grasp. She'd had enough of people grabbing her. "Now, I'll get that kettle on. Where should I look for a dry shirt?"

"There should be a sweatshirt in the laundry basket just inside the bedroom door," he said, sagging against the pillows. His posture looked defeated, but the glint in his eyes said this conversation wasn't over.

"I'll be back in a sec. Keep an eye on him, Beau."

After setting the kettle on the stove, she dashed upstairs, forgetting the key in her haste, but she was able to unlock the door the way she had the downstairs door and Emily's. Oh dear, she really did have powers. She wondered what she could do other than open locked doors. The NYPD sweatshirt was where he said it would be, lying in a basket of clean clothes. She grabbed it and ran back downstairs.

The kettle was just starting to boil when she got to it. It was too late in the evening for tea, so she rummaged through the cabinets and found a box of cocoa mix. Good, she needed a dose of sugar after all the shock, and it didn't require the water to be fresh off the boil. She turned off the stove, then turned to focus on Michael.

"I can dress myself," he grumbled as she approached with the sweatshirt.

"Do you really feel up to that?" He glared at her and eased his right arm out of the sling, then struggled to lift the hem of his long-sleeved T-shirt. When she couldn't stand watching anymore, she snapped, "Oh, come on, no one's going to give you a medal for changing shirts by yourself, and you'll exhaust yourself trying." As she helped him pull his arms out of the sleeves, she reflected that this was her first time to undress a man. She was glad the shirt was over his head so he couldn't see her blush at the thought. Not that this was *that* kind of situation. It was more like helping a child get into his pajamas.

He had a lanky build, but he had a decent set of muscles, like he'd put some work into staying in shape. His ribs stood out, though, so he must have lost weight since being hurt. The upper right side of his chest was swathed in gauze bandages and surgical tape. "Do you need to change these bandages?" she asked.

"No, I'm fine. I saw the doctor earlier today, so these are fresh." She helped him get the weaker arm into the sleeve of the sweatshirt, then left him to get the shirt the rest of the way on while she went to make cocoa. She put one mug into his hand, wrapped an afghan around his shoulders, and sat next to him.

He was breathing better, she noticed, and he wasn't quite so gray. "You need to take better care of yourself," she scolded.

"You're one to talk. What happened, Sophie?"

"No one mugged me, if that's what you're worried about."

"What about trying to abduct you?"

There was no way she could answer that question in a way that didn't sound alarming without lying, and she knew he'd know she was lying. Even so, she looked him in the eye and said, "It's not what you think."

"How do you know what I think?"

"Oh, honey, trust me, there is no *way* you can be thinking this." She couldn't hold back a laugh that sounded borderline hysterical.

"Care to share?"

"It has nothing to do with you."

"Does it have anything to do with Emily? Nobody's threatening you or asking for ransom, or anything like that?"

"I'd tell you if that were the case."

"Would you? You're lying to me about everything else. What about your meeting with our prime suspect earlier in the evening?"

She wavered between tackling that head-on and trying to deny it. Either way, it would look bad. "I see Detective Tanaka has talked to you," she said. "It's not what he thought. It wasn't the same guy." Metaphorically speaking, that was true. The first time she'd encountered the fairy, he'd been an enemy, but this time he seemed to be an ally.

"You can tell me off the record if you need help with something and you're afraid to involve the police."

"I appreciate your concern, really, I do, but this isn't a police matter, and there's nothing you can do to help. I'm not up to anything illegal, if that makes you feel better."

"Are you in trouble?"

She paused, thinking, then shook her head, "No, no, I don't think so." With a bitter chuckle, she added, "I may be the one causing the trouble, but that's usually the case." She placed a hand on his arm and said, "You don't need to worry about me. I can take care of myself." The memory of taking down her would-be abductors and flinging them around magically flashed before her mind's eye and it took all her self-control not to burst out laughing.

"Just like they don't give medals for changing shirts by

yourself, they don't give prizes for self-sufficiency. You don't have to do everything."

She sighed. "Yes, I do. Otherwise, it doesn't get done." She stood and nodded toward his mug. "Are you finished with that?"

He handed it to her, and she took both mugs to the sink, then turned to face him. "Can you make it upstairs by yourself, or do you need help?"

He grinned suddenly and shook his head in disbelief. "Look at you—you act like you have to do everything for yourself, and yet you're the first one to offer help."

"Okay then, when you're back to full strength, I'll let you carry me up the stairs."

He got off the daybed, groaning only slightly, then stood still for a moment to steady himself. As he let her take his arm, he said, "I'll hold you to that." She had a vivid mental image of him scooping her into his arms and sweeping her up the stairs, and when she met his eye, his expression told her he'd seen a very similar image. Both of them quickly looked away, and she could hardly wait to get him up the stairs so she could take her arm from around him. She should have outgrown the hopeless crush phase years ago, so this was awfully silly of her.

Upstairs, he unlocked his apartment door and hesitated a moment with his hand on the knob. "Here, let me help," she said.

"No, I've got it." He took a deep breath and opened the door, then turned back to face her. "I think I'll be okay from here."

"Let me know if you need anything," she said with forced brightness. She felt about a ton lighter once his door closed behind him and she returned to the shelter of Emily's apartment.

And then she wished she'd kept him around because now she didn't have anything to distract her from all the thoughts raging in her head—the lost dreams, pointless sacrifices, unnamed debts, and uncertain future.

Twenty-Eight

"Such insolence!" Maeve sputtered at Eamon. "You owe me obedience. I don't need to explain myself to one such as you."

Eamon glared at Maeve. "I am not a member of your court." He straightened his shoulders, and it seemed to Emily that he grew taller. "I would never bow to you."

Maeve's eyes went so icy that they could have emitted freeze rays. Her voice dropped to a sinister whisper. "If you are not a member of my court, why do you spend so much time here?" Her gaze flicked to Emily, who shivered at the sudden blast of cold that struck her. "It's the girl, isn't it? You've become fond of the human girl."

She moved forward in a walk that was practically a slither until she was eye-to-eye with Eamon. "When you enter my court, you come under my rule, and I will not tolerate traitors," she spat. Then she raised her voice and shrieked, "Seize him! He will tell us how to find Sophie Drake."

Before Eamon could react, he was swarmed by henchmen, one of whom bound his arms against his sides with a silver chain.

Another moved his hand, and Eamon slumped limply to the ground. The henchmen hauled him away.

Without thinking, Emily rushed forward and slapped Maeve hard across the face. "You bitch!" she screamed. "You have no *right*! He's free!"

The look on Maeve's face should have scared Emily, but she was too outraged to feel fear. Was this what it was like to be Sophie? Whatever it was, they could sell this feeling as a drug. She was invincible. "And while I'm at it," she continued while Maeve was still too stunned to speak, "you had no right to grab me. You also have no right to whatever it is you want from my sister, and I am sick of getting caught up in your stupid little power trip."

Instead of yelling, Maeve smiled sweetly. "You ignorant, insignificant, pathetic little human," she said in a voice that made saccharine seem sour in comparison. "You have no idea what is happening here, no idea at all. Stay out of matters that don't concern you."

Still riding the adrenaline high, Emily snorted in derision. "Don't concern me? This concerns me a lot, in every meaning of the word. Considering that I'm being held prisoner and you're trying to do God knows what to my sister, yeah, it concerns me. And I'm pretty damned concerned about what all this means."

"I have had enough of your insolence." Maeve reached out and touched Emily's forehead. The last thing Emily heard as the darkness closed in was Maeve's voice saying, "Your sister will pay for her defiance."

Twenty-Nine

The Antique Shop
Friday, noon

Sophie did not want to join the enchantresses. She had so much more to worry about than humoring a pair of dotty old ladies. Yes, the magic had been helpful the night before, but she didn't think that committee meetings about how to handle the fairy situation would be of much use. Unfortunately, the fairies took debts and obligations very seriously, and if she didn't carry through on what she'd promised Tallulah, she might be asked for something even worse. She went to the antique shop the next day.

As the bells on the door jangled at Sophie's entrance, Athena looked up. She was dressed in gingham and denim trimmed with eyelet lace today. Sophie let Beau off his leash, and he went straight to his bed.

"You've reconsidered?" Athena said.

"I have."

Athena clapped her hands excitedly. "I knew you'd come around."

"I wouldn't really say that I've come around," Sophie said, already regretting this move. She suspected it was about to complicate her life even further. "It's more of an obligation."

Athena made a "tsk, tsk" sound and said, "I'd have thought you'd know better than to oblige yourself to their kind."

"This is a very old obligation." Sophie sighed. She might as well come out with it instead of wasting time talking in circles. "It turns out I was wrong, about everything. Tallulah didn't take Emily, and Emily wasn't the price for my training. It's Maeve who has Emily, and no one seems to know why. But Tallulah has called in the debt I owe her, and she said I had to accept the offer I was extended yesterday. So here I am. Quite reluctantly, to be honest."

"Oh, my. I'd better call Amelia. But in the meantime, you can start learning some basics." She went behind the counter and brought out a stack of binders. "I created a curriculum," she said as she handed the binders to Sophie.

Of course you did, Sophie thought. She opened the first binder with some trepidation, not sure what to expect of a magical training course. It turned out to be along the lines of "Dick and Jane Learn to Channel Mystical Forces," complete with short, simple sentences and colorful illustrations on laminated pages.

"I wrote that for Amelia's daughter, years ago," Athena said. "I don't mean to insult your intelligence. You can sit at that table over there and I'll be back in a moment."

Sophie sat and read about how Hortense realized she had magical power when she knocked her brother Mortimer away from her toys without touching him. Her mother then taught her to use her power properly. Younger brother Mortimer mostly served as the person Hortense didn't magically kill for being an idiot. Sophie got the impression that Amelia's daughter had a younger brother who'd been in danger of being turned into a toad.

"Oh, Hortense, honey, there are so many other ways to deal with younger siblings," Sophie muttered as she read. Or were there? Had everything she'd done actually been magic and not just intimidation and wits?

She looked up to see Athena standing in front of her. "Amelia should be here soon. Do you have any questions about what you've read?"

"I think I figured out most of this for myself without realizing it involved magic."

"You have good instincts, and your association with the fairies may have taught you more than you realized. I'm surprised they didn't recognize what you were. When did you stop visiting the fairy realm?"

"Before I was eighteen."

"Ah, that explains it. Your power wasn't fully developed then. You may have had stirrings, but they wouldn't have thought to look for magic in you."

"*I* didn't think to look for magic in me, but it's probably always been there. For instance, I've always thought I just had a forceful personality. People usually do what I want them to do. I suppose I was making them do it."

Athena nodded. "Yes, Emily told us that about you."

"Before last night, I'd never consciously tried to get through any door I knew was locked, but I've also never been locked out of the house or my car—or have I?"

"And I would bet that things generally go your way. You get what you want."

Sophie sighed dejectedly. "I just thought I was clever and good and people liked me—or feared me."

With a wry smirk, Athena asked, "Is it any worse that you were doing magic all that time?"

"It makes me reevaluate everything I thought I knew about myself."

Athena patted her reassuringly on the shoulder. "All of us should do that from time to time, magic or not."

The bell on the door rang, and they looked up to see Amelia entering. "I hear you've agreed to join us," she said to Sophie.

"For the time being. I don't know yet if this will have to be a permanent arrangement."

"I suppose that will depend on what else Tallulah demands of you," Amelia said, taking a seat at the table.

"I briefed her," Athena said, joining Sophie and Amelia at

the table. "Now, why don't you tell us what happened last night to change your mind about your magical abilities?"

Sophie was about to deny that anything other than Tallulah's demand had happened, but she recalled letting it slip that she hadn't tried opening a locked door until last night. *Drat.* She must have really been rattled. "As I mentioned, I had a meeting with Tallulah. While we were talking, two fae men who'd been part of Tallulah's group tried to capture me." She went on to describe the fight in detail. In spite of her earlier reluctance, it felt good to get it off her chest, to verify that it hadn't been a nightmare. "It seemed like I was able to undo any spell they tried on me, and I could also affect them," she concluded.

Amelia nodded. "Our magic usually trumps fairy magic. Their magic is actually rather ephemeral. It's mostly about illusion."

Sophie rubbed the burn on her wrist, which was starting to itch. "It felt real enough."

"Oh, it can be real. It's just that they're more accustomed to glamour than to doing anything real, which means they're not as good at it. We could do glamour if we wished, but we focus on practical matters."

"Would that include opening locked doors?"

"Yes," Athena said. "Magic allows you to manipulate things as well as people."

"How do you resist the temptation to use magic all the time?" Sophie asked.

"Who says we do?" Amelia asked with graceful shrug. "We don't make a show of it, but we may simplify our lives somewhat."

"Isn't that cheating?"

"What do you call what you've been doing all along?"

"I didn't know I was using magic. I was just being me."

"Using magic *is* just being me. It's a shame to waste a gift."

"Yes, it is," Sophie said with a sigh, though she wasn't talking about magic. One of the many things she was trying not to think about was the fact that she'd given up her dance career for what turned out to be a misconception. Her heart would break if she let herself consider what she'd lost. A thought occurred to her, and she asked, "Does Emily have this power?"

"A little," Athena said. "If our priority hadn't been protecting her from the fairies, we might have tried teaching her, but she wasn't our ideal candidate, for a number of reasons. The magic is much stronger in you, just as her hair is redder."

"And she's so much taller."

Athena looked at her for a moment before saying, "Yes, I suppose she is. I hadn't thought about that, but then I've never seen you two next to each other." Sophie stared at her, waiting for a laugh or some other sign that she was joking, but she seemed to be deadly serious. The height difference was usually the first thing anyone noticed about the Drake sisters.

The tinkling of the bell on the door interrupted the conversation, and the sisters got up to greet the customer. The customer was a ditherer, unable to choose between a blue or a pink flowered teapot but not willing to listen to the shopkeepers' suggestions about which piece was more valuable. At this rate, she'd never leave, and Sophie had more important things to deal with. She thought it was as good an opportunity as any to test her magical persuasive ability. In the past, she'd always spoken with people when convincing them to do what she wanted, but this time, she sent out a silent suggestion that the customer pick the blue teapot and get out of there. A moment later, the woman held up the blue teapot and said, "I'll take this one."

When the customer was gone, Amelia turned to Sophie and said, "If you hadn't done that, I would have, though I would have played fair and suggested the less expensive item."

"I didn't see the price tags. I was going by the colors she wore. I thought she'd like that one better," Sophie said.

The sisters exchanged a look, and Athena said with a grin, "I told you she'd be good."

They returned to the table, and Amelia said, "Now that we've discussed Sophie, I have news. There's a market tonight at Belvedere

Castle. That's our best chance to gather intelligence and see what Maeve's up to. You'll join us, of course, Sophie."

"What do we have to trade?" Athena mused, knitting her brow in concentration. "If I'd had more warning, I could have made something."

"We won't bring anything," Amelia said. "We've got all the currency we should need."

"Do we?" Athena asked, then she followed her sister's gaze to Sophie. "Ah, yes."

"Are you going to trade me to the fairies?" Sophie asked.

"No, but you are a fairy-taught dancer. The fairies love nothing more than a good dance. Ballet should enthrall them, especially danced by one with fairy skills."

"I might as well get some use out of it," Sophie said, swallowing a lump in her throat. She rose and snapped her fingers to summon Beau. "I suppose I'll see you tonight at midnight at Belvedere Castle."

Athena walked her to the door. "I'm looking forward to seeing you dance. Emily said you're wonderful."

Sophie gave her a smile, then hurried out the door and up the stairs before any of the tears welling in her eyes could fall. She let them spill silently as she walked back, wiping them away when she reached Emily's block. She was letting herself into Emily's apartment when Michael appeared on the upper landing. "Sophie," he said, his voice grave. "I've just heard from Tanaka." Instead of finishing the thought, he came downstairs, moving slowly. He was dressed to go out, she noticed.

"What is it?" she asked.

"Let's go inside."

"No, tell me now."

She knew it was bad when he took her hand in his good one. Then he said, "They may have found Emily."

Thirty

As a detective, Michael had seen a number of people go through the experience of identifying a loved one's body. He'd even gone through it a few times himself, when they found a body that someone thought might have been Jen's. Sophie was as eerily composed in this situation as he'd expected her to be.

She did go terribly pale when she saw the sheet-covered body, so pale that he saw for the first time that she had a slight dusting of freckles across the bridge of her nose. He put his arm around her shoulders and was surprised when she didn't step away or shrug it off. She nodded to the attendant, who pulled back the sheet covering the corpse's face.

As soon as he saw the face, Michael's breath caught in his throat. He wished he'd learned to swear so he'd have the vocabulary for dealing with a situation like this. *No, no, no, no, no,* he repeated inside his head instead of swearing. The tangle of red curls lying on that slab, the waxy pale face that not too long ago had been grinning at him while forcing him to eat soup, it was all wrong, so horribly wrong. This wasn't how it was supposed to go.

Then the initial shock ebbed enough for him to remember that this wasn't about him, that he was standing with his arm around Emily's sister. He squeezed Sophie's shoulder, pulling her tight to his side. "I'm sorry, Sophie," he whispered hoarsely. "We'll get whoever did this."

Tanaka caught Michael's eye, and Michael nodded grimly. Sophie still hadn't said anything. "Sophie?" Tanaka said gently, "We need you to make an ID for us. Is this your sister?"

Sophie looked up at Michael with dry eyes and an expression that said quite clearly that she thought he was crazy. She gave the body a sidelong glance, looked back at him, and then she gave a tiny gasp followed by a long exhalation, as though she'd just realized something. She turned back to face the body, shook her head and said, "That's not Emily."

Michael closed his eyes and stifled a groan. Victims' loved ones sometimes clung desperately to denial. He could have fingerprint, dental record, and even DNA matches, and they'd swear they'd never before seen that body in the morgue. Sophie hadn't struck him as the type to go into denial, but everyone had a breaking point. "Sophie, I know this is tough," he began, but then he did a double take at the corpse. It *wasn't* Emily. There were superficial similarities, but when he really looked at the body, it wasn't much at all like her. "No, it's not Emily," he agreed.

It was Tanaka's turn to do a double take. "Are you sure? She looks just like the photo you gave me." He frowned as he looked at the body. "Then again, yeah, I can see the differences now that you mention it. I'm sorry to drag you in here and put you through this, Sophie."

"I understand," she said softly. "You needed a definite answer. Thank you for trying."

"She might be one of the other missing girls," Michael suggested.

"She does fit physically," Tanaka said. "We'll contact the families of the other missing women and see if any of them can identify her. Thank you for coming down here, Sophie. I'll talk to you later, Rev." He gave Michael a look and a head gesture that said very clearly, "Take care of her," and Michael nodded.

"Are you okay?" Michael asked as they waited for a cab. "I know it's rough going into that place, and looking at dead bodies is never fun, even if it's not someone you know."

"I'm just tired," she said with a weak smile. "This hasn't been the best week ever." A cab arrived a moment later, cutting off his chance to follow up on that.

She went quiet again once they were in the cab. As they rode uptown in silence, he couldn't help but notice the red mark on her wrist. It didn't look as bad as it had the night before, but he had to wonder what had happened. It wasn't a rope burn from the dog's leash, that much he was sure of. It was too neat a wound, not ragged at all. The mark on her face wasn't quite as visible, but it looked like she'd covered a bruise with makeup.

"Detective Tanaka called you 'Rev.' What does that mean?" she asked abruptly.

"Cops love nicknames. My dad's a minister, and I guess he rubbed off on me, even if I didn't go into the family business. I'm more of a straight arrow than your typical cop, so they started calling me 'The Reverend.' Over time, that became 'Rev.' To make matters worse, Saint Michael the archangel is the patron saint of cops, and they manage to fit that in, too."

"That would explain the very interesting collection of refrigerator magnets you have."

"You should see my desk. I have to rotate them to the fridge at home to leave room for the new ones. If anyone finds anything with an angel on it, it'll end up on my desk."

The tiny ghost of a smile that touched her lips made him feel that spilling that story was worthwhile, even if it was a little embarrassing. Then again, he could barely stay on his feet for five minutes without leaning on her, so it wasn't like she'd ever seen him as particularly macho.

When they got back to his building, she paused at Emily's door and said, "Thank you for going with me."

"No one should have to go through that alone."

"I appreciate it. Do you have any sisters, Detective?"

"Michael," he corrected. "And no, no sisters. But I have two brothers."

"Older or younger?"

"Both older."

She nodded and gave him a wry smile. "You're the third brother. If you were in a fairy tale, you'd be the lucky one, the one who marries the princess and inherits the kingdom. Though, really, it's not so much luck as it is good karma. The youngest is the nice one who helps the people and creatures the older ones ignore, and they then help him succeed in his quest."

"So the moral of the story is that I should be nice to people?"

"It doesn't seem to me that you have to work very hard to do that." It was hard to tell in the stairwell's dim light, but he thought she might have turned a little pinker. She ducked her head and turned toward the door, saying, "I'd better see to Beau. He'll be hungry."

She opened the door, and Michael called to her, "Sophie!" She looked back, and he hurried to say, "If you need help, please tell me. Don't get yourself in trouble."

"I'm not in trouble," she insisted. "I can take care of myself, believe me." She chuckled softly, as if at some secret joke. "Oh yes, I can take care of myself. Good evening, Michael."

He wasn't sure why, but he felt like he really ought to get upstairs. And then he should probably take one of his pain pills and get some rest. Yes, that was what he should do. His chest hurt again, and he was very tired. He trudged up the stairs, got to his apartment, and was just about to open the pill bottle when he stopped and shook his head. He didn't hurt all that badly, actually. He was feeling much better. The compulsion went away entirely and he put the bottle down. Instead, he fumbled with the coffeemaker to make a pot of coffee. If Sophie was up to her usual nighttime activities, he wasn't going to lose her this time.

Thirty-One

Emily woke gradually with the feeling that there was something important she needed to tell her sister. She knew she was supposed to call Sophie and tell her what the reviews said, but that wasn't it. What was it?

Her eyes flew open and she sat up with a gasp as it all came rushing back to her. She wasn't at home. She was in an empty, dimly lit room. It looked like a basement utility room, only without the utilities, just a bare concrete floor and cinder-block walls, all painted a stained and faded industrial gray. Given that most of the room's appearance was likely a glamour, Emily was impressed that they'd bothered to make the place look dank and depressing.

It wasn't so empty, after all, she realized once her eyes adjusted to the light and she saw Eamon slumped against the wall on the far side of the room. "Eamon!" she cried as she rushed to his side. He looked like hell, his skin an ashy color and the silver in his hair dimmed to a dull gray. She soon saw why: They'd shackled him with iron handcuffs. "Oh no! How could they do this to you?" she asked, placing her hand on his cheek. She then had to yank her hand away because his skin burned so hot that it felt like it would scorch her.

His eyelids fluttered open. "Emily Drake?" he croaked. "You're awake. I was worried. You slept a very long time."

"A girl needs her beauty sleep," she said with a shrug that she tried to make look casual to hide the fact that she wanted to hug him. Where had that feeling come from? A kiss or two was one thing, but this was real caring. She must have developed a bad case of Stockholm Syndrome. But no, though he may have kidnapped her, he'd proven to be a real friend once he'd realized his mistake. "We need to get you out of these cuffs."

She'd seen people unlock things with hairpins dozens of times in movies, and the lock on these cuffs looked simple enough that it might even work–if they weren't magically locked. What she needed was a hairpin. They put dozens in her hair every night to hold it in the Grecian-style bun of the Regency era, and though she took her hair down after the show, she was always finding stray hairpins later because they disappeared into her thick curls. With any luck, this would be one of those times. She raked her fingers through her hair, frantically searching, until she came across a pin. "The unruly mop saves the day. Now, let's see if I can make this work."

She stuck the pin into the keyhole and wiggled it around. She wasn't sure what she was supposed to do beyond that. Eventually, she felt a click, and the cuffs popped open. She yanked them off him and hurled them to the opposite corner of the room. The skin on his wrists where the cuffs had been was blistered. "Oh, you poor thing," she said, cradling his hands in hers.

He tried to sit up, shuddered violently, and sank back to the floor. She caught him and pulled his head into her lap, where she used the hem of her T-shirt to wipe the sweat off his forehead. "Thank you," he whispered.

"Don't mention it," she said, making her voice sound cheerier than she felt. Then she realized what he'd just said. "Wait, you thanked me."

"You saved my life. I am truly in your debt." His voice sounded stronger, but she didn't think he'd be back on his feet for a while. Did fairies have medicine or doctors?

"I guess we're even now," she said, forcing a smile as she smoothed his hair back from his face. "You kidnapped me, and then I saved your life. No, wait. I think you still owe me. But considering we're both prisoners, we can worry about settling who owes whom later."

"Yes, I would prefer to defer that discussion."

Her stomach growled, and as close to her as he was, he heard it. "You are hungry," he said.

She bit her lip and cringed before saying, "Yeah, a bit. But I'll live. Depending on how long we're stuck in here. Considering there's no fairy food, either, we're in the same boat."

Both of them were quiet for a moment. Emily wondered if he was contemplating starving to death while locked in a small room with a human. He eventually said, "Do you think you could unlock that door the way you unlocked the cuffs?"

She wanted to smack herself on the head. "Oh, duh! I should have thought of that." She helped him sit up–he already seemed stronger–and then she found the hairpin and went to the door. One quick look at the handle dashed her hopes. "It locks from the outside," she reported. "The hairpin doesn't do any good. I'm afraid we're stuck until Maeve wants to gloat at us."

He leaned his back against the wall. "Then perhaps we should prepare to greet her or her minions." He grinned in a way that reminded her of Sophie when she'd spotted someone's weakness and was about to pounce. "And she seems to have locked a large piece of iron in here with someone who can handle it."

She followed his gaze to the iron handcuffs lying in the corner where she'd thrown them. "I like the way you think. One booby trap, coming up."

Thirty-Two

Near dusk, Michael lurked by the window, waiting to see if Sophie made another one of her nightly trips. She'd walked Beau earlier, returning after about fifteen minutes. Beau had never been game for more than one walk in the evening, so if she went out again, it would probably be for her own agenda. He waited until well past nightfall, but she didn't go out.

When he went to bed–fully dressed, just in case–he left the window open. His bedroom window was directly above the front door, so he'd hear if that door opened or closed. He slept lightly, waking at every sound. Once, just after ten, he heard the door, but it was someone coming home. The next time he heard the door, it was nearly eleven-thirty, and he got to the window in time to see Sophie and Beau going down the front steps. She was fully dressed, with a tote bag on her shoulder, so he doubted it was a case of Beau needing a late-night potty break.

Michael ran to his front door, grabbed his keys, and went down the stairs as quickly as he could without falling. He had to pause and catch his breath at the bottom of the steps. Following

Sophie would be a challenge late at night when there were no crowds to hide in, but unless she vanished into thin air again, she wouldn't have anywhere to hide, either.

She went straight to the park. What was she doing in the park at this time of night? While it wasn't the dangerous crime zone it used to be, it wasn't a good idea for a woman to walk alone this late, even with a dog. He didn't feel so safe, himself, not as weak as he was and without the reassuring weight of his service weapon on his hip.

Sophie seemed to be heading to Belvedere Castle, or perhaps going through the castle in an attempt to lose him on his way to somewhere else. She walked quickly enough that he had trouble keeping up with her in his weakened state and often lost sight of her as she moved between the pools of light cast by lampposts along the path.

A mewling sound near his feet startled him, and he barely held back an exclamation of surprise that would have given him away. He saw a flash of white on the ground and bent to see a small white cat tangled in what looked like a makeshift wire trap. He was in a hurry, but he couldn't bear to leave a defenseless creature like that. Smiling slightly to himself as he remembered what Sophie had told him about third brothers in fairy tales, he knelt and whispered, "Easy, it's okay, let's see what I can do, and then I guess we'll see what you can do for me." The wire was wound too tightly for him to untangle it with one hand, so he got out his pocket knife and cut the wire. He was surprised by how calm the cat was. A trapped animal would normally hiss and claw, but this one seemed to understand that he was trying to help. When he got it free, it purred and rubbed against his ankles, then ran down the path Sophie had taken. It paused to look back at him, as if to say, "Aren't you coming?"

He made his way up the stairs to the terrace in front of the castle and when he rounded the landing, he pulled back into the shadows. Sophie sat on the terrace, putting on ballet shoes while two women stood nearby. He got the impression that they were elderly because their hair appeared white, but that could have merely been a trick of the light because they didn't move like old people. The three women were engaged in what looked like a spirited discussion. He would have loved to hear what they were talking about, but there was no way he could cross the open expanse of the terrace without revealing himself.

What was Sophie doing putting on ballet shoes in the middle of the night in Central Park? She didn't seem to see the women as threats—she showed neither fear nor bravado with them—but who were they, and what did they have to do with her? A nearby snort startled him out of his surveillance. He glanced down to see that Beau had noticed him and had come to greet him. "Go away, you crazy dog," he hissed as Beau flopped wearily down at the top of the stairs. Michael hoped Sophie didn't go looking for the dog, but she seemed to be preoccupied.

She was doing what looked like warm-up exercises, bending and straightening her knees, swinging her legs, and popping up to her tiptoes and then back down again. Then she did a few dance steps, balanced on one toe with her other leg held straight out behind her, and spun so that her full skirt flew out around her hips. She stopped the spin and nodded to the women as if to say, "Okay, I'm ready."

And then, in a heartbeat, everything changed. It was like someone had set off a flare. The castle, its balconies, and the terrace in front of it blazed with light. The terrace was no longer empty. It was filled with booths, like a festival or marketplace, and the most beautiful people Michael had ever seen thronged the aisles. Most of the people were tall and willowy, with hair that glowed in the bright light. Wild music and exotic scents filled the air.

In all his years on the force, he'd never heard of any midnight festivals in the park. They couldn't possibly have a permit. An event like this required security, and that would mean a few uniforms on the scene. There wasn't a uniform in sight.

Not that he planned to shut it down. He was on medical leave, and it didn't look like they were doing any harm. Besides, it was... Well, the only word he could think of was magical. It was like something out of a storybook. Or a dream.

He'd momentarily forgotten Sophie in the surprise of seeing

a festival appear out of thin air right in front of him, and he craned
his neck, looking for her. With all this commotion, he might be able
to get close enough to find out what she was up to. She was hard to
find in this crowd, though. She wasn't as tall as most of these people,
but she was willowy and had bright hair, so she blended in. He finally
spotted her standing with the two women, talking to another person.
He climbed the rest of the stairs to the terrace and headed toward
her, Beau at his heels.

As soon as he entered the brightly lit marketplace, a woman
in a white dress brushed his arm with her hand, then took his hand
and tried to pull him into a dance. He shook his head apologetically,
indicating his sling. He wasn't up to anything that energetic. She
smiled, released his hand, gave him a little curtsy, and danced off
with feline grace.

A man came out from behind one of the booths and offered
him a tankard of a drink that smelled like Christmas. The heady
mix of spices was intoxicating even at arm's-length, but before he
could take the tankard, Beau rushed at the vendor, barking, snarling,
and growling furiously. "Beauregard! No! Don't be rude," Michael
scolded, but Beau didn't back down. He stood squarely between
Michael and the man, growling. "Sorry about that," Michael said to
the vendor. "I've never seen him do that before. He's usually too lazy
to be aggressive."

The man bowed as he backed away. "No apologies are
necessary, my good sir. Please forgive the intrusion." The man acted
like he'd been caught doing something wrong.

"What was that about?" Michael asked Beau. The dog snorted
before giving one last growl. Michael found a spot behind a rack
displaying silk scarves where he could lurk and listen to Sophie and the
women without being seen, and settled in for a spot of eavesdropping.

"I may have heard something," said the man talking to Sophie
and the women. He'd have looked like he'd crawled out of a bush
where he'd been hiding since 1968 if he hadn't appeared no more
than twenty years old. Had flower children come back into vogue?

"Would you care to share?" Sophie asked sweetly, but Michael heard the steel underneath her tone. If the flower child knew what was good for him, he'd spill, and fast.

Apparently this guy was made of sterner stuff. "That kind of information will cost you."

"I can pay," Sophie said. She gestured to the musicians nearby, and they changed their tune to a lilting dance. Then Sophie went into action. She spun, leapt, and did an odd little step on her toes that made her look like she was fluttering across the floor, and it was absolutely mesmerizing. She was more ethereal than any human being had a right to be, all while exuding a sense of power and strength. Surely a normal human body couldn't do these things. The dance ended far too soon, and Michael realized he'd forgotten to breathe while watching. The twinge in his wound reminded him forcefully.

As short as the dance was, it was apparently enough for the flower child, for he beckoned Sophie and the women to come closer. Michael edged out of his hiding place as far as he dared so he could hear. "Rumor has it Maeve announced that she's found the throne and will take it soon," he said, glancing around as if to make sure no one saw him sharing this information.

"Well, that's silly of her," Sophie said. "That's only warning her enemies in time to stop her. I'm assuming she has enemies."

"Everyone has enemies," he said before slipping away into the crowd.

When he was gone, Sophie said, "I knew Maeve was ambitious, but making a bid to rule the Realm is big, even for her. You said nobody's done that for centuries, so why her, why now, and what does this have to do with Emily or me?"

"We need more information," the taller of the two older women said. She headed into the marketplace, returning with a woman who looked like she'd stepped out of a badly colorized old movie. The taller woman nodded at Sophie, who gestured to the musicians and began dancing again, much to Michael's delight.

It didn't take long for her to get caught up in the music, and it was like seeing a flower bud open as she truly came to life for the first time since he'd met her. He got the feeling he was getting a rare look past all her barriers into her soul. He'd considered her very pretty, but too restrained to be alluring. Now, though, she was beautiful. Behind all that control lurked a deep well of pent-up passion. She made a chain of quick-fire turns on the point of her toe, leapt so that she seemed to hang in the air, and spun on her toe with her other leg whipping around.

At the end of the dance, the colorized woman nodded, as if accepting the payment. "She made a public announcement," she said when Sophie rejoined the group. "But she has made no moves since then, other than sending out her people to try to capture someone. Even before her announcement, she had people in our court, seeking a fugitive."

"Do you know whom they sought?" the smaller of the two women with Sophie asked.

"No. I have heard rumors of mighty battles, though."

"Winter is upon the Realm, isn't it?" Sophie asked, and apparently the question was as much a surprise to her cohorts as it was to the woman they were questioning because they turned to stare at Sophie.

"Whatever made you ask that?" the taller woman asked.

"Winter?" the colorized woman asked.

"The Realm is the Summer Country, the land of endless summer," the smaller woman said, as though pointing out something obvious. "It's *never* winter."

The colorized woman glanced around nervously, then said so softly that Michael had to move further out of his hiding place to hear her, "Some say that things are changing, even that the Realm is dying. That is why some support Maeve. The Realm may die without a queen, and although few of us would choose Maeve, anyone who can find the throne would save us all."

"Find it?" Sophie asked.

"I've said enough," the woman said.

"Now really, I did ten fouetté turns," Sophie argued, grabbing the woman's arm. "That should count for something."

The woman seemed to go through an internal struggle, then

blurted, "The throne has been lost—the palace has been lost. One would have to find the throne to win it, and no one knows how to win it."

"Presumably Maeve has figured it out," Sophie said, but the woman jerked out of her grasp and ran. "And it must have something to do with my sister or me, unless the timing is pure coincidence," she concluded, seemingly speaking as much to herself as to the women with her.

Michael slunk back into concealment, more confused than ever. It sounded like Sophie knew who had Emily, but why hadn't she shared that information with the police? Were they threatening her? Was that where her injuries came from?

He noticed a new group entering the market. This group looked a little more normal than the other people at the festival—though that was in relative terms. They were at least in real clothes instead of dressing in spiderwebs and flowers. It looked like the Rat Pack had invaded. The men wore slim-cut suits with skinny ties while the women wore dresses that were either tight through the body and with full skirts or tight all over so that they walked in mincing steps on high heels.

The woman at the center of the group was a living department store mannequin, with an impossibly perfect face and figure and hair so golden that it couldn't have been natural. The crowd parted for her, but it looked like the distance had as much to do with distaste as it did with fear or respect. There was a lot of muttering around the marketplace, and those who hadn't noticed the group's arrival were elbowed or tapped on the shoulder until made aware.

"Speak of the devil," Sophie muttered, heading toward the newcomer so quickly that the women with her were left behind. Michael didn't quite manage to turn away as she passed, but she was so intent on the newcomer that she didn't see him. When she was within earshot of the woman, she called out, "Maeve, it's been *ages*," in a drawl heavy with sarcasm. "Let's see, when did we last see each other? Why, I do believe it was the last time you tried to kidnap my sister. We've *got* to stop meeting like this." The crowd parted to clear a path between her and Maeve, and she moved forward slowly, walking as though she was still dancing, her leg extended and her toe pointed with each step. When she was face-to-face with Maeve she glared up at the much taller woman and said in an iron-hard voice, "Let her go."

Maeve laughed again. "Didn't you already find her in the morgue?"

Moving so quickly that Michael didn't quite see how she did it, Sophie had the other woman on the ground and was holding her there with one foot on her throat. The pink satin ballet shoes might have looked delicate, but the toes were strong enough to support a woman's weight. "Did you really think I'd fall for your little trick?" she asked, her voice low, but still carrying. "It was bad enough that you took my sister, but trying to trick me into thinking she was dead? That's low, even for you. The sad thing is, it didn't fool me for a second."

A crowd had formed around the combatants, and while Maeve had her entourage, most of the rest seemed to be on Sophie's side—or at least were opposed to Maeve. Michael left his hiding place, picking up Beau's leash to drag him forward, and blended in with the spectators.

The two women who'd been with Sophie caught up, and the taller one caught Sophie around the waist, lifting her away from her victim. "Harm her, and you may not get your sister back," she said. Sophie must have seen reason because she didn't struggle. The smaller woman handed Sophie her tote bag, as though with the hope that the bag would keep her hands too busy for another attack.

Maeve's entourage rushed over and helped their leader to her feet. "I can see why you're reluctant to hand over your prize, considering you need her to take the throne," Sophie said.

Maeve froze, then with a weak laugh she said, "Why would I need a mere human girl?"

"If you could have done it on your own, you'd have gone for it already." Sophie shook her head and moved closer to Maeve. "I'm not yet sure why, but you can't do this without Emily." She frowned for a moment, and then a light dawned in her eyes. "Or is it Emily? You've had her for a couple of days, and you haven't yet done anything. Meanwhile, your minions have tried to grab me every time I've gone near. She was just bait for your trap. I'm the one you need." She shook her head in mock pity. "Maeve, honey, what makes you think you could hold the Realm, even if you won the throne?"

The crowd behind Sophie liked that. They laughed and cheered, and Michael moved further forward so he could see and hear better. He had a feeling Sophie was too busy at the moment to notice him there.

Maeve pulled herself together with visible effort and spat, "What do you know, little human girl? Dancing with us doesn't make you one of us. Even with our teaching, what have you achieved? Those we taught have graced the greatest stages in the world. And then there's you. Where is it you dance now?"

That didn't seem to bother Sophie—at least, not visibly. "I've had other priorities," she said with a shrug.

"Ah, yes, protecting your sister. You've done such a good job of that. Where is she now? As I recall, she's been kidnapped."

That didn't rile Sophie, either. "Well, yes, that's why I'm here." She moved another step closer to Maeve and asked sweetly, "How long did it take you to get your hands on my sister? And how many wrong women did you grab along the way? But at least you had a real reason. I thought you were after payment or revenge."

This exchange raised a lot of questions for Michael. For one, what throne? Was this some secret society they all belonged to? He was missing a lot of context. He searched for a friendly-looking face to ask what was going on. As a cop, he was good at spotting those who were eager to show off what they knew, and while these people were like nothing he'd ever seen before, he hoped he still had the instincts to find good sources.

Then he noticed a small group nearby. A couple of women in the group looked different from the other people, more substantial and less like imaginary beings.

"Her majesty is not going to be happy," one of the women said.

"She doesn't need this girl," the other one said.

At the sound of her voice, he froze. He knew that voice. He still had it on an old voice mail message he couldn't bear to delete.

The woman was tall and red-haired, and she was...she was... "Jen?" he blurted, stepping toward her like he was moving in a dream. He couldn't seem to catch his breath, and his body didn't want to obey him.

She didn't even turn her head. It was like she hadn't heard him or didn't recognize her own name. Instead, she wrapped her arm around the man standing next to her and leaned her head against him. Michael's blood felt like it started flowing properly again, hitting him in a rush. He went up to her, faced her directly, and said again, "Jen!"

She took a step backward, hiding behind her escort, then turned to exchange a glance with the other woman. This close, he knew it was definitely Jennifer. She looked exactly the way she had when she disappeared, though her hair was in a different style. He grabbed her arm. "Jen, it's me, Michael. Your husband?" He twisted his wrist so that she could see his wedding band. "Where have you been all these years?"

She looked at him like he was a complete stranger. "I'm sorry, I don't believe we've met," she said, pulling her arm out of his grasp. "My name is Emma."

"No, it's Jennifer," he insisted desperately. "Your name is Jennifer Murray."

"I don't like him," the woman with her said in a stage whisper, and one of the guys with them stepped forward to block Michael from following as the women walked away.

Michael struggled against them, but they were stronger than they looked and he wasn't at full strength. "Jen, wait!" he shouted, but one of the men shoved him so hard he lost his footing. He landed awkwardly on his bad side, and the muscles in his chest weren't strong enough to support the weight that landed on that arm. He was afraid he felt something tear, and he was too winded to get up.

One of the men loomed over him like he was ready to finish him off, but then something flung the attacker backward. "Get away from him," a firm voice said, and Sophie moved to stand between Michael and his assailant.

Thirty-Three

"Is she ever going to come back?" Emily griped as she paced the cell. Attacking Maeve's people with their own iron shackles when they came to retrieve or torment the prisoners had sounded like fun when she and Eamon came up with the plan, but after hours of waiting, the fun had faded into boredom. "What if she's forgotten us?"

"She won't forget," Eamon said. His voice was stronger, though still a little hoarse with pain. "Not you, at least."

"Yeah, I'm her worm to bait the hook. But what happens to the worm when the fish don't bite? It gets dumped in the lake." She could tell he had no idea what she was talking about, but she didn't think it was worth explaining the concept of fishing to him. Or did fairies fish?

She stopped pacing and leaned her back against the wall. "Since Sophie's not dancing to her tune, she's probably just leaving me to rot." She slid down the wall to sit beside him.

He took her hand. "Isn't that what you wanted?"

"To rot?"

"For your sister to stay away so Maeve can't use her."

"If Maeve has Sophie, she doesn't need me. She could just leave me here."

"Do you really think your sister would be here without freeing you somehow?"

"Not if she could help it," Emily admitted. Forcing a smile, she added, "And we'd have heard the explosions. Even if she went down, she'd have gone down fighting."

He leaned his head back against the wall. "In the meantime, we may as well relax and enjoy the peace and quiet. Maeve is giving me the opportunity to rebuild my strength."

"Speaking of which, how are you doing?" She lifted the hand that was still clasped around hers so she could examine the wounds on his wrist. The blisters were healing, but the wrist was still a mess. The other one looked similar. She placed her hand on his forehead. "The fever seems to have gone down."

"I am much better," he said in a hoarse whisper. His silvery eyes locked onto hers, and her breath caught in her throat. She slid her hand down to rest against his cheek, and then she moved to kiss him. This time, she hadn't fallen under a spell and she wasn't trying to find a way to thank him. She simply wanted to kiss him because she liked him and she'd gone through far more with him than with any other man she'd known.

"Emily Drake," he breathed against her lips as he returned her kiss. He cupped her cheek in his hand, and his cool touch made her shiver all over. "You're so warm," he murmured.

She pulled back, shaking her head. "What are we doing? This is crazy. Romeo and Juliet just had families who hated each other. We can't even live in each other's worlds. Once I get home, I may never see you again—that is, assuming I get home."

"But we're here together now," he said, drawing her back to him. "We may as well make the most of whatever time we have."

ﾂHirty-Four

Sophie reminded herself to keep her cool as she faced Maeve, even though all her instincts cried out for a good, old-fashioned catfight. "If you don't need me and you don't need my sister to take the throne, then let her go."

She held her breath, waiting for the response. If she remembered Maeve at all, her ego wouldn't let her appear to need any help—unless she truly needed the help.

Maeve took a long time to respond, which Sophie took as a sign that she had to think about it. At last, Maeve pulled herself to her full height, and maybe a little higher, then looked down her nose at Sophie and snarled, "How do you know that your sister didn't join me willingly?"

Sophie couldn't fight back a smile. Maeve had just told her everything she needed to know. "If she's happy with you, then perhaps you'll allow me to visit her sometime."

A ruckus from the other side of the market distracted them before Maeve could respond. A group of Maeve's people moved threateningly toward a tall, dark-haired man, threw him on the ground, and encircled him. "Michael?" Sophie gasped. *How did he get here?* she wondered as she rushed toward him. He shouldn't even have been able to see this market.

With a thought, she flung his attacker backward. Positioning herself between Michael and Maeve's people, she shouted, "Get away from him!" She realized a moment later that she'd just used her magical abilities in front of Michael, but if he was at the market and fighting with Maeve's people, he was in on the secret and had to know that there was something odd about her. As if he didn't already suspect that.

One good look at the group of Maeve's people clustered nearby told her exactly what the fight was about. She recognized one of the women–a human woman–from the wedding photo in Michael's apartment. He'd found his long-lost wife, and from the looks of things, she either didn't remember her husband or wasn't inclined to go with him. *Oh dear,* Sophie thought, *this could get ugly.*

Maeve sauntered over and joined her people, smirking at Sophie. "So, your sister isn't the only one you care about."

"I don't like seeing anyone get hurt," Sophie shot back. "Honestly, all your goons, ganging up on an injured man?"

Behind her, she heard Michael struggling to catch his breath. She wanted to go to him, but she was afraid to turn her back on Maeve and her people. Then again, she probably needed to restrain Michael before he tried to go after his wife. She could hardly blame him; if Emily had been at this market, she knew she wouldn't leave without her, even if she had to carry her out over her shoulder. But if his wife was part of Maeve's court, and if she didn't want to go, the chances of him getting away alive with her were extremely slim, even with Sophie's help.

A low bark from below her knees told her she wasn't entirely alone. She'd nearly forgotten about Beau, who must have joined Michael while she was busy. Out of the corner of her eye she saw Amelia and Athena come over to flank Michael. The odds looked a little better. The big question was what the free fairies would do.

As if Sophie had any doubt about what–and whom–Maeve

wanted, Maeve turned to her men and said, "That's the one. Take her, or else! I am tired of failure!"

Maeve's goons moved toward Sophie, one of them sending a silver chain flying at her. *Not this again,* she thought as she raised a hand and sent it back at him to wind around his neck. He stumbled backward, bumping into his colleagues. They tried to move forward but the air between them and Sophie shimmered and they bumped into something. A glance to the side showed Sophie that Amelia and Athena had sprung into action, creating the shield.

While they held off the fairies, Sophie crouched beside Michael and got her arms around him to pull him to his feet. "Are you okay?" she asked.

"Jen," he gasped, struggling to get away from her. "They have Jen. She's with them."

"I know, honey," she murmured. "But we have to go, *now.*"

"I'm not leaving without her."

"I understand, trust me, but that could be a bit of a challenge."

By this time, the rest of the free fairies had come to see what all the commotion was about. Some of them attacked Maeve's people, others stood by as spectators, and a few joined in the attack on Sophie. Meanwhile, Maeve and her people were trying to dissolve the enchantresses' magical shield. "Get him away from here!" Amelia shouted over her shoulder.

"Easier said than done," Sophie muttered. She grabbed Michael by the chin so she could look him directly in the eyes and said as forcefully as she could, "We've got to get out of here. Can you walk?"

"I'm not going anywhere without Jen."

The shield wavered. Beau snarled, barked, and growled, and Sophie was getting desperate. "She won't go with you right now. She can't," she said, pleading. "But we need to get out of here. I can find her later."

"No!" His eyes were bright with tears. "I've been looking for her for seven years, and I'm not leaving her now that I've found her."

She hated to do this to him, but it was for his own good, as well as hers. "I'm sorry," she whispered as she reached into his mind and made him feel suddenly very tired, so tired that he needed to go home immediately. His eyes glazed, his eyelids drooped, and he sagged against her. Then he struggled away from her again, and she groaned. He was a husband who'd just found his long-lost wife and didn't want to lose her again, so his will was strong.

She pushed again to put him into a trance. "Okay, I've got him," she said to Athena and Amelia. "Now we just need to get away." She hoped they were up to some good defensive spells because it was taking everything she had to keep Michael from going after his wife.

That was when the shield fell and the goons rushed at them. "Oh, dear," Sophie murmured, wishing for once she'd learned something stronger to say in situations like this.

Amelia and Athena were now fighting off attackers individually. A few of the free fairies put themselves between Maeve and Sophie, but some of the goons got past. Sophie didn't think she had it in her to do any magic while she was controlling Michael, and she didn't dare let him go because he'd head straight for his wife, and then she wouldn't be able to save him. With the arm that wasn't supporting him, she reached into her bag and grabbed her iron skillet by the handle. It was heavy enough to knock aside attackers, and because it was iron, any fairy who got hit stayed down. Soon, they learned to give her a wide berth.

Athena and Amelia and a few of the free fairies had created a clear path for her, so she called, "Beau, come!" and headed for the stairs. Sophie couldn't run with Michael's weight on her. She glanced over her shoulder to check on signs of pursuit and saw several of Maeve's people get past the enchantresses to launch themselves over the castle terrace wall and land with catlike grace on the ground below.

Sophie tightened her grip on the skillet. She couldn't outrun the fairies, she couldn't use magic without losing her tenuous grip on Michael, and her only weapon was a cooking implement. This situation was almost as bad as a preschool ballet class with mommy separation anxiety.

Then a sprightly woman in white with flowing white hair to

match darted out from the trees, calling, "Here!" as she pointed to a gap in a nearby wall. Sophie wasn't sure she and Michael together could fit through that small opening, but somehow they did, and then Sophie realized where they were: the Borderlands. She didn't think they were any safer there, but at least their pursuers weren't hot on her heels. Eerie sounds nearby made her heart beat faster. She'd never entered the Realm this way, but she'd heard about the things that lurked on the edges.

To make matters worse, a group of fairies appeared ahead of them, and Sophie muttered a heartfelt, *"Drat!"* before recognizing Tallulah. She didn't think Tallulah would join in the kidnapping, but why was she there? "This is *not* a good time. I'm kind of busy here," she told the fairy. On the bright side, the eerie noises had ceased at Tallulah's arrival.

Tallulah walked straight up to her and touched her lightly on the forehead. "I have one more task for you. You must stop Maeve."

"That was my plan."

"Your plan was to rescue your sister, but even if you don't achieve that, you must keep Maeve off the throne."

"I don't suppose you have any suggestions on how to do that?"

"You already have everything you need." Her voice intensified. "Keep Maeve off the throne. If you fail, I will ask another payment, and you will not like it." She gave Michael a long, appraising glance, then turned back to Sophie with a sly smile before gesturing for Sophie to follow her.

Tallulah led them to a gateway, and they came out on the edge of the park, near the street. Sophie wondered how safe they really were. Would Maeve's people dare leave the bubble of the market to go after them in the real world? She only let herself relax when they'd crossed Central Park West and Beau stopped growling.

Her next challenge was getting Michael home. In addition to his emotional anguish, he seemed to be in physical pain, and his breathing didn't sound good. She had his good arm draped across her shoulders and her arm around his waist, but the weight dragged on her. To make matters worse, she hadn't changed out of her pointe shoes, and they weren't designed for long walks. She'd have a mess of blisters after this adventure.

Fortunately, his apartment wasn't that far away and there weren't that many people out to notice her half-carrying a man. Not that New Yorkers would care. They'd just think he'd had one too many and she was getting him home. Beau led the way down the sidewalk, dragging his leash. She wondered if that would count as adhering to the leash law. It wouldn't do to attract police attention while she was hauling around an incoherent police detective.

At Michael's building, she paused to catch her breath before taking him up the front steps. She unlocked the door magically, then it took the last of her strength to get him up the stairs to his apartment, where the door flew open at a thought. Beau headed inside first, and she willed the door shut behind her. She got Michael to his bedroom and dropped him on the bed, found the bottle of painkillers on the nightstand, and made him take one before arranging him into a more comfortable position.

Only then did she release her control over him. He tried to sit up, calling out, "Jen!" but she pushed him back down onto the pillow.

"Hush," she cooed. "Easy, easy. Hush." She sent a soothing impulse to him, and she felt the tension in him ease. Poor thing, she thought, sitting beside him and stroking his hair gently. Imagine, finding his wife again after all that time, and in that way. But how had he seen her? He shouldn't have been able to see the market at all, nor anyone in it. When he settled down, she bent to remove her shoes, then flexed her feet and sighed with relief.

"She didn't even recognize me," he whispered, drifting back into consciousness.

"That happens," she said. "I'm sorry."

"Sophie, what's going on? What was that place?"

"We'll talk about it in the morning. You won't remember anything I say right now."

"It's real, right? It wasn't all a dream?"

"It was real," she confirmed.

He started coughing, and she propped him up until the

coughing spell stopped, then settled back against the headboard with his head pillowed on her shoulder and her arms around him.

He tried to get up again. "I have to go get her."

She pulled him back. "She won't be there." To distract him, she asked, "How did you two meet?"

He relaxed against her. "I was working foot patrol. She had an audition, and she couldn't find the place, so she asked me for directions. She got the part, so she found me later and said I was her lucky charm. Whenever she had an audition, she looked for me, and she got the part if she talked to me first. Then she invited me for coffee. She gave me a keychain with a four-leaf clover in it." His voice trailed off wistfully. "I still carry it."

That explained it. Carrying a four-leaf clover was one way to see the fairies. "And coffee led to more?"

"Yeah, it did. I proposed six months later." He sighed. "And she's been gone longer than we were married, longer than I knew her before she vanished. Maybe that's why she forgot me."

Her heart broke for him. She felt tears trickling down her face. "No, that's not it. She can't help it, where she is. It's not just you she forgot. I doubt she remembers who she is."

"They brainwashed her?"

"Something like that."

He sighed again, deeply, and she felt the last of the tension flow from his body. The painkiller must have kicked in. "Is that where Emily is?" he asked, his words slurring even more.

"Probably."

"Does she remember who she is?"

"I think so. She knows what to do."

"I don't understand."

"I know. It's hard to understand. Now hush and rest. I'll still be here with you."

He was silent for a long time, and she thought he'd fallen asleep, but then he said, "Sophie, who were those people?"

"They were fairies. But we'll talk about this in the morning."

His fingers folded around hers, squeezing as if he was hanging onto a lifeline. His breathing gradually evened. She wondered what she should do. She might be able to blur his memories so he would think it had all been a dream, but would that be fair to him?

"Can you get her back, Sophie?" he asked after another long period of silence when she thought he'd fallen asleep.

"I don't know, honey. I don't know. I'll try, I promise."

She doubted he'd let her make him forget. He'd cling to this memory with his last ounce of strength. Which meant that she needed to be ready to teach Fairy 101 the next morning.

⌐oThirty-Fiveⲟ⌐

A scratching sound at the lock woke Emily. She raised her head from where it rested on Eamon's shoulder and saw that he, too, was awake. "Looks like it's go time," she whispered, then she fought back a groan as she stiffly moved away from the wall where they'd been leaning. She grabbed the iron shackles from the far corner of the room and flattened herself against the wall next to the door. The door opened, and one of the guards stepped inside. She was about to swing the shackles when she caught the quick shake of Eamon's head and held back. She saw why when Maeve appeared in the doorway.

Emily swung out with all her might, striking Maeve square across the face with the iron. Maeve's scream was so terrible it almost made Emily feel bad for her–but then she remembered what the shackles had done to Eamon and got over her pity. Even so, Maeve's screams made Emily's skin crawl. The sound bypassed her ears and went straight to her nerves.

While screaming, Maeve rolled on the floor, clutching her face. Her guards rushed to her aid, and Emily took that as her chance to make a run for it. She moved to help Eamon up, but he was already on his feet. Emily took the lead, holding the shackles in front of her as a shield. She vaulted Maeve, fended off a guard with the shackles and found herself in the lobby, which was full of Maeve's courtiers. She cleared the way to the front door by waving the iron. Fairies scattered, but the door was still guarded, and possibly still enchanted.

Emma and Leigh, the other human captives, stood blocking the door, and the iron didn't scare them. Emma looked particularly upset. She had tear stains on her face, and Leigh had a comforting arm around her shoulders. Upset or not, Emma stood her ground. "Her majesty didn't give you permission to leave," she said.

"Why, you traitor!" Emily said with a gasp of surprise.

"You're the traitor! Her majesty has tried to be nice to you, but you've ruined everything. And now your horrible sister has made things even worse." Emma's voice broke in a sob, and Leigh patted her shoulder.

Emily supposed she should have been touched by the woman's tears, but all she heard was the insult against her sister. She might say a lot of things about Sophie, but nobody else was allowed to. "What did you say about my sister?"

As upset as she was, Emma had the good sense not to repeat it. Iron might not be poisonous to humans, but it could dent a skull, and Emily was swinging the shackles like she really wanted to hit someone with them. "Something bad happened at the market," Leigh explained with another soothing pat on Emma's shoulder. "There was a man there with your sister, causing trouble, and he accused Emma of being someone else."

A man there with Sophie? That had to be Michael, and if he'd been shocked about a human woman with the fairies... She felt like she'd been shot in the gut as she realized that with a different hairstyle and a wedding veil, Emma would look exactly like that photo in Michael's apartment. "Holy crap, you're Jen!" she blurted. "So, that's what happened to you! Oh my *God!*"

That was the wrong thing to say. Emma/Jen shouted, "I am not! Stop saying that! I don't know who this Jen person is, but that's not me and I wish people would quit calling me that." Which confirmed Emily's suspicions.

By that time, the guards had caught up with them. They surrounded her from a safe distance, unable to get their hands on Emily while she was armed with iron. She and Eamon were badly outnumbered, but she had iron and he could use fairy magic. She glanced over at him to see what he was doing and was shocked to see him escaping through the front door. The guards ignored him as they focused on her.

That *bastard*, she thought. After she'd just saved his life. She'd thought they'd *bonded*. And now he was abandoning her? Maybe Sophie really was right about fairies. Of course she was. Sophie was right about everything.

The guards closed in on her. She waved them away with the shackles, but she could only face one direction at a time, and while she threatened some of the guards, others snuck up on her from behind. She kept turning in circles, but she was getting dizzy.

It was hard to concentrate on defending herself when she couldn't get over what Eamon had just done. Maybe he'd gone to get help, she told herself, and she wouldn't have been able to get through the door. Although she liked having company in captivity, he could do far more for her when he was free. He was merely being practical. At least, she hoped so. She didn't like to think that he'd just saved his own skin while leaving her to rot.

She lashed out at a guard who got too close, and then someone tackled her from behind. While she was on the floor, Emma came over and picked up the shackles. Emily felt betrayed all over again, so she struck back in the only way she could while the guards had her pinned down. "Your husband is my upstairs neighbor," she said. "He really misses you."

"I have no husband," Emma spat, turning away.

The guards dragged Emily to her feet and marched her up the stairs to Maeve's living room, where they shoved her onto the sofa.

Emily had to bite the inside of her lip to keep from grinning when she saw the result of her handiwork on Maeve's face. An ugly red mark marred the fairy's perfect beauty, which had become much less beautiful the more Emily saw of her. Her mother was right: pretty is as pretty does, and someone as nasty as Maeve couldn't be truly lovely, no matter how perfect her features were.

"I am losing patience with you," Maeve snarled. "I am sick of you and your sister and your inability to cooperate. Your arrogance astounds me."

Pot, meet kettle, Emily thought, but knew well enough to keep her mouth shut.

"Apparently, I can't count on your sister's help," Maeve continued. She leaned forward, looming over Emily, who forced herself not to shrink back. "You will have to do."

Maeve straightened abruptly, then whirled away to pace the room. "Tell me about your grandmother," she ordered.

That wasn't what Emily had expected, but it seemed harmless enough. It shouldn't hurt anyone, and any stalling she could do might give Sophie time to pull off whatever she was working on or Eamon time to get help. "You mean Nana?" she asked. "I don't know her that well. She's got Alzheimer's, so she's not all there anymore, and Mama says she was crazy even before that. Was there anything in particular you wanted to know?"

"Did she ever teach you songs?"

This had to be the weirdest interrogation ever, Emily thought. She shrugged and said, "Not that I can think of. She sings with Sophie. That's how Sophie keeps her calm."

"Do you know their songs?"

Emily shook her head. "Not really. I haven't been home in years."

She couldn't stop herself from flinching away as Maeve leaned over her, so close that Emily's eyes crossed when she tried to focus on Maeve's face. "Think about the songs. Try to remember. Your life may depend on it."

While Emily was catching her breath, Maeve left.

So, wait, Maeve had gone through all this trouble to get her hands on Sophie to learn a *song?*

~Thirty-Six~

Michael woke to the worst pain he'd experienced since he'd been shot. His chest throbbed, and the rest of his body didn't feel so hot, either. He felt like he'd been in a big fight and come out the loser. When he finished assessing the aches and pains, he became aware that he wasn't alone. His hand clutched another, smaller hand. It was the first time in nearly seven years that he hadn't awakened alone.

Then the events of the night before came rushing back, and he remembered why he hurt all over. He also recognized the irony of waking up with someone else the morning after seeing his wife again. Opening bleary eyes, he turned to see Sophie Drake lying next to him, looking uncharacteristically vulnerable in sleep. She lay on her side, facing him, her right hand under her pillow and her left hand in his, one leg bent and the other stretched, her toes pointed even in sleep. A stray curl lay on her cheek just on top of the faint bruise on her cheekbone.

Then he noticed that Sophie's eyes were open and watching him. "It's early and we were up late," she murmured sleepily, her eyes fluttering closed. "Go back to sleep."

She'd thrown a blanket over him, but she lay uncovered, so he moved the blanket over to cover her, too. He hadn't thought he could get back to sleep, but the next time he woke, it was nearly eight thirty and Sophie was sitting up and stretching, catlike.

He lifted his head from his pillow, then let it fall back when it proved to be too much effort. "Did I have a really weird dream last night, or did something strange actually happen?"

She pulled her legs to her chest and rested her chin on her bent knees. "I have no idea what you dreamed last night, but yes, you stumbled into something that must have seemed really strange."

He closed his eyes and groaned. "I thought I might be having some kind of ICU psychosis attack. So I really saw Jen?"

"You certainly seemed to think you saw her, and there's a good chance that she was there, if I'm right about what I suspect happened to her."

He tried to remember the details of the night before, focusing on the concrete things. He could sort out the weird stuff later. "It was her voice, that was what I noticed. It sounded just like her." He frowned. "But how could she have been in the city this whole time, with every cop in the department keeping an eye out for her, without anyone even seeing her once?"

She studied him for a moment, like she was assessing him. Then she said, "Do you want the easy explanation, or do you want the truth? Let me warn you, you won't like or want to believe the truth. The easy explanation will let you go on the way things have been. The truth will change everything, and you can never go back."

"That sounds ominous."

"It is, believe me, it is."

"I don't think I can make a decision like that before coffee."

"Both of us could probably use some breakfast. I don't suppose you have any eggs."

"I may. Emily was making me breakfasts after I got out of the hospital."

"And I've got the skillet with me." She unfolded her legs and swung around to sit on the edge of the bed, then looked back over her shoulder at him. "There's just one thing. I don't know how to make coffee." She seemed sheepish about it. "I don't drink it, so I figure there's no harm in not learning to make it. But I could give it a shot."

"I can make coffee with one hand tied behind my back." He moved in an attempt to get up, but sitting up was more than he could manage. Reluctantly, he said, "The coffeemaker is self-explanatory, and right now, I'm not going to be a critic. You could give me some grounds to chew on, and I'd be happy."

She gave him a sweet, almost shy smile and stood. "Okay, then, you stay put, and let's see what I can come up with." She paused on her way out of the room and spoke toward the floor. "Do you need to go out, or are you okay for now?" An answering snore told him that Beau was sacked out at the foot of the bed.

Michael wasn't sure how long it took, but it didn't seem like long enough before she returned with a mug of coffee. She put it down while she helped him sit leaning against the headboard, then handed him the mug. He took a tentative sip, and that was enough to wake him up. He pictured his hair standing on end, like in a cartoon.

She gave a worried grimace. "It's awful, isn't it? I'm so sorry."

He took another swig before shaking his head. "No, no, it's fine. I like it strong. Strong is good." He drained the mug and handed it back to her. "I'll take another, if you don't mind." She took the cup warily and went back to the kitchen. He couldn't help but grin. It wasn't exactly *good* coffee, but it was as strong as the coffee in the precinct when it had been left on the burner overnight, only without the burnt taste, and that made it practically gourmet to him.

While he let the caffeine work through his system, he tried to recall the night before. He remembered following Sophie to the park. It got weird after that, with a marketplace full of strange people on the grounds of Belvedere Castle, Sophie dancing, a confrontation between Sophie and a weirdly beautiful woman, and Jen, who didn't recognize him. The mental images were so dreamlike that he wasn't sure any of it was real. Things grew even hazier after he saw Jen. He remembered pain and fear and falling asleep in Sophie's arms. He didn't remember how he got home.

Sophie returned with a tray loaded with two plates of pancakes, which she set next to him. She went back for his second cup of coffee and a mug of tea, then joined him on the bed, sitting so gracefully that she didn't disturb the tray.

She took a bite of pancake, chewed deliberately, swallowed, and took a sip of tea before asking, "Have you decided whether you want the easy answer or the truth?"

The caffeine had made it to his brain, so he felt qualified to say in no uncertain terms, "The truth, the whole truth, and nothing but the truth. What, *exactly,* happened last night?"

She took another bite and drank more tea, clearly attempting to delay the inevitable. Finally, she composed herself, looked him straight in the eye, and said, "You must have followed me again, and you found a fairy market, a place where the world of the fae meets the human world."

Michael blinked in surprise. Of all the things he'd thought it might have been, this wasn't it. "Wait, *fairies?* Like Tinkerbell? Are you kidding me?"

"Real fairies aren't like Tinkerbell or like the things you see on greeting cards. They're not little and cute with dragonfly or butterfly wings. They're supernatural beings who live in a realm below our world, but in a parallel universe, or something like that. I know how to go there, but I'm not entirely sure what the place is or how it works. They have magical powers that they mostly use to create illusions and make themselves beautiful. Don't let the beauty fool you, though. They're ugly to the core. They can be cruel, just for the fun of it."

He laughed and shook his head in disbelief. "You're talking about these things like they're *real.* Tank didn't put you up to this, did he?"

She raised an eyebrow. "What did you see last night?"

"I saw a market on the terrace in front of Belvedere Castle."

"Was it there when you got there?"

"They hadn't turned the lights on yet, so I couldn't see it until they did."

She narrowed her eyes at him. "*Really?* Is that what you saw?

If you expect me to tell the truth, the whole truth, and nothing but the truth, you have to do the same."

In his mind's eye, he saw her sitting on the empty terrace, putting on her dancing shoes. If there had been enough light to see Sophie, there would have been enough light to see the market being set up. "No, it wasn't there," he admitted. "And then it appeared."

"When?"

"Midnight," he said as he realized the truth. "Suddenly the place was full of booths and people."

"What were the people like?"

"They were beautiful. A lot of them looked like hippies, all floaty rags and flowers and leaves. Then there were some dressed like something out of an old Rat Pack movie."

"Did they look human to you?"

"Yeah. They had funny-colored hair, and they looked kind of surreal, but they were human. No pointy ears or wings."

"That's what fairies look like—or the way they want you to see them. You only saw that market because of the four-leaf clover on your keychain. Otherwise, you could have walked through that whole terrace without realizing anything was going on."

"You're serious?" He regretted eating breakfast because it threatened to come back up.

"Quite serious." He held eye contact with her for a long moment, but she didn't waver or show the slightest sign of amusement. Nothing pinged his internal lie detector.

"So, assuming for the moment that fairies are real, that woman you were sparring with, she's the one who took Emily?"

She nodded. "Yes. The same group also has your wife, and likely those other missing women you mentioned."

He shook his head, willing this to make sense. "But why? What do they want with them?"

She closed her eyes and looked like she was in pain, then opened her eyes and said, "They've wanted Emily all along, and they took other women they thought might be Emily. To them, all humans look pretty much alike. They first tried to take Emily fourteen years ago. That was one of the reasons I wanted her to go to New York. I thought she'd be safe here, far away from home. But it turns out that our geography is meaningless to them. Here may as well be Louisiana. You just have to find the right gateway and know how to use it."

"Why do they want Emily?"

She started doing all the things she hadn't when Tanaka interviewed her. She glanced down, smoothed the bedspread, straightened the folds of her skirt around her legs, and tucked her hair behind her ear before answering without looking directly at him. "That's the big question, but I think Maeve actually wants me. She's never been able to catch me, but she knows if she has Emily, I'll come for her. She's trying to take the throne to rule the entire fairy realm, and it's possible that she thinks I'll be useful for that, but I don't know how or why." A cold, hard smile crossed her lips, then vanished. "But I believe it's wisest to stay out of her grasp, regardless."

Anger bubbled up in him. "You've known all along where Emily was? Why didn't you say something? You let me play the worry card to get the police on the case right away, when you knew?"

"I never asked you to do anything," she protested. "I wouldn't have even rung your bell if I'd known Beau had someone looking after him. I'd have taken care of it all by myself. What would you have done if I had told you?" She deepened her accent and raised the pitch of her voice to a girlish tone. "Oh, Detective Murray, there's no need to call the police. Emily was kidnapped by the fairies and taken to their realm, and I'm afraid that's out of the jurisdiction of the NYPD. You just sit tight, and I'll take care of it." She gave a surprisingly unladylike snort of laughter, then said in a more normal voice, "I can't imagine that would have gone over well."

"I'd still have called the police," he admitted, "and probably Bellevue." Even now, that sounded like a wise course of action, though he'd have to have himself committed while he was at it because he couldn't deny what he'd seen. "What about Jen? Did you know where she was, too?" He could forgive her for keeping information about Emily to herself, but not Jen.

She chewed on her lower lip for a moment before saying, "I suspected, once I saw the wedding picture. There were too many similarities for it to be coincidence. But I didn't know for sure until last night. I am sorry about that, but, again, what could I have possibly said that you might have believed?"

"Were you ever planning to tell me?"

"The plan was to get both of them back and then make it look like they'd just found their way home."

"That's why you've been sneaking out every night, to go into this fairy realm and look for them?"

"Yes."

"That's where you were the other night, when you were out all night and you said you were only gone a couple of hours?"

She nodded. "But to me it really was only a couple of hours. Time does funny things in the Realm. A whole night went by out here in a couple of hours there."

"You lied about someone trying to kidnap you."

"Maeve's people tried to get me, but I escaped."

"That's how you got all those scrapes and bruises and that burn on your wrist the next night, another kidnap attempt?"

"Yes. I'm sorry I lied to you, but I ask you again, what could I have said? You don't even believe me after seeing it for yourself."

"I don't know what I saw."

"Now you're just being dense. But that's how their existence has remained nothing but legend for thousands of years. People are all too eager to rationalize what they've seen with their own eyes."

"But I didn't see anything that can't be explained—well, other than that market appearing out of thin air, which is pretty big, I'll admit, but I didn't see any fairies or magic."

She sighed. "Yeah, you were out of it for the good stuff. You even missed our shortcut through the Realm."

He pointed at her accusingly. "See, that's just it, you're telling me about all this stuff that I didn't see. How do I know you didn't make up this whole story?"

With a groan, she shook her head sadly. "You were the one

who asked for the truth. I would have been perfectly happy giving you an easy, rational explanation. You would have been happier, too. So, you want to see magic?" She raised her hand, and the bottle of pills on his nightstand flew to her. "You could probably use one of these right now."

He ignored the pill she held out to him as he gawked at her. "What are you?" he gasped.

Instead of having a quick answer for that, she shrugged and said with a soft laugh, "I have no idea anymore."

That admission from the incredibly self-assured Sophie took him aback. "What?"

"I knew about some of this before. I'd met fairies when I was a kid and knew how to deal with them. The rest is new to me. I learned only the other day that I'm supposedly an enchantress. I've just started learning about that. I get the feeling there's something else that nobody's telling me–if they even know the whole story. Apparently, I'm quite the mystery."

She ran her fork through a pool of syrup on her plate. "You know, all this time, I thought that people actually liked me–or feared me–and it turns out I was using magic to manipulate them. I wonder what would happen if I turned it off entirely. Who would I be?"

"Did you put the whammy on me?"

"I have. A couple of times on purpose." She looked up at him and shrugged. "I don't know what I might have done unconsciously. I don't know what parts of my life have been real. To be honest, I'm not sure how much of all this I believe."

"You believe in fairies. You were just trying to convince me that they were real."

"Because I've experienced them. Doing magic, that's different."

"What do you call what you just did?"

"Telekinesis? Maybe it's some kind of psychic ability, not real magic. It's the women Emily worked for at that shop who say I'm an enchantress. They know about the fairies, but I don't know if they're right about everything else."

He realized he was shaking. "I can't take this. You can't expect me to believe it. Maybe I'll wake up soon."

"Then here's the easy answer: Emily, and Jen before her, ended up with some cult of holdover hippies who like to party in Central Park in the middle of the night. They're probably keeping them drugged so they don't remember who they are and so they can't escape. Does that work better for you?"

"Not really. I don't know what you are or what you're up to, but I don't like any of it."

"Then, if you'll excuse me, I've got a lot to do." She slid off the bed, picked up the breakfast tray and carried it to the kitchen. A burst of classical piano music from somewhere on the floor brought her back to the bedroom to get her phone. She looked at the screen and groaned before answering it. "Hello, Mama," she said perkily. She listened for a while, then her eyes went wide with alarm. "What's wrong? Oh no. But what about Bess, can't she do anything? What set her off? Maybe if I talked to her."

She sat on the end of the bed, biting her lip and pulling one foot up under her. In a soft, gentle voice, like someone would talk to a scared small child, she said, "Hello, Nana, it's Sophie. I went to New York to visit Emily."

She chewed on her lip while she listened, and then she said, "Easy, easy, Nana. I'm okay. I'm safe. I'm visiting Emily. It's okay. I'll be home soon. Why don't we sing a song together? It'll be just like I'm there." She ran the back of her hand across her eyes, brushing away tears, before she started singing what sounded like an old folk song.

Michael felt like he was eavesdropping on a private moment, so he forced himself to his feet and staggered into the kitchen, where at least he wasn't watching her, even though he could still hear everything. He should make tea, he decided. She sounded like she could use another cup. He filled the teakettle and put it on the stove. Soon, the rattle of the kettle drowned out some of Sophie's voice so he didn't feel so much like he was eavesdropping.

She was still singing when the kettle boiled and he poured

hot water over a tea bag. Her voice was very different from Emily's. Emily had a big, powerful voice that could reach the back row of the upper balcony. Sophie's voice was soft and sweet, a voice made for singing lullabies, which, he realized, was what she was doing. Her song reminded him of "Scarborough Fair," the old Simon and Garfunkle song his mother had liked, with its repetitive pattern and seemingly nonsensical list of impossible tasks. It wasn't a likely choice for a lullaby, but maybe it was an old song Sophie's grandmother remembered from her youth.

She was finishing the song when he returned to the bedroom. She looked up in surprise, then nodded in thanks as she took the mug from him. Her voice trembled slightly as she asked, "Is she better now?"

Standing this close to her, he could hear the voice on the other end of the phone saying, "She's quit screaming and yelling, but you should still get home right away. You don't need to be playing in New York when your grandmother needs you."

And that, right there, made things add up. Now Michael understood her—that is, the human part of her life, the reason someone like Sophie had stayed in a small town instead of pursuing her ambitions. He put his hand on her shoulder in a gesture of silent support. "But I can't, Mama," she said. "My return flight isn't until next week, and you know how *impossible* it is to make changes these days."

"She's your grandmother. She's not any relation of mine, and I can't deal with her. She won't listen to anyone but you."

"I just need a few days, okay, Mama? I haven't had a break in ages, and Emily needs me right now."

A deeper, richer voice came on the line after a brief, muffled argument. "You stay right where you are and have a good time. We'll be fine. Just call and talk to your grandmother every so often, you hear?"

Sophie gave a shaky smile. "Thank you, Bess. And please let me know if there's a problem."

"I'll do that."

Sophie gave a long, shuddering sigh after she ended the call, then she took a sip of tea and glanced up at Michael. "Sorry about that. I believe I have now dumped all my family drama in your lap."

He sat next to her. "Is it Alzheimer's?"

She nodded. "It started about a year before Daddy died—it's his mother. She moved in with us then. She and Mama never got along, and it only got worse after he died. I can certainly understand Mama's position. She got stuck looking after a mother-in-law who never approved of her."

"But you were the one who had to take on the responsibility," Michael concluded.

"We were always close. I don't mind, really, but it's the last thing I need right now."

"Does your mother know? About the fairies, and all?"

"Oh, heavens, no! My grandmother does, but nobody but me believes her."

"That's why you didn't tell your mother Emily was missing."

"Precisely. You don't believe me, with what you've seen. My mother would refuse to believe out of sheer spite."

He wanted to reassure her that he did believe her, but it wouldn't be true. He sat in silence while she picked up her bag and called to Beau. He was still sitting there when he heard his front door open and close.

With her gone, the last fragments of his belief dissipated. He was still pretty sure he'd seen Jen, and he had a feeling that would lead him to Emily. It was worth looking into. He picked up the phone, dialed the precinct, and left a message for Tanaka.

Thirty-Seven

Emily was convinced that Maeve was completely, totally, out of her mind. Maybe there had never been any rhyme or reason to why she wanted or needed Sophie. Maybe it was just some wacky revenge fantasy and she wanted Sophie there to see her moment of triumph. It wouldn't be the first time that an old rival of Sophie's had dreamed of that day coming.

Maeve's obsession with songs Emily knew from her childhood was the final proof that she was nuts. "You know a song!" she kept repeating. "Sing it for me!"

And, since her life and maybe even the freedom of the fairy world depended on it, Emily sang. It was like the audition from hell, but because she was a singer, she knew a lot of songs, and if Sophie needed her to buy time, then time she would buy.

She started with the alphabet song, but Maeve cut her off midway through. "No, that's not it," she said with an impatient wave.

Unlike at an audition, she couldn't just leave after being told no thanks. She had to try again, opting for "Twinkle, Twinkle, Little

Star." Maeve sat forward with some interest at first before cutting Emily off.

That led to "I'm a Little Teapot," complete with the arm movements. The rest of the fairies liked that one, but Maeve shook her head. Emily moved on to "Itsy, Bitsy Spider," doing the hand motions that went with it. A few of the fairies tried to imitate the way she made the spider walk by touching the pinky of one hand to the thumb of the other and then swiveling her hands, but Maeve was not amused.

Just to be obnoxious, Emily belted out "Tomorrow" from *Annie*, a role she'd been born to play—she hadn't even needed the red, curly wig. In the theater world, she'd have been pelted with rotten vegetables for that one, but the fairies liked it. Maeve just shook her head.

"Old MacDonald Had a Farm" was a hit with the fairies, who sang along with the "E-I-E-I-O" part. Maeve frowned carefully as she listened, like she was trying to pick hidden meanings out of the words. Emily was glad when Maeve cut off that one because she'd forgotten a lot of it. To go with the farm theme, she sang "The Farmer in the Dell." Again, Maeve listened intently, but eventually shook her head.

The first verse of "Lavender's Blue" made Maeve's eyes go wide, and she leaned forward eagerly. She let Emily sing the whole song, and when Emily finished the song, Maeve paused, thinking, before finally shaking her head slowly.

"That is not it," she said. "Do you not know other songs?"

"I know hundreds of other songs," Emily said, her voice rasping from strain and dehydration. "This is what I do." A human servant approached with a glass filled with a sparkling liquid, beads of condensation on the outside showing that the liquid was nice and cold. Emily stared at it for a moment, sorely tempted, but waved it away. It wasn't worth being trapped in fairyland. Maeve would just have to get used to her sounding gravelly.

"It's a song you knew from childhood," Maeve said. "Something you and your sister learned together."

"That doesn't narrow it down much. I come from a musical family. Do you maybe know the tune or the first line?"

Maeve came off the sofa and loomed over Emily. "You will give me this song."

Refusing to be cowed, Emily put her hands on her hips and stared up at her. "I'm trying. I just don't know which song you want. My sister sang a lot of songs with me."

It took some effort to maintain eye contact without blinking or doing anything else that might make her look like she was lying, because Emily was starting to suspect which song Maeve meant, and although she had no idea why the song mattered to Maeve, she had no intention of sharing it. She didn't remember details, but she had a vague memory of Sophie and Nana singing something together. It was a simple, repetitive melody, but Emily couldn't remember the words, even though she could hear Sophie's sweet, soft voice singing it in her memory.

But what could a song have to do with becoming queen of the fairies?

Thirty-Eight

Michael was too restless to sit around, so he took a shower, dressed, and headed for the park. He still felt wobbly and sore and couldn't move very quickly—a possible sign that his adventures had been real—but he needed to do this. He had to know.

On a Saturday morning, the park was an entirely different place than it had been the night before. It was full of people enjoying the last weekend in August. Kids ran around, laughing and yelling. People walked dogs, sat on benches and read, or just strolled along the paths. He headed straight for Belvedere Castle, ignoring all the other park activities.

He wasn't sure what he expected to find—maybe a scrap of that spiderweb silk clothing or a sign that those booths had been there. Instead, the place was painfully normal, crowded with Saturday-morning park-goers. He stood in what he estimated to be the spot where he'd seen Jen. He could picture the scene in his mind, as vivid as if it were still happening. Had he dreamt it, or was Sophie telling the truth?

The park didn't hold any answers for him. The market might as well have taken place on the moon. With a weary sigh, he headed down the stairs. At the foot of the stairs sat a small white cat–the cat he'd helped? It stopped grooming itself and approached him, rubbing against his ankles and purring. Apparently, that much had been real. The cat then trotted daintily over to a hedge and turned to see if he'd followed.

Caught in the hedge were several scraps of fabric. One looked like it had been torn from the shirt he'd worn the night before. Another seemed to have come from Sophie's dress. A third looked like it had been woven from spiderwebs. All that told him was that he and Sophie had been here, along with someone else who dressed like Sophie's so-called fairies. It still didn't mean that there was a fairy realm hidden beneath this world.

He looked around for the cat, but it was gone. "Did you lose something?" a soft voice from right next to him asked. He jumped, startled, and turned to see a woman wearing a flowing white dress. Her hair was white-blond and sparkled with sunlight even though they were in the shade. She looked vaguely familiar, but he couldn't quite place her. "Or perhaps you lost some*one*." There was a faint sibilant hiss to her speech.

"No, no, I'm fine," he said.

"You lost your lady. I could help you find her. You saved my life. I owe you a favor."

He backed away warily. "What? You must have mistaken me for someone else."

She made a purring sound deep in her throat. "I make no mistake. I helped you last night, but that was because I do not like Maeve and we must protect the enchantress. I still owe you a life debt."

Michael figured he had two options: He could faint, let the park's medical personnel deal with him, and then pretend that none of this had ever happened and resign himself to never seeing Jen again, or he could accept all the evidence and do something to get his wife back.

"Maybe later," he told the woman, who flicked him a smile before sauntering away.

He headed home, moving as quickly as he could without straining himself. He needed to talk to Sophie.

Thirty-Nine

Sophie barely had a chance to shower and put on clean clothes before there was a knock on the door. She opened it to find Amelia and Athena. "We need to talk about what happened last night," Amelia said as the two of them brushed past her to enter the apartment.

"Please, come in," Sophie said dryly, shutting the door behind them. They were already seated at the table by the time she rejoined them. "I see you made it out okay," she added.

"Did you get Detective Murray home?" Athena asked, wringing her hands anxiously. "That poor man, finding his wife again like that."

"Yes, he's fine, more or less. I'm not sure how well he's coping with what he's just learned, but he'll come around." She dragged Emily's desk chair over to the table, then decided she'd had enough pleasantries. It was time to get down to business. "I need to stop Maeve."

"Well, yes, of course, that *is* our job," Athena said. "We are to keep the throne empty, at all costs."

"I take it that means you will join us," Amelia said.

"For this," Sophie agreed. She didn't feel it necessary to tell them that her mandate to stop Maeve had nothing to do with their roles and everything to do with settling an old debt. "I need to stop Maeve and get Emily back. Then I'll think about what to do next."

"Don't forget about Jennifer Murray," Athena added.

"That may be more difficult. But first things first. We need to figure out why Maeve needs me to win the throne. If we know that, then we should know exactly how to stop her. I don't suppose it's as easy as wrapping myself in iron and staying well away from any gateways."

"You'd have to do that for the rest of your life," Amelia said. "You also might not get your sister back. No, we need to put a stop to her so she won't keep trying."

"You are most likely the key," Athena said. "What is it that you know or can do that might be useful?"

Sophie ran her hands through her hair and rubbed her throbbing temples with her thumbs. It was hard for her to concentrate when she was constantly, painfully aware of Emily's state of distress. Something was wrong, wherever she was. "I can dance. I've known Maeve most of my life, but I don't have any good blackmail material on her. She never made much of an impression on me until she kidnapped my sister. She's not particularly special or powerful."

A knock on the door interrupted her train of thought. "Excuse me," she said as she got up. She opened the door to see Michael filling the doorway. Speaking without thinking—a sure sign that she was under too much stress—she blurted, "What are you doing here?"

"I want to help—whatever it is I can do. I've got something at stake here. I may not be of much use physically, but I'm a cop, so I'm used to thinking analytically. And I'm in on the secret now, so there's no excuse for lying to me anymore about what you're up to."

"You've decided you believe me?"

"You told him?" Amelia asked, her voice rising in pitch to what in any other woman would have been a screech.

Sophie glanced over her shoulder to see that the sisters had joined her in the entryway. "He was there, he saw it all. I had to explain," she protested.

"But if he didn't believe, it would have been easy enough to smooth his memories," Amelia said.

"He deserved to know. He's affected." Sophie turned back to Michael and added, "But I don't need your help. What I need is one less person I have to protect." She fixed him with a direct gaze while making a conscious effort not to influence him magically. "I know you want to help, and I understand why, but there isn't anything you can do." Less stridently, she added, "You should probably be resting."

She tried to close the door, but he stepped inside before she could shut him out. "You can't drop all this crazy stuff on me and then leave me out of the loop," he said. Turning to Amelia and Athena, he added, "I'm the youngest of three brothers. Isn't that supposed to mean something in this sort of thing?"

"Wrong kind of fairy tale," Sophie said, but Amelia took his good arm and led him into the apartment and over to the daybed.

"Please join us, Detective," she said. Sophie opened her mouth to protest, but Amelia glared her down. "There is a pattern to such things, and it isn't just in stories that the youngest of three brothers has power. He could be helpful." Michael shot Sophie a triumphant smile as he sat. Amelia placed a hand on his shoulder and said, "Besides, I rather enjoy having a handsome young man around. I am Amelia Abernathy, and this is my sister, Athena Abercrombie. Emily works at our shop when she's between shows, and your lovely wife was a regular customer. It's such a pleasure to meet you."

Athena rolled her eyes and coughed while Michael turned pink. Sophie could have cheerfully strangled them both. She didn't need any distractions, and Michael had become increasingly distracting after she'd spent hours with him in her arms. Even though it had been perfectly innocent, it had been the kind of feeling she was afraid she could get used to. Not that she would, since it was utterly impossible. But she kept her mouth shut and dragged the dining chairs over to the daybed so they could all sit together.

"What I'm curious about, Detective," Athena said as she sat beside Michael, "is how you found the market last night. You shouldn't have seen that."

"He has a four-leaf clover on his keychain," Sophie answered for him.

"I assume Sophie has explained some of this to you," Athena said to Michael.

He nodded. "She briefed me. I understand you need to stop Maeve to get her captives back."

"And we're getting nowhere," Sophie said. "I can't think of what it is about me, something I know or have, that Maeve needs."

Michael said, "Well, what do you know or have?"

She sighed in frustration and resisted the urge to run her hands through her hair. "That's the problem. I don't *know*."

"Try listing a few things," he encouraged. "I've got an outsider's perspective, and remember, this is what I do. I sift through information to find the key facts."

"Okay, then. There's the dancing. I make an amazing peach cobbler. I boss people around. Somehow I doubt she needs any help with that."

"You said your grandmother knows about the fairies. Did she teach you anything?"

"She told me stories. But they're just fairy tales, not histories."

"Are you so sure?" Amelia asked, leaning forward with interest.

"None of them were about taking a throne. Most of the stories were about people escaping from fairy captivity," Sophie said. "I *really* don't think Maeve wants that."

"Was there anything about finding a lost person?" Athena asked. "A story can be a metaphor, and a lost loved one could stand for something lost by the fairies."

"That's it!" Michael cried out. He turned to Sophie. "What about that song you sang to calm your grandmother this morning?" He glanced sheepishly among the three women, then continued, like he was trying to justify his theory, "It was about finding a lost love, and it sounded like it had instructions in it."

Sophie laughed out loud and launched herself at him, throwing her arms around him and hugging him fiercely. "You're brilliant!" she said with another laugh. "I can't believe I didn't think of that."

Then she realized that she was practically sitting in his lap and jumped up and back to her own seat. She grabbed a notebook and began writing down the lyrics. "Now that I think about it, my grandmother was very intent that I learn this song. She said her mother taught her to sing it, and her mother had taught her. I always thought it was just some old folk song, but maybe Michael's right, and all along they've been passing on the instructions."

"How would Maeve know about it?" Athena asked, leaning over to read what Sophie had written.

"When I was little and went into the woods to dance with the fairies, Maeve was part of that group. Sometimes I sang as I danced. This was the song I knew best." She shook her head in disbelief. "And I bet Maeve figured it out when she heard it—or maybe it stuck with her and she figured it out later. Though it might have helped if Nana had told me what it was about."

"She may not have expected you to ever use it," Amelia suggested. "You may have been meant to be just another link in the chain passing the knowledge along."

"But how did my family get this knowledge?"

"It wouldn't be the first time fairy knowledge was entrusted to humans," Amelia said. "Most of the things enchantresses have learned about using magic originally came from the fairies. We had our own power, but we had to learn to use it. If you inherited your magical abilities from your grandmother, it makes sense that the knowledge went with the power."

Athena finished reading the words to the song and said, "These instructions are rather precise. I bet Maeve doesn't remember them exactly, so she'd need Sophie to give them to her." She gasped. "Oh my, does Emily know this song?"

"I don't know. I don't remember my grandmother singing it to her. She may have heard it, but Nana won't let me forget it. Even now, when she gets agitated, the best way to calm her is to sing the song to her."

"Maybe she knows more about the song," Athena suggested.

Sophie shook her head sadly. "She has Alzheimer's. She doesn't seem to remember much of anything, other than making sure I remember the song."

Michael said, "This is good, right? You know what to do, so you can stop Maeve from doing it."

"That depends on how much Maeve remembers–or how much Emily remembers and Maeve manages to get out of her. She won't know that she's not supposed to tell, but Em is pretty stubborn. She may withhold information just because she's annoyed about having her life messed with."

"If Maeve remembered precisely, she wouldn't need Sophie and she wouldn't have taken Emily," Athena said.

Then Sophie reread the last stanza of the song and realized that Athena was wrong. There was a reason other than the song that Maeve might need Sophie. The last line went, "My heart it bleeds for my one true love, and with her blood she'll win my heart."

If Maeve thought the song was the key, and if she thought it was significant that Sophie was the keeper of the song, then she'd think she needed Sophie's blood to seal the deal. And if she thought that Emily's blood was the next best thing... Well, she didn't think Maeve would stop at a drop or two, and if that was the only thing she remembered about the song, she'd spill blood just to see what happened.

And that meant Sophie had to do the one thing she knew would prevent that.

Forty

Emily was running out of songs to sing for Maeve. She'd resorted to commercial jingles and television theme songs so she could keep stalling for time. Her throat felt like someone had run a cheese grater across it, and her mouth felt full of sand and cotton. She would have killed for a sip of water, but she kept rejecting the drinks the fairies offered her.

An attendant entered and whispered something to Maeve. Emily strained to hear as she kept singing, but all she could tell was that it wasn't good news. "Enough!" Maeve shouted, waving for her to stop singing. Emily was so tired that she sagged with relief even as panic seized her.

She rasped, "But your majesty, I know more songs."

Maeve ignored her and snapped her fingers for an aide, then said, "Send out a raiding party to find Sophie Drake. You must find her immediately. Both Niall and Fiontan are raising armies, and I must get there before they do. Bring her now! I don't care what condition she's in."

"I just need a little break, and then I'm sure I can find the right song for you," Emily pleaded. She might be singing bass by then, but she had to keep Maeve occupied.

"I don't have time for this. And besides, it's painful to my ears." She turned away from Emily to give more instructions to her flunkies.

In desperation, Emily tried to think of something, anything, she could do to keep Maeve away from Sophie. She might have joked about how difficult it would be to capture Sophie, but a big enough group of fairies ambushing her in the city might do it. She thought she knew the song Maeve wanted, and maybe if she sang just enough, she could keep Maeve on the hook. She opened her mouth and sang, "I had a love, then she was lost." All that came out was a faint whisper, and Maeve didn't even notice that she was singing.

The last beverage she'd been offered still sat on the table next to her. It was a clear, sparkling liquid, and beads of condensation trickled down the outside of the glass, making the drink look cool and refreshing. But it was a fairy beverage, and even one sip might trap her here for good, or else make it impossible for her to adjust to life in the real world again. Even if she did make it out, everything else she drank from this point on, from the sweetest fruit juice to the finest champagne, might be drab and tasteless.

But her sister's life, the fate of the fairy realm, and maybe even the fate of humanity was at stake. It would be a small sacrifice on her part, and it would save her a lot of money if all drinks tasted like water from now on. Hoping her sister would understand and forgive her, she picked up the glass, then squeezed her eyes shut as she brought it to her lips.

The liquid was the coolest, most refreshing thing she'd ever had. It tasted the way television commercials made bottled water or sodas look. Her sore throat instantly felt better, and a surge of energy rushed through her entire body. It took every ounce of self-control she had to put the glass down after two sips instead of guzzling the whole thing.

Now she felt she could sing. She tried again, raising her voice like she was singing to the back of the upper balcony. "I had a love, then she was lost. I dream she'll find me once again." At those words, Maeve's head snapped around, and all conversation in the room stopped. Emily pretended not to notice as she kept going with the first verse. "It won't be long 'til she'll hear my song, and she will know the way to my heart."

Maeve slowly rose to her feet. "Yes! That is the song. Sing me that song."

"I'll have to think about it. I don't remember it all," Emily said. That wasn't a lie. She couldn't remember much past the first verse.

"Then think!" Maeve demanded. She settled back onto the sofa and called back her flunkies with a gesture.

Emily hummed the melody, inserting the occasional word, and she wondered how long she could keep this going without either giving away too much or frustrating Maeve into taking impulsive action.

⌒Forty-One⌒

Once they'd figured out that the song was the key, Amelia and Athena insisted they go to the shop and cross-reference their fairy information with Sophie's song so they could figure out what to do to stop Maeve. Michael felt out of his league, since he knew nothing about magic or fairies, and he felt completely out of place in the small, low-ceilinged shop full of fragile things. Instead, he focused on Sophie. She acted like this was all in a day's work, but he could see the strain on her face. She reminded him of the more stoic class of crime victim, the ones who insisted they were fine but who were barely hanging on.

He was suspicious of how little she involved herself in the planning. The two old women scurried around with books and papers while Sophie did a lot of nodding. Her focus was on those lyrics she'd written. Even though she'd written them from memory, she looked like she was trying to memorize them.

"You're able to pass into the Realm yourself," Amelia said to Sophie, startling her enough to make her jump. "I think it would be best if we came with you for this, though. Once you open the gateway, you may be able to bring us through with you."

"I suppose so," Sophie said. "I've never tried it with another person, other than getting Emily out."

"I still wonder how you do that at all," Athena said, resting her chin on her hand. "We can't do it, so it's not an enchantress power." She kept staring at Sophie, then her eyes narrowed slightly. "I wonder...I wonder what happened to the last queen. They're immortal unless they're killed, so she didn't die of old age. If she'd been murdered for her throne, someone would be on the throne now. It's like she just disappeared."

"Maybe she retired to Florida," Michael quipped. "After a few centuries of ruling, she might have wanted a break."

Instead of laughing, Athena tilted her head and went, "Hmmmm."

"Right now, I don't care what happened to the last queen," Sophie said, sounding like her temper was fraying. "I just want to get Emily back."

Speaking of getting Emily to safety, there was one question Michael had to ask. "So, Jen, if they have her, can we get her back, too?"

She sighed deeply, then said, "I'm sorry, but I don't know. The longer someone's in the fairy realm, the more difficult it is to leave. The real world looks pale and dim in comparison. The first time they took Emily, I spent that night sitting on her to keep her from trying to go back, and she was there less than an hour. Eating fairy food can also trap a person. They start to magically belong to the place. They're transformed a little. It *is* a beautiful place, one big nonstop party, and it would be easy to fall under its spell."

"That's why she doesn't remember me. Why she didn't even know her own name."

"Her old life would feel like a distant dream. But now that she's seen you, memories may return."

"So there is a chance of getting her back?"

She hesitated. "Maybe."

"When, exactly, did she disappear?" Amelia asked.

"It will be seven years at Halloween."

"Then there's still a chance," Athena said with an encouraging smile. "Seven years is generally the point of no return. Or, in some stories, it's the term of imprisonment, after which she may be freed. And you haven't remarried or fallen in love with anyone else, which is one of the barriers in the folklore."

He realized he was staring at Sophie as he considered what Athena had said. Until a day or so ago, he could have said without a doubt that he was in the clear. Now, though… No, he decided, it wasn't love. He liked Sophie. He was intrigued by her. There was maybe even a small side order of lust–it had been a very long time, and she could do some amazing things with that taut little body. But he wasn't in love with her, not like he still loved Jen. "Well, that's good," he said. "There's still a chance."

"I'll do whatever I can to get her out," Sophie said, "but you have to realize that she may not want to leave, and she may never be happy again in the human world."

"Is she happy there?"

"If she's forgotten, then, yes, she probably is."

"And Emily still stands a chance?"

"Emily knows not to eat the food. I may have to borrow your handcuffs for a few days, but I'm pretty sure she could go back to normal life."

"Let's focus on that first. You need to stop Maeve, we'll get Emily back, and then we'll worry about Jen."

She raised an eyebrow. *"We?"* Then she shook her head. "No, you're staying out of this."

"They have my wife!"

"You're hurt, you're not at full strength, and you have no idea what you're dealing with. You're a liability, not an asset. You've already helped more than enough by thinking of the song." She shoved her chair back and stood up. "I have a splitting headache and I need to lie down for a while. I'll see you this evening around sunset. We'll meet at the park. Come on, Beauregard."

The dog blinked awake at the sound of his name, got up,

stretched, and went to her. While her back was turned, Michael reached across the table and palmed the sheet of lyrics, tucking them into his sling just as she turned back to give a half-hearted wave. She frowned for a second, as though trying to remember something, then shook her head and departed. As soon as the door closed, Michael turned to the two women and said, "She's up to something."

"What makes you think that?" Amelia asked.

"Do you really think a headache would slow *her* down, at all? I'm not sure she'd even admit to feeling pain. Going to lie down for a headache? I don't buy it."

"What do you think she's up to?" Athena asked.

"I think she's going to ditch us and attack Maeve directly, on her own."

The two women looked at each other, then back at him. "She wouldn't!" Amelia said.

"How long have you known her?" Michael asked.

"About as long as you have."

"Anticipating what people are likely to do is part of my job." He gestured toward the door where Sophie had disappeared. "She's got a plan that doesn't involve us." He pulled the sheet of lyrics out of his sling, and his eyes went right to the word "blood." A chill went down his spine. "I think I know what she's up to," he said. "There's something here about needing blood. If she thinks Maeve might resort to using Emily's blood, Sophie will give herself up."

Both women looked alarmed. "That can't happen," Amelia said. "That would allow Maeve to win the throne. We have to stop her."

Michael stood with some awkwardness and said, "I'd better go keep an eye on her."

Amelia wrote a number on a scrap of paper and said, "That's my cell number. Call us if you notice her sneaking out."

"Just a moment," Athena said. She disappeared into a back room and returned with a small bag. "Take these," she said, handing him the bag, which was heavier than he expected. "They're iron nails–good weapons against the fae. I may have some iron bullets around here somewhere. What caliber weapon do you carry?"

"Athena," Amelia warned. "I've told you about those bullets. They're not a good idea." To Michael she added, "They're ancient. I'm not sure they'd even work in modern firearms, or that they wouldn't just blow up in your face."

"Iron nails should be enough," Michael said, hefting the bag in his hand before sliding it into his sweatshirt pocket. He folded the lyrics and pocketed that sheet, too.

When he got back to his building, he paused by Emily's door. He could hear Beau snoring from inside, so if Sophie had gone anywhere, she'd left Beau behind. She might really have wanted to rest. Or else she'd left a recording of Beau's snores playing on a loop to fool him.

He got some rest, himself, keeping an ear open for sounds of anyone coming or going. When he knocked on Emily's door again a couple of hours later, there was no answer, and now he couldn't hear Beau. He had a bad feeling about that. He went upstairs to get his cell phone and anti-fairy ammo, then called the sisters as he went down the stairs. He was just ending the call when he opened the front door and found himself face-to-face with Gene Tanaka.

"Hey, Tank!" he said, trying to sound a lot more casual than he felt. "What's up?"

"I don't know. You called me."

Michael didn't have to fake confusion. It had been a day full of life-changing discoveries and revelations, so the morning seemed to belong to another lifetime. "Oh, yeah, I guess I did," he said, weighing his words carefully. Tanaka was an even better human lie detector than he was, so he had to avoid any outright falsehoods. "Last night was pretty bad, probably the worst since I've been out of the hospital. The painkillers either knock me out cold or give me wild, vivid dreams—the kind where it takes you a while after you wake up to realize that they were just a dream." That was all entirely true. "I think I dreamed about Jen last night, and I must have called you while I was still not sure what was real." That was technically true, but if he'd given that testimony under oath in a courtroom, he'd have perjured himself. "Sorry about that."

Tanaka nodded slowly, and Michael tried not to hold his breath while waiting to see if he bought it. "Emily's disappearance must have your brain going back to Jen," he said at last.

"I guess so. I can't believe people take those drugs for fun."

"There are also people who watch home remodeling shows, and they give me nightmares, so it takes all kinds." Just when Michael was starting to relax, Tanaka asked, "Now, where are you off to?"

Michael fumbled for an answer that wouldn't be a lie. "I thought some fresh air would be good for me. I still can't be up long, but getting up and around every so often is good for preventing pneumonia." That was true, in a broad sense, though not about this specific moment. He hoped that was good enough not to trigger the "lie" buzzer in Tanaka's brain.

Tanaka studied him again for a beat too long. "Are you sure you're okay? Is there something you want to talk about, off the record? I'm not your training supervisor anymore, but I'm still your friend. I know this has to be rough for you."

"I appreciate that, Tank, I do. I won't say I'm fine, but I'm okay." And he was going to lose Sophie entirely if he didn't get away from here. With any luck, those two old ladies would be able to stop her.

Tanaka patted him on his good shoulder. "Okay, then, you hang in there, kid. Call if you need me—but only if you need me, not if you have a dream about needing me."

Michael gave a rueful grin and waved good-bye as Tanaka got into his double-parked car and drove off. As soon as he was gone, Michael headed for the park, aiming straight for the place where he'd lost Sophie before, but she wasn't there—either not there yet or long gone. He was startled when he heard her voice behind him. "What do you think you're doing?"

He turned around slowly. "I could ask you the same thing," he said. "I thought the plan was for us to do this together."

She glared at him. "I don't need you here."

"You need backup."

"You're too sick to be at work. You've got one good arm.

You're in obvious pain. And I don't even know if I can get you into the Realm."

"Plus, you're planning to turn yourself over to Maeve."

It was the first time he'd seen her look truly shocked. Her mouth opened, but no sound came out. Sophie Drake was at a loss for words. She shook her head. "Of course not. I wouldn't do that," she eventually stammered.

He pulled the sheet of lyrics out of his pocket. "It looks like blood is required, and you're afraid she'll use Emily's."

She seemed to sag inwardly. With a helpless shrug, she said, "She's my sister. What would you do?"

He nodded. "Yeah, I see your point. But you're willing to let Maeve win?"

A bit of her usual spark came back. "Have you met me? There's still a lot about this I don't know, and I think Maeve does or she wouldn't have recognized that the song fits. What's the best way to find out what she knows?"

"Once you're in her custody, you'll have her where you want her?"

"Something like that." Her smile was wicked, but it didn't last long. She paused for a moment, worrying her lower lip with her teeth, then stepped forward and held out Beau's leash. "Take care of Beau. Now that I think about it, I don't think he'll be that helpful in this situation."

"Is he ever helpful?" He took the leash, but said, "I should go with you."

"You'd just be in danger." She spun away from him and took off.

"Sophie!" he called out, hurrying to catch up with her, but before he reached her, she vanished into thin air. Beau gave a single harsh bark. "Yeah, me, too," Michael muttered as he caught his breath. He tucked the end of Beau's leash into his belt, then fumbled for his cell phone and called the sisters again to let them know where he was and what had happened.

They arrived so soon after his call that they had to have been very close by when Sophie disappeared. Just a few seconds, he thought,

a few seconds sooner and maybe they could have stopped her. "Now
what do we do?" he demanded as soon as they were in earshot.

"We can't get into the Realm," Amelia said. "There's nothing
we can do. I'm sorry."

"It's up to Sophie," Athena said.

"She has a plan. She's not just giving up," Michael said, as
much to boost his own spirits as to reassure them.

Athena nodded. "I wouldn't be surprised. I would just feel
better if she weren't alone."

He saw a glimpse of white out of the corner of his eye and
turned to see a little white cat, like the one he'd freed the night before
and seen again that morning. It ran up to him, hissed when Beau
barked at it, then twined itself around his ankles. He knelt to scratch
it behind the ears. "Hey there," he said softly.

"What is that?" Athena asked, leaning over.

"Last night when I was following Sophie to the market, I
found this cat tangled up in some wire. I helped it out."

The women exchanged a look. "He *is* a third brother," Athena
said with a smile.

The cat stepped away, heading toward the rocky embankment
beneath the park's walls. It paused to glance back at them and flicked
its tail.

"Is it my imagination, or does it look like it wants us to follow
it?" Michael asked.

"It's worth a try," Amelia said. "It's an animal that was helped
by a third brother. Let's see where it takes us."

With Beau leading the way, they followed the little cat, who
waited for them to catch up before continuing. "Okay, it definitely
wants us to follow it," Michael said. The cat led them to a gap
between two large stones.

"This could be a passage," Amelia said. "There are physical
passages into the Realm, but you have to be careful with those because
the Borderlands between our world and theirs are dangerous. Take
the wrong passage, and you might never actually make it into the

Realm. We've never dared enter the Realm that way because we lack the crucial information." She addressed the cat. "Is it safe?"

The cat meowed and ran between the rocks. "She seems to think it's safe enough," Michael remarked. "I'd better go in first, though."

"Which of us has magical powers and two good arms?" Athena replied with a wryly raised eyebrow. "I'm not even sure you'll fit."

"You're not leaving me behind."

A meow echoed from the passage, and Beau headed between the rocks. "Here goes nothing," Athena said, taking Beau's leash from Michael and crawling in after the dog. Amelia followed her. Michael hesitated, realizing that Athena had a point. It was going to be a tight squeeze, and crawling on one arm wouldn't be easy.

It turned out that the gap between the rocks was the hard part. Once he was all the way through, he was in a larger tunnel—too large to be hidden in Central Park. A light flared, and he blinked to see that Athena had a flashlight. "Come on," she called to him.

The flashlight barely made a dent in the darkness. He hardly noticed when they left the tunnel because it was too dark to tell that the walls were no longer an arm's length away. He could only tell that their footsteps made a different sound.

All he could see was a shining woman in white who waited near the end of the tunnel—the woman he'd seen in the park that morning and, now that he thought about it, who had tried to get him to dance the night before. "Come," she said. "I will guide you safely through the Borderlands."

"Lead on," Amelia said with a regal wave to the woman, who darted ahead into the darkness. To Michael, she added softly, "Don't thank her directly. Direct thanks and direct payment are avoided here. She's obligated to help you to release the debt she owes you. They don't like owing anything. But if you thank them, that makes you obliged, and that's not a position you want to be in. Now, keep your eyes and ears open. It could get dicey around here."

They were walking through what seemed to be a very dense forest full of thick, twisted tree trunks. Then he realized that the trunks were actually the roots of trees above. "Are we *under* the park?" he asked.

"In a sense," Athena answered. "We're between worlds."

"I'm assuming you know how to get out of here."

"We retrace our steps," Athena said with a too-casual shrug. "But that's a worst-case scenario. With any luck, we'll have Sophie to help us out."

The woman came to a stop and said, "I must leave you here. I can go no farther into the Realm. Follow the light." She raised her hand, and a small spark floated upward and hung in front of them.

"Th–" Michael began before remembering Amelia's lecture. "You've been a big help."

"As were you." She ran one small, white hand up his arm before running back the way they'd come.

"Now what?" Michael asked the sisters.

"We follow the light," Amelia said. The spark moved forward through the dense root forest. Michael was sorely tempted to chant about lions, tigers, and bears, but he suspected the women wouldn't be amused. They moved confidently forward, following the pinpoint of light and neatly stepping over any roots on the ground. Michael wasn't as sure of his footing, and since his feet were bigger than theirs, he couldn't step between roots as easily as they did. Once he stumbled so badly he nearly fell. Amelia caught him by his good arm and held him upright. "Are you sure you're up to this?" she asked.

"To be honest, no. But I have to do it."

"Very well, then. Watch your step. We can't carry you."

"Is there anything else I need to know while we're here?" he asked, mostly because the dead silence was getting on his nerves, but also because he had a feeling that the slightest mistake could be dangerous in this place.

"Don't drink or eat anything a fairy offers you," Athena said. "Eating the food here can trap you. Don't assume they're all enemies, but don't assume that the friendly ones are your friends. Their idea of morality is different from ours, and a 'good' fairy is generally one whose goals coincide with yours at that moment. Don't harm any trees or bushes or pick flowers. Be careful about gifts. They often comes with strings attached or with strict rules."

They moved onward. Something rustled in the darkness nearby, and he stifled a gasp. "What was that?" he whispered.

"I'm not sure," Athena whispered back. Beau barked at the sound, which soon stopped. "Good boy," Athena said to the dog.

It might have been Michael's imagination, but it seemed to be growing lighter. There were real trees growing out of the ground mixed in with the root trees. "Looks like we're almost there," he said.

"Be on the lookout," Amelia warned.

"For what?" He'd barely completed the question when something jumped on his back, on his left shoulder where he couldn't reach it with his right arm in a sling.

Forty-Two

Sophie steeled herself as she entered the Realm, expecting to find Maeve's people lying in wait for her. No one was there, but she suspected Maeve's ever-present spies would know the moment she arrived. Sophie supposed she should act as though she was going somewhere. They might get suspicious if she just sat there, waiting for them to catch her.

It was even colder than it had been the last time she was in the Realm, and the grass around her was dry and brown. Snowflakes fluttered to the ground, dusting it with a fine coating of white. Winter had come to the summer country, and that couldn't be good. She thought she heard a faint chorus of voices saying, "My lady," but she didn't see anyone nearby, just a never-ending expanse of dead grass. With the feeling she wasn't getting the whole picture, she lowered herself into a crouch to get a closer look, and then she couldn't hold back a gasp of surprise.

There was a whole world down there, populated with its own breed of fae creatures. These were tiny, no larger than her index finger. They wore bell-like flowers as clothing, but these creatures were nothing like the little flower fairies from a preschool ballet recital. They were ugly, more stick insects or praying mantis than human. Still, they had a glow about them so that from a distance they looked like fireflies flitting from place to place, and that gave them their own kind of beauty.

"My lady," they said, speaking as one, but not quite in unison. "We would offer our aid to you." Sophie wondered how they could possibly help her take down Maeve and free her captives. Maeve could grind them to dust with one stomp of her foot.

The grass around Sophie rippled subtly, then began to glow softly as more and more of the tiny creatures gathered around her. It might have been the effect of the glow, but the grass seemed to have come back to life. "Thanks, I've got things under control," she said.

A bluebell-clad creature that looked like a wizened stick insect flew up to her and perched on the hand she held out to it. "We are many. We may help," it said in a reedy voice.

Feeling like she was trapped in some twisted version of a Disney cartoon, she addressed the creature perched on her finger. "If I need you, I'll let you know."

"Call upon us whenever you wish," the creature said. The creature fluttered back to the ground, and Sophie stood and brushed the dirt and grass from her skirt. She'd be in dire straits, indeed, if she needed to be rescued by creatures such as that. Now, where were Maeve's goons? Did she have to wait around all night? Honestly, how did Maeve expect to rule the entire Realm when she couldn't manage to capture someone who was *trying* to turn herself in?

It looked like she'd have to meet Maeve halfway. Even in the Realm, she had to take care of the important things for herself. Now very conscious of how she placed her feet, she began walking, heading in no direction in particular but hoping that moving around would bring her within sight of one of Maeve's spies.

Finally, when she was ready to look for a place to sit down and rest, she saw movement out of the corner of her eye. One of

Maeve's Rat Pack goons lurked behind some nearby trees. Sophie's instinct was to prepare to defend herself or to go on the attack, but she squelched it.

Another goon showed up in a cluster of trees on her other side, and she was fairly certain there was yet another ahead of her, while she felt the itch between her shoulder blades that told her someone was watching her from behind. So far, though, they were all keeping their distance. She was tempted to play damsel in distress and say loudly, "Oh my, here I am, all helpless and alone," but after her previous encounters with Maeve's people, she had a feeling they'd think it was a trap. And it was, just not in the way they thought.

It looked like she'd have to make at least a token show of resistance before they'd make a move. She whirled as if just becoming aware of the follower, saw him, and took a few steps backward, feigning shock and fear. She felt the others close in on her, but they still kept their distance. When the silver chain flashed out from the hand of one of the men, it took all her willpower not to repel it or catch it and use it to disable her attackers. Instead, she shuddered as it circled her, binding her arms to her sides. Only when they had her securely bound did they approach her. Two of them grabbed the chain from either side and forced her to move forward.

"We're taking you to her majesty," one of them said, making it sound like a threat.

Sophie bit her tongue rather than say, "Finally!"

Forty-Three

"No, that's not it!" Maeve shouted as Emily botched yet another verse of the song.

"That's how I remember it," Emily said with a shrug. Two small sips of the fairy water had left her so energized that she felt she could keep this up for days. It was actually kind of fun.

The apartment's front door opened and a cluster of goons entered, surrounding a prisoner. Had they recaptured Eamon? The lead goons looked awfully pleased with themselves. They knelt in front of Maeve and said, "Your majesty, we have done your bidding." Then the goons parted, revealing their bound prisoner, and Emily's heart sank. It was Sophie.

"No!" she couldn't stop herself from blurting. This was the worst possible thing that could have happened. If her sister had swung in through the terrace doors with a dagger in her teeth, that would have been risky, considering that Sophie seemed to be the key to Maeve gaining power, but at least Sophie would have been in control of the situation. As a prisoner, with her arms bound... Well, that was a worst-case scenario.

But then Emily noticed that Sophie's hair was barely rumpled and her dress was only slightly wrinkled. Her captors were unharmed. Emily remembered how the others who'd tried to capture Sophie had looked after their ordeal, and she knew her sister fought like a wildcat when cornered. Sophie had to be up to something.

Emily tried to catch her sister's eye to verify her suspicion, but Sophie avoided looking at her directly, instead facing a Maeve who was too stunned with delight to speak. "You needed me. Now you have me. You don't need my sister anymore, so let her go, and then I'll help you win the throne," Sophie said, her voice calm and conversational, but with that bitchy undercurrent she got when dealing with someone who got on her nerves.

Maeve laughed harshly. "You would like that, wouldn't you?"

"Well, *yes*," Sophie drawled, sounding like she was losing patience. "That *was* why I asked for it. Now, do you want to be queen, or what?"

Maeve approached Sophie and loomed over her. "No, I think I'll keep her awhile longer, in case I was mistaken about you. She will come with us." She turned to address her court. "As will all of you! You will see my moment of triumph."

Maeve waved her arms, and her glamour shifted so that she wore a gown that looked like it had been woven from spun gold. It had a low-cut bodice and the kind of high collar usually worn by a Disney villainess. The long sleeves came to points on the backs of her hands. A snug straight skirt hugged her body, and a puffy half skirt flared out behind her, trailing onto the ground. Emily was pretty sure she'd seen a dress like that in a movie, but she couldn't recall which one. Maybe it was pieces from various movies.

A flicker of a smile crossed Sophie's lips when Maeve wasn't looking, confirming Emily's suspicions that Sophie was up to something. She probably had a whole fairy army lying in wait for a major ambush that would rescue all the human captives. When Maeve least expected it, Sophie would open a can of whoop-ass and do her thing. Emily actually felt sorry for Maeve. She thought she had Sophie trapped, but Sophie wasn't someone you wanted to catch. It would be like setting a trap for a kitten and instead snaring a wild bobcat. Even freeing the cat could be hazardous to your health.

Maeve gestured for her guards to open the front doors. Two of them led the way. Maeve swept after them, and the other guards brought Sophie behind her. Emma/Jen and Leigh hooked their elbows through Emily's, bringing her along with them. They passed through the lobby, where the rest of the court joined the procession.

After walking for some time, they entered a narrow gap between tree-crested hills. It was the perfect site for an ambush, and Emily readied herself for a fight. She scanned the hillsides, looking for evidence of hidden warriors, but either they weren't there or they were very well hidden. She looked to Sophie for a cue, but Sophie was walking with her usual grace that made her look like she was floating, even with her arms bound against her sides. Nothing happened. There was no signal, no war cry, no sudden flurry of chaos.

And then the whole procession was out on the other side, totally unscathed. Emily felt the first stirrings of dread. Was Sophie really sacrificing herself for her?

The procession stopped at a wide, weed-choked stream. On the other side lay a tangled mass of thorny vines that might have had a wall beneath it at one time. Emily wouldn't have been surprised if Sleeping Beauty's castle lay behind those vines. Maeve made a good candidate for the role of evil fairy in that story.

The guards shoved Sophie forward to face Maeve, who was gloating so hard she glowed even more brightly than normal. "Here we are!" she said with a gesture toward the water and the vines on the other side. "This is why I will be queen. The other rulers don't even know where to find the palace, but I found this long ago. All I needed was to learn how to get into it."

"And that's where I come in," Sophie said, sounding suspiciously calm. Maeve didn't know her well enough to recognize the danger she was in from that tone, but Emily had heard it before. That tone tended to come up when Sophie let others talk about what they wanted to do before she let them know that she already had everything arranged.

Maeve gave a laugh that sounded more than a little unbalanced. "Yes, that is where you come in. You never knew what treasure you held, all this time. Your grandmother's song that you sang so sweetly to us when you were a mere child is the key to winning the throne." Her tone grew darker and she seemed to grow as she moved closer to Sophie and bent to stare her straight in the eye. "And now you will give that song to me."

Forty-Four

It took every ounce of Sophie's formidable self-control not to reveal the turbulence inside her. She had to count to five with each breath to keep from gasping. Michael *had* been right about the song. It was instructions. And here was the lost palace, behind the vine-covered walls.

So, now what?

She needed to keep Maeve from using the instructions in the song to take the throne and she needed to free the captives. Stopping Maeve wouldn't be too difficult, given that the instructions in the song were hardly clear and were, in fact, impossible. But there were too many of Maeve's courtiers around for her to be able to just grab Emily and make a run for it.

Maeve glared at Sophie and said, "The song?"

"Oh, it's been *ages* since I've heard it," Sophie lied. She had no intention of just rolling over, whether or not the song could help Maeve.

Maeve came closer to her, her lips twitching slyly. "Don't lie to me. I know you won't have forgotten this. You had to learn it for a reason. Now, tell me the first part. I remember it having something to do with how to cross the river."

Acting as though she was deeply reluctant, Sophie sighed, took a deep breath and sang, "To reach my side, tell her to cross a river wide that has no bridge. If she can cross not wetting her feet, then she will know the way to my heart."

Maeve turned to study the river. "That is easy!" she said after a while. "I am fae. I can fly across." She spread her arms and a wind stirred the outer skirt of her gown. She rose slowly into the air and moved forward. Sophie bit her lip as she watched. She'd forgotten to factor in magical powers when ruling the tasks impossible. In the Realm this might be considered child's play. She consoled herself with the knowledge that there were other tasks before they got to the part involving blood. She had plenty of time to stop Maeve.

Before she was over the river, Maeve seemed to hit an invisible wall that knocked her onto her backside. Sophie barely restrained herself from doubling over with laughter. Even some of the most staunch members of Maeve's court appeared to fight back smiles.

Maeve's skin-tight inner skirt made it impossible for her to stand with any dignity. She held her hands up and snapped, "Will someone help me?" It took two of her courtiers to pull her to her feet. A couple of women rushed forward to straighten her gown and brush the dust off it. Once she'd regathered her dignity, Maeve turned to face Sophie. "You did that!" she snarled. "I have heard about your enchantress powers. Do not thwart me, girl!"

"I had nothing to do with that," Sophie said primly, even as she mentally berated herself for not having thought to try. "It would seem that you can't use magic to complete these tasks."

"Do you know a way across?"

"Why should I? Until a few moments ago, I thought it was a silly nonsense song." Sophie eyed the distance between Maeve and the water. One good shove and Maeve's feet would get wet, which would presumably render this whole exercise moot. She gathered her magical resources and focused on the chain binding her, loosening it so that she'd be able to pull her arms free. When Maeve turned to study the river, Sophie made her move, letting the chain slide to the ground and then grabbing one of her captors to shove him at Maeve.

He checked himself just in time, lurching aside rather than hitting Maeve. Sophie prepared to spring at Maeve, but a voice behind her called, "Stop!" Sophie whirled to see the other human woman—the one who wasn't Jen Murray—with her arm tight against Emily's neck, choking her. "If you hinder her majesty, we will hurt your sister." Jen still held onto Emily's arms. Emily's face was turning red, but Sophie couldn't tell if that was because she couldn't breathe or because she was furious.

Sophie had thought she wouldn't have to worry about a hostage situation with fairies because it wasn't in their nature, but she'd neglected to factor in what their human allies might do. She took a step away from Maeve and raised her hands in surrender. Only when the woman lowered her arm slightly and Emily's color returned to normal did Sophie turn to face Maeve.

Maeve smiled in smug triumph and said, "Now, if you want your sister to live, you will help me win my throne."

For the first time, Sophie felt a real surge of panic because she had no idea what to do.

Forty-Five

The Borderlands
Meanwhile

Michael shouted when he felt the thing jump on his back. He tried to keep the panic out of his voice because it was wrong for an experienced cop to be more frightened than two old ladies, but this was beyond anything he'd experienced. Facing enemies he couldn't see and couldn't defend himself against was scarier than confronting armed thugs.

Amelia raised a hand and he felt the thing leave his shoulder. The area around them suddenly grew quieter. "There, that's better," she said with some satisfaction. "I don't know how long it will hold, so we'd better keep going."

They'd almost made it to the light when a great whirring roar surrounded them. "What's this, the flying monkeys?" Michael asked.

"Can you run?" Athena asked in reply.

"To get away from this? I'll try." He felt things pulling at his clothes and his hair.

"Then run!"

They took off, Beau putting on more speed than Michael would have believed possible. The sound dimmed as they drew closer to the light, but he still felt like some of those things were attached to his clothes. He wanted to keep running when he ran straight into Athena, who had stopped.

"It's okay, it's over, I think," she said, sounding only slightly out of breath. He gasped for air while an invisible vise clamped down on his chest. It was a forcible reminder of why they didn't even want him working at a precinct desk yet.

A voice calling, "You!" caught their attention. Michael looked up to see a silver-haired man approaching.

"I think this is the guy who kidnapped Emily," Michael said between gasps, wishing he had his gun with him.

"Yes," the man said matter-of-factly. "I am Eamon. And you are Sophie's friend, the man with the badge of office. Where is Sophie?"

Michael shook his head in confusion. "You kidnapped Emily and you've talked to Sophie and you're still alive?"

"I am trying to help. I explained myself to Sophie. Where is she?"

"She's here. We were coming to help her. I think she's gone to Maeve."

Eamon looked alarmed. "She was warned to stay away from Maeve," he said. "She's the one Maeve needs."

"She knows that, but she's trying to protect Emily," Athena said.

"Do you know how to find Maeve?" Amelia asked. "I believe that would be the best starting point."

"I believe I know where Maeve will go if she has Sophie." Michael noticed that his wrists were horribly burned. He wasn't sure exactly how fairy people were supposed to look, but this guy looked like hell.

"You've found the palace?" Amelia asked.

"Maeve did. Emily found her map, and I think I can locate the palace now. If Maeve has Sophie, we must get there first." He turned to go, the others falling in behind him. Michael hadn't had nearly enough time to catch his breath, but he forced himself to continue.

When they left the woods, they came out into a parklike land dotted with trees. Michael wasn't sure how fairyland was supposed to look, but this wasn't it. Everything was drab and brown. "Try not to get too caught up in it," Athena warned. "It can be very alluring."

"Only if you're into winter."

The others turned to stare at him. "Is that what you see?" Amelia asked.

"Yeah. You don't?"

"He has a four-leaf clover," Athena said. "Sophie said the Realm was dying."

"What does it look like to you?" Michael asked.

"It's bright and colorful, like a Technicolor movie," Amelia said.

"It's a glamour to hide the true state of things," Eamon said. "Most of us prefer not to see the truth."

They stopped at the edge of a forest, beyond which a grassy expanse sloped down to a river. Across the river was a towering wall of thorny vines. Michael started to ask why they'd stopped, but then he saw that they hadn't arrived first. Maeve was already there in what looked like a showdown with Sophie. Michael felt a pang when he saw Jen and another red-haired girl with a bedraggled-looking Emily between them. Not only was Jen not trying to escape, but she was helping hold Emily. She couldn't possibly realize what she was doing, he told himself. More fairies dressed in that Rat Pack style were part of the group.

"Now what?" Michael asked Amelia. He doubted that two old women, a sick fairy, a wounded cop, and a bulldog would be able to free the captives, but he felt like they ought to do *something*.

Amelia frowned in thought for a moment before giving a very Sophie-like smile. "Let's see what happens."

Forty-Six

Sophie tried to buy time by saying, "Let me think about it."

"Why do you need to think?" Maeve snapped.

"You're fae and you don't know what to do," Sophie pointed out. "What do you expect of a human?"

"My people will hurt your sister if you don't give me what I want."

"Yes, I quite understand that." Sophie doubted that Tallulah would see Emily's peril as a valid excuse for not honoring an obligation. Even so, she wasn't going to let harm come to her sister. The problem was, she had no clue how to get Maeve across the river without getting her feet wet, not if flying didn't work. A boat, maybe? But where was she supposed to get a boat?

Then she noticed the water. It sparkled the way wind-whipped water did when the sun hit it at the right angle, but there was no wind. She stared longer at the sparkling water and realized that the light was coming from below the surface. It was the small creatures she'd seen earlier and so casually dismissed. They must have followed her. Could they help? They were small, but there were a lot of them. And she was desperate. Swallowing the lump in her throat, she said,

"It might be nice if I had some help with this. I may not be able to do it alone."

"Do it, or else," Maeve warned.

Hoping the small fairies had understood her plea, Sophie went to stand at the water's edge. A large lily pad emerged from the water in front of her, like a stepping stone. It didn't look like it would support human weight, but she hoped this was the help she'd asked for. Taking a deep breath while trying to look totally calm and confident, she stepped out on to the lily pad. Another one immediately appeared in front of her.

She turned back to Maeve. "It looks like all you need is a little faith," she said. That applied as much to her as to Maeve. Stepping into the unknown with her fate entirely in someone else's hands wasn't in her nature. Without waiting to see what Maeve would do, she forced herself to step forward onto the next lily pad. Another appeared in front of her.

Maeve wrestled with indecision for a moment, then she waved her hands over her dress until it shortened and the skirt flared. Her shoes changed into flats similar to those Sophie wore, but gold like her dress. She stepped onto the lily pad, and Sophie stepped onto the next one. They moved across the river that way, one lily pad at a time, with Maeve stepping directly behind Sophie.

Just before Sophie reached the shore, Maeve pushed her from behind. Sophie's balance was excellent, but the lily pad dipped dangerously to one side. Getting her feet wet didn't worry her, since she didn't care about gaining the throne for herself, but she didn't want to fall into the water. Then the lily pad shifted, rising higher so she remained dry. With a silent thanks to her allies, Sophie jumped off the pad onto the shore, then turned to see a scowling Maeve step onto the final pad, which quickly dipped. Sophie was sure she saw water lapping over Maeve's foot, but Maeve acted as though nothing had happened as she stepped onto the shore. All the lily pads disappeared beneath the water. Sophie caught a glimpse of glimmers under the water near the shore where she stood.

She turned to see the vines on one section of the wall parting slowly, uncoiling from each other to reveal a drawbridge. When the vines had moved completely, the drawbridge creakily lowered, bridging the river and opening a portal through the walls into a wildly overgrown garden. They'd made it past the first task, but she didn't celebrate. After all, she'd brought Maeve one step closer to the throne.

Maeve called across the river to her people, "Bring the captives here, and then keep anyone else from crossing this bridge." Two of the guards escorted Emily, Jen, and the other redhaired woman over the bridge, and while they were halfway across, Maeve grabbed Sophie's arm and hustled her through the doorway into the garden. As soon as all of them passed through the entry, a heavy golden portcullis dropped behind them with an ominous clang.

Sophie had the sinking feeling that no one would leave these walls until a new queen had been crowned. Even if she stopped Maeve, they might not be able to escape.

Forty-Seven

When the drawbridge fell, Amelia turned to the others and said, "Be ready to run for it." Michael wasn't sure he was up to much more running, but he thought he could handle the hundred or so feet between him and the drawbridge. His heart gave a painful lurch that had nothing to do with his gunshot wound when he saw Jen and that other woman walking Emily across the bridge, and then he had to bite his lip to keep from shouting when the golden bars filled the entryway, trapping Jen and the others inside.

Amelia muttered a very unladylike curse as the portal closed. To make matters worse, Maeve's people moved to block the bridge, like they were expecting invaders.

The sound of a hunting horn rang out, and Eamon groaned.

"What is it?" Michael asked.

"Fiontan and Niamh are coming," Eamon explained. "They are among the other rulers. They must have followed Maeve."

Athena smirked. "Hang on to your hat. This will get interesting."

"How interesting?" Michael asked.

"War," Eamon answered.

Men on horseback topped the nearby hill and rode full-on toward Maeve's people. Michael couldn't tell how many there were, they rode by in such a furious blur, but he got the impression of great numbers.

Then yet another group appeared. These looked less fierce. They weren't on horseback and they didn't carry lances, swords, or spears. They looked more like they were set to party everyone to death, and they were dressed like something out of a badly colorized black-and-white movie, but then one of the men pulled a Tommy gun from inside his coat, and Michael realized they were serious. "I knew Niall and Orla wouldn't miss this," Eamon said with a nod. Still more groups arrived, all in historical attire from various eras. It was like a mob war had broken out on Halloween.

"What do we do?" Michael asked anyone who might have an answer.

"Nothing," Amelia replied. "We let them fight it out, and if we get a chance, we run for the drawbridge."

If Michael had any illusions about how dangerous fairies were, they were shattered by the battle that broke out among them—a battle that stood between him and Jen, Sophie, and Emily.

Forty-Eight

The Keep
Meanwhile

Emily flinched when she heard the portcullis drop. A few moments later when she heard the hunting horn, she was glad she was locked inside. She might have been stuck with Maeve, but she was also with Sophie, and when things got sticky, it was always best to be near Sophie.

The garden looked like what grew around the ruins of antebellum mansions back home, something that had been planted with care but which had gone wild since then. Hedges of rosebushes grew well above her head on either side of a white path, with other plants scrambling for position at the base of the hedges. The air was heavy with the perfume of the roses.

"Now the path," Maeve said to Sophie. "Sing that part."

"To reach my side, tell her to walk down a path of shale and shell. But she must not step upon a shell or she won't find the way to my heart," she sang, then added, "And, no, it doesn't say how. Presumably, those who are worthy will be able to figure that out for themselves." Emily could hear the suppressed laughter in Sophie's voice as she added, "Somehow I doubt flying is the answer."

Maeve bent to study the pathway. "But the stones are all intermingled," she said. "It is impossible to walk without treading on shells, not even the way you dance on your toes."

Sophie shrugged. "Well, if you want to give up…"

Maeve straightened and whirled on Sophie, grabbing her by the arm. "You know how to do it, don't you? I demand that you tell me." Emily held her breath, knowing they were in dangerous territory and things were likely to get ugly very soon. She looked for something to hide under or behind and wondered if she could maneuver her two captors to be between her and whatever explosion Sophie set off.

But Sophie allowed herself to be shaken like a rag doll. When Maeve stopped shaking her, Sophie said calmly, "I can clear a path." She reached with her free hand and delicately removed Maeve's fingers from her arm before turning to face the pathway. She raised her arms toward the path and sang something that Emily recognized as a list of ballet steps in French. She bit her lip to stop herself from giggling. Oh yeah, Sophie was up to something, and she couldn't wait to see what it was.

Whatever Sophie did couldn't have been total nonsense, though, because a glowing spot appeared in front of her on the path. The glow then shrank from the middle of the spot, leaving a ring. Sophie stepped into the ring and another glowing spot appeared in front of her. She turned back to Maeve. "This works like crossing the river. Follow in my footsteps, but be careful."

Maeve glanced over her shoulder at Emily and the others. "May they follow?"

"If they're not trying for the throne, I imagine it won't matter where they step once we've gone down the path."

Sophie moved on to the next glowing spot, and Maeve cautiously followed her onto the first spot. Emily thought she saw a bit of the glow dart back into the center before Maeve stepped. When Maeve had taken a few steps, she called back to the others, "Follow us. I want witnesses to my triumph."

As they moved onto the path, Emily heard the sounds of battle outside the walls. She'd seldom doubted her older sister, but this time, she really hoped Sophie knew what she was doing. If she didn't, the consequences could be dire.

Forty-Nine

Outside the Keep
Meanwhile

Maeve's people weren't able to guard the bridge for very long once they were drawn into the battle. Unfortunately, the battle also kept Michael and the others away from the bridge. Although the various factions had very distinct attire and weapons, in the melee it was hard to tell who was on which side. "Who do we want to win?" Michael asked Eamon.

"We want them to destroy each other," the fairy said, his voice ice-cold. "It will be better for the Realm if all of them are weakened."

Athena tugged on Michael's sleeve. "I think we can make it now," she said. A path had opened, but the fighting was so chaotic that Michael wasn't sure how long it would remain open. He was still recovering from a gunshot. He had no desire to add a sword wound.

Keeping his bad arm tight against his chest, he ran behind the two old women and Beau as Eamon brought up the rear. When they reached the drawbridge, Michael turned back and fished in his pocket, coming up with a handful of iron nails. "Go on," he told Eamon before scattering the nails on the ground at the end of the bridge. Then he crossed the bridge and joined the others.

Now they were on the other side of the river, but they were still trapped outside the keep. He wasn't sure that they were in a better position, other than having a river between them and the battle. "Can we get past that?" he asked.

"Give us a moment," Amelia said, then she and Athena put their heads together. Peering between the golden bars, Michael spied Jen, Emily, and the other redheaded woman heading down a path between walls of overgrown rosebushes toward the center of a wild garden.

Fifty

The Garden
Meanwhile

Sophie reached the end of the path, then turned to watch Maeve finish following in her footsteps. A faint flutter of glow receded into the hedges, and Sophie sent another silent thanks to her tiny allies. As much as she hated to admit it, it was rather nice to not have to do everything for herself. But was it cheating to get help?

No, she decided. Fairy tales were full of stories about people who succeeded because they got help like that. Maybe that was even the test. One had to prove worthiness to rule by admitting one couldn't do it all and by recognizing the contributions of the tiniest and ugliest members of the Realm. Besides, it wasn't as though *she* was trying for the throne. She was merely making it look like she was helping Maeve while still blocking her.

Maeve came to the end of the path. "Isn't there supposed to be a maze?" she asked, staring at the unbroken wall of hedge that created a dead end.

"Yes, and the song gives instructions on getting through the maze," Sophie replied.

"But how do we enter the maze? The hedges must have grown

up. There has to be an entry in here somewhere." Maeve stuck her hands into the hedges and tried to push the branches apart. It would have been lovely if the hedges had bit her arms off at the elbows, thought Sophie, but all they did was snag on Maeve's sleeves.

"The song tells how," Sophie said.

The others caught up to them. "Why are you helping her, Sophie?" Emily asked. Sophie resolutely avoided looking at her sister.

Maeve answered for her. "If she wants to take you back home, she has to help me."

"Sophie, it's not worth it!" Sophie caught the faint trace of amusement in Emily's voice. Now Sophie *really* had to avoid looking at Emily, lest the two of them break down in giggles the moment they made eye contact.

The only problem was, Sophie wasn't sure what she could do to keep Maeve from winning the throne while also saving Emily and the others. Her allies may have helped by wetting Maeve's feet and putting a few shells in her path, but was that really enough to disqualify her, or was that just poetic license to make a better song?

"Sing the next verse," Maeve ordered.

"To reach my side, tell her to find a perfect rose to offer me. The petals fall and pave the way to open wide the door to my heart," Sophie sang.

Maeve stared with dismay at the walls of rosebushes surrounding them. "Which one is perfect?" she asked. "There must be some trickery here." Gesturing at her people, she demanded, "Help me search. Look for a perfect bloom." Sophie suspected that wasn't the way to go. The only thing picking a perfect rose got anyone in a fairy tale was captivity in the home of a hideous beast. But what would the perfect rose be in this situation?

She saw one full-headed bloom lying on the ground. As she knelt to study it, she heard Jen call out, "This one looks perfect!" Whatever she'd found, it couldn't be as perfect as the one Sophie had noticed. This rose had opened fully, and the velvety red petals had darkened almost to black. It was a rose that had lived a full life.

She cupped it gently in both hands and stood. Maeve and her

people were severing a bloom from a bush at the head of the path. Maeve grabbed it as soon as it was free from the bush, then waved it at the hedge that dead-ended the path. "Open for your queen!" she shouted.

At the same time, Sophie opened her hands and let her rose fall in a shower of petals. They lingered in the air, drifting slowly to the ground, as the branches of the hedge parted to form a doorway.

Maeve shouted in triumph and grabbed Sophie by the elbow. Her other hand still held the rose by the stem. "Guide us through the maze," she ordered.

"To reach my side, tell her to turn always looking to the right," Sophie sang. She moved into the maze and took the first right turn, and then each right that came up after that. Maeve, Emily, and the rest followed. It was a complex maze that could easily befuddle anyone who didn't have directions. Sophie didn't notice any skeletons lying along the pathways, and she wondered if anyone had ever made it this far. Instead of leading to the center, this maze took travelers to the other side. When she could see only one wall of hedges remaining, she sang, "One last left turn will bring her home, where she will find the way to my heart." She turned to the left there, and they were out of the maze.

They came out in front of a wall whose veil of thorny vines was even denser than that of the outer keep. "This is *so* Sleeping Beauty," Emily remarked. "What we need now is a prince with a magic sword."

Maeve released Sophie's arm and shoved the rose into her hand. Sophie winced as a thorn dug into her skin. "There has to be a way inside," Maeve said, moving forward to study the wall. "What does the song say?"

Sophie hummed it to herself, then said, "It doesn't say anything about this."

"There's a door here," Maeve said. A glittering knife appeared in her gloved hand, and she hacked at the vines until the doorway was clear. The door opened easily, without the slightest squeak or creak of hinges even though the door most likely hadn't moved in centuries. Maeve reached back and grabbed Sophie's arm to pull her through the doorway with her. It was such a jolt that Sophie momentarily lost her balance and put out a hand to steady herself on the door jamb as she passed. She left a slight smear of blood from the prick of the rose's thorn, and she sent a quick mental apology to whomever was maintaining this place.

As soon as she was over the threshold, the door slammed shut behind her. Both she and Maeve whirled at the sound, and Maeve tried to open the door again, but it refused to budge. She turned back to Sophie with an evil glint in her eyes. "All the better. When you win my throne for me, no one will be the wiser."

"I'm telling you how to win the throne for yourself," Sophie said, refusing to back away from Maeve's menace. "I'd think you'd want witnesses for that."

Maeve laughed madly. "You do not know, do you? You have no idea what you are. Do you think I wouldn't have seized the throne the moment I heard your silly little song if that had been all it took?"

"I know it takes blood," Sophie said, glancing at the smear she'd left on the door jamb.

"The key is whose blood it is. Now, come. We must go through yet another garden if we're ever to find the palace."

Sophie barely managed to stop a double take. As far as she could tell, they *were* in a palace. There were marble floors and gilded walls in a corridor that seemed to go on forever. There wasn't a garden in sight. As she followed Maeve, their footsteps echoed, and all Sophie could think of was what the requirement of blood might mean for her.

Fifty-One

The battle raged on the far side of the river, and Michael watched in sick fascination while he waited for Amelia and Athena to find a way past those golden bars. Eamon gave a clinical running commentary, sounding like a play-by-play analyst on a football broadcast. "That seems to be the last of Maeve's people to fall," he said. "Even if she wins the throne, she will have to fight to keep it, for she will have little support."

"Would there be a revolution?"

"There has never been one in my time, but I would not be surprised."

"Just how old are you?" Michael couldn't resist asking.

"It is difficult to say, since time passes differently in the Realm, but I remember a time before the Church came to Ireland."

Michael was still staring at him, trying to remember when Saint Patrick lived, when Amelia and Athena cried out in triumph. He turned to see the portcullis slowly rising. "Hurry, run through!" Athena panted. "We can't hold it long."

Michael and Eamon ducked underneath, then the two women and Beau barely made it before the portcullis dropped with a resounding clang. Michael felt like he'd been imprisoned. He tried to adjust his perspective to think of himself as having escaped to the outside of the bars, but he still felt trapped.

"Now, down this path," Amelia instructed. Michael was so out of breath he had trouble keeping up with the two old women, and Beau strained at his leash, trying to go even faster.

At the end of the path stood a head-high wall of hedges with a doorway cut into it. Michael reached for the sheet of song lyrics in his pocket. "I think the song gives the key to the maze," he said. "There's something about keeping to the right."

Without speaking, Amelia raised her hand and pointed at the hedges ahead of them. A passage appeared down the middle. "I prefer to take the direct route," she said with a wink. "After all, we aren't trying to win the throne."

They arrived in a courtyard outside another vine-covered wall just in time to see Sophie disappear through a doorway. Jen, Emily, that other woman, and a couple of guards rushed toward the door, but it slammed shut in their faces and the vines snaked across the door, blocking access. One of the guards tried unsuccessfully to cut the vines away.

"The door won't open until a ruler is chosen," Amelia said, and the group turned to face the newcomers.

Emily's face lit up, and she jerked her arms away from the women on either side of her to rush forward. Michael braced himself for a hug, but she ran past him to Eamon. She stopped in front of the fairy as her grin faded to a scowl. "I thought you'd abandoned me."

"I saw no reason for both of us to remain captive."

She nodded, considering that. "Okay, I can see that. And you did bring help."

"As well as spread the word of Maeve's plans."

Emily's grin returned, and she threw her arms around him in a joyous embrace that looked suspiciously affectionate. Michael exchanged a worried look with Athena and Amelia. He doubted

Sophie would like her sister hooking up with a fairy, no matter how helpful he was.

It wasn't his problem, though. He'd let the Drake sisters fight it out, assuming they all survived this. Beau took care of things in the meantime. He wandered over to Emily and butted her in the leg with his head, forcing her away from Eamon until she bent to hug her dog.

Michael had his own problem to deal with, the wife who still stared at him like he was an unwelcome stranger. "Hello again, Jen," he said softly.

"That's not my name," she insisted.

"It used to be," he said. "That's what I called you."

She shook her head. "I don't know you. I don't even know your name."

"I'm Michael."

She moved closer, frowning. "You wore a uniform."

His heart leapt. "Yes! When we met, I was a patrol officer, and I wore a uniform."

She smiled up at him and said, "Her majesty will soon rule the entire Realm, and I will be in her court. I'll be a princess."

He fought not to groan in disappointment. How could he hope to compete against being a fairy princess? "That's nice," he said blandly.

She spun away and flounced over to one of the guards, wrapping her arm around his waist and resting her head on his shoulder. "And you will be my prince," she purred. Michael closed his eyes from a pain that was worse than his throbbing gunshot wound.

"You're all that's left of Maeve's court," Eamon said, his voice cutting harshly through the mood. "The others have been slaughtered outside."

"The other courts will suffer when her majesty is made queen," the other woman snarled.

Emily glanced at Michael and rolled her eyes. "They drank the Kool-Aid," she said. "Literally."

"Sophie's alone in there with Maeve?" Michael asked.

"Yeah. But I think she's up to something. I've never seen her that quiet and passive. That means an explosion is brewing. I wonder if there's a fallout shelter near here."

"What do we do?" Michael had never felt so helpless, not even after he was shot and lying in that hallway bleeding and fighting for breath.

"We wait, Detective Murray," Athena said with a pat on his arm. "We wait and see just how formidable our Miss Drake really is."

ᘺFifty-Twoᘺ

The corridor finally ended in a great hall so massive that Sophie couldn't see the ceiling. Slender windows that went from the floor all the way up the walls would have filled the hall with light if they hadn't been covered with vines. Through gaps in the vines, shafts of light dappled the marble floors.

In the hall, a great feast had been laid out. The food looked fresh, not like it had been sitting for centuries. Even if she hadn't known that eating fairy food was dangerous, Sophie would have been suspicious of this magical feast.

"Ah, refreshments!" Maeve said, moving toward the table. She filled a goblet from a pitcher of wine and drank deeply. Apparently, fairies didn't have fairy tales, Sophie thought. Maeve didn't keel over immediately, but that wasn't generally the way things like this worked. There was no telling what the spell might be. "Such a strange place for a feast, though," she remarked as she took a handful of grapes from a bowl. "Here, in the middle of a garden."

"It's a picnic," Sophie said, trying to keep her tone even and calm in spite of her inner agitation. There was only one verse left in the song, the one involving blood that would presumably secure the throne, and she didn't know if she—or her allies—had done enough to thwart Maeve. Sophie was on her own once more. Her tiny helpers appeared to have been locked outside, and she was surprised to find that she missed having backup.

While Maeve ate, Sophie glanced around the hall, assessing her surroundings. There, at the very far end of the hall, which was practically on another continent, stood a tall silver throne. Without realizing what she was doing, she walked slowly toward it.

In spite of the distance, it seemed like no time before she stopped in front of the steps that led up to the dais where the throne sat. From this angle, the throne towered above her, gleaming in the dappled light. For such a large, heavy object, it looked surprisingly delicate. Its back was a tall Gothic arch, and it was carved and filigreed in a pattern that looked like it was woven from ivy vines and then turned into silver. She began climbing the steps, drawn inexorably toward it.

As her foot landed on the top step, she got a prickling feeling between her shoulder blades and spun just in time to see Maeve rushing toward her.

"You will not take my throne!" the fairy shrieked, her eyes wild. She grabbed Sophie's arm and threw her to the ground. Sophie didn't have a chance to react before Maeve's knife flashed at her, slashing across her inner wrist and sending blood gushing to the surface. Maeve clasped Sophie's bleeding wrist and brought away a hand gloved in blood. Shoving Sophie away, she approached the throne.

First she raised her bloody hand in triumph, then she placed her hand on the arm of the throne and shouted, "It is mine! At last!" Slowly and regally, she lowered herself onto the throne and gripped the arms.

Sophie held her breath, waiting to see what would happen while she pressed the hem of her skirt against the bleeding wound on her arm. *Something* should happen to verify that the throne had been taken. Otherwise, why bother with all those tests, trials, and obstacles? There should be flashing lights or royal trumpets. At the very least, the vines should disappear from the windows as the castle came back to life.

But none of these things happened. Even Maeve seemed disconcerted, like she wasn't sure it had really worked. "You," she hissed at Sophie. "You did something. You tricked me."

"Maybe," Sophie admitted through teeth gritted against the pain in her arm. She was starting to get lightheaded, though surely she couldn't have lost that much blood yet. Slitting one's wrists was supposed to be an ineffective suicide method. You had to do it in warm water to keep the blood from clotting before you bled out. Not that she'd studied suicide methods. She'd merely watched more than a few crime shows on TV. Her father had liked those. Then she realized her mind was wandering and forced her focus back to the present.

Maeve leaned forward, half rising out of the throne, but thought better of that and sat back down. "What have you done? Why is the throne not accepting me as its rightful ruler?"

"Maybe because you *aren't* its rightful ruler. Did you think you could trick something like this?"

"What didn't you tell me?" Maeve demanded.

Feeling more and more lightheaded, Sophie laughed. "I was the one who asked them for help, and they only helped me," she said. "They got your feet wet, and I'm fairly certain they moved a few shells back into your path. Oh, and I was the one who found the right rose. But your rose helped, too." She held up the thumb that had been pricked. "That's what brought us into the palace."

"We aren't in the palace," Maeve thundered. "We're still in the garden. There is no palace."

"You don't see it? We've been in the palace ever since we came through the door. I suppose my blood only works for me." She forced herself to rise to her knees. "And you have to think that with something like this, there's a penalty for cheating. In all the stories, bad things happen to unworthy people who try to steal power."

It was difficult to tell when someone with porcelain skin went pale, but Maeve's skin took on a chalky look, and she lost all her fairy radiance. Then she pitched forward. Although the throne didn't move at all, it looked as though it had ejected her. Sophie barely rolled out of the way so that Maeve didn't fall on top of her. Her vision was growing blurry, and she heard a roaring in her ears. She'd feel so much better if she could just rest for a while. Maeve wasn't moving, so it should be safe. She closed her eyes with a sigh.

As she drifted off, she thought of her sister, of Michael and his wife. Maeve might have been thwarted, but this wasn't over. She forced her eyes open and struggled back to her knees, but she was growing weaker and weaker. Could she really have lost that much blood already? It wasn't a large wound, but it had possibly been an enchanted knife. Losing her balance, she reached out her bloody hands for the nearest object on which to steady herself: the throne.

A burst of strength shot through her. She got to her feet, then practically fell onto the throne. It was as though the throne had pulled her to it. Then the universe exploded.

When her vision cleared, the hall was entirely different. The vines were gone from the windows, so the odd Realm light streamed through. Courtiers milled about in diaphanous raiment. The distant front doors to the hall flew open, and a cluster of guards moved forward. When they were halfway to the dais, she could see that they surrounded a human man dressed in what she guessed to be Renaissance attire. He showed no sign of fear, in spite of being a prisoner. In fact, he gave the impression that they'd done exactly what he wanted.

"So, you have come to slay the queen of the Realm," she heard herself saying. Although the voice wasn't hers, the words seemed to come out of her mouth. She had the sense that she found the man interesting. With his bright red hair and beard and his aura of power, he might have been fae, himself.

"I've come to empty the throne, one way or another," he said in a rich Irish brogue.

"Why do you care about the affairs of a Realm in an entirely different plane of existence?" she asked.

"Because your people have been invading our world and causing no end of trouble."

"And you think that removing me from my throne will stop that?"

"If the Realm isn't united, the fae will have other things to worry about."

She laughed. "And I won't go riding through your world, scooping up dreamers, collecting the fealty that's owed to me, or stealing babies. Is that it?"

"That's the sum of it, yes," he said.

Smiling to herself, she asked, "How do you plan to remove me from my throne?"

He raised his arms, flinging the guards aside magically, and rushed up the dais steps, grabbed her hand, and pulled her to her feet. "Something like this," he said with roguish grin that gave her a flutter like nothing she'd felt in a very long time. Holding the courtiers and guards at bay with his magic, he pulled her behind him toward the exit.

She resisted, saying, "No, this way," and they ran together down a side corridor to the garden, where they lost themselves in the maze. There she faced him and said, "What if I agree to stop the raids and the processions through your world? I cannot promise there will be no incursions, but I will no longer demand tribute from your people."

"You expect me to trust the word of the fairy queen?"

"We do have a reputation for untrustworthiness, I will admit. What must I do to prove my word to you?"

"Leave the throne."

"That would divide the Realm as others try to take it. You do not know what you ask of me, enchanter."

They talked for hours, and to Sophie it seemed as though she was fast forwarding through the scene. In fact, it soon seemed to be another meeting between the two, this time more an assignation between lovers than a parley between foes. She greeted him with great joy in her heart, and when he was gone, some of the light went out of her life. At yet another meeting, she took his hands and said, "I can give you what you want."

With a saucy gleam in his eyes, he said, "You already have, my love, many a time."

"What you want in your role as enchanter. I will leave the throne."

"That's not necessary. You've been true to your word."

"I want to leave. I have ruled for so long I scarcely remember a time before. Your coming has been the only thing to change the unending days. I want to go with you, to be with you always."

"My always is rather different from yours," he said somberly.

"But yours has more life in it."

"You would give up your immortality for me?"

"For you, and for me, as well. I can hide the throne so no one can take it, and I can pass on the knowledge to our children, and they to their children, in case it ever needs to be found."

They ran away, hand in hand, as vines began growing over the castle they left behind.

And then Sophie was back in the hall the way it had been earlier, seated on the throne, with a woman facing her. Even though she'd never seen the face of the woman in the vision she'd just experienced, she knew exactly who she was: the fairy queen. She was tall and lithe, with flame-red hair. "My daughter," the queen said, "you have found my throne."

"Daughter?" Sophie whispered. Had she just witnessed the courtship of her ancestors? If so, they were countless "greats" removed, but then there had been something familiar about the man, an echo passed through the generations that she'd seen in her father, her grandmother, and even her own mirror. Any resemblance to the fairy queen was harder to find, but her eyes were the same silvery gray as Sophie's odd left eye. "That explains me, then—both enchantress and fae," she said with a nod of understanding. "That's why no one knows what to make of me—or knew but wouldn't tell me." It also explained so much more, too much for Sophie to process at the moment, especially as lightheaded as she still felt. She wasn't entirely sure this moment wasn't also a dream. She felt like she was floating in a hazy mist.

"And now you have come to take your rightful throne."

That jolted Sophie out of her fog. "No! I came to keep someone else out of it."

"You must live your heritage, my daughter. The Realm needs a queen."

"Like a fish needs a bicycle."

The queen's brow creased in confusion. "I do not understand."

"They've gotten by without you for centuries, and as I'm far more human than fae, my sympathies lie with the outside world." Hoping to appeal to something her ancestor might understand, she added, "Have you considered that I might be in love? You wouldn't deny me the chance to do what you did."

The queen laughed again. "You, in love? You have not known a man."

Sophie cringed. Did she have a sign on her back? Flashing "virgin" lights on her forehead? "That doesn't mean I don't love," she whispered as her thoughts went unbidden to Michael. Michael who had just found his wife again, she reminded herself firmly. There was no point in developing a hopeless affection for an unavailable man.

"The Realm needs a queen," the former queen repeated. "Haven't you noticed that it's dying? I did not realize that would be the consequence of my departure."

"It's not exactly an urgent consequence, since it's taken at least five centuries," Sophie pointed out.

"That is but a blink of an eye to our kind. You must take the throne or the Realm will die and be no more."

Something in Sophie snapped. "Why is that my responsibility?" she shouted. She would have come off the throne if it had let her, but it had her in its grip. "It's enough that my family and my town can't—or won't—do without me, but now there's a whole Realm that will die unless I rule it? At some point in my life I was hoping that I would get to *have* a life."

"The entire Realm, all its people, depend on you. I know we have long plagued your kind, but we have also brought much to you. Without us, who will inspire the artists, the musicians, the dreamers—and, yes, the dancers?"

"Oh, great," Sophie groaned. "Now I'm not only responsible for the entire Realm, but also the arts in the real world? If I told anyone this, they'd claim I was a raging narcissist. I can't be that important."

"You are the rightful heir to the throne. You won it through blood, knowledge, and the loyalty of your subjects. This is where you belong." The queen paused and frowned. "But you are not yet crowned. Why did you take the throne without being crowned?"

"It was more like the throne took me."

"You have very little fae blood." The apparition of her distant ancestor was fading, and the light in the hall grew dimmer as darkness closed in on Sophie. "I had not planned for that. You have much human magic, but so little of ours. The palace may not accept you properly." If she said anything beyond that, Sophie didn't hear it because her surroundings had disappeared entirely, leaving her lost in eternal blackness.

⟔Fifty-Three⟔

Michael felt like he'd spent so much time waiting helplessly that he'd nearly given up hope that anything would ever happen. When it did happen, it took him totally by surprise. With no warning, the vines shrank back on themselves, retreating into their roots and revealing a towering castle.

"Her majesty has done it!" the other redheaded woman rejoiced.

"I suppose that's true, considering that whichever one did it would now be 'her majesty,'" Athena muttered.

"It's got to be Sophie, right?" Emily asked. "She had a plan, I'm sure."

Amelia strode forward and opened the door. "Let's find out." One of Maeve's guards moved as though to stop her, but she held him back with a smile. "Oh, come now, do allegiances really matter at this point?"

He glared at her and entered the palace, the others following him. Michael tried to stay near Jen, but she was focused on her fairy friend. He reminded himself that they had other things to worry about right now, such as what had happened to Sophie and Maeve.

They found themselves staring down an impossibly long hallway. "This way," Eamon directed. "I know this place."

The hallway ended in a giant chamber that could have held Yankee Stadium, with room to spare. A table loaded with suspiciously fresh-looking food for a place that smelled stale with disuse stood nearby, but otherwise the room was empty. "Up there!" Athena said, pointing. At the back of the hall stood a throne on a high dais. The woman sitting on the throne didn't seem to notice their arrival.

When they reached the foot of the dais steps, they saw that it was Sophie on the throne. Although she sat upright, she appeared to be unconscious. Maeve lay motionless at her feet. Emily ran up the steps to her sister's side, calling her name. Maeve's people and Jen rushed to their fallen ruler and knelt around her in dismay. Michael ignored them, figuring that the fairies would know what to do about one of their own. He focused on Sophie. Her clothes were covered in blood, which worried him. The left sleeve of her sweater was soaked and there was a giant bloody patch near the hem of her skirt, but he didn't see any wounds.

He and the elderly sisters climbed the steps more slowly than Emily had. When he reached the throne, he searched Sophie's neck for a pulse, but found nothing. Her skin was too cold even for death. He'd seen her alive too recently for her body to have cooled that much. "Something's wrong," he said, in what he was sure was the understatement of the year.

"I don't believe she's dead," Athena said, studying the motionless Sophie. "The castle woke, and I don't think that would have happened if she were dead."

"I don't think she's alive, either," he said. "Not exactly."

"She's on the throne," Amelia said, frowning.

"Well, yeah," Michael said.

"It is our mandate to keep the throne empty."

"Better her than Maeve," Emily said. "You know if Sophie's in charge, there *will* be changes around here."

"Let's worry about that later," Michael said. "I think the

priority for now should be to figure out how to revive her. Then we can find out what happened."

Athena smiled mischievously as she said, "A kiss from her protector and defender usually awakens the sleeping princess."

Michael felt his cheeks growing warm. "You want me to kiss her?"

"You're the only mortal man here, and it needs to be a mortal to bring her back to mortality."

He couldn't bring himself to kiss another woman in front of his wife, even if his wife was currently snuggled against some other man. She was brainwashed. He had no such excuse. Maybe a kiss on the forehead would work, like he might kiss a sister or a child. But then something occurred to him as he leaned over her.

"Wait a second, I haven't been her protector or defender at all. If anything, it's been the other way around. But she has had a mortal defender." He patted his leg and called, "Here, Beau." The bulldog trotted over eagerly. Michael glanced at Amelia and Athena. "Or is he mortal? He seems to be in on the secret."

"He's mortal," Amelia confirmed. "Animals don't try to rationalize what their senses show them, so they're more aware of reality than humans tend to be."

Emily boosted her dog into her sister's lap. "Now, give your Auntie Sophie a big kiss." Under her breath, she added, "And I hope she doesn't kill me for this."

Beau licked Sophie's cheek and whined. Her eyelids fluttered, then opened, and then she smiled. "Well, hello there, Beauregard," she said. The dog licked her again, and she wrapped her arms around him in a hug while pressing her nose to his.

"Are you okay, Soph?" Emily asked.

"Yes, of course," Sophie replied, but her voice sounded vague and unsure. She glanced around like she was looking for someone and frowned. "Maeve?"

"Down and out, but I don't know if it's permanent."

Sophie let the dog go, and he jumped back down to the ground. She placed her hands on the arms of the throne and took a deep breath before shoving herself upward. For a moment, she seemed surprised to be standing, and then her sister caught her in an enthusiastic embrace. "I knew you'd come for me, I knew it," Emily said, burying her face against Sophie's neck. As they pulled apart, Emily added, "Though I'll admit that I wasn't expecting all this."

"Overkill?" Sophie asked.

"It wouldn't be you if it wasn't." Emily draped an arm around her sister's shoulders. "But maybe you could learn something about not using nukes in a flyswatter situation."

"I think this may actually have been a nuclear situation," Sophie said wearily. "But it's a long story for another time. Now we just need to get out of here."

"That's okay with me," Emily said with deep feeling.

Sophie turned to look at Maeve, who still had Jen and her other people kneeling around her. "What should we do about her?" Amelia asked.

"I don't think she'll be a problem," Sophie said, still sounding a little dazed. "If I know anything about fairy lore, she won't be able to leave the palace."

"What do you mean?" Emily asked, clutching her sister's arm.

"I don't like the idea of leaving her in the palace," Amelia said. "That puts her dangerously close to the throne."

"The throne won't have her," Sophie said, heading down the dais steps.

"But why can't Maeve leave?" Emily asked, keeping up with Sophie.

"She drank the wine," Sophie said with a gesture toward the banquet table.

"Silly her," Emily said, her voice tight.

Michael and the others had to jog to keep up with Sophie. He could hardly blame her for wanting to get out of there, but he had unfinished business. "What about Jen?" he asked.

She stopped abruptly. "Oh, yes, I'm sorry."

She'd just started to turn back to the dais when a voice said, "Very well done, little one." They all turned to see a tall, red-haired fairy who looked vaguely familiar to Michael, like he'd seen her in his dreams.

"Are we even now?" Sophie asked with a sharp edge to her voice. "I did what you asked. I kept Maeve off the throne."

"I think you know what more you need to do," the fairy said.

Sophie shook her head. "No. Not that."

"You were willing to give yourself up to me and stay forever not too long ago."

"This is different."

The woman studied Sophie shrewdly. "You know, you wouldn't have to stay here all the time. The throne can remain vacant and occupied at the same time."

"Sophie, what's she talking about?" Emily asked.

"The last fairy queen was our ancestor. She left the throne and the Realm to be with the enchanter who was supposed to slay her. I guess you could call it the ultimate Romeo and Juliet story, except they managed to pull it off. And that makes me a rightful heir to the throne."

"The Realm needs a queen now," the fairy woman said.

"No, it doesn't, and we're here to see that the throne remains empty," Amelia said, moving to stand between the fairy and Sophie.

"The Realm is dying and will die without a queen," the fairy insisted.

"It's winter here. It should never be winter here," Sophie said with a solemn nod.

"Except in your footsteps," the fairy said. "There, summer returns."

"Really, Soph? That's kind of cool," Emily said. "And maybe she's right. You could commute instead of living here full-time." She turned to the elderly sisters and added, "Better her on the throne than any of the other fairy rulers. Trust me, I've run into some of them."

"You do owe me a debt, and believe me, this is the option that will be least painful to you personally." The fairy turned to face Michael, and the look she gave him made him shiver.

"Okay, then, what do I need to do?" Sophie asked with a resigned sigh. "I've taken the throne, but apparently that wasn't enough."

"You must be crowned."

"But where's the crown?"

"Usually, that comes before the throne."

"I didn't choose to take the throne," Sophie snapped. "It was all the throne's doing."

A burst of light shot through the hall as the great doors at the far end opened. Michael had to shield his eyes with his good arm. "I was afraid of this," the fairy woman said. "They were bound to notice that the castle had come back to life."

"What is it?" Michael asked.

"We need to hide," Emily said urgently. "These are some of the other fairy rulers, and I've seen what they do to their prisoners."

⌒Fifty-Four⌒

"Would they really–" Sophie started to say, but then she noticed that Tallulah and Eamon had already vanished. She ducked behind the banquet table while Emily dragged Michael to safety behind a pillar. The two older sisters found their own hiding places.

It seemed like forever before she could hear footsteps approaching. She crawled to the end of the table and peered between the chairs and the table legs to see white-haired and black-clad fairies striding forward as though they were entering their own palace. She could see why Emily had suggested hiding. These fairies dropped the room's temperature by several degrees just with the look in their eyes.

She crawled under one of the massive chairs when the footsteps stopped next to the table. "Ah, refreshments. How hospitable," a woman's voice said, and Sophie had to stifle a laugh. The fairies really needed to be better about reading their own press so they'd know the rules.

Maeve's voice rang through the hall. "Fiontan, Niamh, you are the first to come swear me fealty."

"Maeve? You?" a male voice said from nearby as Sophie scrambled to the other end of the table so she could see Maeve. Maeve was on her feet again, standing near the throne but not touching it. Her people, including the human women, were kneeling before her as though she was a crowned queen.

Maeve spread her arms, gesturing at the seemingly empty hall. "Who else do you think woke the palace?"

Light shot through the hall as the doors opened again, and this time footsteps on the marble floor weren't the only sound. Sophie heard the clang of weapons and shouts of battle approaching. She risked rising to her knees to peer over the table and see what was happening. The black-clad fairies put down their goblets and placed their hands on their weapons.

Sophie still couldn't see who the new arrivals were, but it sounded like there were a lot of them, and they were already fighting each other. Then something else caught her attention. The filigreed base holding a bowl of fruit was glowing ever so slightly, and now she saw that it looked like a crown. It was like the answer key to one of those "find the hidden objects" puzzles she'd liked as a child, with the hidden objects highlighted. The crown of the Realm was holding up a bowl of grapes.

But she couldn't get to it, not with one of the fairy factions standing right next to it and at least two more factions battling their way forward. While the fairies were all focused on each other, Sophie darted behind the pillar where Emily, Michael, and the enchantresses had hidden. "I found the crown," she whispered. "See, under the bowl of grapes."

"That trivet?" Emily asked.

"The one that's glowing," Sophie said.

"I don't see a glow."

That was a relief to Sophie. If she was the only one who saw the crown that way, it was less likely that any of the fairy rulers would spot it. "Trust me, it's there," she said. "Now if they would just move away from the food and drink for a moment."

But, no, that would be too easy. Not only were more fairies heading to meet those standing at the table, but Maeve had come down from the dais. "I will have no warfare within my hall," she commanded.

"*Your* hall?" one of the newcomers, who was improbably dressed in a tuxedo, snarled, though he did lower his weapon.

"How else do you think the palace returned to life? I said I knew how to find and take the throne, but none of you believed me. Now, please, refresh yourself at my table."

"You're not wearing the crown," a fairy woman in a blood-spattered evening gown said.

"It would mess up my hair," Maeve said. "Besides, it's merely symbolic. The important thing is that I brought the castle back."

Some of the newcomers poured themselves goblets of wine, but the tuxedoed man refrained. He still stared warily at Maeve in a way that made her twitch with unease. "Please, Niall, have some wine," she said, her voice a bit shrill.

"I feel I shouldn't take your hospitality without first swearing fealty to you as my queen," he said. He gestured to the others. "We all should kneel to you before we sit at your table."

"Yes, you should," she said, gesturing to the floor in front of her.

"Ah, but these things should be done properly," Niall said with an unctuous smile. "We must kneel before the throne to recognize you as rightful queen of the Realm."

"That's really more of a tradition than an obligation," she said with a nervous laugh.

"Humor me," he said, the charm in his voice turning to steel. "Or is there a reason you don't want to sit in the throne you've so valiantly won?"

Maeve hesitated a moment too long, and in that time, the others all put their goblets down and drew weapons. Soon, Maeve faced a variety of knives, swords, arrows, and guns—an arsenal of the ages. "If you insist," she said stiffly and began walking toward the dais like a bride with cold feet heading to the altar. The others followed close on her heels.

Halfway there, she made a break for it, darting toward the corridor that led to the garden. She wasn't fast enough for the other fairies, and they moved to block her. Her guards joined the melee. Swords clanged, bowstrings twanged, and shots rang out as the fairy factions fought each other and Maeve's people.

Sophie saw her chance and rushed to the table, where she tossed the bowl of grapes aside and picked up the crown. "Okay, now it looks like a crown," said Emily, who had joined her, along with the others. Eamon had reappeared at some point and stood next to Emily. "So, now what? You put it on?"

"Well, usually someone else puts the crown on, but I don't see any archbishops around, so I suppose I'll have to pull a Napoleon," Sophie said. She lifted the crown and placed it on her head. Although it had seemed delicate and light, it weighed heavily on her.

"Should something happen?" Michael asked. "How will we know if it worked?"

Sophie glanced around. "Nothing seems to have changed. Maybe I have to sit on the throne while wearing the crown."

"To get there, we'll have to get through them," Michael said with a glance at the fight.

"This is starting to make the American electoral college system look like the simple way of choosing a leader," she muttered. Then she gave Michael a direct glare. "And there is no 'we' to this. You stay here. I can get to the throne."

She was weighing the relative merits of staying under as much cover as possible by running from pillar to pillar until she was nearly at the dais as opposed to just making a run for it when Michael grabbed her wrist. "You're not going to get anywhere while you're wearing that thing. They'll know what you're up to."

Wincing, she reached up and removed the crown. "What should I do with it?"

He held out his hand. "I can hide it in my sling."

"That's just a ploy to get in the fight," she accused.

"Well, it won't fit in your bra," Emily said, snatching the crown out of Sophie's hand and giving it to Michael.

"It's not too heavy for you, is it?" Sophie asked as he tucked the crown into his sling.

He acted like that was a surprising question. "No, not at all. Now, come on."

The battling fairies still hadn't noticed them, but that didn't last long. When they saw a cluster of humans rushing toward the dais, they stopped fighting each other and turned to the interlopers. "We'll take care of this," Amelia said. "Go!" She and Athena took up defensive positions, firing off bursts of magic to keep the fairies at bay. Sophie tried to ignore the arrows flying past as she ran.

They'd just reached the dais steps when Michael cried out and sagged against Sophie. She caught him before he fell. "What hit me?" he gasped. "My good arm, it's gone numb. I can't move it."

"Sophie?" Emily begged in distress.

"It's probably elf-shot," Sophie said. "I know how to treat it, but I don't have the supplies."

"Go," Michael urged. "Take the crown."

Her heart wrenched at the thought of leaving him lying there, injured and helpless, but she remembered her mission. She reached into his sling, took out the crown, and ran up the steps toward the throne.

Some of the fairies had made it past Amelia and Athena, and Maeve was racing Sophie to the dais. Maeve got to the throne first and stood blocking it, but Sophie took a couple of running steps and launched herself into the tour jeté of a lifetime. She hadn't just been boasting about the kind of air she could get. She kicked up with one leg, hitting Maeve square in the jaw, then twisted her body around in the air, scissoring her legs, and landed on one foot on the edge of the throne's seat. As soon as she'd caught her balance and had both feet under her, she placed the crown on her head, hoping that standing on the throne counted.

It must have, for the palace truly came to life. When she'd sat on the throne earlier, it had merely removed the outside barriers. Now it was as though the electricity had been reconnected. Light shone from above onto gleaming surfaces. At the same time, a wave of *awareness* swept over her, and she suddenly knew and understood so many things that it was as though her mind had lit up along with the palace.

Every head in the room turned to face the throne, and Sophie realized that standing on the furniture was hardly dignified, so she gracefully lowered herself into the seat. "Now, y'all stop it right there," she ordered in her best scolding teacher voice, like she was making a student spit out her gum. "Drop the weapons." Much to her surprise, they complied, and then they all knelt without her even having to give the order. Maeve was already on the ground, wiping blood away from her mouth, so Sophie couldn't tell if she meant to be kneeling, but she figured it was safe to assume the others now all knew Maeve wasn't the rightful ruler, and that was the important part.

"As you can probably tell," she continued, "the throne is now occupied. Whether or not I'm here, you can consider it occupied, so there's no point in all this fighting." They all bowed their heads in acknowledgment, and she had to stifle a smile. She could get used to this.

She allowed herself a sigh of relief when she saw that Amelia and Athena were tending to Michael, and he was moving his good arm again. With a sense of satisfaction, Sophie stood and said, "And now I'm taking my people home, but I will be back." The knowledge pouring into her brain told her what to do. She removed the crown and placed it in the throne's seat. A glowing bubble formed around the throne, sealing it and the crown safely out of reach.

Tallulah, who had reappeared at some point in all the commotion, met her at the foot of the dais. "Very good, little one. Our debt is cleared, and you are welcome to dance with us at any time, with no additional obligation."

"I should think so," Sophie said, "considering I'm now your ruler."

Tallulah didn't kneel, but she did bow her head with a smile as Sophie brushed past her. Emily and Eamon helped Michael to his feet, and they and the enchantresses joined Sophie. "Let's get out of here," Sophie said.

"Please!" Emily said with great enthusiasm. "I hope you know how to get us home."

"More now than ever," Sophie said. "I can create a gateway, but we'll have to get outside the palace to do so." Sophie and her friends headed for the doors at the end of the hall, and all the fairies followed behind. Now that taking the throne was no longer an option, they were jockeying for a position close to the queen.

When they reached the massive front doors, Sophie opened them with a gesture and prepared to enter her Realm.

Fifty-Five

Michael couldn't tell if the fairies were blindly following their new ruler or if they were up to something, but he braced for another fight. His left arm still tingled, but at least he could move it, thanks to Athena's balm. He got through the doorway, as did Emily with Beau, Eamon, the two old ladies, and a few of the fairies, who made a hasty departure from the scene. He couldn't help but look back to see if Jen was coming, too, and then he saw Jen, Maeve, and most of the fairies clumped together in the doorway. "Sophie?" he called softly.

She turned and smiled with a wicked gleam in her odd eyes. "Never take food or drink from strangers, especially strangers you can't see," she said. "It looks like you're stuck in the palace."

"You're going to leave us here?" Maeve whined.

"I'm not sure even I could free you. It wasn't my spell." Sophie moved forward until she was practically on the threshold, face-to-face with Maeve. "And why should I? You kidnapped my sister–twice. You can expect no help from me. In fact, I think my palace needs staff." In an instant, all the fairies' fanciful clothes turned into servants' uniforms–and not cute French maid stuff, either. They looked like the downstairs staff in the costume dramas Jen used to watch. In spite of the dire situation, Michael almost smiled to himself. If that didn't lure Jen out of the palace, he wasn't sure what would. She'd hate being forced to dress that way.

That seemed to be Sophie's plan. She turned away from Maeve and gestured toward Jen and the other woman, her expression softening. "You two can come with me. You didn't eat or drink in the palace, so you aren't bound here. I'm afraid Maeve can't hold true to her promise to make you a princess. But I could, if you come with me."

Michael held his breath to see what would happen. He wondered if he should say something or if he should leave it to Sophie. When Jen glanced to him, he couldn't stop himself from speaking. "Jen, please," he said, surprised by how badly his voice shook.

For a heartbeat, he thought he'd actually reached her, but then the other human woman hooked her arm around Jen's, and Jen's fairy paramour put his arm around her shoulders, shooting Michael a defiant glare. Maeve smiled smugly at Sophie. "It seems your power isn't absolute," she purred.

Although Michael was exhausted and sore, and just a few minutes ago he wasn't sure how he'd make it home from the park, a surge of adrenaline shot through him as his body geared up for a fight. "Why don't you just let her go?" he shouted at Maeve.

Maeve turned to him, acknowledging his presence for the first time. "I'm not doing anything," she said, her eyes wide with feigned innocence. "She's making her own choice."

Michael would have sprung forward to attack or to grab Jen or to do *something*, but an arm caught him around the waist and held him back as the giant doors slammed shut.

"You can't get to her like that," Sophie said.

She was small, but she was too strong for him to break her grasp. "I'm not leaving her."

"We'll have to get to her another way." With the slightest of smirks, she added, "I know people here, people in very high places. I should be able to get something done."

But he couldn't go, not when he was so close. "I'm not leaving her," he repeated, his voice breaking.

"I'll figure something out, I promise. Now, let's get Emily home, okay?" He still couldn't bring himself to move, and she said gently, "Michael?"

"Don't you dare enchant me," he said, turning on her with a snarl.

She didn't flinch from his anger. "Okay, I won't, if you'll be reasonable," she snapped in response. "Do you want to stand here looking dramatic and tragic, shouting to the heavens, or do you want to accomplish something worthwhile?"

Her appeal to common sense made it past the red haze filling his mind, and he took a few deep breaths before saying, "I guess you're right."

"Of course I am." Keeping one arm around his waist, she gently turned him back to face the others. "And now I desperately need to eat something and sleep for about a week, so let's get Emily home." He noticed as he walked with her that she was leaning on him almost as much as he leaned against her, and he slid his good arm around her shoulders to offer support. Whatever it was she'd done back there couldn't have been easy, and there was all that blood. This hadn't been easy on any of them.

He felt like he was leaving his heart behind as they moved away from the palace.

Fifty-Six

They walked along a great terrace overlooking the river. Below, on the other shore, the battle had stopped and the soldiers were dispersing. A few stayed and knelt, somehow recognizing their new ruler, even without her crown. Emily wanted to crack a joke about Sophie finally getting the treatment she'd always felt she'd deserved, but this was so far beyond a small-town queen bee scenario that the joke wouldn't be all that funny.

She kept an eye on Michael as he walked leaning heavily on Sophie. She wasn't sure how he remained vertical after all he'd done in his condition. Maybe the Realm's magic had given him a boost. Or Sophie had. He seemed to be a little stronger since Sophie had put her arm around him. Emily didn't want to speculate on what he might be going through emotionally. Somehow she doubted this was the closure he'd been looking for.

"Wow, it's really changed since we were inside," he said. "It's all Technicolor now. I feel like the Munchkins are going to come out and greet us with a song-and-dance routine."

"It's always like this," Emily said.

"Not when I came in here, it wasn't. It was like winter, everything dead and dry."

"So Sophie really did bring the place back to life." It was slowly dawning on Emily that her sister was a big deal here—and merited it.

"I merely facilitated it," Sophie said primly.

Emily asked, "How long have I been gone?"

"It was Saturday afternoon when I entered the Realm."

"That long? It only felt like about a day to me. I don't suppose there's any chance we could return last Wednesday."

"That would require time travel for me, and I don't think I can do that. But your mysterious disappearance has been great for publicity, so I doubt you'll be recast. They even had a candlelight vigil."

"That's what Eamon said. Did it make the news?"

"I'm not sure. There was a news crew there, but I didn't watch."

"Sophie! You should have recorded it."

"I was busy."

Even as they bantered, Emily's dread grew. She'd have to tell Sophie she'd disobeyed the rules and taken a drink. The fairy world was lovely and had its own delights, but Emily really and truly wanted to go home, back to her usual life. She hoped Sophie would know what to do.

Sophie stepped off the walkway onto the grass, released Michael, and waved her hands in a sweeping arc, leaving a shimmering space in the shape of a broad doorway. With the gateway formed, Emily knew this was her last chance to come clean. She blurted, "Um, well, there is something we need to talk about before we can go home." She hesitated, then plunged ahead before Sophie could ask her what was wrong. "I took a drink. I know I wasn't supposed to, but I was trying to buy time by singing every song I knew for Maeve, to string her along while she waited for the right one, and I hadn't had anything to drink in ages. I couldn't sing anymore without some water, and when I stopped singing she talked about sending gangs into the city to kidnap you, so I had to sing the first verse to stop her, and I took a drink—just a couple of sips, but I could tell it did something to me." When the words stopped tumbling out of her, she felt as breathless as if she'd just done a tap number while singing. If she hadn't been panting, she'd have held her breath, waiting for Sophie to respond.

"What does this mean? Is she trapped here, like Jen?" Michael asked.

Sophie shook her head. "I don't know. Most of my information is folklore. I do know that eating or drinking within the Realm makes it harder to leave, but I don't know what the threshold is. A couple of sips may not be enough to make a difference, and you do have some fairy blood. That may matter."

Emily swallowed the lump in her throat. "Okay, worst-case scenario, what happens?"

"You're stuck here for seven years."

"*Seven years?* That will kill my career."

"Then again, I am queen of the Realm, so you'd think I have some pull, so long as you want to go back."

"I do, believe me, I do."

"Well, since I'm queen, that means I represent the Realm. If you're with me—if you're attached to me—then maybe that counts as being in the Realm even if you're outside."

"And by attached, you mean…?"

Sophie turned a little pink and glanced down at her shoes before saying, "You'd have to swear fealty, more or less that you belong to me."

Emily put a hand on her hip and glared at her sister. "You have *got* to be kidding."

"It's just a formality. It's not like it means anything."

"What do I have to do?"

"Start by kneeling."

"You're enjoying this way too much," Emily muttered as she knelt in front of her sister. She started to think that this was just formalizing the way things had always been, but then it occurred to her that though Sophie was bossy, she was usually the one doing things for others. She was never the one being waited upon. "I swear to serve you for seven years, your majesty," she said, then added as she stood, "And you'd better not take advantage of me."

"I told you, it was merely a formality."

"So I'm okay now?"

Sophie pulled off her sweater and handed it to Emily. "Here, put this on."

Emily held it distastefully at arm's length. "It's covered in blood."

"I know, but giving the captive an article of your own clothing to wear is another way of getting someone out of the Realm. I don't want to take any chances." As Emily reluctantly struggled into the too-small sweater, Sophie turned to Eamon and asked, "Do you have any other ideas?"

"She is likely to pine, with or without having drunk." He clasped Emily's hand in his and added, "But perhaps if I go with her, she will feel the loss less."

"That could work," Sophie said with a nod. "Like fairy methadone, a little bit of the Realm to help overcome the addiction to the Realm itself. Okay, then, everyone, hold hands. I think I need to be connected to all of you to get you through the gateway."

Sophie and Eamon stood to either side of Emily, so she was flanked by the two strongest in fairy magic. If they couldn't get her home, Emily didn't think anyone could. Athena held Eamon's other hand, with Amelia on her other side, holding Beau's leash. Sophie put her arm around Michael, and Emily thought those two looked awfully comfortable like that.

That thought distracted her so that she barely noticed when Sophie stepped forward. The next thing she knew, she was in a world that was dull and flat. She fought to go back, but then Eamon touched her cheek, and she looked into the swirling colors of his mercury eyes. He, at least, had color in this drab place. As long as she focused on him, she was okay. She looked to her other side and saw that her sister was as bright as ever–brighter, even–with her strawberry blond hair standing out against a muted landscape.

"Okay, this isn't so bad," she said with a sigh of relief. Then the worst pain she'd ever felt struck, and she felt like her limbs were being ripped out of their sockets.

Fifty-Seven

Michael had just allowed himself a sigh of relief at being back in the real world when Sophie abruptly jerked away from him, like something had pulled her. He turned to see her throwing her arms around a snarling beast. "Help me hold her, and whatever you do, don't let go," Sophie shouted. He might have asked why or how, but the queen in her came out in her tone, and it wasn't the sort of order one disobeyed.

Michael got his good arm around the beast, and only then did he notice that Emily wasn't with them. "Didn't Emily make it?" he asked.

"This *is* Emily," Sophie said as the beast turned into a bear. "It's a spell. Hold her!" Amelia and Athena joined in, but Eamon stood back. Emily changed from snarling lion to hissing snake to fire-breathing dragon and just about every other creature in the menagerie. At last, she turned back into Emily and sagged against Sophie. Michael lent his support, and the two of them held Emily upright.

"What happened?" Michael asked, breathless from the exertion.

"I've read about this sort of thing, but I thought it came from longer captivity," Sophie said, sounding a little breathless, herself.

"It's the Realm's way of keeping its captives," Amelia said, stroking Emily's back. "One last test for the rescuers. You must be truly devoted to hold on to someone through all that. If you fail that test of devotion, you lose your loved one for good."

"Was that because she drank?" Michael asked.

Sophie shook her head. "I don't know. Maeve may have enchanted her to keep her from escaping. If she knew what I am, then she might have thought Emily could have the same power to leave the Realm."

Michael didn't want to ask the next question, but he had to know. "If we get Jen out of the palace and get her through a gateway, will this happen to her?"

"Almost certainly," Athena said with a sorrowful nod. "And it will be worse if she isn't going willingly. Emily didn't try to escape from our grasp. Imagine holding on to the beasts while they're trying to get away."

"So, we will need to bring sturdy gloves on that rescue mission," Sophie said briskly.

"Is it over?" Emily asked, still clinging to her sister.

"Yes, sweetie, I believe it is. Now, let's get you home."

Emily tried to move out of Michael and Sophie's grasp and nearly fell. Eamon stepped in to support her. Michael couldn't tell if her glassy look was because of what she'd just gone through or because she wasn't adapting well to the real world. They bustled her home and up the stairs to Michael's apartment, where Eamon eased her onto the sofa. She seemed oblivious to her surroundings, just staring vaguely into the middle distance.

As usual, Sophie took charge. "Water first, then she needs some food–preferably as strong a flavor as we can find."

"My partner's mother sent me some enchiladas," Michael suggested.

Eamon had to coax water between Emily's lips, and then Sophie fed her the first few forkfuls of reheated enchiladas like she was feeding a child. Emily's color gradually returned, and her eyes regained some focus as she took the fork from Sophie and fed herself. She still didn't look like her usual self, but when Sophie let out a long, slow breath, Michael got the impression that the worst might have passed.

Now that the immediate life-or-death matters had been handled, he realized they had other problems. "What about Tanaka?" he asked. "This is a missing person case. How do we explain where she's been and the condition she's in?"

"Obviously we can't tell the truth," Athena said.

"We could tell a version of it," Sophie suggested. "She was kidnapped, then escaped, but she's fine."

"That could bring up a host of other problems," Michael said, shaking his head. "Tank would have to investigate and try to track down these nonexistent kidnappers."

"They exist," Sophie said, quirking an eyebrow. "And he doesn't stand a chance of finding them. But I think I can make it a little less drastic for him."

"Are you sure you're up to it?" Amelia asked.

"It shouldn't take much more than a nudge, since I'm not sure how valid a case he ever thought this was."

"I think he's already a little scared of her," Michael put in.

Amelia and Athena looked at each other and seemed to come to an agreement. "Very well. We'd better leave before the police arrive," Amelia said. To Sophie, she added, "And I presume you will be working with us now?"

Sophie rubbed a weary hand across her forehead. "I don't see why you need me. Your job is keeping the throne empty, and I've got that taken care of for the rest of my lifetime. I need to get back home before my mother has a nervous breakdown."

Amelia and Athena exchanged another look, but they didn't argue. Athena just said, "I do hope you'll stop by before you leave, and let us know if you need help with Emily."

The two china dealers/enchantresses/whatever said their good-byes and left. "You'd probably best not be here, either," Michael said to Eamon. "It's your description that's been circulating as the prime suspect."

"I can change my appearance," Eamon said.

"No, Michael's right," Sophie said. "The fewer oddities around here, the better it will work."

Eamon gave Emily's hand a squeeze, and she turned to look at him. For the first time since her return, she seemed to notice another person. "You'll come back, won't you?" she asked, pleading.

"I will come back," he assured her, dropping a light kiss on her forehead. She reluctantly released his hand as he moved away.

When he was gone, Michael said to Sophie, "You'll have to make the call. I've already cried wolf once today, and I'm not sure Tank will believe me if I call again."

Sophie got out her cell phone and punched in the number Michael gave her. When she got an answer, she put on her most honeyed drawl to say, "I'm so sorry to call you on a weekend, but Detective Murray assured me you wouldn't want me to wait, under the circumstances." She took a deep breath, then blurted, "Emily's back. She just came home. She seems to be okay, just a few scratches and bruises, and she's tired and hungry." She bit her lip while listening, then said, "No, I'm afraid she's not clear on that." Another pause. "Are you sure that's absolutely necessary? It could wait." She winced while she listened, then said, "Okay then, if you insist, we're at Detective Murray's apartment. Thank you so much."

She ended the call and said, "He's on his way over."

Michael frowned at Sophie. "Might I suggest that you change clothes before the cops get here? You being covered in blood is going to bring up questions."

Sophie glanced down at her dress and groaned. "You're right. I'll be back in a moment. Don't let her go anywhere."

Emily turned to watch Sophie go, then said, "You know, this explains so much about my childhood. I should have known she had magical powers."

Fifty-Eight

Emily's Apartment
Saturday, 9:00 p.m.

Sophie was glad of the excuse to go downstairs and be on her own for a moment. She still hadn't processed everything that had happened, and she suspected that would take a while. Once she'd washed off the blood on her arm, she was surprised to find no trace of the knife wound. It had healed itself–or perhaps she'd healed it unconsciously. She peeled off her bloody clothes and put on a clean dress before heading back upstairs.

"Are you all set?" she asked Michael and Emily.

Emily gave her a mock salute. "Yes, your highness. We have discussed the cover story."

Her sister's words were slightly slurred, but at least she was talking and showing signs of life. "You sound like you're drunk. Are you okay?"

"I'm exhausted. I haven't had much sleep. Maybe if I act weary, the cops will leave me alone."

There was a knock on the door, and Emily muttered, "Places, everyone!" Sophie gave her a quick glare before going to open the door.

"Detective Tanaka," she said, ushering him inside. "Thank you for coming so quickly."

"Not a problem. I love it when a case resolves itself." He went to the sofa, bent over Emily and said, "And I take it this is Miss Emily Drake? It's good to have you back with us. I'm Detective Tanaka, and I need to ask you a few questions."

Emily grinned up at him with the smile that had audiences eating out of her hands. "Wow, Detective Tanaka was on my case?" She turned to Sophie. "He's like Michael's Yoda."

Tanaka visibly fought a grin, but lost. "I thought I was more of an Obi-Wan."

He sat in the chair facing the sofa, and Sophie sat next to her sister, with Michael to her other side. The questions were along the lines of what Sophie had expected, but she concentrated on getting into Tanaka's mind instead of on listening to the conversation. It was a little more difficult than working with Michael. Tanaka was more guarded and didn't have the residue of painkillers or extreme emotional turmoil, but finally she found the way in. She nudged him to accept all of Emily's answers and to be satisfied with the outcome. In no time at all, he wrapped up his questions and stood to go.

Sophie walked him to the door, pausing to say, "I appreciate all you've done for us."

"I have to confess, I was mostly worried about Michael."

"I understand. This has been very difficult for him."

"It's too bad that the connection with Jen's case didn't pan out. He had such high hopes."

"Yes, that is a shame," she agreed. When the door was safely shut behind him, she leaned back against it and let out a long breath.

"Way to go, Soph!" Emily said. "Oh wait, do you do that all the time, to everyone?"

"I don't think she can help it," Michael said, but he was smiling a little, almost fondly. Sophie couldn't hold back her own smile in response.

"Well, I don't know about you two, but I am dead. I could use an epic nap," Emily said, stretching and yawning.

"You can use my bedroom," Michael said.

"That way we can keep an eye on you," Sophie added.

"Maybe you should also lock the door," Emily suggested with a grimace.

Acknowledging that she was struggling was a bad sign, and it worried Sophie. "Michael, do you have your handcuffs?" she asked, trying to keep her tone light.

"It's not that bad," Emily said.

"Beau, you go with her," Sophie said to the dog.

Once Emily and Beau were safely on the other side of the bedroom door, Sophie struggled with what to do next. There were too many things to deal with, and no matter how magical she was, she couldn't be in more than one place at a time. Then she remembered the tiny creatures who'd helped her win the throne and the lesson she'd learned about asking for help. Forcing herself to disregard a lifelong habit, she turned to Michael and said, "Do you think you can keep her from trying to escape for a while?"

"She won't get past me," he assured her.

"I need to go take care of a few things, but I'll be back." She headed toward the door, stopped, and turned back toward him. "Thank you for everything you've done. I'm sorry I wasn't able to help more."

"At least I know she's alive, and she seems to be happy, even if she isn't quite herself."

"I'll do everything I can," she assured him. She moved to hug him, then thought better of it. She wasn't sure she'd be able to make herself let go.

She left the apartment, hurried down the stairs, and went back to the park. The information that had come through the crown remained in her brain, granting her the secrets to the Realm. Emily had been right about her being able to commute, but not just between the real world and the Realm. As she stepped onto the grass in the park, she created a gateway, and then once in the Realm again, she opened another one, this one to her backyard in Louisiana.

She eased open the kitchen door and called out, "Mama? I'm home!"

Her mother met her at the doorway between the kitchen and the hall. "Why didn't you tell me you were coming back?"

"I caught an earlier flight, but I'll have to go back to New York again. Emily needed me to bring her some things. Now, how's Nana?"

"She's been asking for you all evening."

Sophie made her way to the parlor that now served as her grandmother's room. The frail old woman sat huddled in her armchair, singing softly under her breath. Sophie recognized the song and joined in as she sat on the footstool facing her grandmother and took the wizened hands in her own.

Her grandmother looked at her with eyes clearer than they'd been since Sophie was a teenager. "You did it, then," she said.

"Yes, Nana, I did it. Thanks to you."

"Now we can stop singing that gosh-darned song. I was beginning to get tired of it. When you pass it on to your daughters, come up with something new. Tell it as a story."

"A fairy tale," Sophie said with a smile.

Her grandmother squeezed her hands. "Yes, a fairy tale."

The End

Thank you for reading *A Fairy Tale* by Shanna Swendson.
Please enjoy the following excerpt from the second book
in the series, *To Catch a Queen.*

One

Michael Murray ducked under the crime scene tape his partner held up for him and asked the uniformed officer at the scene, "What've you got, Milton?"

"Dead body. You'll have to wait for the M.E. to know if it's natural causes or not, but it is weird."

"Define weird." Michael's threshold for "weird" had shifted radically in the last couple of months.

"See for yourself." Milton gestured toward the body lying sprawled in the grass nearby.

At first, Michael didn't notice anything obviously out of the ordinary. Then again, he didn't consider fairies and magic to be all that strange, these days. It was his partner, Marisol Lopez, who spotted the anomaly. "Well, they do say that disco is dead," she quipped.

That's what was strange. The body looked like it had fallen through a time warp from sometime around 1977. It wore tight white bell-bottom trousers and a shiny shirt with a huge collar. The clothes looked new, but the body didn't. Michael guessed that the dead man was in his sixties, old enough that he might have worn these clothes back in the heyday of disco when he was of an age to hit the town for a little Saturday-night fever.

"This stuff isn't coming back in style, is it?" Michael asked Mari.

"God, I hope not," she replied, then winced. "Sorry. I guess I owe a dollar."

"I'll just stand over here where the lightning bolt won't hit me." Michael had given up trying to talk his colleagues out of teasing him for his goody-goody reputation by charging a fine for swearing in front of him. At least it meant the precinct got a free lunch every so often when they emptied the penalty jar.

Michael leaned closer over the body. The dead man looked aged, but not weathered, and his skin was so pale that either he was religious about wearing really good sunblock or he hadn't seen the sun in decades. Even his hands were free of liver spots. His hair was white, but worn in a longish, feathered style that matched his wardrobe.

"He looks scared," Mari commented as she, too, studied the body. "And not just 'Ay! My heart!' scared."

"Detectives!" Milton called out. Michael looked up to see a few uniforms struggling with a man dressed similarly to the dead man. He looked to be about the same age, with the same lack of weathering. "We just found this guy hiding in the bushes over there. Think maybe they're connected?"

Michael and Mari went over to the captive, who looked nearly as frightened as the dead man. "Please, let me go back!" he babbled. "I'll be good, I promise! Let me back in. I don't want to stay here. I don't like getting old."

"What's he talking about?" Mari asked.

"No telling," Milton said. "I don't smell booze on him. Actually, he smells pretty good for a guy wandering through the park and babbling."

"Sir, do you know that dead man over there?" Michael asked.

The man's eyes filled with tears. "He's my brother."

"I'm sorry for your loss. Did you see what happened to him?"

"They made us leave." His voice broke. "We were happy, but they sent us away, and then we got old." His eyes went wild—wilder—with terror. "Are they still coming after us?"

"He may not be drunk, but I bet a tox screen comes up with something," Mari muttered.

"Should we take him in?" Milton asked.

"Yeah, at the very least he's a person of interest, and we probably need to get him some medical attention," Michael said. He had a funny feeling, though, that the tox screen would come up clean. There was something about this man that seemed familiar, an aura he could barely detect. When he slipped his hand into his pocket and clutched his keychain, the aura became stronger, almost a halo.

"Is something wrong, Rev?" Mari asked him.

"You mean other than the dead body?"

"The dead body is all in a day's work. You look troubled."

He rubbed his shoulder. "My old PTSD is acting up again."

"You should get that looked at. But while you have your flashback, or whatever, I'm gonna take a look around. Let me know if you need a hug or a slap."

"Will do," he replied, his voice already trailing off because of what he'd just noticed. The park around him was full of fae creatures, but he was getting used to seeing that. What caught his eye was another man sitting with his back against a tree. Milton and his buddies had walked right past him without noting a potential witness. Michael squeezed his keychain again and the closer contact with the laminated four-leaf clover in the middle of it showed him the reason why. It was a fairy not even bothering with a human glamour. In fact, he looked like he was barely able to conceal himself from humans. Not that most humans would have recognized him as a fairy if they'd seen him.

Real fairies weren't the cute winged creatures of little girls' Halloween costumes. They looked more or less human—both more and less. They were too beautiful, too ephemeral, and too odd to be truly human, with the kind of coloring that didn't occur in nature. And that was just what Michael could see. He had a feeling that even with his enhanced senses, he couldn't see down to the heart of what they truly looked like.

Walking as though he was looking for clues on the ground, Michael made his way over to the fairy and crouched beside him.

"So, what's your story?" he asked. "I take it you have something to do with those two." He gestured with his head toward the body and the man who was being put in the back of a squad car.

The fairy blinked in surprise. "You see me?"

"Four-leaf clover. And I've spent a little time in the Realm. I'm friends with the queen."

That got a reaction. "I've done nothing wrong!" the fairy insisted frantically. "I don't deserve exile. You must tell her majesty."

"Exile? The queen cast you out, and those men?" That didn't sound like something Sophie Drake, the current queen of the fairy Realm, would have ordered, Michael thought. She hadn't shown any signs of forcing anyone out. In fact, Michael was getting a little frustrated with her about that. On the other hand, the fairy looked terrified, which was common in people who'd dealt with Sophie.

"Her men did, under her name. The humans had to go, as did others who refused to swear fealty." He jerked as though startled and whipped his head around like he was looking for pursuers. "They're still after me," he said in an anguished whisper as he clutched at Michael's arm. "And I am so weak in daylight."

Michael would have said the fairy was paranoid, but he sensed something malevolent. It wasn't visible to the naked eye, so none of the nearby police had noticed, but Michael felt it, and he wasn't armed against the fae. He hadn't thought it necessary in daylight. Glancing around to make sure no one was watching him, he reached into his coat pocket and brought out the half-eaten sandwich from his interrupted lunch. "Please accept this offering," he said, holding the sandwich out to the fairy.

The fairy accepted it greedily, without thanks, unwrapped it, and gobbled it up. Then he suddenly stood and whirled, emanating a flash of something that looked like an almost-visible sound wave. The sense of threat dissipated, and the fairy ran away without a word to Michael.

Michael took a moment to catch his breath and had just risen to his feet when Mari approached.

"Find something?" she asked.

Since she didn't mention the odd man Michael had just been talking to or the brief magical battle, he assumed she hadn't noticed any of it. "I thought I saw something on the ground, but it was nothing."

Her phone rang, and he took advantage of that opportunity to place a phone call of his own. Turning his back to his partner and walking a few yards away, he found the number in his directory. As usual, the call went into voice mail after three rings. "Sophie, it's Michael Murray. I have a question for you," he said after the tone. "And no, it's not about Jen, though that deadline is getting awfully close. I'm working on a case that may fall into your Realm. That's the one with the capital R. Call me, please."

He didn't hold out much hope, unless he'd piqued her curiosity enough to get her to stop dodging his calls. Maybe her sister would be able to reach her, he thought. Just then, his phone rang, with Emily Drake's name on the caller ID. He shook his head as he took the call. Those Drake girls really were uncanny.

"Hey, Emily, what's up?" he asked.

"I was wondering if you could look after Beau for me. I probably won't make it home between the matinee and the evening show, and I might go out tonight. I don't want to leave him there alone all that time."

"No problem. I'll stop by and get him when I get off work."

"Thanks, you're a lifesaver."

"It's funny, but I was just about to call you. Have you talked to Sophie lately?"

"We mostly exchange voice mails. But she hasn't forgotten you. She is working on it."

"I know." He'd found the baked goods left on his kitchen table several times a week, noticed the missing wedding photo with a note left in its place. He had evidence that Sophie was still around. He just never saw or spoke to her. "But that's not why I wanted to talk to her. I'm working on a case that falls into her area of expertise, and I wanted to pick her brain."

"Homicidal ballerina?"

"No, her other area of expertise."

"Huh. But I wouldn't be surprised if one of those bunheads

went postal. They're pretty highly strung. If you can't reach Sophie, maybe you could talk to Amelia and Athena. They probably know as much as Sophie does in that area."

"Good idea. Thanks. And how are you doing? I hardly see you anymore, and you live right below me."

"Well, you know, being a superstar keeps me busy." He'd have bought that, considering that she was Broadway's latest sensation, but her tone was a little too bright. She sounded like someone working hard to fake a normal good mood and overshooting the mark by a mile. That worried him. He'd promised Sophie to keep an eye on Emily after her sojourn in the fairy realm, and he didn't think one could break a promise to Sophie Drake and escape lightly. He'd just recovered from one critical injury. He didn't want to sustain another.

"Okay then, but take care of yourself, and let me know if you need anything other than dogsitting. If you talk to Sophie, ask her to call me."

"Will do!" As he ended the call, he made a mental note to leave Sophie a message suggesting she check on her sister.

"You okay, Rev?" Mari asked, startling him out of his thoughts.

"Why wouldn't I be?"

"You look a little pale."

"And you sound like your mother."

"Ouch, that's mean. But seriously, are you okay? Do you need to sit down and take a break?"

"I'm fine. Back to one-hundred percent, cleared by the doctors, and all. You don't have to worry about me."

They started heading toward the car. "Oh, but now that I've seen you bleeding and gasping for breath, the light fading from your eyes, there's no going back. You'll always be helpless and vulnerable to me."

"Helpless, vulnerable, and armed," he warned. "You know, if you went through the same thing I did, it would be a real bonding experience for us as partners. I could arrange that if you keep this up."

"Yeah, but you'd try to counsel me and save my soul before you pulled the trigger," she said, opening the passenger door of their sedan for him.

"I did that once. And it worked," he shouted while leaning across to open the driver's side door as she came around the car.

"And that's why you'll always be the Right Reverend Saint Michael," she said, sliding into the driver's seat. He braced himself as she took off and joined the flow of traffic. She was a native New Yorker who navigated the city streets like a veteran cabbie, so he never bothered asking to drive.

"So, whattaya think about this case, Rev?" she asked, expertly steering around a stopped bus and ignoring the symphony of car horns that followed her maneuver. "Murder or natural causes?"

"I suspect this is going to turn out to be a case for the fashion police, not us." At least, that's what it would look like to normal people if it turned out to be what he thought it was.

"Still, you've gotta love finding a geezer in disco gear in Central Park. I wonder if any clubs are doing a seventies night tonight. I'm suddenly in the mood for that. Want to join me?"

"No thanks. Not really my scene."

"You know, it wouldn't hurt you to get out. You only play an old married man on TV."

"It wasn't my scene when I was single. And I do have plans. I won't be sitting at home alone."

"Yeah, I bet you've got a really rocking Bible study going on."

"Something like that." He couldn't help but smile at the thought of how she'd react if she knew what he did have planned.

About The Author

Shanna Swendson is the author of the Enchanted Inc. series of humorous contemporary fantasy novels, including *Enchanted, Inc.*, *Once Upon Stilettos*, *Damsel Under Stress*, *Don't Hex with Texas*, *Much Ado About Magic*, *No Quest For The Wicked*, and *Kiss and Spell*. She's also contributed essays to a number of books on pop-culture topics, including *Everything I Needed to Know About Being a Girl, I Learned from Judy Blume*, *Serenity Found*, *Perfectly Plum*, and *So Say We All*. When she's not writing, she's usually discussing books and television on the Internet, singing in or directing choirs, taking ballet classes, or attempting to learn Italian cooking. She lives in Irving, Texas, with several hardy houseplants and a lot of books. Visit her Website at http://shannaswendson.com or find her on Facebook at www.facebook.com/shanna.swendson.

Made in the USA
San Bernardino, CA
02 January 2015